Professor Bernard Knight, CBE, became a Home Office pathologist in 1965 and was appointed Professor of Forensic Pathology, University of Wales College of Medicine, in 1980. During his forty-year career with the Home Office, he performed over 25,000 autopsies and was involved in many high profile cases.

Bernard Knight is the author of twenty-three novels, a biography and numerous popular and academic non-fiction books. *A Plague of Heretics* is the fourteenth novel in his highly acclaimed Crowner John Series.

You are welcome to visit his website at
www.bernardknight.homestead.com

Also by Bernard Knight

a plague
of heretics

Bernard Knight

POCKET
BOOKS

LONDON • SYDNEY • NEW YORK • TORONTO

First published in Great Britain by Simon & Schuster UK Ltd, 2010
This edition first published by Pocket Books, 2010
An imprint of Simon & Schuster UK Ltd

A CBS Company

1 3 5 7 9 10 8 6 4 2

Simon & Schuster UK Ltd
1st Floor
222 Gray's Inn Road
London WC1X 8HB

www.simonandschuster.co.uk

Simon & Schuster Australia
Sydney

A CIP catalogue record for this book is
available from the British Library

ISBN: 978-1-47113-252-0

This book is a work of fiction. Names, characters,
places and incidents are either a product of the
author's imagination or are used fictitiously.

Typeset by Hewer Text UK Ltd, Edinburgh EH10 7DU
Printed and bound in Great Britain by
CPI Group (UK) Ltd, Croydon, CR0 4YY

acknowledgements

I would like to thank Dr John Morgan Guy of the University of Wales, Lampeter, for his expert advice about medieval ecclesiastical matters and Alex Wallis for reading a draft and spotting errors.

Also sincere thanks to Kate Lyall Grant, Gillian Holmes, Emma Lowth, Libby Yevtushenko, Florence Partridge and all at Simon and Schuster, as well as my agent and good friend Sara Menguc, for steering Crowner John through fourteen adventures.

As always, heartfelt thanks to my wife Jean for acting as my inhouse constructive critic and eagle-eyed proof-reader.

AUTHOR'S NOTE

All through history, plagues of various types have been recorded, the most catastrophic being the influenza epidemic of 1918–19, which killed up to a hundred million people worldwide. Due to lack of accurate diagnosis until modern times, the causes of many plagues are unknown, but the notorious 'Black Death' of 1347, which killed a quarter of the population of Europe, is attributed to bubonic plague carried by rat fleas. However, some epidemics were called the 'yellow plague' due to the obvious jaundice, which is not a feature of bubonic plague. There are several mentions of the yellow plague in medieval Welsh annals, such as the *Dylyt Melyn* of AD 547, which killed Maelgwn Gwynedd, an early king of North Wales, and caused some Welsh saints to flee to Brittany. Ten years earlier, according to the *Annales Cambriae*, in the year that Arthur died at the battle of Camlann, 'there was plague in Britain and Ireland'. The cause is uncertain, but mosquito-borne yellow fever is a possibility, known to have occurred in Europe, including England, in the 1700s. Virus hepatitis, malaria or Weil's disease, also contracted from rats, are other possibilities.

*　　*　　*

'Heresy' may be defined as the expression of any opinion which runs counter to the beliefs of the majority 'Establishment' and is most commonly applied to conflicting religious views. Almost every religion has its heretics and the Christian faith is no exception, with over forty different heresies being listed. Most challenged the entrenched views of the Roman Catholic Church right from its inception, including Arianism, Gnosticism, Catharism and Pelagianism. Further details are given in a note at the end of this book, though no doubt Thomas de Peyne will lecture you en route!

One of the problems in writing a long series, of which this is the fourteenth, is that regular readers will have already become familiar with the background and main characters, perhaps becoming impatient with repeated explanations in each book. However, new readers would wish to be 'brought up to speed' on the general situation and on some of the historical aspects, so a glossary is offered with an explanation of some medieval terms, especially those relating to functions of the coroner, one of the oldest legal offices in England, established in 1194.

Any attempt to use 'olde worlde' dialogue in a historical novel of this period is as inaccurate as it is futile, for in late-twelfth-century Devon most people would have spoken Early Middle English, which would be totally incomprehensible to us today. Many others would have spoken 'Western Welsh', a Celtic tongue similar to Welsh, Breton and Cornish, while the ruling classes would have spoken Norman-French. The language of the Church and virtually all writing would have been Latin.

The only money in circulation would have been the silver penny, apart from a few foreign gold coins known as 'bezants'. The average wage of a working man was about two pence a day, and coins were cut into halves and quarters for small purchases. A 'pound' was 240 pence and a 'mark' 160 pence, but these were nominal accounting terms, not actual coinage.

All the names of people in this book are authentic for the period, being either real historical characters or taken from the Exeter Crown Pleas Roll of 1238. Unfortunately, though the identities of sheriffs and senior churchmen are known, history has not recorded the names of the Devon coroners until the thirteenth century, so Sir John de Wolfe had to be a product of the author's imagination.

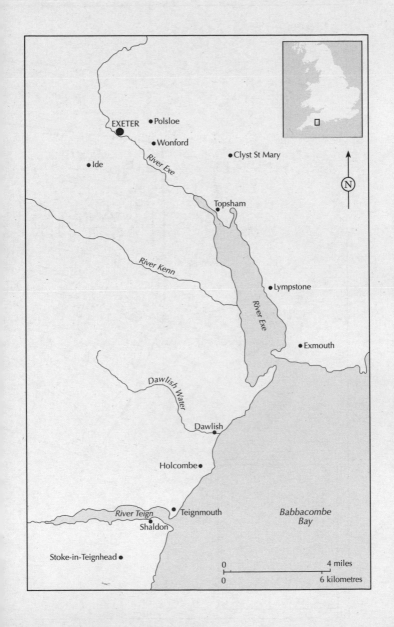

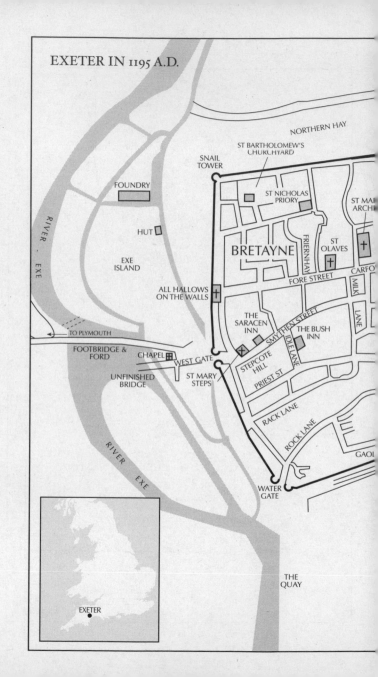

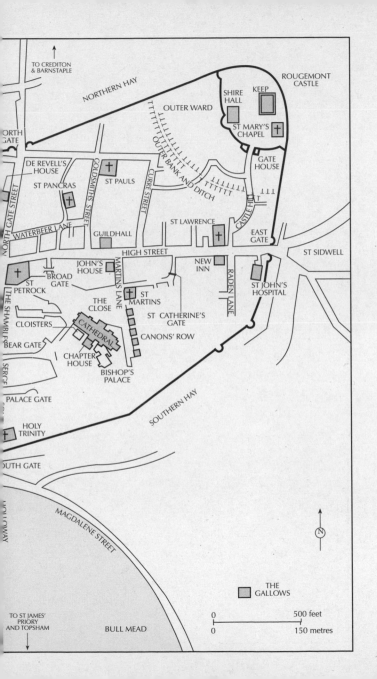

TO CREDITON & BARNSTAPLE

NORTHERN HAY

ROUGEMONT CASTLE

SHIRE HALL

KEEP

OUTER WARD

NORTH GATE

ST MARY'S CHAPEL

DE REVELL'S HOUSE

GOLDSMITHS STREET

ST PANCRAS

ST PAULS

OUTER BANK AND DITCH

CURRE STREET

GATE HOUSE

NORTH GATE STREET

WATERBEER LANE

GUILDHALL

ST LAWRENCE

CASTLE HILL

EAST GATE

HIGH STREET

ST SIDWELL

JOHN'S HOUSE

MARTINS LANE

NEW INN

BROAD GATE

ST PETROCK

ST MARTINS

RADEN LANE

ST JOHN'S HOSPITAL

THE SHAMBLES

THE CLOSE

ST CATHERINE'S GATE

CLOISTERS

CATHEDRAL

CANONS' ROW

BEAR GATE

SERGE

CHAPTER HOUSE

PALACE GATE

BISHOP'S PALACE

HOLLOWAY

HOLY TRINITY

SOUTHERN HAY

SOUTH GATE

MAGDALENE STREET

THE GALLOWS

TO ST JAMES' PRIORY AND TOPSHAM

BULL MEAD

N

0   500 feet
0   150 metres

GLOSSARY

ABJURING THE REALM

A criminal or fugitive gaining sanctuary in a church had forty days grace in which to confess to the coroner and then 'abjure the realm', that is, leave England, never to return. France was the usual destination, but Wales and Scotland could also be used.

He had to dress in sackcloth and carry a crude wooden cross to a port nominated by the coroner. He had to take the first ship to leave for abroad and if none was available, he had to wade out up to his knees in every tide to show his willingness to leave. Many abjurers absconded en route and became outlaws; others were killed by the angry families of their victims.

ALBIGENSIAN

See 'Historical Note'.

ALE

A weak drink brewed before the advent of hops. The name derived from an 'ale' which was a village celebration, where much drinking took place, often held in the churchyard. The words 'wassail' and 'bridal' derive from this.

ANATHEMA
An extreme form of excommunication used by the Early Christian Church, implying complete banishment from the Church.

APOSTASY
The voluntary rejection or abandonment of a person's religion, who then became an 'apostate'. In strict Islamic law, apostasy is punishable by death.

APOTHECARY
A medieval medicine seller and herbalist, who also offered medical aid and advice, as physicians were very rare outside large cities. Much medical aid was provided by monks and nuns.

ARIANISM
See 'Historical Note'.

BAILEY
Originally the defended area around a castle keep, as in 'motte and bailey', but later applied to the yard of a dwelling.

BAILIFF
Many different types, but in medieval terms, was the officer of a manor lord responsible for organising all the agricultural work. Other senior servants in towns and other establishments could be termed bailiffs.

BARON
A lord who was a 'tenant-in-chief', holding his land directly from the king, who owned the whole country. A 'Baron of the Exchequer' came to mean a judge of the royal courts, not connected with the actual Exchequer.

BURGESS

A merchant or property-owner in a town or city, his house and garden being his 'burgage'. The burgesses of a borough elected the council and the portreeves and, later, the mayor.

CANON

A senior priest in a cathedral, a member of the chapter, deriving his living from the grant of a parish or land providing an income. Exeter had twenty-four canons, most having an entourage of vicars and secondaries who often attended the nine 'offices' (services) each day on their behalf.

CAPON

A castrated male chicken, known since Roman times to be more tender than a farm fowl, which was thought suitable only for peasants.

CATHAR

See 'Historical Note'.

CHAPMAN

Also known as a packman, he was a travelling pedlar, who hawked his wares, mainly needles, threads, ribbons and other haberdashery, around the towns and villages.

CHAPTER

The administrative body of a monastery, priory or cathedral, consisting of canons, prebendaries and priests, which usually met daily in the chapter house. The name derives from the practice of having a chapter of either a monastic Rule, such that of St Benedict, or of the Gospels, read at every session.

COB

A building material made from clay, lime, ferns, dung, etc. (also see 'wattle and daub') made into walls or plastered over panels of woven twigs supported by oak frames.

COG

The common sea-going sailing vessel of the Middle Ages, derived from the Viking longship, but much broader and higher, with a single mast and square sail. There was no rudder before the twelfth/ thirteenth centuries, but a steering oar on the 'steerboard' side.

COIF

A close fitting helmet of felt or linen, worn by either sex and tied with tapes under the chin.

CONSTABLE

Several meanings, the custodian of a castle, but also applied to a watchman who patrolled the streets.

CORONER

Though there are a couple of mentions of a coroner in late Saxon times, the office really began in September 1194, when the royal justices at their session in Rochester, Kent, proclaimed Article Twenty, which in a single sentence launched a system that has survived for over 800 years. They said '*In every county of the King's realm shall be elected three knights and one clerk, to keep the pleas of the Crown.*'

The reason for the establishment of coroners was mainly financial; the aim was to sweep as much money as possible into the royal Exchequer. Richard the Lionheart was a spendthrift, using huge sums to finance his expedition to the Third Crusade in 1189 and for his wars against the French. Kidnapped on his way home from Palestine, he was held for well over a year in prisons in Austria and Germany and a huge ransom was needed to free him. To raise this money, his Chief Justiciar, Hubert Walter, who was also Archbishop of Canterbury, introduced many measures to extort money from the population of England.

Hubert revived the office of coroner, which was intended to raise money by a variety of means relating to the administration of the law. One of these was the investigation of all deaths which were not obviously natural, as well as serious assaults, rapes, house fires, discovery of buried treasure, wrecks of the sea and catches of the royal fish (whales and sturgeon). Coroners also took confessions from criminals seeking sanctuary in churches, organised abjurations of the realm (q.v.), attended executions and ordeals (q.v.) and trial by battle.

As the Normans had inherited a multiple system of county and manorial courts from the Saxons, the coroner also worked to sweep lucrative business into the royal courts. This gave him the title of 'Keeper of the Pleas of the Crown', from the original Latin of which (*custos placitorum coronas*) the word 'coroner' is derived.

It was difficult to find knights willing to take on the job, as it was unpaid and the appointee had to have a large private income of at least twenty pounds a year. This was supposed to make him immune from corruption, which was common amongst the sheriffs. Indeed, another reason for the introduction of coroners was to keep a check on the sheriffs, who were the king's representatives in each county ('shire-reeve').

COVER-CHIEF
From the Norman-French 'couvre-chef', a linen or silk cloth that covered a lady's head, the ends hanging down the back and then forward over the bust, usually secured by a head-band. In Saxon times, it was called a 'head-rail'. Usually worn with a wimple, which covered the neck and sides of the face.

CURFEW
The prohibition of open fires after dark for fear of starting conflagrations. Derived from 'couvre-fue' from the covering or banking-down of fires at dusk. During the curfew no one was supposed be on the streets without good reason and the city gates were closed from sunset to dawn. One thirteenth century mayor of Exeter was hanged for failing to ensure this.

CURIA REGIS
The Royal Council, composed of major barons, judges and bishops, who advised the king.

DESTRIER
A large war-horse, capable of carrying an armoured knight.

EXCHEQUER
The financial organ of English government, where all taxes were received in coin twice-yearly from the sheriffs. Originally in Winchester, it moved to Westminster in the late twelfth century. The calculations were performed with counters on a large table spread with a *chequered* cloth to assist accounting, which gave rise to the name.

EXCOMMUNICATION
The suspension of membership from a religious community, depriving a person of communion and participation in any of the sacraments. The excommunicant could not partake of the Eucharist or get married or buried in a Christian church.

EYRE
A sitting of the king's justices, introduced by Henry II in 1166, which moved around the counties in circuits. They later gave rise to the Assize Courts and in modern times, these became the Crown Courts.

FARM
The taxes from a county, collected in coin on behalf of the sheriff and taken by him personally every six months to the Exchequer. The sum to be raised was fixed annually by the Exchequer and if the sheriff could raise more, he could keep the excess, which made the office of sheriff much sought after.

FLUMMERY
A blancmange-like soft dessert made by straining boiled oatmeal and flavouring with fruit and honey.

FRUMENTY
A dish of wheat boiled in milk with sugar and spices such as cinnamon. Meat such as venison could be added.

HERETIC
See 'Historical Note'.

HOSE
Long stockings, usually single-legged, secured by laces to an underbelt. Worn under the tunic and sometimes having a leather sole in place of a shoe.

HUNDRED
An administrative sub-division of a county, with its own monthly court. Name derived either from a hundred houses or a hundred hides of land.

INFIRMARIAN
A monk with some medical skills, appointed to run the infirmary in a religious house.

KIRTLE
A woman's gown, the ankle length equivalent of the male tunic.

MANTLE
A cloak, usually formed of a large rectangle of cloth, secured at a shoulder by one corner being passed through a ring or brooch, or by a chain passing below the neck.

MURRAIN
A disease or epidemic amongst sheep or cattle, though sometimes applied to people. It was a blanket term, as the actual diseases were not identifiable in the Middle Ages.

ORDEAL
An ancient ritual intended to reveal guilt or innocence. The subject of the enquiry, in the presence of the coroner and a priest, had to submit to painful procedures, such as walking barefoot over nine red-hot ploughshares, taking a stone from the bottom of a vat of boiling water or licking a red-hot iron. If the affected part had healed well after three days he was adjudged innocent. Women were tied up and thrown into deep water – if they floated, they were guilty! The ordeal was abolished by the Vatican in 1215.

OSTLER
A servant who attended to the care and stabling of horses.

PALFREY
A small horse for riding, especially used by ladies.

PAPAL BULL
A edict or charter issued by the Pope, named after the 'bulla', or leaden seal, attached to the document.

PAPAL LEGATE
The representative of the Pope appointed to a foreign country.

PELAGIANISM
See 'Historical Note'.

PELISSE
An outer garment worn by both men and women, with a fur lining for winter wear. The fur could be sable, rabbit, cat, marten, etc.

PORTREEVE
Originally a medieval customs officer, who ensured that taxes and duty were paid at markets and ports – later they became representatives of the townsfolk and led the town council until mayors were introduced.

POSSET
A drink made from hot spiced milk curdled with wine and sweetened with sugar or honey.

POTAGE
Soup or stew, a staple part of the diet in medieval times,

when a cauldron was often permanently simmering, vegetables and meat being added when available.

PREBENDARY
A priest, usually a member of a cathedral chapter, who derived his income from the benefice of a church or parish.

PRECENTOR
A senior monk or priest in a cathedral or abbey, who organised the choral services and music as well as the library and archives.

PRESENTMENT OF ENGLISHRY
At coroner's inquests, a corpse was presumed to be Norman, unless the locals could prove 'Englishry' by presenting evidence of identity from the family. If they could not, a 'murdrum' fine was imposed by the coroner, on the assumption that Normans were murdered by the Saxons they had conquered in 1066. Murdrum fines became a cynical device to extort money, persisting for several hundred years after the Conquest, by which time it was virtually impossible to differentiate between the races.

PROCTOR
A senior priest or monk responsible for discipline in an abbey or cathedral. He had lay servants or bailiffs to carry out his orders, who policed the ecclesiastical enclaves.

REMOVE
A 'course' in medieval dining. Two or three 'removes' might have been offered, each having a variety of dishes, which were removed before the next round.

ROUNSEY
A general purpose horse, used for riding or as a pack-horse.

RUSH LAMP
Illumination given by a lighted reed, made by soaking a peeled reed in waste animal fat. This light was the only illumination available to most of the population, as candles were expensive.

SCRIP
A pouch carried on a belt.

SECONDARY
A young man aspiring to become a priest when he reached the minimum age of twenty-four. Secondaries assisted canons and their vicars in their cathedral duties.

SERGEANT (or SERJEANT)
Several meanings, either a legal/administrative officer in a Hundred or a military rank of a senior man-at-arms.

SHAMBLES
Where animals were slaughtered in the street and meat displayed for sale by the butchers. As the blood and offal was discarded on to the ground, the name gave rise to the expression for great disorder.

SURCOAT
A loose garment worn over the tunic or, in women, the kirtle. Originally, it was meant to cover the coat of mail of the warrior, especially to shield it from the sun in hot climates, and also to carry identifying symbols over the anonymous chain mail (a 'coat of arms'). Later became a common article of wear.

TONSURE

Shaving of the head of persons in religious orders, to demonstrate the renunciation of worldly fashion. The usual Roman form was a large circular area on top of the head, but the Celtic Church adopted shaving the hair forwards from a line joining the ears.

TRENCHER

A thick slice of stale bread, used as a plate on the scrubbed boards of a table, to absorb the juices of the food. Often given to beggars or the dogs at the end of the meal.

TUNIC

The usual wear for men, a long garment belted at the waist, the length often denoting the wearer's status. Working men usually wore a short tunic over breeches.

VICAR

A religious representative, such as a priest in a parish who represents the bishop – or in a cathedral, one who attends services on behalf of his canon, sometimes called a 'vicar-choral'. One who represents the bishop in administrative or legal matters was a vicar-general.

VULGATE

The early Catholic version of the Bible, written in Latin in the early fifth century, much of it attributed to St Jerome.

WATTLE AND DAUB

A building material plastered over woven hazel withies set between the house-frames. Usually made from clay, horsehair, straw and even manure (q.v. 'cob'.).

WIMPLE
A cloth of linen or silk, pinned at each temple, framing a lady's face and covering the throat up to the chin.

PROLOGUE

November 1196

The chapman could see that it was an unusual sort of funeral, even for such an outlandish place as Lympstone. There were corpses, bearers, mourners and a grave, but it was nothing like he had ever seen before.

He shrugged his bulky pack from his back and set it down with some relief on the dusty road outside the church gate. Behind him, the track led down to a primitive wharf, where the river lapped against the muddy banks of the estuary of the River Exe. From where he stood, he could see over the low hedge around the churchyard to a corner well away from the existing grave-mounds. Here a flat farm-cart had just arrived, with a patient ox between the shafts. Six sheeted bodies lay on its bare boards, but there was no sign of coffins. Two of the shrouded shapes were pitifully small.

At the side of the cart lay a large pit, a dozen feet square and almost the depth of a man. Some distance away, three labourers leaned on shovels, their noses and mouths swathed in rags, knotted at the backs of their necks.

As the pedlar watched, he saw four other men, swaddled in cloaks and gloves, with hoods over their heads and cloths tied around their faces, begin to carry the bodies to the gaping pit. Near the east end of the small church, from which a bell tolled mournfully, a group of silent people watched, taking care not to come within fifty paces of the cart. The only exceptions were a tall man, dressed in sombre grey, and a diminutive priest with a slightly humped shoulder. On the side of the pit, the tall one stood, his black hair blowing in the breeze as he held the edge of his cloak across his mouth. The little priest took no such precautions, but was standing boldly on the very edge of the grave, reading loudly in Latin from a small book, his other hand making the sign of the cross as each corpse made its final short descent down into the earth.

The chapman turned to a burly man standing next to him, the foul smell from his soiled leather apron marking him out as a fuller.

'What's going on, friend? What tragedy was this?' he asked.

The fuller looked suspiciously at the pedlar. 'Where've you been these past few weeks?' he snapped.

'Just got off a boat down at the quayside.'

The other fellow backed away, his suspicions deepening. 'Not from abroad, are you? From foreign parts?'

His aggressive tone made the packman hurriedly shake his head.

'No, I've come no further than from Paignton, down the coast. Hoping to sell more of my needles and threads up this end of the county.'

The fuller relaxed with a grunt. 'The yellow plague is back again, no doubt brought in by seamen from across the Channel. Twice it's struck this village since last month.'

He nodded towards the churchyard, where the last body was being laid in the common grave. 'A whole family there, laid low inside three days. Yellow as gorse flowers, the lot of them.'

They both watched as the men with spades advanced on the heap of red earth alongside the pit, preparing to fill it in without delay.

'So who are the two men at the graveside?' persisted the pedlar, a naturally inquisitive soul.

'The tall one is the king's coroner from Exeter, Sir John de Wolfe. The bailiff called him because there were six dead in one house. Why he was summoned, I can't fathom, for it's obvious that it wasn't foul play.'

'The other one's the parish priest, I suppose?'

The fuller spat contemptuously on the ground. 'Not him! Our craven bastard's too scared to go near anyone with the plague, even to shrive them. That brave little fellow is the crowner's clerk.'

As the crowd in the churchyard began to drift away, the chapman shouldered his pack and trudged away from the village, heading for open country. Weary though he was, he had no desire to stay around Lympstone, if the yellow sickness was stalking its lanes.

CHAPTER ONE

In which Crowner John consults the sheriff

'You can't keep riding around half of Devonshire just to look at folks dying of a murrain,' objected the sheriff, pouring de Wolfe some wine from a pitcher on his table. 'There's no profit in it for the king's courts if there's no crime – and sooner or later you'll catch it yourself!'

As he picked up the cup and drank, the coroner grunted, his favourite form of response. 'I agree, but what do I do when I get a message from a bailiff or a Serjeant of the Hundred? The law obliges them to notify me of any unusual deaths.'

Henry de Furnellis, a grizzled old knight almost a score of years older than John, shook his head. 'Now that this yellow distemper is becoming more common along the coast, we'll have to tell the local officers not to bother you with such deaths. I hope to God that it doesn't spread further inland.'

The coroner, sprawled in a leather chair with his long legs sticking out towards the hearth, nodded his agreement. 'The folk down there are blaming it on vessels coming in from across the Channel, but from what my shipmasters tell me, at the moment there's no such disease in Normandy, Brittany or even Flanders.'

De Wolfe was a partner in a thriving wool-exporting business in Exeter, which had three vessels that regularly sailed back and forth to the places he had mentioned.

'Well, just be careful, John!' rumbled the sheriff. 'We don't want to lose you again, after just getting you back in harness.'

After being the county coroner for two years, de Wolfe had recently spent a few months in London at the king's command but was now back and, three weeks earlier, had resumed his old duties.

They were sitting in the sheriff's chamber in the keep of Rougemont, Exeter's brooding castle in the upper corner of the old walled city. Outside, the November morning was grey and cold, with an easterly wind hinting at early snow. John usually called upon his old Crusader friend each day, to discuss cases, politics and generally grumble about the world going to the dogs, in the way that older men do, though de Wolfe was only forty-two. Together they were the main law officers in Devon, the sheriff being the king's representative in the county, responsible for keeping the peace and the collection of taxes, while the coroner had a multitude of functions, including the complicated business of bringing cases to the royal courts.

'Are you settling back in again, John?' asked his grey-haired colleague solicitously. He looked across at de Wolfe, who he thought was looking a little drawn and haggard. At the best of times, the coroner was hardly a cheerful soul, but now his long face, large hooked nose and the deep-set eyes below the dark eyebrows looked even grimmer than usual. His jet-black hair, worn long and swept back, unlike the neck-crop of most Norman gentry, was still without a trace of grey, but de Furnellis thought he detected signs of ageing in the coroner's face.

'I'm glad to be back home,' said John in his deep, sonorous voice. 'Westminster didn't suit me. There was too little work and too much palace intrigue for my liking.'

'And Matilda? How is she taking her return home?'

He spoke carefully, for he was well aware that this was a delicate subject. The coroner's scowl deepened.

'Bloody woman! Without her, life would be so much easier. She's trapped with me, just as I am trapped with her.'

'The convent didn't suit her once again?' probed Henry, though he knew the answer well enough.

De Wolfe shook his head, swallowing the last of his red wine before replying. 'They won't take her back again in Polsloe, that's for sure. Twice she's gone in there and twice she's left. The beds are too hard, the food is too plain and they wear dowdy raiment, she says! What the hell does she expect in a nunnery?' Moodily, he banged his wine-cup back on Henry's desk.

'Her main complaint now, one that's eating her up inside, is that I deprived her of living in the royal court of Westminster when I resigned as Coroner of the Verge. She'll never forgive me for that, as long as she lives.'

The sheriff decided to back away from such a sensitive subject, and he was saved further embarrassment by his chief clerk entering, to hover with a sheaf of parchments and an impatient expression on his lined face. De Wolfe took the hint and pushed himself to his feet to pick up his wolfskin cloak from a nearby bench.

'I'll see you in the Shire Court tomorrow, then,' he promised. 'I've only one case to present, left by Nicholas de Arundell.'

The mention of that name caused de Furnellis to shake his head sadly. 'A nice young man, but not cut

7

out to be a coroner,' he said. 'I've never seen a man so relieved when he was told that you were taking over once again.'

John gave a lopsided grin. 'He wasn't the only one! Even though I have to stay up in that damned draughty chamber in the gatehouse, it's better than staying home with Matilda!'

He swung his cloak over his shoulders and loped out into the great hall of Rougemont.

The little priest who had braved the risks of pestilence in Lympstone was having his hair cut. This was a very public process, as he sat on a stool at the edge of Exeter's High Street near Carfoix, where the four old Roman roads crossed at the centre of the city. The portly barber, who also pulled teeth and cut toenails and corns, charged half a penny for a haircut, though in Thomas de Peyne's case this was hardly a bargain, as much of his thin lank hair was already shaved off for his priestly tonsure, a wide, bare circle on top of his head. Short of stature, Thomas had a thin face, a pointed nose and a weak chin, as well as a lame leg from the effects of spinal phthisis as a child, but an agile mind and a good education more than compensated for his poor physique.

As the man snipped away with his rusting scissors, Thomas's attention was drawn to a small crowd on the opposite side of the crossing. They were listening with varying degrees of attention to a man standing outside a baker's shop, earnestly lecturing them, with many flourishes of his arms. Due to the rumble of carts and barrows and the constant cries of stallholders yelling the merits of their goods, it was difficult for Thomas to follow what he was saying, but what he could hear obviously had some religious significance. However, the words 'free will' and 'man makes his own destiny' were enough to tell the little priest that the man haranguing his unresponsive audience was one of those who followed an alternative path to God from that offered by the Church of Rome.

When the barber had brushed off the remaining hairs from his worn cassock and relieved him of his halfpenny, Thomas dodged a porter jogging past with huge bales of wool balanced on his shoulder-pole and limped across the narrow street to listen to the orator. His interest was mainly professional, as Thomas was a conventional, devoted servant of the Church, faithful to all its tenets and rituals. However, though his faith was rock solid, he had an academic interest in the beliefs of those outside the Roman Church, ranging from Mohammedans to the various critics and non-conformists within the Christian world itself.

As he neared the fringe of the dozen people, including a couple of matrons clutching market baskets, he heard mutters of discontent from some.

'It's blasphemy. It ought not to be allowed!' came a wavering voice from an old grey-bearded man.

'The cathedral should lock him up, the scurrilous bastard!' came a more forthright comment.

Thomas stopped to listen for a few moments, as the crowd shifted, some leaving and a few more stopping as they passed along the crowded street. He heard nothing he had not heard before, as mild heresy was not that uncommon, either from unguarded tongues loosened by drink in alehouses or more discreet discussions behind closed doors. The present exponent, an emaciated fellow dressed in poor clothing, was broadcasting his beliefs about the way in which the Father and Son should be worshipped. It was somewhat unusual, and certainly risky, for such views to be shouted abroad in a city street, but Thomas had no intention of doing the cathedral proctors' work for them by denouncing or arresting the fellow.

He listened for a few moments and decided that the arguments that the man was setting forth were typical of those heretics who declared that all men had free will and that the Catholic Church was corrupt.

'Man can only be saved by knowing himself, not by intercession with the true God only through the priesthood,' the man brayed.

Thomas sighed at the obviously Gnostic preachings of the poor fellow and moved away from the crowd, who were becoming more irate at the blasphemies of the speaker. If the onlookers did not beat him up, then the orator was in danger of being picked up by the emissaries of Bishop Marshal, thought Thomas, especially if some canon or vicar happened to be passing by.

As he made his way back up the crowded High Street, he consoled himself with the thought that Rome had had to contend with heretics for almost a thousand years and that some poor crank yelling on an Exeter street was hardly likely to bring the Christian Church crashing to its knees.

It was still only about the eighth hour of the morning and he had no duties at the cathedral until two hours before noon, when he was due to teach Latin grammar to a class of unruly choirboys. A couple of months had passed since the coroner's team had returned from London, and since his master had been reinstated in his old job they had returned to their long-established routine of meeting each morning in the bleak chamber at the top of the castle gatehouse.

He limped along the High Street and then up the steep slope of Castle Hill and across the drawbridge of the dry moat, to the inner gate of Rougemont. A young soldier, who looked hardly old enough to handle sharp weapons, was on guard duty and waved him through with a cheerful greeting. Inside the arch, Thomas turned into the guard-room, where three more men-at-arms were squatting on the earth floor playing dice. They ignored him as he crossed to a low doorway and laboriously began to climb a stone staircase set into the thick wall. Two floors up, he pushed through a curtain of sacking meant to reduce draughts and went into a barren room with two arrow-slit windows that gave a view down over the city.

'Here's our favourite dwarf!' cackled a huge man sitting on the sill of one of the window embrasures. He had tangled ginger hair and large pair of drooping moustaches to match. A ruddy face with a large bulbous nose was relieved by bright blue eyes. Gwyn of Polruan was the coroner's officer, a former Cornish fisherman who had spent the past twenty years as John de Wolfe's bodyguard, squire and faithful friend. He had a very large body, encased as usual in coarse serge breeches and a tattered leather jerkin.

The priest scowled at Gwyn, for although they were firm friends he sometimes tired of the Cornishman's jibes at his small size and puny muscles.

'You've had your hair shorn,' grunted de Wolfe, almost accusingly, staring at his clerk's head. 'Is it some sort of religious penance?' He glared up from where he sat at his trestle table.

'No, Crowner, not at all!' replied Thomas indignantly. 'It's just that I wanted less cover for fleas. My lodgings are infested with them.' The clerk shared a room with a cathedral secondary in a house on Priest Street in the lower town.

He pulled a stool up to the table, which along with the coroner's wooden chair and a small charcoal brazier was the only furniture in the spartan chamber.

Sir Richard de Revelle, the previous sheriff and de Wolfe's brother-in-law, had grudgingly allotted John the least desirable room in the whole castle, as a token of his contempt for the new office of coroner, which he looked on as usurping his own authority.

As Thomas spread out his writing materials on the table, John resumed his conversation with Gwyn. Usually, the pair conversed in the Celtic tongue, as Gwyn was Cornish and John had learned Welsh at his mother's knee. However, they reverted to English in deference to Thomas.

'Some claim that this yellow curse is brought into the ports by ship-men from abroad,' growled the coroner. 'Did you ever see such outbreaks in Cornwall?'

Gwyn shook his massive head. 'Not myself, but my grandfather told me of such deaths many years ago. They were around Falmouth and Newlyn, so maybe they're right about harbours giving it entrance into the country.'

'I've heard people blaming rats for the plague,' contributed Thomas as he smoothed out a sheet of parchment.

The Cornishman scratched his crotch ruminatively. 'Odd you should say that, for my father used to be a tinner before he took to fishing at Polruan. He said that in tin workings where there were many rats, men used to get sick with yellow skin and eyes and some died. But they didn't pass it on to other men, as far as I could make out.'

He squinted out of his narrow window opening at the roofs of the city below, where a cold east wind was swirling a few flakes of snow about.

'Are we going out to every death from this pestilence, Crowner?' he grumbled. 'If it spreads, we'll have no time for any other work, especially if it reaches other more distant ports, like Dawlish or Dartmouth.'

He almost bit his tongue as he let slip 'Dawlish', for that was where his master's woman lived and he had not meant to mention the possibility of the yellow death endangering her there. But de Wolfe was phlegmatic about the risks.

'Thank Christ it's almost the end of the sailing season, so there'll be few vessels coming in there from abroad until the spring.'

'It's said that very cold winter weather freezes out the contagion,' said Thomas consolingly. 'So let's pray for plenty of snow and ice this year.'

'Looks as if it's starting already,' growled Gwyn, staring out through the embrasure. 'I'll have to scrounge another brazier from the barracks. This bloody chamber gets cold enough to freeze the balls off those rats of yours, Thomas.'

'They're not *my* rats, you Cornish lump!' retaliated the clerk, but John cut short their frequent bickering.

'You asked about holding inquests on these deaths, Gwyn,' he said. 'The sheriff was talking about that earlier. It seems that the Justices in Eyre have declared that unless there's anything suspicious, we can dispense with investigating them.'

His officer pulled his thick jerkin more closely around him, as the strengthening wind blew more persistently through the unglazed window slit.

'That's a blessing. I don't fancy taking the curse back to my wife and sons at the Bush,' he muttered.

The coroner, also feeling the sudden cold, rose from his seat behind the rough table and draped his dark cloak around his shoulders. 'I'm going down to the Guildhall. I want to talk to Hugh de Relaga about our vessels. Talking of Dawlish, I think that two of the ships are there now, so I want to know if they can make any more voyages before being beached for the winter.'

As he made for the doorway, the mischievous Gwyn added a helpful suggestion. 'Best go down to the coast and see for yourself, Crowner!'

Though his expression was blandly innocent, de Wolfe knew that he was slyly hinting at an excuse for visiting the delectable Hilda of Dawlish.

The Guildhall, recently rebuilt in stone, was in the High Street, only a few hundred paces from de Wolfe's house in Martin's Lane. He strode down from the castle, conscious of the biting wind, though the snow flurries had ceased. If this was the weather in early November, thought John, we might be in for a hard winter – perhaps all to the good, if it damped down this threatened epidemic.

The narrow street was as crowded as usual, stalls and booths obstructing each side. The middle, with its central culvert that carried filth downhill, was filled with handcarts, porters pushing barrows and ox-carts piled with bales of wool or straw. The rest of the space was clogged with jostling humanity, all buying, selling, talking, shouting and cursing.

The coroner, a head taller than most men, pushed his way through to reach the wide door of the hall, which was the centre of the economic and civic life of Exeter. As well as providing accommodation for the various trade guilds, it housed the city council, the group of burgesses who ran the administration, under the leadership of the two portreeves. There was talk of electing a mayor, a continental practice which had recently been adopted by London and a few other towns, but for now Hugh de Relaga and Henry Rifford led the more prominent merchants and tradesmen who governed the city.

Almost all the building was taken up by the main hall, parts of which were divided up by movable screens to form alcoves to accommodate a variety of guild and business functions. A number of merchants and tradesmen were standing around, chattering and gesticulating as they conducted their business. At the back was a pair of small rooms, one of which was for the portreeves and their clerks. The two leaders came in at least once a day, though they had their own profitable businesses to run elswhere in the town. Hugh de Relaga was a prominent dealer in wool, and his colleague, Henry Rifford, was a leather merchant and tannery owner.

John was pleased to find Hugh at his table in a corner of the chamber, poring over a list of accounts just supplied by his chief clerk. As a trader, it was essential to be literate – a rare accomplishment in a society where few but those in holy orders could read and write.

'I trust we are making a fortune, Hugh!' he called from the doorway.

The rotund merchant rose from his chair with a broad smile and waved de Wolfe to a nearby stool. He was an unfailingly cheerful fellow, with a fondness for gaudy clothing. Today he wore a yellow linen tunic under a surcoat of bright red satin, with a mantle of green velvet draped over the back of his chair. His head was swathed in a turban-like coil of red brocade, the free end hanging down over one shoulder.

'We're doing very well, John, though these outbreaks of distemper may affect the transport of goods,' he said breezily. 'However, our long voyages will soon be ending for the winter.'

He was repeating John's earlier remark to Gwyn about their ships being laid up for the season. They were vital for their business venture, as when Hilda had been widowed the previous year she had brought her late husband's three ships into the existing partnership between de Relaga and the coroner. They used them to move their wool and cloth around the Channel ports as far distant as Flanders and the Rhine.

The portreeve sent one of his clerks for wine and pastries, and over refreshments he gave John a summary of their present trading position. Though de Wolfe was a 'sleeping partner', he took a healthy interest in the fortunes of their firm. He had invested the wealth he had acquired over years of campaigning into their joint business and had benefited considerably from the thriving expansion of Exeter's commercial life.

Hugh pushed aside his parchments and smiled benignly at the coroner. 'So you'll not starve this month, John. We are doing quite nicely. But tell me how other matters are going with you – have you settled back fully into your old harness?'

The coroner set his cup on the table and wiped his lips appreciatively. Trust Hugh to have only the best wine from the Loire.

'It hardly seems as if I've been away for those months,' he said candidly. 'At least, it does as far as my duties go. At home it's a different matter!'

The portreeve nodded sympathetically. It was a little difficult for him, as he was about the only friend of John's that Matilda would tolerate, mainly because he was rich, well dressed and always made a point of flattering her. But he knew the situation in Martin's Lane and was sad that his friend felt so frustrated and unhappy with his lot. He decided to avoid the subject and stick to John's coronership.

'You found Westminster not to your taste?' he asked.

'Like living in a bloody hive full of bees!' grunted de Wolfe. 'All gossip and scandal and intrigue, but very little actual work for me.'

He had been Coroner of the Verge for only a short while, posted there on the direct orders of King

Richard, but after dealing with an extraordinary crime he decided that he wanted to leave, partly from feelings of guilt at not having done enough to solve it.

They spoke a little more about the sporadic cases of the yellow plague that had been cropping up, and John told him of the most recent one in Lympstone. For once, Hugh looked seriously concerned. 'Lympstone! That's getting uncomfortably close to Topsham.'

This was the port at the upper end of the estuary of the River Exe, where much of their goods were handled. If the disease hit Topsham, then their shipments would be badly disrupted. Like so many worried people around the southern coast, they began discussing possible causes of the yellow curse, without any hope of an answer.

'Why don't you ask the opinion of your new neighbour?' suggested Hugh. John looked at him blankly for a moment, then realised what he meant.

'The new physician? I've hardly said a word to him yet, though my wife seems to think that he's some kind of saint.'

Three months earlier, while John was away in London, the house next door in Martin's Lane had found a new tenant. Empty for well over a year since the silversmith who lived there had been murdered, it had been bought cheaply by the former sheriff, Richard de Revelle, John's brother-in-law. Always striving to make yet more money, Richard had rented it out to Exeter's first resident physician, Clement of Salisbury, who had recently arrived in the city to set up in practice.

Apart from muttering an occasional greeting when they passed in the street, John had kept clear of his neighbours, not being a very sociable individual. However, from the limited conversation he had with Matilda, he gathered that the new doctor and his wife were welcome additions to the upper levels of Exeter society.

Clement was a good-looking man of about John's age, who dressed exceptionally well, as did his handsome wife. Best of all in Matilda's eyes, they were very devout and already constant attenders at the cathedral. Now Matilda had invited them to her own church of St Olave's in Fore Street, for additional services during the week.

'Perhaps I'll have a few words with him when I next see him,' muttered de Wolfe. 'Though I doubt he'll know any more about plagues and distempers than the monks at St John's Hospital. He seems to be more interested in dancing attendance on the wealthier folk in the city.'

As he spoke, he realised that his friend was one of those wealthier folk, but de Relaga was not one to take offence. They spoke for a little while longer, until the clerks began to get restive as they hovered about the portreeve with sheaves of parchment. John finished his wine and rose to leave, his final query to Hugh being about his brother-in-law.

'Have you seen anything of Richard de Revelle lately?' he asked. 'I've not set eyes on him since I returned – not that it distresses me, but I always feel uneasy if I don't know what mischief he might be up to!'

The portreeve grinned. 'Have you not heard that he's become a pig farmer now?'

John stared at him, suspecting some jest, for which Hugh was well known. 'A pig farmer? The last I heard, he was making money with that private school of his down in Smythen Street.'

De Relaga nodded, the length of brocade wound around his head bobbing as he did so. 'He's still got that, but he's found a new way of making yet more money. He has several acres of mud down near Clyst St George and another somewhere about Dartmouth, where he has hundreds of swine.'

John almost gaped in surprise. 'I can't see that dandified creature pouring buckets of pigswill or shovelling manure!' he exclaimed.

The portreeve shook his head. 'I doubt he's ever even seen the damned hogs! He'll have ill-paid slaves to do that for him.'

'So what's he up to, for God's sake?'

'As I said, making money! He discovered that the king's army in France needed feeding, so he's supplying salted pork and smoked bacon by the ton. No doubt at inflated prices, but the soldiers have to be fed. He sends shiploads of the stuff over to Barfleur and Honfleur, mainly out of Exmouth, Topsham and Dartmouth.'

'Well, well! It's a change to see that rascal engaged in some honest trade for once,' grunted John. 'But I'll wager there's some mischief somewhere – bribing royal purveyors to give a higher price or some such crafty deceit.'

Hugh shrugged. 'Perhaps he's seen the error of his ways at last. I even considered offering to carry some of his cargoes across the Channel in our ships.'

'His money is as good as anyone's, I suppose,' conceded John. 'I'll leave it to you, as long as you watch the bastard like a hawk!'

CHAPTER TWO

In which Crowner John visits the Bush Inn

John de Wolfe went out into the cold wind and the crowded streets, this time walking to Carfoix near where Thomas had had his hair cut and seen his heretic. The coroner marched across and down the slope of Fore Street, past the tiny church of St Olave's, where his wife worshipped almost every day. Then he turned left into even narrower lanes and came out into Smythen Street, where his brother-in-law owned a small college which taught logic, mathematics and theology to a handful of earnest young men.

Further down, a side turning crossed some weed-filled land which had lain barren for several years since fire destroyed a row of wooden houses. Now logically known as Idle Lane, the only structure left was a stone-built tavern, the Bush. Since he had returned from the Crusade four years ago, this inn had been as much a part of John's life as his own house. It was here that his former mistress Nesta had reigned as landlady until she left for Wales to get married. Now Gwyn's wife Martha was in charge, as John had bought the inn and set them up to run it for him.

He ducked his head to enter the low front door, set in a whitewashed wall under a steep thatched roof. The whole of the ground floor was a single ale-room, with a large loft above where straw pallets provided lodging for anyone wishing to spend the night. The Bush was one of Exeter's most popular inns, with a reputation for good food, excellent ale and clean mattresses. A large heap of logs glowed in the firepit near the centre of the room, the smoke finding its way out through the eaves under the edge of the thatch, which was barely above head height. The eye-watering atmosphere was compounded by the smell of cooking, sweat and spilled ale, but unlike many of the other alehouses in the city there was no stench of urine and the rushes on the floor were changed regularly.

He made his way to his usual seat, a bench at a table near the firepit, sheltered from the draughts from the door by a shoulder-high wicker hurdle. His bottom had hardly touched the bench when an old man materialised, sliding a pottery ale-jar in front of him, filled with a quart of the Bush's finest brew.

'God and His Blessed Son be with you, Sir John!' bleated Edwin, the tavern's 'potboy', though he was well past sixty. An old soldier, he had lost an eye and was crippled in one leg from wounds suffered in Ireland. Usually, he called the coroner 'captain' in deference to his military reputation, but Gwyn had told John that he had recently become very religious, probably as an insurance against hellfire as he felt his final years approaching. Now Edwin eschewed all mention of warfare and violence, mouthing pious platitudes instead, much to the ribald amusement of many of the Bush's patrons, who for years past had been used to his barrack-room oaths and blasphemies.

'Gwyn's out in the yard. I'll tell him you're here,' he said as he moved off with some empty mugs, his collapsed and whitened eye rolling horribly as he tried to wink at the coroner.

John settled down to enjoy his quart, nodding to acquaintances and exchanging a word with others he knew, who were seated at the few tables scattered around the room. Almost everyone in Exeter knew de Wolfe by sight. He was admired as an ex-Crusader and respected as one of the few honest officials in the county. Not a few feared him, as though he was an almost obsessional champion of justice he was not a man to cross, as he came down hard on any wrongdoing.

A moment later Martha bustled in through the back door, which led to the cook-shed, the brewing hut and the laundry, set outside in the muddy yard at the rear, which they shared with the privy, the pigsty and the chicken run. Gwyn's wife was a large, matronly woman, brisk and efficient in spite of her bulk, which was emphasised by her voluminous dress of brown wool, covered by a tent-like linen apron. She had a broad, genial face, already lined from forty years of hard work. A fringe of iron-grey hair hung below the linen cloth that enveloped her head, but her small, dark eyes were as bright as buttons.

'Sir John, can I get you some victuals?' she demanded in her broad Cornish. 'We've a new smoked ham – none the worse for coming from your brother-in-law's piggery!'

John grinned up at her amiable face. 'I've only just heard about his venture with hogs and sows. Let's hope he's better at making bacon that he was at being sheriff!'

He declined the offer of a meal, saying that as it was approaching noon he would soon have to go back to Martin's Lane, where Mary, his cook-maid, would have prepared his dinner.

As Martha moved away to greet her other patrons with her easy manner, de Wolfe was reminded of how

Nesta used to do the same, both of them able to chaff and tease their customers without giving offence, but also capable of dealing firmly with those who had drunk too much and became either overfamiliar or aggressive. The thought of his former Welsh mistress made him pensive for a moment, as she so often used to share this very same bench with him, as well as the little room directly overhead in the loft, where they had spent so many tender and passionate hours.

Suddenly, Gwyn was looming over him, rubbing his spade-like hands on a cloth. 'Sure you'll not have a bite to eat, Crowner?'

John shook his head, then sniffed at a strong smell of ale that exuded from his officer. 'God's bones, man, have you been drinking the inn dry? I thought you were still up at the castle?'

The ginger giant grinned. 'I've just come back down to start off a new tub of mash. Haven't touched a drop of ale since breakfast! What you smell is the fruit of my new career – apart from being the coroner's officer,' he added hastily. 'My good wife has appointed me brew-master. A job made for me in heaven!'

He explained how he was now in charge of making the ale, except when called away on coroner's duties. 'I'm sticking to the recipe that dear Nesta used to use. Everyone says she made the best ale in Exeter, so I see no reason to change.'

Once again, the spectre of the woman he had loved rose up, but John was nothing if not a realist. Hilda of Dawlish was equally dear to him now, and the very thought of her made him eager to throw himself on to his horse and canter off down to the coast to see her. Even the dozen miles that separated them were far too many. She refused to move to Exeter, even though he could well afford to find another house for her. Matilda was entrenched in Martin's Lane, so he seemed doomed to pound the road to Dawlish, back and forth like the shuttle in a loom.

His reverie was broken when he realised that Gwyn was talking to him again.

'I've just heard a rumour that some folks down in Bretayne have fallen sick with the yellow plague. If that's true, then it's getting uncomfortably close to us.'

John noticed that the low murmur of talk in the taproom had suddenly altered. There seemed to be a wave of more urgent conversation sweeping across the few dozen customers, people huddling closer to hear the news brought in by a couple of porters who had just arrived.

'Are we keeping clear of it, if there are deaths, Crowner?' asked Gwyn, worried about his wife and two young sons.

'Unless there's anything untoward about any of them,' said John reassuringly. Though there was no written law on the matter, the vague declaration of the king's justices in September two years ago, which had set up the office of coroner, had been refined piecemeal by the judges ever since when problems had arisen. It seemed clear that while murder, accident, suicide and sudden or suspicious deaths fell within the coroner's purview, the majority of deaths from obvious disease or old age were excluded, as long as they occurred in the presence of the family. A few of the men in the ale-room were now rising and making for the door, with worried expressions on their faces.

'Best get home and warn my wife and daughters,' said one as he passed, a shoemaker whom John recognised. 'Tell them to keep indoors until we know the truth of this tale.'

De Wolfe could well appreciate how easily panic could spread in a closed city like Exeter, where more than four thousand people were packed together inside a few acres within the walls. He downed the rest of his ale and got to his feet.

'Perhaps that's good advice, Gwyn,' he said. 'Keep your boys at home for now, until we hear whether this is just some false rumour.'

He realised that it was a rather futile gesture, given that Gwyn and his family lived in one of the most popular taverns in the city, where outsiders and strangers were coming and going all the time, possibly bringing contagion with them. Something Hugh de Relaga had said that morning came back to him.

'Maybe I will have a word with that quack who's come to live as my neighbour,' he muttered as he swung his cloak about his shoulders and went out into the city streets, which suddenly seemed to have a menacing feel about them.

Meal-times had never been a very cheerful occasion in the de Wolfe household, but since John had returned from Westminster they had all the charm of a funeral. Matilda, already in a chronic state of sulky depression, had been bitterly disappointed when her husband had voluntarily given up his appointment as Coroner of the Verge. At a stroke, she had been deprived of the chance to live at court and flaunt John's position as coroner to the Royal Household, a position granted to him personally by King Richard – though John would have considered 'thrust upon him' more accurate than 'granted'. Now, as they sat in the gloomy hall which occupied almost all of the high, narrow house in Martin's Lane, she tried to behave as if her husband did not exist. Each sat at the opposite ends of the long oaken table, concentrating on the food brought in by Mary, the dark-haired young woman who was their cook and maid of all work about the house. Matilda had her own personal handmaiden, if such a title

25

could be used for Lucille, a skinny, snivelling girl from the Vexin in northern Normandy.

As Mary placed a wooden bowl of mutton stew in front of her master, she gave him a surreptitious wink, for she was more of a wife to him than Matilda. She cooked his food, washed his clothes, cleaned his house, listened to his woes – and in the past, on occasion, had even lain with him.

When she left the hall to go through the small vestibule and around the outside passage to her cook-house in the backyard, the only sound left was the steady champing of jaws, for Matilda's moods never seemed to affect her appetite. John now and then attempted to start a conversation, though his wife usually only opened her mouth to complain or to deride him.

He had almost given up trying to revive any intercourse between them, as his efforts were usually met with a snub or ridicule – or more often just stony silence. De Wolfe knew full well that she had a long-term strategy to punish him, not only for his infidelities, but for his destruction of her adoration of her brother Richard. John had, in the course of his duties as a law officer, repeatedly exposed de Revelle as a charlatan and traitor, until eventually he was ignominiously dismissed as sheriff of Devon. And now, of course, the final indignity was his depriving her of her moment of glory as wife of the coroner to the king's court.

Mary returned to clear away the bowls and place before each of them a thick trencher of yesterday's bread carrying a trout grilled with almonds. When she had refilled their pewter cups from a jug of Burgundian wine and departed through the draught-screen, John made a new effort to break the oppressive silence, this time at least with some useful motive in mind.

'There is talk of the yellow distemper arriving in the city,' he began. 'I hear that a family in Bretayne may be affected, so perhaps it might be wise if you kept clear of St Olave's until more definite news is known.'

Matilda's favourite church was on the edge of Bretayne, the worst slum area of Exeter. It was so named because centuries ago the invading Saxons had pushed the Celtic British inhabitants out of the higher parts of the city down into the less desirable north-west corner of the Roman walls.

The mention of her beloved St Olave's forced his wife out of her sullen silence. 'I'll not be dissuaded from attending the House of God by some fever,' she snapped.

'It would be wiser to find some other House of God while this danger lasts,' he said mildly. 'Why not stick to the cathedral?'

To his credit, it did not even cross his mind that if Matilda succumbed to the plague it would solve many of his problems.

'The Lord will protect me and those who worship Him in the face of adversity,' she said sententiously. 'What is this ailment that people are speaking of, anyway? We have managed to survive all the fevers and sweats over the years, as well as the gripes that turn one's bowels to water!'

'It's the yellow distemper, woman,' he said impatiently. 'It was well known in former days but has not been seen for many years.'

The topic, for once, seemed to catch Matilda's attention. 'What causes it, then?' she demanded. 'And is there any cure?'

John picked some fine fish bones from his tongue before answering. 'No one knows where it came from, but many suspect that it is brought in from abroad by ship-men. For it to appear inside the city is a new departure. Some blame rats for spreading it, but I can't see why foreign rats should come within the walls of Exeter.'

She had fallen silent again and, as John raised his wine-cup to wash down the remaining bones, he looked across at her, wondering why fate had cast them together. She was a stocky, thickset woman with a square face and a mouth like a rat-trap. In the house she wore no cover-chief, and her wiry brown hair looked like the head of a mop, in spite of Lucille's efforts to tame it with a brush and tongs.

He made an effort to start the sparse conversation again. 'I thought to ask our new neighbour if he has any opinions on the matter. Maybe as a physician he has some advice about avoiding the contagion.'

This immediately revived his wife's interest. Apart from anything connected with food, drink and the Church, social advancement was her major concern. 'Doctor Clement? Yes, he would be aware of all there is to be known about it. His wife told me that he had attended two of the best medical schools in Europe,' she enthused.

Her small eyes suddenly narrowed as she glared at her husband.

'But you told me that you did not much care for him, you barbarian!' she snapped. 'We at last get a respectable next-door neighbour, instead of a murderer, and you snub him!'

John capitulated; it was the easiest path. 'Well, he's not so bad, I suppose, if he dropped a little of his airs and graces. His wife is a handsome woman, I'll admit.'

Matilda snorted. 'Trust you to notice a good-looking woman! Don't you get any of your usual lecherous ideas about her; she's a most devout and chaste lady.'

She attacked the rest of her trout fiercely, wielding her small eating-knife as if she were cutting out her husband's heart with a dagger. After a further long silence, she abruptly restarted the stilted conversation.

'If you really want to talk to the doctor, I'll invite them in for supper tonight. I doubt I can get that lazy, useless maid of ours to prepare a decent meal, but as you refuse to get anyone better, we'll just have to put up with her.'

De Wolfe went back to Rougemont after his dinner and again went to see Henry de Furnellis in his chamber in the keep. On the way he met Thomas de Peyne, who was coming out of the tiny garrison chapel of St Mary in the inner ward, and learned from him that there was indeed an outbreak of the yellow plague in Bretayne.

'Five dead and several more very sick in a couple of huts just below St Nicholas Priory,' he reported. 'They are digging a grave pit in St Bartholomew's churchyard, rather than risk hauling the corpses over to the cathedral Close.'

The cathedral had normally enforced a monopoly of all burials in the city, even though there were twenty-seven other churches within the walls. John was already on his way to talk to the sheriff about this new hazard and Thomas's news only made it the more urgent. In a city where the inhabitants were packed in so closely together, there was a real danger of a widespread epidemic. He said as much to the grizzled old warrior when he reached his office.

'Henry, is there anything we can do to lessen the risk of this plague taking a hold in the city?'

The sheriff shrugged, his weathered face wrinkled in despondency. 'Years ago I saw disease rampage through a town in France. Nothing seemed to stop it, even burning down the afflicted houses. Though that wasn't this yellow curse, it was vomiting and flux of the bowels.'

John shook his head. 'This is different. Their skin and eyes go yellow, almost green in some cases. I'm going to do what you suggested, have a word with this new physician; maybe he has some more modern ideas.' He scratched an itching point in his scalp. 'I don't care for the fellow, but this is too serious a situation to pass up anything that might help.'

'What about this rat business that people are talking about?' asked de Furnellis. 'Should we start a war against the little bastards?'

De Wolfe shrugged. 'God's guts, Henry! There are a hell of a lot more rats than people in Exeter. You'd need an army of rat-catchers and dogs to clear out half of them.'

The sheriff sadly agreed. 'I take it you needn't get involved with inquests down in Bretayne, John?'

De Wolfe shook his head. 'This is a doctor's business, not a coroner's! Let's hope more cold weather will kill whatever poison that's causing it.'

As he went down the wooden steps from the first-floor entrance to the keep, he could certainly vouch for the cold weather. The east wind had risen more strongly and was moaning through the battlements on the top of the castle wall. There was no snow, but patches of ice glistened on the ground, where water had frozen in the ruts formed by cartwheels and horses' hooves.

To avoid going home, he sat for a while in his lofty chamber, but in spite of the small charcoal brazier which stood on a slab of stone on the wooden floor, the cold soon drove him out. He left Thomas there, muffled up in an old Benedictine habit over his thin cassock, as he sat at the table carefully penning the last of the parchment rolls for presentation at the Shire Court next day.

'Don't stay too long, lad,' he said kindly as he lifted the hessian draught-curtain. 'I don't want to come here in the morning and find your corpse frozen to that stool!'

Back at Martin's Lane, he hung his cloak on a wooden peg in the small vestibule behind the front door and sat on the solitary bench to pull off his boots. Though today he had only been walking around the city, he had worn his riding boots to try to keep his feet warm. With a pair of soft house-shoes on his feet, he opened the door to the hall and went into its gloomy cavern, relieved to find that Matilda was not there, only his dog sleeping by the fire. He went across to the hearth, which was his pride and joy, being copied from a house he had seen in Dol in Brittany. Instead of the usual central firepit, with its smoke rising into the room to water the eyes and irritate the throat, he had replaced the back wall of the wooden hall with stone and had a conical chimney added, which took the fumes up through the roof.

There was a good fire of oak logs burning across the iron dogs in the hearth, and with a sigh of contentment he sank into a wooden monks' chair, rather like an upright coffin, with a high back and side wings to divert the draughts. Giving his old hound Brutus a friendly prod with his foot so that he could drag his seat a little nearer the flames, he stretched out his long legs on to the stone slabs of the hearth.

A moment later the latch rose on the door, but he was happy to see that it was Mary rather than his wife.

'I thought I heard you come in,' she said, almost accusingly. 'The mistress has gone to church. I'll mull you some ale.'

She spoke in English, heavily accented with the local Devon dialect. Her mother was a fair Saxon, but from

31

her own dark hair, her father was probably a stranger. No one knew who he might have been, as he only stayed for the conception.

She brought him a heavy pottery mug, filled with ale from a pitcher on a side table and thrust a red-hot poker into it, which she had left in the fire in anticipation of his return.

When the sizzling had subsided, he sipped it appreciatively.

'I don't know what I'd do without you, Mary,' he said sincerely. 'If it was left to my dear wife, I'd starve and go around in rags.'

'I'm glad to see you back from London, that's all I know,' she retorted. 'I lived here alone for months, worried that you'd never come back and I'd be thrown out into the street.'

John cupped his hands around the mug to warm them. 'I told Matilda not to go down to that damned church – it's too near Bretayne, now that there's been an outbreak of the sickness there. You watch out, too, my girl!'

'And how am I going to do that, pray?' she snorted. 'I have to go out to market every morning to see that you are fed. In fact, I'll have to go out again now, as the mistress wants some fancy food to give those people this evening.'

She went back to her kitchen, Brutus following her, as he decided that the possibility of some scraps outweighed the attractions of a good fire. John sat with his ale, looking around the hall, whose interior rose right up to the rafters that supported the high roof of wooden shingles. The walls, partly wooden planks and partly wattle-and-daub panels inside heavy oak frames, were hung with faded tapestries, their indistinct patterns showing biblical scenes. There was a window low down on the street wall, glassless but covered with yellowed linen inside the hinged shutters. The floor was flagstoned, a novelty insisted upon by Matilda, who considered the usual rushes strewn over beaten earth too common for her station in life.

Soon, the warmth of the fire and the quart of ale combined to send him into a peaceful sleep, where he dreamed of his boyhood down near the coast at Stoke-in-Teignhead, where his mother, sister and elder brother still lived at their manor. William, his brother, was a totally different character from John, though he looked remarkably like him. He had never been a warrior like his younger brother and was devoted to managing their two estates of Stoke and Holcombe, especially since his wife and infant had died in childbirth a few years earlier. Under the will of their long-deceased father, a quarter of the income of the manors came to John, with which he was well content.

The scenes in his mind shifted to their other demesne a few miles away at Holcombe, where he had first become enamoured with Hilda, the daughter of the manor-reeve. In the way that dreams do, the scene suddenly jumped forward a quarter of a century, and as he dozed before his hearth he found himself locked in a passionate embrace with the beautiful blonde until the clatter of the door latch jerked him back to the present. It was Mary, ushering in the large figure of Gwyn.

'Your man is here to see you,' she announced. 'He's brought you some work, by the sound of it.'

She slipped out again and his officer advanced to the hearth. John knew that Mary must have assured him that Matilda was not at home, or he would not have ventured into the house. Relations between the two were frosty in the extreme, and Matilda usually referred to Gwyn as 'that Cornish savage', typical of her Norman disdain of anyone who had Celtic blood

– which included her husband, whose mother was half-Welsh.

'We've got a murder, Crowner,' he proclaimed with almost a gleeful air. 'A real nasty one, too.'

John rubbed the last of the sleep from his eyes and hauled himself out of his chair. 'Where is it? If I'm taken out of town and miss these folk coming in from next door, I'll never hear the last of it from her.'

Gwyn shook his head, his wild auburn locks shaking like the head of a sheaf of corn. 'Not more than a few hundred paces away! Just this side of the East Gate, in Raden Lane.'

John followed him out of the hall and shrugged on his cloak and a pair of boots, while his henchman gave him some details.

'A pair of urchins found him, lying in weeds down a narrow alley between two houses. I went up for a quick look after Osric came down to the Bush to look for you.' Osric was one of the two constables charged by the city council with the arduous task of trying to keep the peace in Exeter's crowded streets. The coroner and his officer were out in the lane now and facing the biting east wind as they made for the East Gate.

'So who is he and how did he die?' snapped John, knowing that Gwyn was wont to make a short story into a long one.

'I don't know who he is, for in the state he's in his own mother would be hard put to recognise him!'

'So he was beaten up?' demanded John.

'Not that simple, Crowner!' replied Gwyn with relish. 'He's had his throat cut and his tongue ripped out!'

De Wolfe's black eyebrows rose at this. Though he had seen far more horrible mutilations in campaigns across Europe and the Levant, this was unusual in the remote lands of Devon. However, he held back more questions until they reached the scene. Raden Lane was in the most elite part of the city, on the south side of the High Street just before the road ended at the eastern gate. There were a score of large houses there, occupied mostly by rich merchants and burgesses – it was as far away from Bretayne as possible, both geographically and socially.

The two men turned into Raden Lane, where some of the houses were stone-built, set back on plots a short way from the street. Others were made of wood or cob and were flush with the edge of the narrow lane. They were close together but had slim gaps between them, and one of these, halfway up on the left, was an actual path, overgrown with winter-dead weeds. Its sides were formed by the wooden fence-stakes of the houses on either side.

'He's up here, Crowner,' said Gwyn, pushing ahead of him through shrivelled dock-leaves and withered coarse grass. In spite of being a path, it no longer went anywhere, as beyond the long back gardens it had been cut off by a high fence that faced St John's Hospital near the city wall. No doubt its isolation from lack of use had led to its being chosen as a dumping ground for a murdered corpse.

As the coroner followed Gwyn up the narrow corridor, the skirts of his long grey tunic brushing frost from the weeds, he saw figures standing against the tall hurdles of woven hazel-withies which blocked the end. One was the skinny figure of Osric, a painfully thin Saxon, the other his fellow constable, a stocky, rather fat man called Theobald. Both were clutching their long staves and staring down at something on the ground.

The 'something' turned out to be a spectacle that could have been used for a church wall-painting depicting the expected terrors of hell for those who sinned. A man's body lay on its back in the weeds, a molehill under his shoulders throwing the head back to expose a ghastly wound that occupied the whole of his neck, from jawline to collarbones. Most of his face and the upper part of his body was plastered in dried blood, the colour of his tunic being apparent only below his waist. His grey hair was thick with blackening blood clot, and the front end of a deep laceration was just visible above his left ear.

What was even more macabre than his horrific injuries was lying alongside his outstretched right hand. Here a complete tongue and attached voice-box was carefully laid out on a bloody stone, like some piece of offal displayed on a butcher's stall.

De Wolfe stood silently for a moment, contemplating the awful sight. The two constables, though also hardened to blood and gore from dealing with hundreds of street fights and killings, looked rather white around the gills.

'Never seen anything like this before, Crowner!' ventured Osric.

'Any idea who he is?' demanded John.

The constable shook his head. 'Not until he's cleaned up, anyway,' he muttered. 'You can't see his features for blood.'

Osric explained how a lad – or rather his dog – had found him about an hour ago and had run to the constable's hut behind the Guildhall to raise the alarm. 'But God knows how long he's been lying here, as no one comes up this path, for it goes nowhere.'

'Suggests that whoever did it knows his way around Exeter,' said Gwyn. 'He obviously knew of a place where it would be some time before it was discovered.'

'And how long was that, I wonder?' grunted the coroner ruminatively. He snapped off a piece of dead twig from a nearby bush and used it to prod the Adam's apple. It was stuck fast to the flat stone by dried blood. 'That's been shed some long time ago, even allowing for the freezing weather.'

Gwyn gave the thigh of the corpse a shove with the toe of his boot and the whole body moved as if carved from stone.

'Stiff as a board!' he commented. 'But given this frost, it doesn't help much to tell us when he died.'

'You reckon he's been here all night?' asked Theobald, his podgy face starting to recover some colour.

The coroner shrugged. 'He's been dead at least for many hours, I'm sure. But he might have been dead for days!'

Gwyn had hunkered down alongside the cadaver and was studying the head.

'Looks like a real nasty blow there. Shall I shift him so that you can see?' he asked hopefully. The Cornishman always relished a bit of drama and mayhem.

John waved a hand at the two constables. 'One of you run around to St John's,' he commanded. 'They've got that little mortuary behind the hospital, so ask them if they can send a couple of men with a bier to take him away.'

As Theobald left to do his bidding, John instructed Osric to search the surrounding area to see if he could find any weapon.

'If he's had a crack on the head, there may be something lying around that caused it,' he said, then dropped to his haunches opposite Gwyn and waited for his officer to lift up the head. The corpse was so rigid that it came up like a plank, but John was able to see the back of the head. Though obscured by a welter of blood, a deep laceration ran from above the left ear to the back point, above the nape of the neck. He motioned for his officer to lower the corpse to the ground and stood up, after wiping his soiled fingers on some weeds.

'I suspect that's what killed him,' he growled.

Gwyn nodded in agreement – he was always vying with his master over their expertise in matters of violent death.

'All this blood has run down, but there's no sign of spurting,' he said, waving a hand at the surrounding vegetation. 'I reckon he had his Adam's apple cut out after he was dead.'

Before he could enlarge on this macabre observation, there was a cry from down the path and Thomas came hurrying up.

'I heard in the castle that you had been called up here. What's going on?' he demanded. Then his gaze fell on the dreadful apparition on the ground, and without warning the little clerk turned aside and was spectacularly sick against the nearest fence. After two years as the coroner's scribe, he had largely overcome his sensitivity to the various forms of violent death, but the sight of a bloody tongue and voice-box laid out neatly on a flat stone was too much for him.

'Better out than in!' bellowed Gwyn jovially as he slapped Thomas on the back. Then he turned back to de Wolfe and carried on their conversation. 'There would have been blood splashed six feet away, if that wound had been caused while he was still alive,' he boomed confidently. 'I remember seeing a Saracen beheaded outside Acre once – there was a fountain of bright blood as long as my arms could span!'

De Wolfe nodded absently. 'But it all must have been done here. The corpse wasn't brought from elsewhere, or there'd be a trail of blood all the way up this lane.'

'But he could have been hit on the head somewhere else,' observed Osric, who had rejoined them, after having failed to find anything nearby that could have been a weapon.

'Must have been, as I can't imagine anyone coming up this alley of his own free will,' agreed John.

Thomas de Peyne had recovered his nerve a little and after wiping his face with a kerchief came to stand shakily alongside his master, carefully averting his gaze from the corpse. Jerkily, he made the sign of the cross as if this might ward off the horror.

'Who is he, Crowner?' he asked. 'And who would do a terrible thing like that?'

John shook his head. 'Can't answer either of those questions, Thomas. When he's been cleaned up a bit, hopefully someone will recognise his face, if he's a local man.'

A few minutes later a couple of lay brothers came up the path, carrying a canvas stretcher supported by two poles. Behind them strode a tall, gaunt figure in a black Benedictine habit. This was Brother Saulf, the infirmarian of the small priory of St John, which was virtually the only place in the city where the poor could get medical attention. The coroner explained the situation and the monk readily agreed to house the cadaver in the lean-to shed at the priory, which acted as a mortuary. As the lay brothers hoisted the corpse on to the stretcher, Thomas joined Saulf in intoning some Latin prayers over it as the best they could do by way of shriving the dead man.

With an old blanket draped over him, and his tongue tucked under his armpit, the victim went off at a jog down the path, the coroner's trio following more sedately around to St John's.

It was growing dark by the time de Wolfe arrived back in Martin's Lane and, inevitably, found his wife in a bad temper at his lateness.

'Our neighbours will be attending on us in an hour!' she grated. 'You had best change into some decent raiment. I don't want to be disgraced by them thinking we are too poor to have good clothing!'

With a sigh, he went off to the solar where they slept, to rummage in his chest to find something to wear. As everything he had was either grey or black, it was hardly likely to dazzle the popinjay next door, but he was in no mood for a confrontation with Matilda over it.

When he returned, his wife went off to persecute her handmaiden, Lucille. With a face like a rabbit and a timid nature to match, she was servile enough to tolerate Matilda's bad temper. When her mistress had gone into the convent at Polsloe some months earlier, she had been fobbed off on to Matilda's sister-in-law, Eleanor de Revelle, but as soon as she returned to Martin's Lane Eleanor threw her back again like some cast-off slave, with the excuse that she had not been satisfactory.

Lucille lived in a box-like cubicle under the timber supports that held up the solar built on to the back of the house. Now she was hauled out and taken up the outside stairs to primp Matilda's lacklustre hair and array her in a suitable gown for the entertainment of their supper guests.

Supper was another à la mode innovation of Matilda's, who had heard that an evening meal was becoming popular with the privileged classes. For centuries, a noon dinner had been the main meal of the day for almost everyone, but she felt obliged to adopt these new fads so that she could parade them before her matronly cronies at St Olave's.

In due course the physician and his wife arrived and were conducted to a pair of folding leather-backed chairs before the chimneyed hearth, between the two monks' seats. John gravely provided them with his best wine, served in glass goblets he had looted from a French castle in the Limousin and which came out only on special occasions.

If John had not known his wife so well, he might have thought that she had suddenly turned into a different person. From her usual glowering, sullen manner, the arrival of favoured guests had given her an ingratiating smile and a convincing façade of pleasantry. Her stocky body arrayed in a gown of dark red velvet, she had discarded her head-veil and wimple in favour of a net of gold thread which confined her hair. She also wore a surcoat of blue brocade, as in spite of the large fire the hall was cold and chilly.

Though he had met his neighbours before, albeit briefly, John now had time to study them more closely as they politely sipped their wine and listened to Matilda's prattle about the cathedral and her little church in Fore Street. Clement was a handsome man, with a patrician face but rather thin lips. A few streaks of grey showed in the dark hair that was cut in the old Norman style, being clipped short around his neck and temples, with a thick bush on top. His manner was precise and rather imperious, suggesting that he did not take kindly to his opinions being questioned. What struck John most, seeing him at close quarters, were his eyes, pale blue and unblinking. They seemed to have a strange intensity, which reminded John of a cat waiting to pounce on some unsuspecting mouse.

Dressed elegantly in a long tunic of bright green linen, with a fur-edged surcoat of deep blue, he looked exactly what he was, a mature professional man who was sure of his position in society. Then, as he refilled Cecilia's goblet, John – a connoisseur of women – realised anew that Clement's wife was extremely attractive. Considerably younger than her husband, she was handsome rather than beautiful. About thirty, slim and straight-backed, she wore a cover-chief and wimple of white silk, though enough hair peeped out to show that it was as black as his own. A smooth complexion and full, slightly pouting lips convinced de Wolfe that she was a very desirable addition to the scenery of Martin's Lane, especially in her elegant gown of black velvet with a gold cord wound around her narrow waist, the tasselled ends dangling almost to the floor. A heavy surcoat of dark green wool was held across her neck by a gilt chain.

Her presence undoubtedly made him less taciturn a host than usual, and he already felt Matilda's censorious eyes upon him as he fussed over Cecilia's glass of wine. After the usual platitudes about their health and the prematurely cold weather, the physician turned his attention to the news of the day.

'Some sad deaths in the city, I hear,' he observed. His voice was mellow, and John began to wonder if this paragon could have any faults at all.

'You mean the outbreak of distemper in Bretayne?' he suggested.

'And the murder of that woodcarver up in Raden Lane,' added Clement with a slight note of triumph in his voice at being so abreast of the news.

John was once again amazed at the efficiency of the Exeter grapevine, which seemed to be able to relay news even as it was happening, for it was less than a couple of hours since the identity of the victim had been established. When the face had been rubbed clean of dried blood by the vigorous application of wet rags, Osric was able to recognise him straight away as Nicholas Budd, who had lived alone in a rented room off Curre Street, which was not far away on the north side of the High Street. The two constables, who knew virtually every resident of the city, said that he made a modest living carving wood, both for furniture and especially for religious artefacts for churches or to sell to pilgrims. They knew little else about him, as he was a quiet, withdrawn person, with no relatives that they knew of.

Matilda seized upon the news like a terrier with a rat, as John had not bothered to tell her why he had arrived home late that afternoon.

'I have heard of the man. He shaped some parts of the rood screen in St Pancras Church,' she snapped. 'Why should someone want to murder a devout man like that? He could have no riches to steal.'

Clement and Matilda launched on a somewhat patronising discussion about why the good are struck down while the wicked prosper. John, sitting now in one of the monks' seats, was content to watch Cecilia, who so far had hardly spoken a word, except for some polite responses to a few questions about how she liked her new life in Exeter.

As he looked across at her profile, the old adage 'still waters run deep' came into his mind, and he again had to remind himself that an equally attractive woman awaited him in Dawlish. Cecilia seemed aware of his scrutiny, for she turned her head and gave him a slight, almost secret smile. He thought that she must be well used to men staring at her; it could hardly be otherwise. He was jerked from his daydreaming by her husband speaking to him.

'Is there any reason why this man should have been fatally attacked?' he asked. 'As in any town, there are plenty of drunken brawls and knife fights, but this secret killing must be unusual, even for such a large city as Exeter.'

John raised his shoulders in an almost Gallic gesture. 'It is too early to say. I sent my officer around to all the houses nearby, to raise the hue and cry, not that it was of any use as the man had been dead for some time. But no one admitted seeing or hearing anything untoward. We can do no more until daybreak tomorrow.'

He kept the nature of the injuries to himself, but saw no harm in enlarging on the circumstances, as doctors heard things that often no one else could pick up, other than priests in the confessional.

'The victim was severely wounded, so it is probable that the assailant would have been heavily bloodstained. Given this deep frost, it is impossible even to guess at the time of the attack, which must have taken place somewhere else.'

At last, Cecilia joined the conversation. 'How could someone move a body across the city without being seen?' she asked. Her voice was low and pleasant, her Norman-French perfect. Though John knew that they could both speak good English – and no doubt the physician was fluent in Latin – Matilda insisted on always speaking French in the house. Though she was born in Devon and had lived all her life there, apart from a couple of trips to distant relatives in Normandy, she insisted on 'playing the Norman' on the strength of her de Revelle ancestors.

'There are plenty of back alleys and, at night, few people about, except around the taverns,' answered Cecilia's husband. 'Maybe you will never find the culprit, though Almighty God knows and will bring him to his proper reckoning when the Great Trump sounds!' he added piously.

John was more forthright. 'It must have been possible to move him, for indeed it happened!' he declared. 'The dead man was a thin old fellow; he could have been carried quite easily. And for all we know, there might have been more than one assailant.'

Matilda was becoming increasingly fractious at the choice of subject. She wanted to talk of churches, priests and well-known citizens of her acquaintance.

'Do you have to bring your loathsome work home with you, John?' she snapped. 'I'm sure the doctor here does not weary his wife with tales from the sickbed!'

Cecilia smiled faintly but said nothing in response, leaving it to the others to guess whether her husband discussed his patients' problems with her. However, John was not going to be sidetracked by Matilda, for he needed some information.

'Doctor Clement, these outbreaks of the yellow plague,' he began, topping up his guest's goblet. 'Have you experience of them elsewhere? There has not been such a murrain for many years, though it seems that some older people recollect them.'

Clement considered this as he sipped his wine. 'I have never seen this yellow variety, where the bodily humours are stained with bile,' he admitted. 'There are many sorts of fever, as everyone knows, and some seem to pass easily from person to person. But this present ailment is outside my experience.'

'You know there has been an outbreak in the city, with five dead already?'

The physician nodded. 'I had heard that, but they were down in the poorer area of the town, I understand. Where living conditions are bad, then it seems that whatever poison causes it can spread more easily.'

'Is there nothing that can be done to limit the spread of this sickness?' demanded John. 'With more than four thousand people crammed inside these walls, there could be devastation!'

The physician raised his hands helplessly. 'As no one knows the cause or how it is spread, what can we do? I think the power of prayer is our only defence. We must throw ourselves on the mercy of God the Father and His Blessed Son and Virgin Mother.'

At this, the doctor crossed himself, reminding de Wolfe of his clerk's almost obsessional habit – and confirming the fact that Clement of Salisbury was an extremely devout man. Matilda growled in agreement and imitated the physician by making the sign of the cross herself. John noted that Cecilia said nothing and did not join them in their fervent religious gestures.

'I have heard the plague being blamed on an excess of rats about the place, as is more common in slums like Bretayne,' he persisted, doggedly determined to squeeze any useful information out of this professional man. Again, he failed to get any satisfaction, for Clement replied that though it was possible, these distempers could arise anywhere, whether there were rats or not. As without exception those ubiquitous vermin were everywhere, this was hardly useful. Even in this house, old Brutus caught at least one every day, usually in the kitchen or yard, but sometimes in this very hall.

Mary came in with the first 'remove' of the meal, balancing a tray heaped with food. Matilda, with a scowl at her husband to get him out of his chair, conducted her guests to the long table of dark oak and sat them together on a side bench, while she and John took the one opposite. He promptly rose again to fetch a pitcher of different wine from a side table, and while he was refilling his looted glasses Mary began placing dishes on the table. For a small gathering like this, there were only three removes and each consisted of three dishes, from which the diners could choose what they wanted. Again, Matilda had insisted on using pewter plates instead of the usual trenchers of thick bread. There were horn spoons at each place, but everyone also used the small eating-knife they always carried, together with their fingers. There were bowls of lavender-scented water on the table, together with napkins to wipe their hands. Mary was an excellent cook, though she received nothing but grumbles and criticisms from her mistress. This evening, she had started with pastries filled with beef marrow, a large platter of boiled mutton slices and a brewet of veal pieces with a spiced sauce of pounded crayfish tails.

The physician seemed very fond of his food, and his eyes lit up at the sight of the cook-maid's efforts. 'A most attractive menu,' he enthused as he helped his wife to slices of mutton and a couple of the small pastries.

'She does her best, poor girl,' said Matilda deprecatingly, which was an insult to Mary's prowess, especially as she had to cook everything with the primitive facilities of the shed in the yard, which was also her sleeping quarters.

Eating took precedence over conversation, and the food rapidly vanished. The brewet of veal was especially popular, the sauce being provided in small dishes at each place, into which the diners dipped their right little finger to spread upon the meat. Before the harassed Mary could bring in the next course, there was time for more talk and Clement expounded upon his medical practice.

'Salisbury was too small to contain an ambitious doctor like me,' he declaimed. 'I needed to offer myself to a wider clientele, and Exeter is famed for its burgeoning prosperity.'

'My husband has a chamber in Goldsmith Street where patients can consult him,' offered Cecilia, delicately wiping sauce from her finger with a linen cloth. 'Already he has a substantial practice.'

'Entirely among the better class of citizen, of course,' added Clement. Matilda murmured her approval, but

John was determined to put a brake upon the doctor's conceit.

'Perhaps you could spare some of your undoubted talents to helping the less fortunate as well,' he suggested. 'I'm sure that Brother Saulf at St John's Hospital would welcome your expertise with some of his poor sufferers down there.'

The physician put on a doleful expression. 'I would like to do that; it would no doubt be an act of Christian charity,' he said sententiously. 'But unfortunately my practice is growing so rapidly that I would have little time to spare – but I will try to assist them when circumstances allow.'

He went on to speak more honestly. 'Also, I fear that my patients, who come from the higher levels of county society, might not look with favour on the possibility of my carrying contagion to them from the legion of ailments from which the poorer classes suffer.'

Matilda nodded in agreement, but de Wolfe again noticed that Cecilia made no effort to support her husband's selfish attitude.

'So you also wish to keep well clear of any victims of this yellow distemper?' observed John with a harder edge to his voice, which made his wife glare at him.

The elegant doctor made a deprecating gesture. 'What purpose would it serve? There is nothing I or anyone else can do to help. As I said, it is in the hands of God, whose ways are mysterious.'

Any developing dispute was avoided by Mary returning with a large platter of grilled trout and a dish of capons' legs, which the diners seized upon with relish. The cook-maid took away used dishes and returned with a pudding of rice boiled in milk with saffron and raisins, together with fresh bread, butter and cheese. All this occupied them for a further hour, including John's further ministrations with a wineskin of white Loire and a flask of strong brandy-wine. When they eventually left for their short walk home, the physician seemed a little unsteady on his feet, but nonetheless effusive with his appreciation of their hospitality. John thought somewhat cynically that his excessive zeal for religion did not diminish his fondness for good food and drink. Cecilia also thanked them, less enthusiastically, but quite charmingly, for their kindness, and for once Matilda was smiling smugly as they at last said their farewells to their guests at the front door. The moment it closed, however, her amiable mask slipped immediately.

'It would have been a perfect occasion tonight but for your constant ogling of that poor lady!' she snapped. 'Cecilia is too refined and genteel to have men like you lusting after her.'

As she turned away from him to lumber off towards the solar and her bed, John felt his fingers aching to settle around her fleshy neck, to release him for ever from her mean-spirited nature.

CHAPTER THREE

*In which Crowner John talks
to an archdeacon*

Soon after a grey November dawn, when the cathedral bells were ringing for Prime, the coroner made another call upon the sheriff and brought him up to date with the events surrounding the bizarre killing of Nicholas Budd. Then he went across to his chamber in the gatehouse, where he found Gwyn and Thomas huddled over the brazier. The wind had dropped outside, and it was marginally warmer but still miserable.

'A lot to do today,' he announced cheerfully. 'We've got the Shire Court first, though that should be disposed of quickly. Then there are hangings to attend out on Magdalen Street as well as this murder to pursue.' As he stood rubbing his hands above the charcoal glowing in the iron bucket, he sensed that Thomas was itching to say something.

'I went down yesterday to attend the burial of those poor souls in Bretayne,' said the clerk with a return of the slight stutter which afflicted him when he was excited. 'I saw something curious.'

John frowned at him. 'You're a devil for danger, Thomas!' he said sternly. 'First at Lympstone, now here in Exeter. I would be very sad if you took in whatever noxious vapour causes this plague.'

'And I'd be sorrier still if you brought it back to us!' grumbled Gwyn, thinking of his family.

The little priest shook his head stubbornly. 'God will protect me. I was afraid that those people might have been buried without so much as a prayer, let alone a proper shriving.'

'And were they?' demanded de Wolfe.

Thomas looked a little abashed. 'No, as it happens. The old priest from St Bartholomew's was there, God bless his soul. He was sober enough to say a few words as they threw the bodies into the pit.'

'So what was this that aroused your curiosity?' asked John.

The clerk ran a finger over the tip of his sharp nose to remove a dewdrop. 'For some reason, maybe shortage of cloth in that poverty-ridden place, the bodies were not fully covered. Their heads were sticking out from the rags that passed for shrouds.'

De Wolfe sighed, for Thomas was catching Gwyn's habit of spinning out every tale.

'I noticed that four out of the five were as yellow as French lemons, as was to be expected. But the oldest man was still lily-white.'

The coroner and his officer digested this for a moment.

'And you think that has some meaning?' asked Gwyn.

'Well, if this was a plague pit for those who perished from the yellow curse, why wasn't he yellow?' said Thomas defensively.

'Are you suggesting that he might have died from something else?' said John.

The clerk shrugged his thin shoulders. 'It bears thinking about! It would be a good way to get rid of a murdered corpse, putting it in with plague victims, now that they are no longer coroner's business.'

Crafty Thomas knew that this would pique his master, who was jealous of his duty to investigate all suspicious deaths.

'Well, it's too late to look into it now,' boomed Gwyn. 'He's six feet under a layer of quicklime and soil by now.'

'We could get him dug up again,' retorted de Wolfe.

'I doubt any labourer would risk shovelling out a plague pit, even for extra wages,' said Gwyn. 'Especially on such flimsy evidence as the colour of his face.'

John had to agree, but he was reluctant to let the issue drop. 'We must enquire about how he died, but first find out who he was.'

'I already know that, Crowner. I made enquiries on the spot. He was Vincente d'Estcote, from down near the town wall, opposite the Snail Tower. A fellow of fifty-five, an impoverished porter who carried mainly for the fulling mills on Exe Island. He lodged with the family that died and was found dead in the house with them. No one cared about the circumstances; they were too concerned to get them out and buried before the contagion spread.'

Once again, de Wolfe marvelled at the resourcefulness of his clerk, who was worth far more than the three pence a day he was paid for his work.

'This dreadful killing in Raden Lane must be our first priority, but later we must find out more about the death of this fellow,' he commanded.

After attending the single case of declaring outlawry held in the Shire Hall, a bleak barn-like building in the inner ward of the castle, they walked down Castle Hill and across to St John's Priory, tucked away just inside the city wall, which had been built by the Romans, neglected by the Saxons and restored by the Normans.

It was a small Benedictine house, with just a prior and three brothers, devoted to caring for the sick and in schooling a few local children. The only ward was a large room with a row of straw mattresses on the floor down each side, dominated by a large wooden crucifix on the end wall, confirming Clement of Salisbury's claim that God was the only real healer of bodies and souls.

They found Brother Saulf there, a tall, gaunt monk who acted as hospitaller. He had had some medical training in Flanders before entering the cloister and had been very helpful to the coroner on several occasions. Saulf led them around to the back of the tiny priory, where a small shed stood in the shadow of the ancient city wall. Functioning as a store for stretchers and old furniture as well as a mortuary, it now sheltered the corpse of Nicholas Budd, which lay on the ground covered with a sheet. Gwyn pulled it back and they looked down at a face now cleaned of all the blood and clot that had obscured it the previous day. His open eyes stared up glassily and his lips were distorted by the havoc that a knife had wreaked inside his mouth. Grey hair and stubble marked him as being probably in his fifties.

The monk bent down and picked up something wrapped in a rag from alongside the cadaver. 'This is his tongue and throat parts,' he said, unrolling the bloodstained cloth. 'It should be buried with the body, for decency's sake.'

Gwyn poked at it with a finger, while Thomas contrived to look elsewhere. 'Must have been a damned sharp knife, Crowner,' he observed. 'Clean cuts, very little ragged edges.'

'I try to heal bodies, rather than disordered minds,' said Saulf gravely. 'But I would have thought that whoever did this was making retribution for something that this poor man had said.'

De Wolfe stared thoughtfully at the Benedictine. 'You suggest that cutting out the tongue and voice-box, the organs of speech, might mean that the victim had caused offence?'

'Must have been a bit more serious than just telling him to bugger off!' offered Gwyn facetiously.

They examined the body carefully, but apart from the wound on the head there was nothing else of significance. The scrip on his belt contained four pence and a tarnished medallion of St Christopher. The fingers were slightly callused and had some small healing cuts, consistent with his work as a woodcarver. The monk pulled the sheet back over the body when they had finished. 'What happens now?' he asked. 'Did he have any relatives that will attend to his burial?'

De Wolfe straightened his back and moved away from the corpse. 'We will have to make enquiries at his home, then I will have to hold an inquest. I will let you know about disposing of the body as soon as I can.' He offered a dozen pennies to Saulf, which the monk gratefully received as a donation to the funds of the hard-pressed hospital, then left with his two assistants. They made their way down to Curre Street, which was one of the small lanes that led from the High Street towards the North Gate. It was lined with a mixture of houses and tenements, varying in size and shape, some with shopfronts and others being the work premises of various crafts. They found Osric outside a cordwainer's shop, talking to the owner.

'I was just asking about Nicholas Budd, Crowner,' the town constable explained. 'His workshop is next door, and this man says that Nicholas was at home the day before yesterday, but he's not seen him since.'

'Kept himself to himself, did Budd,' volunteered the shoemaker. 'Nice enough fellow, but very quiet. Lived alone, can't say as if I've ever heard of him speak of family. Certainly, he never had no visitors here.'

There was no more to be learned, and Osric confirmed that his enquiries elsewhere along the street had been equally barren.

'Let's have a look in his house,' commanded John, pushing open the door, which was unlocked. Nicholas Budd had occupied the ground floor of the small thatched house, the upper storey being used by a family of six who gained access by steps from the backyard. The woodcarver used the front part of his premises for his trade, with two workbenches, stacks of seasoned timber and a rack of tools on the wall. The floor was ankle deep in shavings and offcuts, but beyond a flimsy wattle partition, the rear part of the premises was clean. A firepit, now cold and dead, occupied the centre, and a table, a stool and a blanket-covered palliasse on the floor were the only furniture in Budd's living quarters. Some food and few pots were on the table, and a small keg of cider stood in one corner.

John sent Gwyn into the yard to look around and to make enquiries among the people upstairs, while he and Thomas looked around the ground floor. There was little enough to study, and within a couple of minutes they had drawn a blank.

'So why was the poor devil so cruelly mutilated?' muttered de Wolfe pensively. 'It seems he had no life other than carving his bloody wood, by the looks of it.'

Thomas nodded, his beady eyes roving around the living room.

'Not even a cross or a pilgrim's badge on the wall. Yet something he did must have caused great offence to someone.'

Gwyn came down to report that the goodwife upstairs had not heard her neighbour since the day before yesterday. 'Usually, she hears him sawing and chopping down here. So it looks as if he met his death the night before last.'

'Did she say anything about relatives who might wish to know of his death – and who might pay for his burial?' asked John.

Gwyn shook his head, his ginger locks swinging wildly. 'She knew very little about him, it seems. Thinks he came here from Bristol a couple of years ago. Doesn't attend any church, which apparently causes offence to some of the neighbours.'

With nothing more to be learned, the trio took themselves off to the castle gatehouse, where they ate some bread and cheese and drank ale mulled with an old sword heated in the brazier.

Thomas was never keen on ale, a great handicap in a world where it was almost the only safe drink, given the dangers of all water, whether drawn from wells, rivers or ditches. However, when heated, Thomas could tolerate it better, though he preferred cider.

'You must round up a jury for this afternoon, Gwyn,' said de Wolfe. 'Osric, Theobald, the lad who found the body and a few folk from Raden Lane who were knocked up by the constables. We'll look on them "First Finders", though as usual they'll know damn all about what happened.'

'Best add that shoemaker and the woman upstairs from Curre Street,' said the Cornishman. 'I wonder if he was in a craft guild – they might pay for his burial expenses?'

'Who did he work for, I wonder?' mused de Wolfe. 'Must be a freeman on his own, I expect. If he carved stuff for churches, maybe my friend the archdeacon might know of him?'

The coroner was correct in this, but not in quite the way he expected.

Some time before noon, John made his way back towards Martin's Lane for dinner, taking his horse

Odin back to the livery stables opposite. He had ridden out to the gallows on Magdalen Street to witness and record the hanging of two thieves and a captured outlaw, a sight which in no way put him off his expected meal. However, on the doorstep he met Mary clutching a basket filled with new bread and a brace of sea fish from the market.

'Your dinner will be another hour, Sir Coroner,' she announced firmly. 'My fire went out, thanks to the damp wood that old fool Simon has been chopping, so I had to relight it.' In spite of her protests, he tore a chunk off one of the loaves and loped away, chewing the warm bread.

'I'll go down to see the archdeacon while I'm waiting,' he called over his shoulder as he headed for Canon's Row. This was where some of the prebendaries of the cathedral lived, only a few hundred paces from his house. It lay along the north side of the Close, the large burial ground outside the huge twin-towered church of St Mary and St Peter.

One of the houses was occupied by Canon John de Alençon, one of the four archdeacons of the diocese. An uncle of Thomas de Peyne, he was the one who several years before had prevailed on John to take on the disgraced and penniless priest as his clerk. He was an old friend of the coroner, an ascetic with a strong sense of justice and piety, his only worldly weakness being a love of fine wines. As usual, he offered the coroner a cup of an excellent Anjou red as a preprandial drink. They sat in de Alençon's study, a spartan room contrasting strongly with the luxurious accommodation beloved of many of the senior churchmen.

'It's good to have you back as Exeter's coroner, John,' said the archdeacon warmly. 'But I hear you have already had a distressing problem?'

'This strange murder up near the East Gate? It's not every day we get victims with their tongues and throats slashed out.'

'Who was he? I've heard no details of the tragedy.'

John took a sip of the luscious red fluid. 'That's partly why I called, to see if you knew of him. He was a carver of devotional objects, so I thought maybe you had had dealings with him.'

De Alençon stared at his friend in surprise. 'A woodcarver? Surely you can't mean Nicholas Budd?'

'You knew him, then? I thought you might and wondered if you could tell me something of him.'

The archdeacon looked suddenly very sombre, his thin face and crinkled grey hair giving him a stern appearance above his black cassock.

'I can tell you a lot about him, John! In fact, Nicholas was due to get into the public eye very soon, though not in the horrific way you describe.'

De Wolfe placed his wine-cup down carefully on the table. This was far more than he expected and he thought again how often chance ideas turned up vital information. 'Tell me, then,' he said, and his friend continued his story.

'The cathedral chapter and the bishop's legal deacon have been debating what to do about Budd for some weeks – and only last Friday, several of the canons gave instructions for him to be arraigned before a special court.'

John's black eyebrows rose. 'What's he been up to? Ravishing the nuns at Polsloe?'

His friend ignored his flippancy; this was a serious matter. 'In the opinion of some of my fellow canons, that would be a trivial offence compared with what they consider his mortal sins. They want him to be tried for heresy.'

'Heresy? I thought that was something that was

known only in France and Germany – not that I know much about it,' admitted the coroner.

His friend shook his head sadly. 'I agree that it is not openly evident in England, where thankfully the rule of Rome is rarely challenged. But under the surface there are still those who doubt or even strongly dispute the right of the Church to be the only channel of intercession between man and God.'

De Wolfe was neither an educated person nor had he much interest in religion, other than a passive acceptance of the inflexible dominance of the Church, instilled into everyone from childhood. He was more interested to know why Nicholas Budd had had his throat torn out.

'So what has this woodworker been doing, to bring down the wrath of your chapter upon him?'

The archdeacon sighed. 'It was not what he was doing, John, but what he was *saying*. One of the proctors' bailiffs heard Budd talking to a group of labourers on the quayside, dispensing the usual nonsense about every man being his own salvation. The proctor told one of my colleagues and he began a crusade against this man.'

He paused to sip his wine and sighed again. 'I'm afraid the matter has escalated since then, as this canon found supporters for his views and has forced the chapter to take the matter to the bishop. It is difficult for me, as I admit to not having such strong feelings about the issue as some of my colleagues.'

The archdeacon paused to top up John's cup before continuing. 'Somewhat to my discomfort, I am the one who will have to deal with this matter, as the bishop appointed me as his vicar-general. Unlike some other dioceses, the bishop here has no chancellor to deal with such administrative and disciplinary matters.'

'But I thought that the chapter dealt with such things?' objected John, to whom the labyrinthine workings of the Church were a mystery.

De Alençon shook his grey head. 'It has been traditional for the archdeacon of the see to be given this duty. In fact, we are sometimes called the *oculus episcopi*, "the eye of the bishop" – which does not increase my popularity with my brother canons, who sometimes suspect me of being Henry Marshal's spy!'

De Wolfe looked at the priest from under lowered brows. 'I get the feeling that you are not as enthusiastic as your brothers about pursuing this man?'

'I am not, John. Our Church has been plagued by such critics since its early days in Rome. Then they posed a more serious threat, but stern measures over the centuries have repulsed them until, certainly in this country, they are mere irritations like the fleas and lice in our hair.'

'I have heard somewhere that in the south of France there are many who challenge the supremacy of the Roman Church,' said de Wolfe.

'That is true. That area has always been full of strange beliefs, such as claiming that the Holy Mother herself fled there with Mary Magdalene – ludicrous, when everyone knows that after the Crucifixion she went to Ephesus to live out her days near St John.'

The coroner did not know that, but he failed to see the relevance. 'Are they not called after the town of Albi?' he asked as he stood up to leave. 'I once rode through there to get to some campaign in Toulouse.'

De Alençon nodded. 'The Albigensians, sometimes called the Cathars. They might pose a threat one day and will have to be dealt with, but I doubt we have many adherents in Devon.' He finished his wine and saw his friend to the door. 'If you want to know more, get my nephew Thomas to give you a lecture! He's always keen to show off his knowledge.'

As they stood on the doorstep, John had a final question. 'What will happen to this enquiry now that Budd is dead?'

John de Alençon shrugged. 'No doubt it will be dropped, as Canon fitz Rogo can hardly press for the prosecution of a corpse.'

With much more to think about than when he came, the coroner left the cathedral precinct and went home to Mary's grilled fish.

The inquest on the woodcarver that afternoon was a brief and unhelpful formality. For convenience, John held it in the yard behind St John's, adjacent to the ramshackle mortuary. Gwyn had assembled a dozen men and older boys for a jury, which included anyone who might be of use as a witness. The enquiry had to be held with a viewing of the corpse, so Gwyn had lifted it out of the shed and laid it gently on the ground. He left the sheet over it for as long as possible, but at some stage the dreadful wound had to be displayed to the jurymen.

There was virtually no audience – different from the usual inquest in a village, when everyone turned out to gawp at a novelty that livened their dull lives. Rather to John's surprise, there was one unexpected onlooker, his friend and partner Hugh de Relaga, dressed in his usual colourful costume, in spite of the sombre occasion.

'What brings you here, Hugh?' asked de Wolfe, taking him aside just before he began the procedure.

'I represent the guilds, John. We were told of this poor man's death and that he has no known family. We shall look after his funeral and see that his property is safeguarded, if he has any.'

Each trade had its guild, which not only regulated the quality of goods, fixed their prices, controlled working conditions and prevented unfair competition but acted as a friendly society for members, looking after widows and children in times of hardship.

'Did you know anything of this particular man?' asked John.

De Relaga's chubby face was framed by a bright green coif, a tight-fitting helmet of linen, tied under his chin with tapes. He looked like some woodland elf, John thought, but it was an effective protection against the cold east wind that had arisen.

'Not personally, as obviously he was in a different guild from mine,' he answered. 'But the warden of the woodworkers who told me of this tragedy this morning said that he had been a very devout man and worthy of all our help.'

The coroner thought it best not to disillusion his friend of the direction of Budd's devotion and moved off to conduct his inquest. Gwyn bellowed his call to order and the jury shuffled into a line facing the coroner. Thomas set up his parchment, pen and ink on the back of a handcart, as far away from the corpse as possible, ready to transcribe the proceedings for future presentation to the royal justices when they arrived for the next Eyre of Assize.

John first called the lad who had discovered the body, who seemed quite unaffected by the gruesome experience. Osric and Theobald told how they had been called, and Gwyn in turn reported that all enquiries so far had found no witnesses to the killing. Nicholas Budd had worked alone, so that there was not even a journeyman or an apprentice to offer any evidence about his habits, mental state or even when he had last been seen alive. The woman from above Budd's workshop was the only one who could state that the carver had been heard two evenings before, but she had nothing else to offer.

Finally, Gwyn paraded the reluctant jurors past the cadaver, demonstrating the neck wound and offering the severed tongue and voice-box to them, in the manner of a butcher trying to sell offal to a housewife. When they were back in line, a few shades paler in the face, de Wolfe harangued them to obtain a verdict, though in fact giving them little choice.

'This is a preliminary enquiry, so that the law may allow the deceased man to be buried,' he snapped, glaring along the row of faces. 'The verdict is yours, but it seems unavoidable that you must find that Nicholas Budd was foully murdered. It cannot be an accident and I doubt he would have cut out his own throat and then laid it carefully on a stone beside him!'

He pulled his wolfskin cloak more tightly around him as an icy gust swept through the yard. Then he stabbed a finger towards the largest man in the jury, a bruiser of a fellow who wore the bloodstained apron of a slaughterman.

'I appoint you foreman, so consult your fellows and give me your verdict.'

He didn't actually add 'And be damned quick about it', but the message was there and within a brief moment the man from The Shambles turned back to mumble their agreement that the woodcarver had been slain by persons unknown.

'When I get further information I may need to reconvene this inquest, but until then you may all go about your business.'

When they had shuffled away, Gwyn covered up the corpse and put it back into the mortuary until Hugh de Relaga sent men to collect it. John took his friend the portreeve aside.

'I don't know what plans you have for a funeral, but I would advise you to keep clear of the cathedral,' he murmured.

The portreeve immediately pressed him for an explanation, but John held up his hand. 'I can't explain now, but suffice to say that it would be best if you have him buried in one of the smaller churches. Better still, go out to one of the nearby country parishes. He has no relatives, so it will make no difference.' He clapped a hand on the shoulder of his mystified friend and made his way back to Rougemont.

'So what do we do now?' asked the sheriff. 'If it was an ordinary killing, some knife fight in a tavern or a robbery with violence, we could arrest everyone within sight and beat it out of them. But with these secret murders, we never seem to get anywhere.'

De Wolfe was amused at the 'we', as Henry de Furnellis rarely stirred himself to go hunting miscreants. He was sheriff for the second time, reluctantly coming back after John's brother-in-law had been ignominiously deprived of office. Now over sixty, he wanted a quiet life and was looking forward to someone else being appointed in his place.

'Surely this heretic business must be involved?' boomed the third man in the sheriff's chamber. 'Why else would someone want to cut the poor bastard's throat out, if he was just an inoffensive woodworker?'

This was Ralph Morin, the castle constable, a man as big as Gwyn, looking like one of his Viking ancestors with his forked beard. Rougemont had always been a royal possession, ever since the castle was built by the Conqueror, and Morin, as castellan and commander of the garrison, was responsible directly to the king.

De Wolfe nodded, as he reached for the inevitable cup of wine, dispensed by Henry. 'I'm sure you're right, Ralph. But I have a lot of digging to do before I can find out why.'

'The archdeacon said that a few of the canons were after this fellow, so are you going to tackle them about it?' asked the sheriff.

John nodded. 'I'll start this very day,' he promised. 'Though if I know these snooty clergy, they'll be reluctant to even give me the time of day. They always shelter behind the power of the bishop or some such excuse.'

'Is he buried yet?' queried the castellan.

'Being put down this afternoon, I think. Probably in St Bartholomew's, where they disposed of those plague victims.'

De Furnellis looked across at John from his seat behind his table. 'There were five more deaths in Topsham last night,' he said sombrely. 'I hope by Christ and all His Blessed Saints that we get no more in the city. Did you get any help from that doctor last night?'

'He was as much use as my hound! Less, in fact, as Brutus can at least catch a few rats if he shifts himself.'

'You think rats might be a cause?' asked Morin. 'I'm afraid of them getting among my garrison. The unmarried soldiers all live close together in the barrack-halls, and if one gets a cough or running nose they all get it.'

'Get a few dogs in, Ralph, and get rid of any rats,' advised John. 'God knows if they are anything to do with the yellow plague, but according to this bloody doctor I've got next door the only prevention is prayer!'

Morin threw down the last of his wine and stood up. 'Apart from Exeter itself, the other cases have been in Lympstone, Dartmouth and now Topsham. They're all ports, so maybe there is something in this allegation that bloody sailors are bringing it in.'

'Well, we can't stop them coming – and half of them are Devon ship-men who live here,' countered Henry.

When the castellan had gone, Henry looked quizzically at de Wolfe. 'I gather you were not too impressed by your new neighbour?'

John gave one of his all-purpose grunts. 'Thinks too much of himself for my taste. He's only interested in the sound of coins jingling in his purse and preaching at everyone about the power of God! Told me to my face that he won't help out at St John's or go near the plague sufferers in case it affects his trade with the high-paying patients.' He thought for a moment, then added, 'But he's got a most desirable wife!'

Henry, knowing his friend of old, clucked his tongue. 'Now, John, none of that! You've got enough problems as it is. Stick to hunting criminals and having a trip to Dawlish now and then.'

It was good advice, and de Wolfe decided to take it. He was overdue for a visit to his family in Stoke-in-Teignhead and Dawlish was on the same road.

He left the keep, clattering down the wooden steps from the high entrance to reach the rock-hard mud of the frozen inner ward. Going back to the gatehouse to collect Thomas, they walked together back to the centre of the city.

'I need to talk to this canon your uncle mentioned,' said John as they went through a lane which came out in the Close.

'Richard fitz Rogo? He was Archdeacon of Cornwall until recently; now he's settled back into being just a canon. He is a rich man, with a private income, apart from his benefice.'

As John expected, his clerk was a walking encyclopaedia, especially where the Church was concerned.

'What sort of man is he?' he asked as they walked through the dishevelled area in front of the cathedral.

Though it was holy ground, it was hardly a haven of episcopal calm. Rough paths led between grave-mounds, some fresh, some weed-covered and others gaping open awaiting fresh customers. Urchins played among the piles of dumped refuse, and dogs romped along with them. A few beggars slumped against the mounds, half-dead with cold, and a drunk wandered erratically past, singing incoherently.

'This place is a disgrace,' muttered Thomas indignantly before answering the coroner. 'Richard fitz Rogo? He is a stern man, an upright pillar of the Church, but not given to much humour or pleasantries.'

'Does he live in a simple fashion, like your uncle John de Alençon?' asked the coroner.

Thomas shook his head. 'He enjoys the luxuries of life very much, as you will see if we can get invited into his dwelling. It is just there.'

He pointed to one of the houses that lined the Close on the side facing the great West Front of the cathedral. It lay behind the small church of St Mary Major and its yard backed on to buildings in the High Street beyond.

John had brought his clerk with him, as he had learned that the presence of a priest was often useful when dealing with the clergy, especially those in the senior ranks. Thomas trotted to the door of the stone-built house and sought out the canon's steward. Many of the lower orders of priest would be in the cathedral now, at one of the interminable services that occupied most of the day, but the less energetic canons had vicars and secondaries to stand in for them. Canon Richard was evidently one of these, for Thomas reappeared and conducted his master into the house, following the steward to a door leading to one of the two rooms on the ground floor.

Inside, he found a comfortable chamber with a large brazier glowing hotly in the centre. Some padded chairs stood around it, and a table, a cupboard and a wine cabinet completed the furnishings, apart from some expensive tapestries that softened the harshness of the stone walls.

A fat man with a bald head hauled himself from one of the chairs and greeted John as Thomas made a brief introduction and then retired to stand inconspicuously against the door. Richard fitz Rogo was pink and fat all over, including his cheeks and puffy neck, which overhung the neckband of his black cassock. A heavy woollen cape hung over his shoulders against the cold, though at the moment his room was probably one of the warmest places in Exeter.

'Sir John, we have not met before, but I have seen you in the distance, attending Mass with your devout wife.'

His voice was strong and resonant, the utterance of a man used to getting his own way. The coroner muttered something neutral and sat down in the other chair, as the canon indicated.

'I have no doubt that you wish to seek my help in respect of this sinner who was found dead yesterday in Raden Lane?'

'You know about that, then?' said John.

'All Exeter knows about it, coroner. Even to the strange injuries he suffered.' Again de Wolfe marvelled at the way in which news passed around the city like lightning.

'You knew this man Nicholas Budd?'

The canon, who had let his corpulent body sink back into the chair, shook his head.

'I had never met him, though I would have done shortly when he was due to be arraigned at the bishop's court – but God took a hand in the matter.'

'So how did you discover that he was deserving of your attention?'

Fitz Rogo smiled indulgently, but his small cold eyes took away any hint of humour. 'Those who deny the authority of the Holy Church cannot conceal themselves for long. They are like rats skulking in the midden, but the hounds of Rome always flush them out!'

This colourful reply did nothing to answer John's question.

'But how came he to be brought to answer for his sins at this particular time?'

The priest ran a finger around his collar to ease away his drooping jowls. 'Let me explain, Sir John,' he said rather condescendingly, as if lecturing a backward chorister. 'Some time ago, the Papal Legate – the Holy Father's representative in England – passed on to every bishop a message from Rome. This expressed concern at the revival of blasphemous and seditious beliefs contrary to the Catholic teachings of the Church, especially in southern France and Germany.'

'And in England?' interposed de Wolfe.

The canon hummed and hawed a little. 'Admittedly, they were not on the same scale as in these other places. But we were all told to be vigilant and to stamp out heresy wherever it may be found, lest these evil seeds take root and blossom.'

He scowled at some private memory. 'I regret to say that Bishop Marshal did not appear to be unduly disturbed by the threat, probably because he is so concerned with the politics of Church and State that he has little time for dangers closer to home.'

He sniffed disdainfully, mindful of his own failed efforts to obtain the mitre. 'In fact, our bishop is rarely in his diocese, as I expect you are aware.'

Even John, uninterested as he was in religious matters, knew from his conversations with John de Alençon that Bishop Henry Marshal was to be found more often in Westminster, Canterbury or Coventry than he was in Devon. But all this was not getting him any nearer to learning about Nicholas Budd.

'But how came you to seize upon this particular man?' he demanded, tiring of the canon's lecture.

'My brother canons – at least, two of them – and myself decided to augment the bishop's lack of enthusiasm by carrying out the Legate's instructions more directly,' explained fitz Rogo with an air of self-importance. 'We instructed the proctors' men to keep a special lookout for any hints of heresy and even to pay agents among the common folk to keep their ears open for the same.'

'You mean you set spies among the people?' said John bluntly, but the canon seemed impervious to sarcasm.

'All means are legitimate in the service of God,' he said piously. 'The devil employs every evil artifice in his campaigns, so we need to follow his example.'

'So what did your spies report to you?' asked John irreverently.

'They found that Budd was seducing people with his blasphemous ideas, both among his customers and folk that he met in the market or the alehouse. And as if this was not blatant enough, more recently he has been meeting secretly with others in dwellings or in the countryside to discuss and elaborate on their foul concepts.'

'How could you know of this, if they were held in private places?' demanded John.

'Our agents passed themselves off as possible converts to this religion of the Antichrist,' boomed the priest. 'In fact, one of them seemed to be so taken with the sedition that he has refused to work for the proctors any longer. We are keeping a sharp eye on him,' he added threateningly.

'Did Nicholas Budd know that he was to be arraigned?'

'Indeed he did. The proctors' men delivered a message to him a week ago, telling of the time and place that he must present himself before the preliminary examination. If he had failed to appear, they would have seized him and incarcerated him in the proctors' cells near St Mary's Church.'

The canon rubbed his podgy hands together, almost in delight.

'But now he has been spared that ordeal – and the Church is rid of one more blasphemer.' Fitz Rogo seemed quite pleased at the outcome.

'If the Church had found him guilty, would he have had his tongue and throat cut out?' asked de Wolfe cynically. 'For that was his fate, and I see no other reason for a quiet tradesman to be so brutally done to death, apart from his beliefs.'

The former archdeacon shrugged. 'Perhaps some citizen more zealous than the Church itself was so incensed by this man's heresy that he took the law into his own hands.'

The coroner felt that he was going to gain very little from this man and his entrenched attitude. 'You say that you have two fellow canons who are equally assiduous in heeding the Legate's warning. Can you tell me who those are?'

'All the priesthood should be equally assiduous, Sir John, in carrying out the orders of the Papal Bull issued some twelve years ago. And, indeed, every Christian man and woman who respects the authority of Rome should be on the lookout for these evil people who would undermine the very fabric of the Church, including yourself, coroner,' he brayed pompously. 'But the leaders in this crusade were Ralph de Hospitali and Robert de Baggetor – and, of course, myself.'

'What about the other canons – there are twenty-four, are there not?'

Fitz Rogo looked slightly evasive. 'Naturally, we are all concerned about this insidious evil – but some of my fellow prebendaries have other duties and other priorities, so it is left to we three to push forward the campaign. And I might tell you, Sir John, this man Budd was but one of many who have fallen by the wayside and absorbed this poison that seeps into the country from abroad.'

The canon's last words rang in John's head as he and Thomas walked back across the Close. 'Poison seeping in from abroad' was all too familiar a phrase, given the possibility that the yellow plague was being imported into Devon from foreign parts.

'So what did you make of that, Thomas?' he asked his clerk as they trudged towards South Gate Street. 'Somehow I can't see that fat priest as a knife-wielding killer.'

His clerk looked shocked at the suggestion that one of his seniors could even be considered as a murderer. 'Indeed not, master! Yet I agree that there seems to be every reason to think that Budd's heretical beliefs were the cause of his death.'

'So we must look elsewhere for a culprit, Thomas. Yet do not dismiss anyone from suspicion, especially those with strong religious convictions. I spent two bloody years of my life at the Crusades, which were all about one faith trying to annihilate another.'

They walked through Bear Gate, then crossed the busy road that led down to one of the main city gates, to reach the warren of small lanes that ran down the slope towards the river.

'I will have to speak to the other two zealous canons that fitz Rogo named,' said John as they walked down towards Priest Street, where Thomas lodged. 'But we can go together in the morning. What do you know about them?'

'Like fitz Rogo, Robert de Baggetor was formerly another archdeacon, this time of Barnstaple. He is a severe man, immovable in his old-fashioned attitudes. I have heard him preach thunderously about those who voice the slightest criticism of the established Church. He is a reactionary in the strongest sense of the word.'

'And the other one?' prompted de Wolfe.

'Ralph de Hospitali? A little younger than the other two, but equally zealous. He is a thin, active man, never still and always wanting to impress upon his juniors the perils of straying outside the strict rituals and formalities laid down by Rome. He is especially insistent that the Vulgate should never be made available in the vernacular, in case common people should read it and not require the interpretation of we priests.'

Thomas sounded bitter about this particular canon, and John suspected that his clerk had suffered a tongue-lashing from him at some time.

They parted at the end of Idle Lane, as John wished to call at the Bush to down a quart or two of his officer's new ale, to see if he had mastered Nesta's recipe. It was still an hour or two until dusk, and Thomas announced that after a prayer and a bite to eat in his lodgings he would walk down to St Bartholomew's to see if there was any more news of the latest plague victims.

'When I told you that one man was not yellowed, you said we must enquire further,' he said with a frown.

'Something worries me over that, but I can't put my finger on it.'

'You be careful, Thomas,' admonished the coroner. 'That part of town is unhealthy, and we don't know how contagious this curse might be.'

His little clerk limped away, the cold weather making his spinal problem worse. John turned off down the lane to the tavern and sank thankfully on to his bench by the fire, where a pile of oak logs was warming the low taproom. The inn was quieter than usual, and John guessed that some of the regular patrons had stayed at home, fearful of possible contagion in crowded places. Edwin came up with a pottery mug of ale and waited until John had passed a favourable comment on Gwyn's efforts.

'Edwin, they tell me that you have become very religious these days,' ventured the coroner. 'What do you know of any people preaching heresy in the city nowadays?'

The old man leaned with his fists on the table, his one good eye fixed intently on de Wolfe. 'It's a scandal, sir, a real scandal that such folk should be allowed to walk the earth!'

He sounded almost viciously indignant, unlike the easy-going, hard-drinking old soldier that John knew previously.

'Blasphemers like those should be hanged – or, better still, burned at the stake, to get them used to the everlasting fires of hell that they are bound to suffer eventually!'

De Wolfe could almost smell the brimstone coming from the potman's nostrils and thought he might learn something useful here.

'Who are these people you speak of, Edwin?'

The potman tapped the side of his prominent nose. 'I know that fellow that was killed was one of them,' he said, again confirming the efficiency of Exeter's gossip-mill. 'I heard him spouting his evil nonsense once, down in the Plough Inn in North Gate Street. There were several of them in there, gabbing about free will and the right of every man to choose his own salvation. Fair makes me sick now, though then I had not seen the light of God's will and knew no better.'

'Do you know of any more like him in the city?'

'I used to hear others, but I never knew their names, back in the days when I was too ignorant to care. If I spotted any now, I'd be straight around to the proctors to denounce them!'

He banged an empty pot angrily on the table, and John marvelled at the change that the prospect of hellfire had on the elderly when they felt that they were soon to come face to face with the Almighty.

'What about in the countryside – are these heretics confined to the towns?' he asked.

Edwin scowled, his dead eye wandering horribly out of line with the good one. 'The bastards are everywhere these days, Sir John! My sisters live out in a village and even there they tell me that some men and even a woman or two refuse to attend the church. They have heard that they meet secretly in a barn, but I don't know if that's true.'

John was willing to clutch at any straw that might further his investigation and asked Edwin where his sisters lived.

'In Ide, Crowner, just a couple of miles outside the city. It's a scandal that their parish priest doesn't do something about it, but he's a drunken sot who can hardly read.'

Just then, Martha bustled in through the back door and Edwin limped away, trying to look busy.

'What nonsense has that old fool been stuffing you with, Sir John?' she asked, but with a smile on her face.

'Since he's taken up religion, that's all he talks about. He'll end up as a bishop before he's seventy.'

'They say that only fools and children speak the truth, Martha. I pick up useful information in some of the most unlikely places.' He turned down her usual offer of food, pleading that he must go home and eat whatever Mary had prepared that night, though Gwyn's buxom wife was also an excellent cook.

'How's that husband of mine behaving himself, Sir John?' she demanded. 'I hope his new passion for brewing ale isn't keeping him from his proper tasks.' She was eternally grateful for de Wolfe's generosity in given them the tenancy of the Bush, which gave them a far better home than the decrepit cottage they had rented in St Sidwell's.

The coroner reassured her that his officer was as diligent as ever, but as they were going through a quiet patch in their duties, apart from this murder, Gwyn was quite welcome to spend time in his brewing-shed, especially if he produced such good ale as today's batch.

With her thanks ringing in his ears, he left for home and another sullen session at the supper table with Matilda. As he reached his front door, he glanced at the neighbouring house, hoping to see the lissom shape of a far more attractive woman that his wife, but there was no sign of Cecilia and with a sigh he went inside to face the bane of his life.

CHAPTER FOUR

*In which John decides against
an investigation*

'I thought there was something I'd missed, Crowner,'
said Thomas next morning. They were in their usual
place in the bleak tower room of the gatehouse,
though thankfully the cold weather had moderated
and instead there was a thin drizzle borne on a westerly
wind.

John looked at his clerk from under his black
brows. Gwyn, perched on his window ledge, waited
expectantly.

'That man in the plague pit, the one who wasn't
yellow,' continued Thomas obscurely. 'I got only
a glimpse of his dead face and I failed to make the
connection then, as I was intrigued by the difference
between him and the other victims.'

'What connection?' demanded de Wolfe, convinced
now that his clerk was becoming as long-winded as
Gwyn.

'I had seen him before, only the previous day. It
had slipped my mind, but he was the man who was
preaching heresy in the street at Carfoix.'

'So what? Even a religious crank is allowed to catch
the plague!' grunted Gwyn, scratching at a flea bite on
his thigh.

'Two heretics found dead on the same day?' mused de Wolfe. 'That's a coincidence, right enough.'

Thomas was impatient with the others for not seeing the full significance of his news. 'Look, I saw him alive and perfectly well in the street at around midday on Tuesday. By the evening, he was dead along with those other poor people. Even this serious plague doesn't kill you within such a few hours. I saw the corpse next morning and he wasn't yellow then, so he can't have died of the distemper.'

John leaned his folded arms on the table and stared at Thomas, his head jutting out like a vulture.

'You're a clever little fellow, Thomas de Peyne,' he observed. 'I wish I had half your brains!'

'What's to be done about it, Crowner?' asked Gwyn.

'I had better get down to Bretayne and ask a few questions. You said you knew this man's name?'

'Vincente d'Estcote, a porter from down there. That's about all I know, except that he was certainly preaching blasphemous opinions in the street.'

De Wolfe rose from his stool and took down his grey cloak.

'No time like the present. Then I'll have to ask your uncle if he knows anything of this man and also talk to the other two canons who seem most involved in this affair.'

'Do you want me to come down to Bretayne as well?' asked Gwyn uneasily. John knew that though his henchman would happily fight a dozen Saracens single-handed, he was reluctant to face some invisible infection.

'You go back to the Bush and try brewing some better ale,' he said roughly. 'That last lot tasted like horse-piss!' He winked broadly at Thomas to give the lie to what he said, and both knew that he was saving the Cornishman's pride at avoiding the hazards of Bretayne.

They went out into the fine rain that made the morning miserable and walked down to the bottom of the High Street.

'This is where I saw the fellow. He was talking to a group of bystanders over there,' said Thomas, pointing across Carfoix. When Gwyn left them a few yards further on, the coroner and his clerk crossed the street and turned right near St Olave's Church into one of the lanes that led down into Bretayne. Slippery with mud and refuse, the narrow alleys were lined with a motley collection of huts and small shacks, all either thatched or roofed with splintered or rotted shingles. Goats, mangy dogs and ragged children abounded, and rats were scuttling freely in the filthy drains between the dwellings.

'Where's the best place to ask for some information, Thomas?' asked his master.

'Try the parish priest, the one we saw when that man was nailed to the tree in his churchyard,' suggested Thomas, referring to a previous drama they had dealt with down here.

At St Bartholomew's, a small chapel set in a neglected half-acre of trees and weeds, they found the sexton, an old man whose face was badly disfigured by cowpox scars.

'Father Robin is not well; he didn't get up this morning,' he told them rather sheepishly. John knew that the incumbent was probably drunk, but the sexton seemed to know plenty of local gossip.

'My clerk here tells me that one of those plague victims had none of the usual yellowness of the skin,' said John. 'Do you recall that?'

The old man, who had a severe tremor of his fingers, pondered a moment, then agreed. 'Not that I noticed much, nor cared. All me and my labourer wanted was to get a hole dug and tip them in as quick as we could.'

'Did you notice anything else about the corpse?' he demanded. 'Any injuries that you could see?'

The sexton shook his head vehemently. 'We had cloths over our heads. I could hardly see nor breathe!' he exclaimed querulously. 'Got 'em down under ground as quick as we could, no time to bloody examine them!'

'Well, it may be that you'll have to dig them up again!' snapped the coroner.

Again the old man shook his head and held up his hands as if to ward off the devil. 'That can never be done, sir!' he wailed. 'You'll not find a man who'll put a spade into that pit, not for a king's ransom.'

De Wolfe argued with him for a few moments, but the sexton was adamant that neither he, his gravediggers nor any sensible fellow would risk disturbing the remains of plague victims.

'Then tell me more about this fellow,' said John. 'My clerk says that he was probably one of these malcontents who preached heresy.'

'That was well known, Crowner,' agreed the sexton. 'Though he was but a common porter, he had a mind above his station in life, did Vincente. Father Robin had great arguments with him, when they sat here in the churchyard with a pitcher of ale between them.'

'And your priest did not denounce him?'

The old man leered. 'Father Robin is one for a quiet life, sir. It would be far too much trouble for him to start something like that.'

The only other useful fact that de Wolfe could get from the sexton was that there were quite a few others in Bretayne who seemed to share Vincente d'Estcote's views and that they sometimes even met in the churchyard to discuss their beliefs. Having exhausted what little the sexton knew, John walked back towards the city centre with Thomas, picking his brains as he went.

'Tell me more about these heretics, before I visit the other canons,' he said. 'I don't want to appear too ignorant.'

The clerk, a born teacher, was only too eager to oblige. 'They disagree with the dogma and rituals of the Roman Church, though, of course, they are still Christians – and often very devout ones, for they care more about their beliefs than the average man.'

That was true enough, thought John, who accepted religion merely as an ordinary fact of life, just like food, drink and sex. 'So what do they believe?' he asked.

'There are many types of heretics – in fact, one could even call the Eastern Church based in Constantinople a heresy, as they refuse to abide by the rules of Rome, as did the Celtic Church of Ireland and Wales, until eventually Rome trod them under foot.'

This didn't answer de Wolfe's question, but he waited for Thomas to continue.

'The early bishops of the Roman Church set down their rigid beliefs and ceremonies in a series of synods in the first few centuries after the death of our Blessed Saviour.'

The little clerk paused to cross himself. 'The main article of faith was that man is born with original sin, derived from the fall of Adam, and can achieve salvation only through the intercession of the Holy Church and its priests.'

John had not heard it put so plainly before, not in all the hundreds of boring sermons he had sat through over the years.

'In other words, Rome claims a monopoly on salvation?' he asked provocatively.

As a faithful servant of the Church, Thomas bridled a little at this. 'And quite rightly so, for we have that power given by God, through the laying on of a bishop's hands during ordination.'

'So what do the heretics say to that?'

Thomas pattered alongside, keeping up with the coroner's long strides. 'There are many different sects of heretics, but most have one thing in common. They deny that all men are born into sin and say that every man has it within him to makes choices that will lead him to his own salvation, without the interference of a priest. In other words, free will can direct him to heaven or hell.'

'Seems quite sensible to me, Thomas,' said de Wolfe, impishly goading his clerk.

'Oh, don't say that, sir!' squeaked the clerk. 'I would never forgive myself if I thought that I had led you out of the path of righteousness.'

'Don't worry, lad, I'm not that concerned with my immortal soul. But tell me, what sort of heretics would these Exeter fellows be likely to be?'

They had reached the cathedral Close by now, where John sat down on a low wall near the little church of St Mary Major that faced the West Front. He motioned Thomas to a place alongside him, as he knew he was panting after the rapid climb up from Bretayne. When he had regained his breath, the clerk expounded his knowledge once more.

'It is hard to say, there are so many different sects, each disputing with the other as to who is correct.'

'Your uncle mentioned the Cathars, from southern France?'

'It is possible, though I doubt that many Englishmen belong to them, numerous though they are in Albi and around Toulouse. If those here are home-grown blasphemers, they are probably Gnostics or some descendants of the Pelagians, who were called the British heretics long ago.'

John's brow furrowed, as his clerk's breadth and depth of learning often left him behind. 'Who the hell are they?' he asked.

'Hell is the right word, master, as no doubt Pelagius has been languishing there for the past eight hundred years. After Arianism, his beliefs were virtually the first to challenge the early Roman Church.'

The coroner wisely decided not to ask about the Arians.

'Why was this heresy called British, then?' he demanded instead, interested in spite of his usual apathy about religion.

'He was a Briton – a Celt like you, sir. In fact, he is also known as Morcant or Morgan – probably a monk from the monastery at Bangor-on-Dee in North Wales, though all his active life was spent in Rome and Carthage.'

'And these heretical beliefs of his gained adherents?'

'Indeed they did!' replied Thomas, gesticulating in the full flow of his lecturing mode. 'In the early fourth century, they spread so widely that at one time it was a possibility that they would gain the ascendancy over Rome. They were especially popular in Britain, so much so that Pope Celestine had to send three bishops, including St Germanus, to try to quell the rise of the cult, which even had many Roman priests convinced of its worth.'

He was now really into his stride. 'Pelagius fled from Rome to Carthage and St Augustine of Hippo strove to overcome his heresy – in fact, the Council of Carthage in 418 set down the nine articles which remain the basic tenets of the Roman Catholic faith, as a direct reaction to Pelagius's teachings.'

This was getting too scholarly for de Wolfe, so he moved the subject on a little.

'So what about these Cathars? Even I heard about them when I was campaigning in France, down near the Languedoc. Some of the other knights were muttering about exterminating them.'

Thomas shook his head. 'They are very different from the old Pelagians – and they are a new breed of heretics, posing a modern threat to Rome. I fear there will be a Crusade against them before many years are out. They believe that all material things, including our very bodies, are works of the devil and that only our souls belong to God. They see no reason for the existence of the Holy Church and also claim that a man must work out his own salvation.'

John rose from the wall, bemused by an excess of knowledge.

'I suppose it matters not one bit which kind of blasphemy our Devon heretics subscribe to, Thomas!' he observed. 'Your masters in the cathedral no doubt tar them all with same brush when it comes to getting rid of them.'

The clerk nodded soberly as he followed the coroner. 'But retribution must be applied through the proper processes – the bishop's court and the like, not by a knife to the throat, Crowner.'

This time, they went across the Close to Canon's Row to find one of the other heretic-hunters, Ralph de Hospitali. He occupied a house three doors beyond that of John de Alençon, and Thomas repeated his actions to get de Wolfe admitted to the canon's presence.

Once again, he found the prebendary living in some luxury, so different from the ascetic home of Thomas's uncle, just along the road. The well-furnished chamber had a blazing fire in a side hearth like the one in John's home, and there seemed to be a surfeit of servants about the house.

Ralph was a younger man than Canon fitz Rogo, only a few years older than John himself. He was tall and lean, with a mop of fair hair around his shaved tonsure. A nervous, overactive man, he seemed unable to keep still, restlessly sitting down and then standing up, calling for wine, which his visitors declined.

'Richard fitz Rogo told me of your visit, and no doubt you need to consult me as well,' he stated in a staccato voice that suited his twitchy nature. He made no effort to seat his visitors, but paced around them like an angry lion.

'I heard of the death of this woodworker, who we were about to bring to account,' he snapped. 'Even my Christian charity cannot stretch to the hypocrisy of expressing sorrow for it, though I would not wish that method of death on any of God's creatures.'

His attitude rankled with John, but he suppressed his distaste with an effort. 'How came you to know of this man's activities?' he asked.

'It was reported to me by Herbert Gale, the senior of our two proctors' bailiffs. He said he had an informant in the city and so personally went down to a meeting in a house where this Nicholas Budd was expounding his dangerous blasphemy.'

'You did not personally hear the man commit heresy?'

The canon shook his head vigorously. 'There was no need! The bailiff's accusation was sufficient to have the fellow called in for interrogation, which was to be in a few days' time.'

De Wolfe stared hard at the priest. 'A servant's opinion was enough for you?' he grated.

'Why not? If the man Budd could explain himself, so be it. If not, he must face the consequences.'

The coroner breathed hard at this cavalier approach to justice.

'Was Budd the only one you suspected of heresy?'

Ralph de Hospitali leaned against the edge of his table and drummed his fingers on the top. 'I suspect many more. It seems obvious that there is a spreading cult of these evil thinkers in Devon, many right here in Exeter. But they will be extirpated, mark my words!' His voice rose in pitch as he became more vehement.

'Do you know more names?' asked John, thinking of the pale-faced man in the plague pit.

'I have suspicions of several, reported by the proctors' men. My brother in Christ, Robert de Baggetor, is compiling a list of suspects, based on the information passed to him by the two bailiffs and their contacts in the city.'

'Does the name Vincente d'Estcote appear in his list?'

Ralph looked blankly at the coroner. 'I do not recall that name, but, as I say, de Baggetor is at present compiling a list and for all I know that person may be included. Why do you ask?'

'I have certain information that he might have been one of these men with very different views from your own,' answered John obliquely.

The canon's sharp wits soon picked him up. 'What do you mean "might have been"? Has he then seen the error of his ways?'

'He is dead as well!' answered John bluntly. 'And I have no means of determining how he came by his demise.'

De Hospitali jerked himself upright and took a step towards the coroner. 'If you have other names, you must give them to me. You have a duty under God to do so.'

'And I have a duty under the king's peace to see that the law is upheld, sir,' retorted de Wolfe. 'Where can I find your bailiff? I need to see this list of his, in case others have met an untimely fate.'

For the first time, Thomas opened his mouth, for until now he had been studiously ignored by the canon.

'Sir, how does the bailiff, who is really but a constable, make a record of these men? Can he read and write?'

Ralph looked down at the clerk as if noticing his presence for the first time. 'Herbert Gale is a former merchant's clerk, who spent some of his youth in the abbey school at Bath. His fellow bailiff is illiterate, but Herbert has some learning. You will no doubt find him in the small building which houses the cathedral detention cells, on the north side of the Close.'

He rang a small bell to summon his steward, an unambiguous sign that the interview was over. Realising that there was nothing more to be gained, John left, his clerk trailing behind him. They walked slowly back along Canon's Row, in silence for the first hundred paces.

'Not very likeable, that fellow,' grunted de Wolfe. 'Is he always like that?'

'He has a reputation for being strict in all matters concerning the observance of cathedral rules and customs,' answered Thomas. 'He is a pillar of the chapter, but it is hard to warm towards him.'

'What about this remaining canon, Robert de Baggetor? What's he like? I've only seen him in the distance, when my wife drags me to the cathedral.'

'Another former archdeacon, this time of Barnstaple. He is older, probably in his sixtieth year. Another proud and somewhat arrogant man, may God forgive me for so saying.' He crossed himself rapidly as a precaution against being struck by a thunderbolt for his disparagement of a senior churchman.

'So where do we find him, Thomas?'

'He lives further along from fitz Rogo on the north side. He is one of the two cathedral proctors who have houses reserved for their use. The other one is William de Swindon.'

'I gather the proctors are responsible for order and discipline within the cathedral community,' said John. 'Is that all they do?' His knowledge of ecclesiastical politics and administration was hazy.

'They are, but much of their function is to deal with legal and ceremonial matters for the chapter and the bishop. They don't soil their own hands with mere physical matters like riot or affray. For that, they employ proctors' bailiffs, who are the cathedral's equivalent of our Osric and Theobald in the city.'

Just then a bell began tolling in the cathedral and several groups of vicars, secondaries and one or two canons appeared from various houses and began converging on the various entrances to the great church of St Mary and St Peter.

'You'll not see him now, master,' said Thomas, pointing to one group as they trod sedately across the Close. 'He's there, off to celebrate Terce, Sext and Nones.' These were the mid-morning offices of the daily devotions.

'We'd best catch him when he comes back for his dinner at noon,' added the clerk. 'I should be there myself, if you don't need me at the moment.'

John waved him away, and Thomas followed the rest of the celebrants into the cathedral. These incessant services were not meant for the benefit of the public except on feast days, as the common folk were served by a plethora of parish churches in the city. The rituals in the cathedral were for the endless glorification of God by the priesthood and their lesser acolytes.

John walked slowly back to his house around the corner, somewhat at a loss as to what to do next. It was too late to trudge back up to the castle and too early for his dinner. Partly from old habits left from the Nesta days, he decided to take Brutus for a walk, his old weak alibi for going down to the Bush. Fetching him from the house, where thankfully Matilda was either in her solar or out somewhere, he walked down to Idle Lane and sampled the new batch of ale, which fully lived up to his expectations.

The big Cornishman came and sat with him, basking in the compliments about his latest efforts at brewing. A fervent dog-lover, he brought a bone from the kitchen-shed for Brutus, who lay in the rushes under the table, gnawing happily while the men above talked.

'The yellow plague has hit Dartmouth now, so a carter told us this morning,' said Gwyn. 'Another port. We don't hear of it happening up on Dartmoor, so it must surely be brought in by ship-men.'

They discussed this for a time, but felt futile and helpless in the face of a disease which struck so rapidly and so randomly.

'That doctor next door to me is useless,' growled de Wolfe. 'I'll have a word with Richard Lustcote, the apothecary. He's a sensible man, though I suppose if there was anything he could do, he would have done it by now.'

His officer, depressed by the subject, moved to another problem. 'What are we going to do about this murder? Where do we start?'

'The heretic fraternity is the only lead I can see,' answered the coroner. 'Unless some fanatic comes to confess to it, which seems as likely as the moon breaking in half, we can only attack the problem by discovering whom the heretics fear or even suspect of such an act.'

'And what about Thomas's pale man in the plague pit?'

John shrugged and took a deep draught of his ale. 'We've no chance of getting him dug up again, in the circumstances. And even if we did and found another bloody great wound in his head, what good would that be in finding out who did it? We've already got one example, and that's taking us nowhere at the moment.'

Gwyn scratched his crotch, which seemed his alternative to Thomas crossing himself. 'So we've got to find us some unbelievers?'

'Unbelievers in the Roman way, certainly – though our clerk says they are more than devout in their own way. Someone said they heard such heresy being voiced in the Plough tavern, so maybe you should do one of your tours around the alehouses and keep those big ears open.'

Where Thomas gained much gossip from among his ecclesiastical colleagues, Gwyn was adept at eavesdropping in taverns, a task that suited him admirably.

'I'll start tonight, Crowner – my goodwife can hardly complain if I'm doing it on behalf of the king and his coroner!'

CHAPTER FIVE

*In which the coroner receives
some bad news*

John spent the early part of the afternoon with Thomas in their chamber, as they had to work on some of the submissions to the royal justices when they came to hold the Eyre in a few weeks' time. As de Wolfe had been away for months, most of the few cases were left over from Nicholas de Arundell, manor-lord of Hempston Arundell, near Totnes. He had reluctantly taken over the coronership when John was posted to Westminster and had now gone back to Hempston with a sigh of relief.

Thomas de Peyne was rewriting some of the scrappy records left by a junior clerk that Nicholas had borrowed from the castle, as his pride would not allow him to put such imperfect parchments before the king's judges. In addition, he had to record a couple of fatal assaults, a rape, two house fires, seven hangings and four declarations of outlawry that John had dealt with since his return. As the coroner could only just about write his name, Thomas took dictation from him and read back any material that John needed to know about. The arrangement worked well, especially as Thomas used his own initiative to improve the content and style of his master's words, without John being aware of it.

As they worked, de Wolfe listened for the cathedral bells, the only way of gauging the time, other than dawn and dusk. The only other means was going to a church that had graduated candles used for timing services.

'That was for Vespers, so we'll wait a while, then go down to tackle this other canon,' he decided.

If de Baggetor had actually graced Vespers with his presence, instead of sending a vicar in his stead, he should be back within the hour.

In due course the coroner and his clerk walked back down to the Close, and Thomas took him to another house a few doors away from Ralph de Hospitali. Here they were again conducted by a steward to a comfortable room with even better furniture than before. De Baggetor was a tall, stooped man of about fifty, with a long, deeply lined face which reminded John of a hunting hound. The canon had an aloof manner which went with a stubborn and inflexible nature.

He offered no invitation for them to be seated, and de Wolfe was again made aware of the antagonism and jealousies that often existed between the clergy and the city. The cathedral precinct was almost a state within a state, as the writ of the sheriff and burgesses did not run in the Close, except along the public paths. Discipline and justice were meted out by the bishop and the cathedral chapter, through the strong arms of the proctors' bailiffs. This had been softened a little by the decision of Bishop Marshal to delegate jurisdiction over serious crimes like murder to the sheriff and coroner, but it was always made clear that the secular powers operated in the precinct only under sufferance.

'You want to talk to me about this slain heretic?' asked de Baggetor. His voice was slow and almost lazy, but was belied by the steely look in his dark eyes. The ring of frizzled hair around his tonsure was grey, but his eyebrows were jet black, like John's.

'It is just possible that we may have two slain heretics,' answered de Wolfe. 'I can't prove it for various reasons, but another man said to have similar beliefs has died suddenly. Does the name Vincente d'Estcote mean anything to you?'

A look of surprise came over the canon's face, which John felt was genuine. 'No, never heard of him. Why do you say that he might also have been a blasphemer?'

'My clerk here heard him addressing folk in the street on the subject. I thought he might have been one of the names that your bailiffs had reported to you. Ralph de Hospitali told us that you held a list of such suspects.'

Robert de Baggetor turned to his table and reached up to a shelf above it, where a number of rolled parchments rested, tied with pink tape. Everything in the room was in meticulously neat order, with nothing out of place. Even the large ebony and ivory crucifix on the wall shone as if it had been polished only an hour before.

He took a thin roll and untied it, before scanning it rapidly and then handing it to John. 'That name is not on there, Sir John.'

The coroner, always slightly sensitive about his illiteracy, slid the curled sheet across to Thomas.

'How did your men come by these names?' he asked.

The canon rubbed one of his eyes, which was red and inflamed.

'On my instructions, they seek out meetings of such evildoers. They also have paid informers who can acquire such names without arousing suspicion. Experience in Italy and France has shown that since the Papal Bull on the matter, threatened exposure can lead to violence and even murder of the investigators.'

John made a mental note to ask Thomas about this notorious Bull, but he did not wish to show his ignorance before this patronising cleric.

'I would like to keep this list – or have my clerk make a copy of it,' he requested.

De Baggetor's dark brows came together in displeasure. 'Impossible! It is for the use of the bishop and the proctors. This is an ecclesiastical matter; it is none of the business of a sheriff or coroner.'

Thomas, emboldened by his knowledge of Church law, ventured to enter the dispute. 'With the greatest respect, canon, the Papal Bull *Ab Abolendum* specifically stated that bishops should seek the aid of stewards, bailiffs and all other officers in pursuing heretics and that such secular authorities were obliged to offer such help.'

The former archdeacon glowered at this little upstart but was unable to contradict him. 'I am one of the cathedral proctors and know the laws as well as you,' he grated. 'But if you think you can find more of these vermin, then make a copy of this list. There is pen, ink and parchment on that table.'

As Thomas, with hidden glee, hurried to take advantage of de Baggetor's climbdown, John had more questions.

'What has occurred recently to bring this matter to the surface?' he asked.

'Events in northern Italy and the south-west of France have caused anxiety in Rome,' answered the canon, who seemed more ready to speak of generalities than his own activities. 'The Papal Legate in England has passed on instructions from the Vatican for all bishops to be far more vigilant in detecting and stamping out the growing cancer that is eating away at the very roots of our Holy Roman Church.'

'So what is intended in regard to these other persons? Are they all to be arrested?'

'There is to be an inquisition, where they will be strictly interrogated. Depending on what arises from that, further action will be taken.'

This sounded somewhat sinister to de Wolfe, but the proctor refused to be drawn on the matter, saying it would be the decision of the bishop and of the chancellor of any court he might set up.

As soon as Thomas had finished copying the list, for there were only a dozen names on it, they left, as de Baggetor made it abundantly clear that he had no intention of telling them any more.

The cloud-filled sky was darkening by now, the November weather already warning of the coming of winter. Again the coroner and his acolyte made their way down towards the lower town, where the old wall gave on to the quayside where smaller ships could get up on the tide past Topsham. John was on his way to the Bush and Thomas to his lodgings, and as they parted at Idle Lane de Wolfe gave him his orders for the morning.

'Tomorrow you must explain to me about this Bull and the demands of the Pope – it's all a mystery to me. Then we'll look at that list you made and decide what to do about it. I smell more trouble coming and we need to be prepared for it.'

The coroner did not stay very long at the inn, as Gwyn had taken him at his word and gone off early on his tour of the taverns, allegedly in search of information. If John knew anything about him, he would get several gallons of ale inside him in the process, but knowing of his capacious stomach and iron head, John had little fear of him coming to any harm.

Dusk was falling, but it was not yet dark when he got back to Martin's Lane and, as he passed the little church of St Martin's on the corner of Canon's Row, he met Cecilia, the doctor's wife. She was swathed in a mantle of heavy green wool, with a fur-edged hood framing her handsome face. Behind her, her young maid lugged a large shopping basket. He greeted Cecilia warmly, for any good-looking woman always melted the usual forbidding expression on his face.

'Best that you reach home and hearth while there's still light, mistress,' he said affably. 'Especially when you ladies are abroad alone in these streets.'

She smiled at him as they stopped to speak, close enough for him to smell a flowery fragrance coming from her.

'At this time of day, my husband sees his patients in his chamber in Goldsmith Street,' she explained, 'so he can never escort me when I wish to visit the booths or the tradesmen's shops.'

For a fleeting moment de Wolfe wondered if this rather unnecessary explanation was a covert message that she was alone at this time every day – but then he discarded the thought, knowing what a godly and upright woman she was. But one could have said exactly the same thing about his Hilda of Dawlish, who was a pillar of her church and community yet had been John's mistress for many years.

'You have been about the king's business today, sir?' asked Cecilia, almost as if she wanted to spin out their encounter.

Being quite happy to dally with her, John gave a brief account of his efforts to track down who might have killed the heretic – and mentioned the possibility that another one of that persuasion might also have been slain.

'Poor people. It seems cruel that they should suffer just because they have a different view of God from the majority,' she said surprisingly. 'My husband has such strict opinions on the matter, but I fear I see them as human beings deserving of compassion.'

'They may well suffer even more soon, if the bishop has to carry out his orders from Rome,' said John grimly. He explained about the forthcoming inquisition of any suspected of deviating from the prescribed pathway laid down by the Pope. 'As the coroner, I have to hold inquisitions, but I fear that the religious variety may be far more harsh than my questioning.'

She shook her head sadly. 'It is wrong that a man's private thoughts and beliefs – or, indeed, a woman's – should be dictated to by others and any transgression punished by violence.'

De Wolfe was intrigued by her words. A freethinking woman was almost unknown, at least any daring to put such thoughts into words.

'You have some sympathy with these heretics, lady?' he asked gently.

Cecilia looked startled, as if she had just realised that perhaps she was speaking unwisely. 'My husband would not favour my expressing such thoughts, I'm sure! He has very strong views on this subject, as on everything else.'

John did not miss the trace of bitterness in her voice and fell to wondering what might go on in the house next to his own. But not wanting to end the meeting, he steered the conversation on to safer ground.

'Your husband is busy, then? His practice is flourishing?'

She smiled wanly. 'I rarely see him except at mealtimes!'

And in bed, thought John – what husband would not wish that? 'He visits his patients at their homes as well as at his doctor's chamber?'

She nodded. 'He is being called from far afield now, to manors and castles all across the county. He keeps a fine horse there, where your great destrier also lodges.' A gloved hand appeared from under her cloak, pointing to Andrew's livery stables opposite their houses.

'I trust he looks to his safety, Mistress Cecilia,' he said gravely. 'Riding the Devon roads can be a dangerous business, given the number of outlaws and malcontents that infest the forests. Even a rough old Crusader like myself rarely rides alone these days.'

'Clement always has a manservant with him, a former soldier,' she said, pulling her cloak around her more tightly. 'And I don't think you are a rough old Crusader, Sir John. You are a gentleman and a brave one at that, by all the accounts I've heard!'

Flushing slightly at her own boldness, she bowed her head and hurried away, her maid trotting at her heels. De Wolfe watched her until she vanished around the corner of his house, for hers was set back slightly from the edge of the lane.

'Well, well!' he thought to himself, feeling a pleasant glow at being flattered by a desirable woman. 'She seems at odds with her husband's opinion. There's a woman with a mind of her own.'

He walked to his front door and, once inside, heard voices in the hall. He sat on the bench in the vestibule to pull off his boots, then, as he hung up his cloak on a peg and put on some leather slippers, he groaned when he recognised the reedy tones of his brother-in-law on the other side of the inner door. Reluctantly, he pushed it open and went between the draught-screens into the hall. As he feared, Richard de Revelle was standing with his back to the hearth, bleating and gesticulating to his sister Matilda, who sat in one of the hooded monks' chairs. Hearing John enter, he jerked up his head and redirected his high-pitched voice towards him.

'It's not good enough, John. You and that lazy successor of mine must do something about it!'

De Wolfe had no idea what he was talking about, but he advanced to the centre of the hall and bobbed his head curtly in greeting. Though he detested the man, he felt obliged as the host to at least be civil and went to his side table to pour some wine, this time into pewter cups, rather than the grand glass goblets that he had brought out for the doctor and his wife.

As he handed one to Richard and his sister, he sighed and asked his visitor what urgent problem had brought him to his door.

'This damned plague, John, what else?' screeched de Revelle.

He was a slim, neat man of average height, a few years older than John. Another dandified dresser, with a penchant for bright green, he had wavy hair of a light brown colour, matching the small pointed beard, a fashion which was more that of Paris than of the Normans, who were usually clean-shaven. John suspected that he grew it to hide the weak chin at the lower end of his narrow, triangular face.

'The plague?' repeated John, still mystified. 'Have you caught it, then?' he asked facetiously. He wished his brother-in-law would stop hogging the fire, as being master of the house John felt that it should be his own cold backside that should be warmed.

'Be serious, damn it!' snapped Richard. 'I mean that it's ruining my business!'

'Why, have all your students in Smythen Street been stricken?'

'Not that business, I mean my pork-exporting venture!' said the other, exasperated at John's deliberate obfuscation.

The coroner feigned sudden enlightenment. 'Ah, yes, I had heard that you were now a swineherd. But what has the yellow disease got to do with that? Are pigs able to catch it?'

With even less sense of humour than John, the former sheriff thought he was being serious. 'Not the pigs, you fool! The men who work for me, of course. Three have died at Dartmouth and half a dozen are sick near to death at my holding near Clyst St George.'

De Wolfe was immediately more concerned. 'There is plague at Clyst? I had not heard that!'

'Nor had I until an hour ago. All the other slaughterers and salters have downed tools and run home. Only one old man has stayed to throw the hogs some food.'

'And it is at Dartmouth as well?'

Richard nodded in agitation, then swallowed his wine in a gulp. 'I have large orders for the king's army to fulfil! How can I carry on with the workers refusing to attend to their duties?'

'They could hardly work if they were sick or dead,' pointed out John. 'Best they stay away from their workplace until the danger of infection is past.'

This only inflamed de Revelle even more. 'Impossible! Think of the money I am losing every day! Unless I can find other men who will take on the tasks, I will be ruined. I cannot feed hundreds of pigs and get nothing in return!'

'So why come to me about it?' demanded John. 'I am a law officer, not a physician or apothecary!'

'Surely there is something you can do, you and that idle fellow now sitting in my chamber in Rougemont!' brayed Richard. 'Forbid ships from entering our ports, as I have heard that it is likely that foreign seamen are bringing the poison. And also make it unlawful for these workers to stay away from their employment. If they were serfs on a manor, they would have no choice but to work for their lord.'

John looked scathingly at his brother-in-law. 'And just how do you think that could be done? Most of the seamen coming to our harbours live there. They are now returning for the winter season. Would you have us ban them from their homes?'

Richard scowled at him. 'Then the workers! Surely they can be put back to their labours?'

'How? Send a troop of men-at-arms to each of your piggeries, to stand prodding the men with their lances?'

He advanced to the hearth and ostentatiously stood close to Richard, easing him away from the fire.

'There's nothing to be done. We all have to make the best of a bad situation and pray that it does not spread to obliterate the city and the county, as has happened sometimes abroad.'

'We must all pray to Almighty God for deliverance,' said Matilda, speaking for the first time. 'For once, John is right. There's nothing that can be done by we weak mortals.'

'And as for physicians,' added de Wolfe scornfully, 'they can only offer the same advice – prayer! We have a smart doctor next door now, but he's made it clear that he won't go within a furlong of a plague victim!'

De Revelle huffed and puffed for a time, but it was apparent that he had no support from either Matilda or John. This was an unusual state of affairs, as though Matilda's former hero-worship of her rich elder brother had collapsed with her realisation that he was a rogue, she normally contradicted her husband on principle.

Eventually, having gained nothing from his visit, he departed, muttering about having to find more men at a higher rate of pay to deal with his pigs.

'He thinks of nothing else but his purse and his treasure chest,' grunted John after the front door had slammed. 'He has two manors and a rich wife, so why is he always pursuing more wealth?'

Matilda hunched in her chair, unwilling to side with her husband any longer. 'At least he is aiding the economy of the county and giving work to many men,' she sniped.

'And what d'you think I and Hugh de Relaga are doing?' demanded John. 'We ship almost half the raw wool that goes from the Exe and a goodly proportion of the finished cloth. It's that that keeps those in this house warm and well fed!'

Matilda sniffed disdainfully, then returned to attack from a different direction. 'You should not cast aspersions on Doctor Clement like that,' she complained. 'He is a professional man and, if he is so busy with his regular patients to attend to the poor, then that is his concern.'

'He's afraid of catching the yellow distemper, that's what!' countered John.

'And who isn't afraid?' she demanded. 'You and that perverted little priest might be foolhardy enough to risk bringing it home to your family and friends, but normal people keep well clear for everyone's sake.'

Another developing row was averted by Mary coming in to ask if they were ready for their supper, as it was now virtually dark outside. John suspected that she had been listening at the inner door and had interrupted to save him becoming enmeshed in yet another futile shouting match with his cantankerous wife.

The prospect of food always mollified her, and soon they were sitting at the table in smouldering silence as they ate their way through venison in broth, carp and eels in a crust and finally frumenty.

Afterwards, John sat by the fire with a pot of ale and his wife dozed in her chair opposite, while a cold wind whined around the shutters and sudden draughts sucked showers of sparks up the wide chimney. It was not a night on which to expect visitors, and John was all the more surprised to hear an urgent knocking on the outer door. Mary usually answered it, but it took her a time to get around the side passage from her hut in the yard, so he went out into the vestibule and pulled open the heavy oak door. A horse was tied to the rail across the lane and a man stood before him, shivering in a damp riding cloak.

'Sir John, it's me, Alfred from Stoke!'

In the dim light from a pitch-brand guttering on the corner of the Close, de Wolfe recognised the reeve from the family manor at Stoke-in-Teignhead, where he had been born and brought up. Surprised and apprehensive, he ushered the man inside and, aware of Matilda in the hall, took him around to Mary's kitchen-shed, where a good fire burned and the man could get warm and have some food. But first Alfred had to give his momentous news.

'I have bad tidings, Sir John. The yellow plague has appeared in the village and two are dead and half a dozen taken sick. I am afraid that your brother William is one of them!'

CHAPTER SIX

In which Crowner John rides to Stoke

At dawn next morning, three riders left the West Gate soon after it was opened and splashed through the ford across the Exe, heading for the coast road southwards. Grim-faced, John de Wolfe was in the lead, with Alfred and Gwyn close behind. Thomas had been left behind, as though he offered to come, he was an indifferent horseman and would have slowed them down on his pony. Even John had left his heavy destrier, Odin, behind and taken a swifter rounsey from Andrew's livery stable to speed his journey. As they cantered down the track towards Powderham and Dawlish, John soberly recalled the events that had set them on this mission.

The previous evening, the reeve had explained how John's mother, Enyd, had sent him to Exeter with the news that his elder brother had been stricken with the fever that had crept into Stoke over the past four days. So far, eight had been afflicted and two of those had died. William, whose solicitude for his free tenants and villeins was well known, had refused to hide himself away in the manor house, but had insisted on visiting the sick and arranging for food and firewood to be supplied to them.

'He forbade the ladies to accompany him, though they both wished to help,' Alfred had said. 'Within a day and a night, he started shivering and soon was yellow, being brought back to collapse on his bed. Only God knows why he was so stricken, when myself, the priest and several others escaped, though we were also helping to aid the sufferers.'

'What of my mother and sister? Do they remain in good health?' demanded John. His mother, Enyd, was a sprightly woman in her early sixties, and Evelyn, six years younger than John, was a placid spinster.

'They show no signs of the curse, thanks be to Christ,' Alfred reassured him. There was no one else in the family to be concerned about, as William's wife Alice had died of a childbirth fever three years earlier.

The horses made good time on the firm roads, as the slight frost that had followed the rain had hardened the mud without being severe enough to leave icy patches. In an hour and a half they reached Dawlish, and it was with reluctance that John trotted straight through the little port without calling on Hilda. A few miles further along the track that hugged the coast, they passed the turning into Holcombe, the other de Wolfe manor, where Hilda's father was the reeve.

'Do they know there about my brother's illness?' shouted John over the noise of the hooves.

'I sent a message yesterday, but told them to stay away from Stoke in case they bring back the contagion,' replied Alfred.

At Teignmouth the tide was ebbing fast out of the river, but they had to wait fretfully for half an hour until the water was low enough for their horses to safely navigate the ford to the sand-spit on the other side. From there it was only a few minutes' canter to reach the head of the wooded valley that held John's birthplace of Stoke-in-Teignhead. The village was unnaturally quiet; no work was being done in the strip-fields and the single village street was empty. Smoke filtered out from beneath the eaves of many of the tofts to prove that people were alive, but the villagers were shunning any unnecessary contact with each other. As they passed two of the small thatched cottages, John saw ominous boards nailed across the doors, with a black cross painted on them.

They neared the manor house at the further end of the village before they saw the first living person walking towards them, the priest of St Andrew's Church. He held up his hand and John reined up alongside, fearful that Father Martin had been to the manor to administer the last rites. Thankfully, the sturdy priest was more reassuring.

'Lord William is no worse, even if not improved, Sir John. He is weak, but still alive, for which I thank the Holy Virgin – as well as your mother and sister, who are tending him like a baby.'

The parson called William 'lord' as befitted the eldest son and holder of the manor title, whereas John was 'sir' by virtue of his military knighthood.

'Is there more of the plague in the village?' asked John.

'Two more of the sick children have died, God save their souls,' admitted Father Martin. 'And two more have fallen ill in another house. I'm on my way to them now, to see if there is anything I can do.'

He looked exhausted, and John suspected that he had hardly slept since the yellow plague had come to Stoke.

They rode on and clattered over the small bridge across the ditch around the house, a defence which had not been needed since before John was born. Inside the stockade, almost an acre of ground held the square stone-built house and the profusion of sheds, huts and barns that made this a working farm as well as a family home.

Though the courtyard had been empty, the sound of their arrival brought boys out of the stables to take their horses. The old steward hurried out to greet them and shepherded John and Gwyn into the house. There was a large central hall, with two pairs of rooms divided off from it on either side and an upper solar built out over a porch at the front. John ordered Gwyn to stay in the hall, as he did not wish to increase the risk of him catching the contagion in the sickroom and taking it back to his family.

In one of the side rooms he found William lying on a low bed and attended solicitously by his mother and sister, with the steward's large wife and a younger servant hovering anxiously in the background. The Lord of Stoke appeared to be asleep, his mouth open and his eyes shut, but his breathing was laboured and a sheen of sweat lay on his forehead and face, in spite of the coldness of the room. His face was yellow, as were the hands that lay across his chest. On a table near the bed were bowls of boiled water, flasks of liniment and cloths to lay on the patient's fevered brow and body. A large bunch of herbs was stuck into a jug, and in the firepit at one side of the room fragrant smoke curled up from where other dried herbs had been sprinkled on the logs. These attempts at treatment suggested desperate frustration that was echoed in the haggard faces of Evelyn and Enyd. They came to embrace him, Evelyn with tears seeping from her eyes.

'He is no worse today, though no better,' whispered his mother. 'All we can do is pray for him.'

They all sank to their knees in the clean rushes that covered the floor, hands clasped and heads bowed. John initially felt he was being false, as he had little real faith in pleading for his brother's recovery when children were lying dead in the village from the same ailment. But as he raised his head and saw his brother's face as he strained to cling to life, a wave of love and pity flowed over him, and he fervently asked for God's mercy on a man who had come from the same womb as himself.

After few moments Enyd rose and took John's arm to lead him back into the hall, where Gwyn was waiting with the reeve.

'You men must be tired and hungry after your journey,' she said firmly.

The steward marshalled a couple of young serving girls to bring food and drink from the outside kitchen, and soon they were sitting eating at a table near the firepit.

'We feel so helpless to do anything either for William or the others in the village,' said a distraught Evelyn. 'There is no physician anywhere nor even an apothecary nearer than Brixham.'

'I doubt it would help much if there were,' said John cynically. 'I have a new doctor living next door to me and he flatly refuses to attend any victims, saying there is nothing he can do for them.'

The steward, hovering behind them with a jug of cider, said that he had heard that morning that new cases were being spoken of in Brixham and Dartmouth, further down the coast.

'All at ports and harbours,' muttered Gwyn. 'It must be coming in from abroad, surely?'

'I seems like it, but how would it have reached Stoke?' growled John.

'We have tradesmen in every day,' answered Evelyn. 'They bring in fish from Teignmouth – and we had a chapman through here last week. God knows where he'd been before coming here.'

John could hear the suppressed panic in everyone's voice, which was also beginning to appear in Exeter.

This was an invisible foe, stalking the streets and fields with a stealth that could not be detected. If disease came from a rabid dog, then it could be slain, but this yellow plague could be neither seen, heard nor smelled, which made it doubly terrifying.

They went back and sat alongside William's pallet for a time, watching helplessly as he lay inert, only his rapid breathing showing that he was still alive. From time to time the steward's wife moved forward and gently wiped his face with a cloth dipped in warm scented water.

'Has he been awake at all today?' asked John.

'He mumbled and muttered some hours ago, but has not spoken rationally to us since last evening. He has passed no water since then, which worries me. The last lot was almost green.'

'Has he drunk anything?'

'We tipped a little watered ale between his lips, but he has swallowed very little,' replied Enyd.

John recalled from his fighting days that wounded men sometimes died of thirst as much as their injuries and, desperate to find some advice to contribute, suggested that they tried harder to get some fluid into his brother.

'I'll try to get that bloody doctor to come down here with me,' he grunted. 'And if that fails, then at least a good apothecary.'

At noon they sat down to dinner in the hall; though the food was ample and well cooked, no one had much of an appetite – not even Gwyn, whose capacity for his victuals was legendary. Afterwards, they sat again with William, who had hardly moved on his mattress, until John's mother decided that there was no point in his staying too late.

'Get you back to Exeter, my son. There's nothing you can do here. I know you will have duties there to carry out.'

'I'll be back tomorrow, later in the day, and will stay until next morning,' he promised. 'If you need me more urgently before then, send Alfred and I'll come, even if it be in the middle of the night!'

As they were climbing into their saddles in the bailey, with the family and servants gathered around, his mother asked him if he was going to call upon Hilda on the way home. Enyd was very fond of the handsome blonde from Dawlish – if there had not been the social gap between the daughter of a Saxon reeve and a knight's son, she would have welcomed her as a daughter-in-law. But her husband wanted John married off into an aristocratic Norman family and had pushed him into wedlock with Matilda de Revelle. Enyd had done her best to accept Matilda, but in return John's wife had never concealed her disdain for his mother, mainly because of her Cornish and Welsh parentage.

John considered her question as he arranged his cloak over the back of his saddle. 'I think not, Mother. I would never forgive myself if I took contagion to her, just for the sake of seeing her face for a few minutes. Alfred says Holcombe is free of it – it would be better if she went to stay there with her parents, rather than keep to Dawlish, with its ships and ship-men coming and going.'

This time, it was only Gwyn and his master who trotted off through the stricken village. John hoped that he would not see Alfred coming again to Exeter, as it would probably mean that he brought news of William's death.

As they rode, Gwyn told him of what he had learned the previous evening from his tour of the taverns. 'I found a couple of men who knew some heretics,' he said. 'They seem to think that there is no law against it, as no one gets punished.'

'Did you get to speak to any yourself?' called John as they rode almost saddle to saddle along the coast road.

His officer shook his bushy head. 'No, those sort are not likely to be great frequenters of alehouses. But I know they meet in various places to discuss their beliefs.'

He said that one group used an old derelict barn off the Crediton road, not far from the village of Ide, which the potman at the Bush had mentioned.

'Who are these people, I wonder?' queried de Wolfe. 'We know our corpse was a woodworker and, if Thomas was right about the other, he was just a labourer.'

'One fellow said that several he knew were foreigners, probably French,' replied Gwyn. 'Maybe they were from the Languedoc; that seems to be a breeding place for these folk.'

They passed through Dawlish, and once again John had to resist the temptation to call on Hilda, though this time the fear of bringing contamination, however small the risk, made it easier for him to pass by. They reached Exeter as dusk was falling, and Gwyn went off to the Bush to see his wife and check his latest batch of ale-mash. John carried on to Martin's Lane to hand back his hired horse, but when he emerged from the stables he did not go straight across to his own front door. Instead, he went to the next house and rapped on the heavy oak with the pommel of his dagger. It was opened by a young maid, but before he could state his business Cecilia appeared behind her.

'Sir John, you are most welcome.' She waved him in and he went into their hall, which was well furnished and better lit than his own, with a large fire flaming in the firepit and a series of tallow-dips flickering in sconces around the walls.

'I am afraid my husband is not here, though he said he will be early this evening as he wishes to attend a special service at the cathedral. It seems that one of the canons is to preach a sermon on the dangers of heresy,' she added with a wry smile.

The doctor's wife looked as attractive as always, slender and erect, with a crisp linen head-cloth and a silken gorget covering her throat up to her chin. She offered him refreshment, which he gravely declined.

'I was hoping to see him to ask his professional advice,' said John and went on to tell her of his brother being stricken by the yellow distemper. Cecilia seemed genuinely upset by his news, holding her fingers to her lips in a gesture of concern.

'Your only brother? That is desperately sad,' she said solicitously, reaching out to lay a consoling hand gently on his arm. Her maid lurked in the background, resolutely chaperoning her mistress. As if in answer to her suspicions, there was a noise from the outer vestibule and the girl hurried out to meet her master, who had just arrived.

Clement of Salisbury handed her his cloak and broad-brimmed pilgrim's hat and came into the hall, looking slightly startled as he saw the tall, looming figure of his neighbour. Cecilia started forward, but John noticed that she did not give him a welcome embrace. Instead, she launched into the reason for him being there.

'Sir John has grave tidings, Clement! His brother, the Lord of Stoke and Holcombe, has been stricken by this plague.'

The physician made sympathetic noises and declared how mortified Sir John must be at the news.

'He is still alive but looks dreadfully sick,' said John.

'You have seen him?' asked Clement, apparently surprised.

'Only a few hours ago – I have just returned from his bedside.'

'Is there anything we can do to help you?' offered the physician.

'I would be very grateful if you would come with me tomorrow to see if you can do anything for my brother. I would naturally pay whatever fee you desire.'

From his previous conversations with the doctor, John expected a polite refusal, but he was confounded by Clement's answer.

'Tomorrow? I think I could manage that, though I would have to desert several of my patients. There is no question of a fee, Sir John; you are my neighbour.'

As the coroner made a rapid revision of his opinion of the physician, they agreed on the details of a late start next morning, then John took his leave, with profound thanks to Clement and a stiff bow to Cecilia.

'I will pray for your brother and your whole family,' she murmured as she followed him to the front door, which the maid opened for him.

He went out into the lane and took a few steps towards his own house, then stopped. Making a sudden decision, he swung around and strode off towards the High Street.

Later that evening the coroner walked down to the Bush, with his old hound weaving ahead of him, enjoying the smells of the odorous Exeter streets. In the tavern he sat with Gwyn at his usual table by the fire, as though the icy weather had moderated it was still a chilly, windswept night and he was glad of the warmth.

By the time Edwin had brought them a quart mug apiece, Thomas appeared, summoned by Gwyn at John's request after returning from Stoke. Almost by habit, the priest sidled into the inn as if entering a den of sin, though he had been there innumerable times before, especially when mothered by Nesta, during his worst period before being restored to the priesthood. Settled with a cup of cider, he asked solicitously after William de Wolfe and fervently promised to pray for his recovery.

'Afterwards, I went up to seek advice from Richard Lustcote and he immediately agreed to come down to Stoke tomorrow with the doctor to see William.'

Lustcote was the senior of the three Exeter apothecaries, who had a shop in North Street. From past experience, John held a high opinion of him, both as a man of integrity and as a good apothecary. Like Clement of Salisbury, he had warned John that there was very little he could do, except perhaps to alleviate some of the symptoms, but he was willing to make the long ride to Stoke for the sake of his friendship with de Wolfe.

John then got down to business, glad to have something to take his mind off his personal problems for a while.

'Gwyn has discovered something about the heretics, Thomas. It seems that one group holds covert meetings not far from the city. Did you glean any more from the cathedral?'

'Not so much about the blasphemers themselves, master, but I did pick up some facts about the people who are determined to stop them.'

He hunched closer across the table, as if he was about to disclose some state secrets. 'The three canons who are the prime movers in this matter are very keen indeed to extirpate any deviation from the rule of Rome. Some of my vicar friends even say that they are totally obsessed by what they see as a crusade.'

'So why have they chosen to start their crusade now?' asked John. 'Surely these critics of the Church have been around for a long time.'

Thomas wiped a drop from the tip of his sharp nose with the back of his hand. The cold weather affected him and he was always sniffing and wheezing. 'Robert de Baggetor spent some time in Aquitaine and Toulouse a year ago, and when he came back it seems he was full of outrage about the rise of the Albigensian heresy in that region. Then he began hearing reports of men with similar sympathies in this county and tried to persuade the bishop to act against them.'

Gwyn yawned and banged his pot on the table to attract Edwin's attention. He was a man of action and Thomas's tales tended to send him to sleep. De Wolfe, however, was keen to learn more.

'I take it that Henry Marshal had more important things on his mind, like plotting with Prince John to oust King Richard?'

Thomas shrugged. 'Probably, but as de Baggetor could raise little enthusiasm in the bishop's palace, he started a campaign of his own. He found two other canons of a like mind and they have been using the proctors' bailiffs to do their spying for them.'

'We know all that already,' grunted Gwyn. 'What we need to know is who is likely to have snuffed out the woodcarver and possibly the man you saw in the plague pit.'

De Wolfe ignored his officer's grumble and jabbed a long finger at his clerk. 'So what are they going to do about it now?' he asked. 'They've lost the man who they were going to haul up before the bishop's court. Are there any others under suspicion?'

Thomas bobbed his head. 'So it seems! They have this list of names which we copied and their bailiffs are actively seeking more. They say they know that several groups meet for discussions and to hold their own type of sacrilegious services. They wish to catch them red-handed.'

This stimulated Gwyn to take more interest. 'If I could learn of one of these meetings, just from visiting a couple of taverns, then the proctors' men can do the same.'

'Have you got that list with you, Thomas?' demanded John.

The clerk scrabbled under his cloak for the pouch on his belt and took out a folded scrap of parchment. 'A dozen names on it, Crowner,' he said, smoothing out the piece of thin sheepskin on the table. 'They mean nothing to me, I must admit.'

'Let's hear them,' commanded the coroner. 'Maybe Gwyn can recognise someone from his tour of the alehouses.'

Thomas began to read out the twelve names, and Gwyn halted him after the fifth.

'Adam of Dunsford! I recall that name, not from a tavern, but from a jury I assembled, just before we went off to London.'

'Why would you recall that particular juror from scores of others?' asked de Wolfe.

'Because he never became a juror – the night before the inquest, he slipped and broke his foot. I had to find someone else to make up the numbers.'

'Where does he live?'

'In Alphington, on the other side of the river. He was a fishmonger, I remember. He had a stall on West Street.'

Thomas read the remaining names and the very last one was familiar to John himself.

'Wait, I know that name! Hengist of Wonford, accused of stealing a chalice from a church. He came before the Commissioners of Gaol Delivery last year, but was acquitted. I recall him because of that strange Saxon name.'

'His parents must have been familiar with the works of the Venerable Bede to give him a name like that,' said Thomas wryly, but his historical allusion was lost on the other two.

'So we can find two of these heretics, if they haven't already been assassinated!' observed Gwyn.

'Why do we need them?' objected the clerk. 'It's the killer we need to find.'

De Wolfe sided with his officer. 'They might know something about who is harassing them most severely. Some may have had death threats, for all we know.'

After more discussion, the coroner finally decided to seek out the two named men in the morning, before he rode off again to Stoke-in-Teignhead with the physician and the apothecary.

West Street was the continuation of Fore Street, as it sloped downhill towards the West Gate from the crossroads at Carfoix. The top end was lined with the stalls and booths of tradesmen, varying from exposed trestle tables to tent-like erections of brightly striped canvas. All manner of goods were on display, though food was the mainstay of this part of the market. Meat which still dripped blood hung on the butchers' stalls, fresh from The Shambles at the top end of South Gate Street, where the slaughterers felled cattle, sheep and pigs at the edge of the road. Many other traders offered vegetables, though the range was limited at this time of year, mainly root crops and cabbage. Between the stalls, women – many of them aged crones – crouched over baskets of eggs or had a few live chickens or a goose trussed at their feet. This early part of the morning was the busiest, as the cooks, house-servants and the city's wives were all out shopping for the day's provisions and the roads were thronged with people. Though the fear of plague was almost palpable, the townsfolk still had to buy the makings of their meals.

The coroner's trio were looking for a fishmonger and they found a choice of four or five. Enquiries took them to a burly, red-faced man who stood behind a table carrying flat trays of fish, some still flapping feebly. Wicker baskets on the ground held other larger fish, as well as eels, crayfish and mussels.

One look told him that a Norman knight, a priest and a red-headed giant were not there to buy fish. Frowning, he finished dealing with a customer, putting ten herrings in the bowl she held out, in exchange for half a penny-piece.

'You are Adam of Dunsford?' asked John as soon as the woman had moved away. The fish-man nodded and wiped his hands on his apron, a length of once-white linen now soiled with fish blood and entrails.

'And you are the coroner, sir,' he answered civilly. 'You are very well known in the city.'

De Wolfe checked to make sure that no one was standing nearby, as this was business that need not be shouted abroad. He lowered his voice a little.

'We have seen your name on a certain list held by the cathedral authorities,' he began. 'That is no concern of mine, except that it may lead me to discover who might have killed Nicholas Budd. I presume that name means something to you?'

The weather-beaten face clouded over, and he became instantly suspicious. 'I know that the poor fellow met a terrible death,' he said cautiously. 'But what business is it of mine?'

John leaned across the table, his fists avoiding fish scales and blood.

'Let's not beat about the bush, Adam. We both know you are on the Church's list of suspected heretics. Budd is dead and we suspect that Vincente d'Estcote may be another. Do you know anything about his death?'

The fishmonger looked furtively from side to side, as if he was afraid that Bishop Marshal might be lurking in the pastry-cook's booth next door. 'Vincente just vanished from his lodgings; no one saw him go,' he muttered. 'He was in good health an hour before, because I saw him myself.'

'He was one of your group, was he?' asked de Wolfe, but Adam shook his head.

'No, he subscribed to the beliefs of the Cathars. He had been in the king's army and had spent time down in France.'

'So what are you, man?' demanded John. 'You may as well answer, you admit you knew him.'

Adam drew in a deep breath, as if committing himself to an irrevocable decision. 'I follow the ways of Pelagius – and I am not alone in that.'

Thomas in his surprise and disbelief made a noise almost like a mouse's squeak. 'A Pelagian! There have been no Pelagians for six centuries!'

Adam regarded the priest placidly. 'It has been revived by many, even if not in name. The principles are well known, and those who disagree with the dictatorship of Rome come together to discuss the True Way.' He held his dirty hands out towards the clerk as if inviting him to put bonds upon them. 'Now you may denounce me, if you wish.'

Thomas seemed nonplussed for once and looked to the coroner for support. 'I am here as an assistant to an officer of the King's Peace. I leave Church discipline to others.'

De Wolfe nodded his agreement. 'I am investigating a murder, Adam, not doing the Pope's work for him. You might be more at risk from whoever killed those men than from the bishop's court. Have you any idea who might have wished them dead?'

'Those canons undoubtedly hate us, but I doubt they would stoop to murder,' muttered the other man. 'His proctors are bullies but are just paid servants, so why would they care?' He shook his head. 'No, I cannot guess who may have done this terrible thing. Perhaps some mad parish priest? We have sympathisers all over the county. Any village parson with an unhinged mind could have taken the law into his own hands.'

The coroner decided to change his approach. 'Where can we find the other men on this list?' he asked. 'We know of this Hengist of Wonford, but maybe the others can help us to track down this killer.'

He motioned to Thomas, who took out his piece of parchment and started to read out the remaining ten names. However, Adam took it from them and scanned it himself, much to the astonishment of the others.

'How is it that an Exeter fish-man can read and be so knowledgeable of Church history?' asked Thomas, slightly affronted that his monopoly of such knowledge was being displaced by a mere tradesman.

Adam smiled wanly. 'It goes to prove that priests are not indispensable in man's dealings with the Almighty,' he answered. 'My father put me as a child into St Nicholas's Priory, intending me to enter holy orders – but he died and I had to leave to support my mother and sisters. In the few years I was there, I learned a great deal, especially how to hate priests, begging your pardon!'

The fishmonger went back to studying the list and nodded at several of them. 'Those three belong to our way of thinking,' he said cautiously, repeating their names. 'I am not sure where they live, but they attend most of our meetings.'

'Are those the meetings you hold in a barn near Ide?' snapped John.

A look of surprise spread over Adam's face. 'How did you know that? It's supposed to be a secret.'

'Fine bloody secret, if you can hear it bandied about in every alehouse!' said Gwyn sarcastically.

'When is your next meeting?' asked the coroner. 'I wish to speak to your fellows there, to see if they know anything useful.'

'Monday, at the end of the afternoon. Those of us from the city have to get back in before the gates close at dusk.'

John took directions to the barn and reassured Adam that he was not coming to spy on them for the bishop or his clergy. Thomas looked a little uncomfortable at this and, when they left the fishmonger's stall, he asked if he could be excused from Monday's venture.

'I could be censured by the bishop if I attended such a meeting and failed to report it, which is my duty as an ordained priest, master,' he said miserably. 'In fact, even knowing what we have just learned is very difficult for me to reconcile with my conscience. These are people whose philosophy is directly in opposition to the Church I serve. I should be doing my utmost to confound them.'

De Wolfe laid a hand on his clerk's shoulder as they walked back up Fore Street. 'I understand, Thomas, believe me! I am only concerned with catching and hanging a cruel killer. What the Church does about its rivals is none of my business. So you stay at home on Monday. No doubt Gwyn will be protection enough for me when I penetrate this den of blasphemers!'

Suiting his actions to his words, he sent Thomas off to his duties at the cathedral and carried on with Gwyn to the livery stables, where they saddled up and set off for Wonford, a village just a mile or so south-east of the city.

They rode through the straggle of dwellings that was spilling out around the thriving city and travelled

121

through a mixture of woodland and strip-fields to reach the hamlet. It was part of a royal manor but rented out to an aged knight who left its running to a bailiff. They overtook a man pushing a barrow of manure and Gwyn reined up to ask directions.

'Where can we find a man called Hengist?'

The villein raised a lined face, with a couple of blackened teeth protruding from under his upper lip. 'Hengist? You may well ask, sir, for he's vanished!'

De Wolfe leaned forward from the other side of Gwyn. 'Vanished? What the hell d'you mean?'

'Just that, sir, he's disappeared. We've been searching for him since yesterday.'

The man picked up the handles of his barrow ready to walk on. 'You'd best speak to the bailiff, sir, he knows most about it. Ask for him in the alehouse.'

He marched away and the coroner and his officer jerked their horses into motion and went on into the little village, where the squat church and the alehouse opposite were the only substantial buildings.

Gwyn slid from his saddle outside the tavern, marked by a bedraggled bush hanging over the door. He stuck his head under the low lintel of the doorway and a moment later came out, followed by a young man with sandy hair and a long brown tunic.

'I'm Robert the bailiff, sir. I understand you are also seeking Hengist?'

'I am indeed, but what's happened to him?' demanded de Wolfe.

'He's our harness-maker and he was in his workshop the night before last, but no one has seen him since,' replied Robert, who John thought seemed an intelligent-looking fellow.

'Does his family not know where he is?'

'He is a widower, sir. His two sons live elsewhere in the vill. One came to visit the next afternoon, but there was no sign of him. We have looked all through the crofts and tofts and the fields – nothing!'

'How can he vanish in such a small place?' grunted Gwyn.

'His sons are now out searching further afield, but beyond our strips, the forest starts. He could be anywhere in there, maybe having lost his wits or had a palsy.'

'We need to find him. Can you show us where he lives, bailiff?'

A lad came out of the alehouse to hold their horses and, with a couple of curious villagers trailing behind them, the bailiff led them on foot across the rutted road and past the church. Here there was a small cottage of whitewashed cob, with a grass-infested thatch. A large open lean-to at the side was his workshop, filled with oddments of leather, ox-harness and a variety of tools.

'Can I ask why you are seeking him, coroner?' said Robert respectfully, as they stood looking around at the crudely equipped workplace.

'I wanted to question him, but now I fear he may be in danger – or worse!' growled de Wolfe. 'Tell me more about him. What sort of a man was he?' Unconsciously, he had already spoken in the past tense.

For the first time the bailiff looked uncomfortable. 'Well, he was an odd fellow. A good worker, but he fell out with the parish priest some years ago and refused to attend church or take part in any of the village festivities. He was a freeman, so we let him go his own way.'

There seemed nothing to find outside, so the bailiff led them into the one-roomed cottage through a shaky wooden door secured by leather hinges and simple hasp and staple, with a piece of twig jammed through to keep it closed.

'No fear of thieves in this village,' said Robert, in an attempt to lighten the mood. Inside, there was again little to see, just a mattress on the straw-covered floor of beaten earth, a small table and two stools, a few shelves with pots and pans, and some food.

Gwyn bent to feel the ashes in the central firepit, which were as cold as the rest of the room. John saw no signs of a struggle or any bloodstains, but, as they were leaving, Gwyn touched his arm and pointed down at the floor just inside the threshold. In the dusty straw were two tracks, each a couple of inches wide and a foot-length apart. They passed out of the doorway and vanished on the harder earth outside.

'They look like heel-marks from someone being dragged,' murmured Gwyn.

John and the bailiff looked at them for a long moment. 'I can't think of a better explanation,' agreed John. He turned to Robert.

'Has anyone visited him lately? Any strangers been in the village?'

'Only the usual folk, a chapman and, a few days back, a man with a cart trying to sell pots and bowls. Oh, and, of course, those men from the bishop, who came to see the priest last week.'

John was instantly alert. 'What did they want?' he snapped.

'I don't know exactly. Father Patrick told us to mind our own business.'

'Were they priests?' asked de Wolfe.

Robert shook his head. 'No, though they wore black tunics. They weren't clerks, for they carried clubs on their saddle-bows, as well as wearing long daggers.'

'The proctors' men,' muttered Gwyn.

'But Hengist has been seen since then?' demanded John.

'Yes, that was more than a week ago. He was seen about his usual business until Thursday.'

The bailiff had nothing else to tell them, and de Wolfe decided to talk to the parish priest. Robert took them to the gate in the churchyard wall and pointed to a small house in the far corner.

'You'll find him there, sir. He's a forthright sort of man, Crowner,' he added, a hint of warning in his voice.

De Wolfe and Gwyn walked between the low grave-mounds, set among a wide ring of ancient yews, to reach the parsonage. The warped boards of the door opened to repeated knocking, and the sleepy face of a rotund priest appeared, having been awakened from sleep, even though the morning was by now well advanced. He was a fat man, with jowls hanging below a bad-tempered face. His tonsure had not been shaved for some time, a grey stubble sprouting over it, matching his unshaven cheeks.

'What do you want with me?' he muttered, staring at his two tall visitors through bleary eyes.

De Wolfe, holding his short temper in check with difficulty, explained who he was and that he wanted to talk about Hengist the leather-worker.

'You know he's missing?' snapped John irritably.

'Of course I do. Wasn't I out half the day and night looking for him with the rest of the village?' responded the priest testily. He spoke English with an Irish accent, reminding the coroner of his campaigning days in that green isle.

Grudgingly, he invited them in to his one-roomed abode, though a back door led into a cubbyhole that was his kitchen. The main feature of his living room was a large box-bed at one side, with sliding doors to keep out the draughts. John suspected that he spent a large part of his time snoring inside it. There were a few books and some writing materials on a table, so Patrick was not illiterate, a failing not uncommon in the incumbents of rural parishes.

'What can you tell us about this Hengist?' he asked as they stood around the near-dead firepit. 'We were told that he had a disagreement with you, some time ago.'

Father Patrick snorted. 'Disagreement! The man was a damned pagan, with his blasphemous ideas. I would have banned him from my church, except that he refused to come anyway!'

'Is that why the proctors' men called on you last week?'

The priest glared at the coroner as if to condemn his prying into his business. 'It was indeed! I had several times reported this Hengist to the bishop, after many months of his refusing to come to Mass or make his confession.'

'So you think he was a heretic?'

Patrick's paunchy face reddened with annoyance. 'Think? I knew! He would argue with me when I remonstrated with him. Gave me a lot of seditious nonsense about free will and the freedom to choose his own path to salvation. To damnation, more like!'

De Wolfe considered this for a moment. 'You said you told the bishop more than once about this. What happened on the first occasions?'

'Absolutely nothing!' ranted the priest. 'They ignored me in Exeter. I heard when I visited there later that the bishop and his staff thought that it was not serious and that in any event they had no time to deal with it.'

'So what did you do?' asked Gwyn, speaking for the first time.

'As no one in the bishop's palace seemed interested, I sought out my archdeacon, John de Alençon, who is also vicar-general, having the bishop's ear. But he, too, said that there was little he could do about it, but he sent me to one of the other canons, who he said had an interest in heresy.'

Now John wondered whether this lone man in Wonford had been the one who had sparked off this witch-hunt. 'Which canon was that?' he asked.

'Robert de Baggetor. He was the first one who listened to me with any concern. He said he and several other members of the chapter would look into the matter.'

'When was this?'

'About a month ago, before the outbreaks of plague started to occur.' He beat a fist into the palm of his hand, animated at last.

'I am not surprised that the Lord has sent this curse. It is punishment for the rise of apostasy in the land!'

John was not clear what 'apostasy' meant and resolved to ask Thomas when he next saw him.

'So why did these proctors' bailiffs visit you?' he asked.

'The canons had eventually persuaded the bishop to investigate Hengist and came to tell me to be in Exeter next week, when he would be brought before his chancellor for interrogation. They also wanted to know if I knew of any others with such heretics' beliefs.'

'And do you?' demanded the coroner.

The priest clutched his shabby bed-robe closer about him. It was cold in here with the fire just a heap of ashes with a faint glow in the centre. 'I know there are more, but not in Wonford. Hengist used to walk out somewhere every week or so, and I suspect he met other blasphemers, but he refused to tell me about them.'

'Did you know what kind of heretic he was?' asked John. 'I understand from my learned clerk that there are a number of different beliefs.'

'We argued about predestination, free will and the right of any man to communicate with God without the intervention of a priest. He claimed that all worldly manifestations arc innately evil. Such dangerous nonsense must mean that he sympathises with these bloody French Cathars.'

De Wolfe was there to investigate a murder and now a missing man, rather than debate theology, about which he was sublimely indifferent and ignorant.

'So as far as you know, there is no cell of heretics within this village?'

Patrick shook his bull-like head, the dewlaps under his chin shaking vigorously. 'Not in my parish, Crowner! Having one evil bastard is more than enough – and I have dealt with him, through the Church.'

'But where do you think he's gone?' demanded Gwyn.

'Run away, that's what! He knew he had to face the God-given power of the Church next week, so he's taken the coward's way out and run off.'

John thought of the drag-marks on the cottage floor and doubted that Hengist had left voluntarily. There was nothing more to be learned from the priest, and they made their way back to Exeter, leaving instructions with Robert the bailiff that he should send them word if Hengist was found, dead or alive.

They called in at Rougemont before going home for dinner and found Thomas there, carrying a message that there had been two deaths reported in the city, one a fatal brawl in the Saracen Inn, the roughest tavern in Exeter. The other was a body recovered from the river at Exe Island, too decomposed to be recognised.

'They'll have to wait until Monday, as it's Sunday tomorrow, but you get down there, Gwyn,' he ordered. 'Get details and the names of those who will

128

be First Finders and who must form a jury for the inquests.'

'I thought I was coming with you to Stoke?' objected his officer.

'Clement the physician and Richard Lustcote are riding with me. I don't know about the doctor, but the apothecary is big and fit and can use a sword if we are waylaid by outlaws. The coroner's duties have to be attended to until I get back.'

After another silent meal with a sullen wife, John prepared to leave to visit his sick brother. This time, as speed was not an issue, he took Odin from the stables and, as arranged, met Clement there, who took out his fine grey gelding. As they rode away down West Street, John noted again, with some surprise and admiration, that Clement was a fine horseman; controlling the frisky grey with considerable skill.

They met up with the apothecary at the West Gate. Lustcote was a tall man, grey-haired and with a calm nature, who never became flustered. He was the city's favourite apothecary, with a flourishing business that employed a journeyman and two apprentices.

Clement seemed a little surprised at seeing that a mere 'pill-pusher' was to accompany them, but he was civil enough to him as they rode towards the coast. Once again John forced himself to trot through Dawlish without calling on Hilda. He hoped that his quick passage through the village would not be reported to her, as she might think that he was shunning her if she did not know of the plague in Stoke-in-Teignhead, though on reflection it was unlikely that her family in Holcombe would not have been unaware of it, as William was also their manor-lord.

They reached Stoke without problems and found his brother in much the same condition as the previous day. There had been no more cases of the

129

plague in the village and none of those who were ill had died.

'He murmurs fretfully in his sleep now and then,' reported Enyd. 'He is still so hot, his forehead feels as if it is on fire.'

Clement examined the victim patiently, now apparently indifferent to the fear of contagion, looking into his yellowed eyes and feeling his pulse. He timed William's rapid, shallow breathing with a tiny sandglass he carried in his scrip, then examined a sample of his urine collected in a small glass vial. Holding it up against the light of a candle, for it was now dusk, he shook it and smelled it. –

'Very thick and dark,' he commented, almost to himself.

Turning to John's mother and sister, he advised them to try to force more watered ale down the patient's throat. 'I know it's difficult, but he needs to flush out the poisons from his system. Don't use wine; that merely dries him up.'

Richard Lustcote also examined William and then had a murmured discussion with the physician, both of them seemingly amicable professional colleagues in spite of their differing status.

With a last sad look at his suffering brother, John went with the others into the hall and sat down to a good meal. When his mother and sister had forced food into them almost to bursting point, they sat around the fire with cups of wine.

The doctor and the apothecary did their best to reassure the family that all that could be done was being done. Clement emphasised the power of prayer and fell into an earnest conversation with Evelyn, who was very religious and who had wanted to take the veil herself.

Lustcote stuck to the medical aspects, speaking to John and his mother. 'I only wish there was more I can do. As we have no idea what causes this distemper, there is no rational way to treat it. I can leave some herbs and drugs to soothe him and try to abate his fever, but it is your nursing and love that will be the best treatment.'

Evelyn, a plump woman, thanked them both with tears in her eyes. 'Does the fact that no one else in the village has since caught this vile disease – and no more of those who are now sick have died – give us hope that it is abating?' she asked hopefully.

Richard was cautious in his reply, but had not the heart to deny her clutching at straws. 'It may be so, lady. It seems that after the first few days the contagion does not pass so easily from one person to another. I most sincerely hope so!' he added with feeling, as they were all at risk.

In the morning little had changed, but William opened his eyes properly for a few moments and briefly seemed to take in his surroundings, before lapsing again into a troubled, mumbling sleep. Clement again checked his pulse and breathing and tried to get another urine sample, but failed.

'His main problem is in not passing enough water,' he repeated. 'Do all you can to force drink into him – spring water, diluted cider or ale, anything to flush out whatever evil humour is infecting his body.'

When there was no more they could do or say, they rode away, leaving a grateful and more hopeful family to wave them off.

chapter seven

In which a fishmonger confers with friends

The following afternoon, the second Sunday in November, the Feast of St Martin, four men sat huddled on the bank of the River Exe, a mile upstream from the city wall. They looked as if they were fishing, but in fact only one had bothered to bait his hook. This was Adam of Dunsford and, as a fishmonger, he felt it was incumbent on him to at least try to catch a fish.

Two of the other men were from Ide, a mile away, and the last one was from further afield near Crediton, a small town a few miles to the north. They met in what they hoped was the least noticeable gathering, just four fishermen whiling away a Sunday afternoon in the most innocent of pastimes. All they needed for camouflage was a short pole, with a length of twine attached to the end to dangle in the brown waters of the river.

As usual, they debated their faith at these meetings, but today there were also more pressing matters on the agenda.

'I had the coroner after me two days ago,' said Adam. 'He wants to attend our meeting tomorrow.'

'And bring men-at-arms to arrest us, I suppose,' said Peter, a thin man with tousled red hair, a shepherd from Ide.

'No, he seemed to have no interest in our faith. He said he was concerned only in solving the murder of Nicholas – and possibly that of Vincente.'

'Was he really killed?' asked Oliver. He was the third man, a small, puny fellow with a face like a weasel. 'I heard today from a carter that one of the Cathars has vanished from Wonford.'

'What's happening to us all? Will we be hanged after this inquisition next week?' Peter's voice was tremulous, as he felt the grip of Rome tightening around them.

Adam shook his head and jiggled his hook in the water. 'They have little power to do anything. I have read something about their disciplinary methods. We can be excommunicated, sure – but we have already done that voluntarily.'

A literate fishmonger was something of a rarity in the West Country, but when young, Adam had had a year's schooling.

'These bloody proctors have summoned us all to the bishop's palace next week, so what can we expect from that?' persisted Oliver. 'In spite of what you say, Adam, I fear for my neck.'

'All we can do is pray for God's mercy,' said the fourth man, who was much older, with a rim of white hair around his bald head. He was Jordan Cosse from Ide, a free smallholder who scratched a living from two cows, some pigs and geese. 'The early Christians died in their thousands for their faith, when it was still untainted by scheming and corruption, so we should not fear dying for our beliefs.'

The others did not seem so sanguine about sacrificing themselves, but they held their tongues.

'Let's see what this John de Wolfe has to say tomorrow,' said Adam eventually. 'For some reason, I trust him. I have heard he is an honourable man and is not in the pocket of the cathedral. Perhaps he can tell us what powers the priests have over us.'

Unexpectedly, he felt a pull on his rod and for a few moments theology gave way to piscatology.

While the furtive opponents of the Pope's hegemony were trying to land a bream on the bank of the Exe, another meeting was taking place in the chapter house attached to the south side of the cathedral. This was an old two-storeyed timber building, though plans were afoot for a new stone building on land the bishop had donated from his garden.

This meeting was not a regular session of the chapter, the governing body of the cathedral which met every morning. The ground-floor chamber, with its circle of benches and raised lectern, was being used for a small private meeting of senior priests. The three canons who were pursuing the issue of heresy were the prime movers, and they had co-opted a rather reluctant John de Alençon. As the archdeacon responsible for the Exeter area, as well as being the bishop's vicar-general, he felt obliged to attend and also hoped that he might be able to dampen down any overenthusiasm on the part of the others. The bishop was represented by his chaplain, his secretary and a deacon, who, though in lower orders, was more a lawyer than a cleric.

They sat on a couple of benches pulled around to face each other, the three canons on one side, the rest on the other. The archdeacon thought irreverently that in their black cassocks they all looked like crows sitting on a pair of fences.

'So who is to officiate on Wednesday?' asked Ralph de Hospitali.

'His Grace will be away, attending a meeting in Wells,' announced his secretary, a prim young cleric with a pasty face and pimples. 'So the archdeacon, as the bishop's vicar-general, will lead the proceedings.'

'Our Brother in Christ John is the obvious choice,' announced Richard fitz Rogo heavily.

De Alençon groaned inwardly but accepted that he had no alternative but to accept his obligations, even if it meant listening to these ranting bigots for a few hours. Immediately, he felt ashamed of his unworthy thoughts and determined to make confession as soon as possible.

'How many of these men are to be brought before the enquiry?' he asked in a resigned voice.

'Four at present, from this coven of blasphemers in Ide,' answered fitz Rogo.

'And how are these men to be persuaded to come before us?'

'Gale and Blundus will be sent to warn them the day before,' snapped Robert de Baggetor. 'They know that failure to appear will lead to their arrest by the sheriff's men.'

'How can that be brought about?' asked the chaplain, an ambitious young man from a noble family, who saw being the bishop's acolyte a useful stepping stone to his political ambitions.

'The *Ab Abolendum* makes it clear that the secular powers must give every assistance to the Church in stamping out heresy,' retorted de Baggetor.

'And where are we to conduct this interrogation?' asked the archdeacon wearily.

'This chapter house seems the most convenient,' responded fitz Rogo. 'No one uses it in the afternoon.'

'That does not seem appropriate,' objected de Alençon. 'This is the business of the diocese, not the cathedral. Bishop's courts are held in the palace, surely.'

Ralph de Hospitali waved a hand impatiently. 'We must not quibble over such details! Heresy is undermining the whole of the Holy Roman Church, so whether it is the diocese or the chapter that fights it seems immaterial!'

There was a murmur of agreement around the benches. 'This is just a preliminary inquisition, not the trial,' volunteered the deacon, keen on airing his legal knowledge. 'But when it comes to definitively trying these creatures, then I agree with the archdeacon that it must be within the bishop's precinct. Perhaps we might even persuade him to officiate,' he added wistfully.

Robert de Baggetor leaned forward. 'These are but four men, though we all know that the poison spreads far more widely. Two of the men on my list are already dead, for the Lord has struck them down, one by murder, the other by the yellow plague. But there must be many more, hiding under stones like slugs and toads.'

'I thought your two bailiffs were searching them out?' said fitz Rogo with a suspicion of a sneer.

'They are, but it is a slow job!' snapped Robert. 'We have informers scattered around, but they are clever, these heretics. But we will find them eventually, just as the hounds flush out the fox.'

'Can we not apply some pressure to the four we know?' suggested de Hospitali. 'Get the sheriff's gaoler to put them to some ordeal to loosen their tongues?'

John de Alençon looked perturbed at this. 'The Church does not allow blood to be spilled – and I hear that Rome is considering forbidding the participation of clergy in Ordeals.'

'There is no spilling of blood in picking a stone from a vat of boiling water,' countered fitz Rogo. 'Nor in iron plates pressing the chest.'

'Nor in walking across nine red-hot ploughshares!' contributed de Baggetor, rubbing his hands in anticipation.

The archdeacon raised his hand for silence. 'You are running far ahead of yourselves, brothers! Let us first see what these men have to say for themselves – and to hear from witnesses. I presume you have some?'

Ralph nodded complacently. 'My bailiffs, of course. And they can produce people to support them.' He gave a broad wink, as if to indicate that the witnesses would provide whatever evidence might be required.

As de Alençon walked slowly across the Close to his house, he tried to analyse his concern over this matter. 'I am a devout and senior priest in the Church of Rome and owe my allegiance to it with every fibre of my body,' he pondered. 'It is my duty and should be my profound desire to stamp out all those who conspire to reduce its power, which is directed towards bringing all men into the Kingdom of God by the pathway ordained by centuries of Popes and their brethren.'

Yet the archdeacon found that a part of his mind respected those who were ardent Christians – probably far more sincere than the majority of people who went automatically through the observances of the Catholic Church – who wished to take their own path to salvation. He disliked the almost savage delight that seemed to emanate from his fellow canons at the prospect of a witch-hunt and he feared for the future if this zealotry became more intense and more widespread, as it was in France and Germany.

Reaching his study, he fell to his knees in front of the large cross on the wall and prayed earnestly for guidance.

Monday morning was a busy one for the coroner. He began by going to the cart-shed in Rougemont, which was used as a mortuary when required. It was just a shingled roof built against the inner wall of the bailey opposite the keep and this morning housed two bodies covered with a tattered canvas.

Gwyn pulled this away to reveal a sodden partly skeletalised corpse that had been washed up on the riverbank. The other cadaver was fresh, but the front of the coarse tunic was soaked in blood from a stab wound in the chest.

'That one could have died in the summer, by the look of it,' said Gwyn, airing his knowledge of decomposition.

The coroner nodded. 'Might have washed down all the way from Exmoor, for all we know.'

Neither corpse provided much of a challenge to his powers. No one knew who the rotted body belonged to and no one ever would, so a short inquest with the finders and few onlookers from Exe Island disposed of the matter and allowed the corpse to be buried in an anonymous pauper's grave. The stabbing from the Saracen, the roughest tavern in the city, had been witnessed by at least a score of other men, and a verdict of murder against another ship-man was returned by his jury in under a minute. The man would be incarcerated in the city gaol in one of the towers of the South Gate – if he survived the violence or disease rampant in prison, he would be brought before the king's justices when they next perambulated to Exeter and John would see him again at the gallows on Magdalen Street.

All the time, de Wolfe was fearing the arrival again of the reeve from Stoke, to tell him his brother was dead. It was impossible for John to keep riding down there every day or two; he had his duties to attend to in the city, as well as the three-hour journey each way being too much to endure on an almost daily basis. As he walked back home for his dinner after the inquests, he pondered on what he would do if William did pass away. His elder brother was an expert at running two manors, a born farmer at heart – while John knew nothing about estate management, having been a soldier all his life. And where would he live – Exeter or Stoke? Much as he disliked Matilda, he could hardly walk out and leave her alone in Martin's Lane for good.

The atmosphere in his house was as gloomy as ever. His favourite dish, roast pork, failed to lift his spirits, even though Mary had provided a side dish of leeks cooked in butter and there was a tart of prunes to follow. When a fresh loaf and a cheese appeared, he silently cut slices of each and slid some across to his wife on a pewter platter, trying to keep up some pretence of good manners, though she never responded with so much as a muttered thanks.

In a desperate attempt to break the silence, he made his first mistake. 'I wonder how my brother is faring?' he asked. 'I must go down there tomorrow afternoon and return the next morning, so that I can attend to my duties.'

This started Matilda off on a familiar tirade about him leaving her alone overnight. 'I suppose you are using the excuse of visiting your brother to call upon your whore in Dawlish,' she spat.

On top of his deep concern for William, this was too much for him to bear, considering that he had resolutely avoided Hilda for fear of taking the disease to her.

'You evil old bitch!' he yelled, pushing back his chair so violently that it crashed over backwards. 'You measure everyone by your own spiteful nature, damn you!'

A furious row broke out, as Matilda gave as good as she got, matching insult for insult. John had a quick temper, and this led to a screaming match that was probably a record for this household. Even Brutus, used as he was to these scenes, crawled away from the hearth and lay down inconspicuously in a corner. Matilda also lumbered to her feet, and they stood on each side of the table, shouting at each other at the tops of their voices.

'Why I've not strangled you years ago, I'll never know!' he yelled at her finally. 'But by God, I'll do it one of these days!'

'Is that so, John? I'll remember that,' came a third voice and, wheeling around, de Wolfe saw his hated brother-in-law standing just inside the door.

'I knocked, but no one answered. Your maid must be hiding away like your hound,' said Richard de Revelle smoothly.

'What the hell do you want?' demanded John. 'Anyone with a little decency would have stayed outside.'

'I thought my sister might need some protection from the threats of her husband,' retorted the intruder.

'And what protection d'you think you could offer?' snarled John. The former sheriff's bravery had been called into question more than once.

'You'll go too far one day, John. Perhaps my sister was safer in Polsloe Priory than living here with you and your threats of violence.'

Matilda, breathing heavily and red in the face, tried to recover her poise. 'Sit down, Richard. John, bring wine for my brother!'

'Let him get it himself. I'm going out!' snapped de Wolfe, abandoning any pretence at hospitality, which he considered would have been the height of hypocrisy.

He moved towards the door to get away from this odious couple, but Richard tried to delay him with an upraised hand.

'John, I came to discover what is being done about the yellow distemper. My pork enterprise is being ruined. I have had to close both those at Exmouth and Dartmouth, as most of the men are dead or sick – and how can I sell meat which has been so near such contamination?'

De Wolfe looked at him incredulously. 'You selfish bastard! Men, women and children are dying by the score, my own brother is near death, and all you can think of is your bloody bacon trade!'

He dragged open the door to the vestibule and stood on the threshold. 'All you can do is pray, Richard! Presumably to the gods of Mammon!'

With that parting shot, he went out and slammed the door so hard that the latch snapped.

Rather aimlessly, John wandered into the cathedral Close, as his bad temper slowly subsided. His feet then almost instinctually took him in the direction of Idle Lane and the Bush Inn. Yet again, he regretted the loss of Nesta, who always had the ability to soothe him with her gentle words and divert him with her loving passion.

In the tavern, Edwin brought him a quart of Gwyn's latest brew and his usual gossip. 'I hear that on Wednesday, some of those faithless creatures from hell are going to get their just deserts,' he announced with grim satisfaction.

'Where did you hear that?' demanded John, again marvelling at how an alehouse potman became privy so quickly to the bishop's business.

'Herbert Gale, one of the proctors' bailiffs, was in here, and he said he had to bring them in from Ide. The other bailiff was supposed to collect one from Wonford, but it seems he's disappeared. Run away, no doubt, when he heard that his blasphemy had been discovered!'

De Wolfe had his own ideas about that, but he was not going to tell Edwin, or it would be common knowledge all over the city inside an hour.

Gwyn ambled in, smelling pleasantly of fresh ale-mash, and sat down to share a pot with John. 'Are we going down to this barn near Ide later on?' he asked.

John nodded. 'We'll leave Thomas out of it, but I need to speak to these men to see if they have any ideas who may be so incensed against them that they resort to murder.'

'It surely has to be a priest or someone in holy orders?' said the Cornishman. 'Who else would care that much?'

De Wolfe shrugged. 'There are some folk who are so devout that they might do anything. I wouldn't put murder past my wife,' he added darkly.

At that moment a small figure appeared alongside them in some state of agitation. It was Thomas, once again venturing into the den of sin that was an alehouse, though in fact Martha was as kind to him as Nesta had been, insisting on feeding him and mending his shabby clothes when necessary.

'Crowner, a man has arrived at Rougemont from Wonford, saying he's the bailiff,' he gabbled. 'He wants you to go there at once. They have found the body of the man who went missing.'

John stared at Gwyn, then held up his hands in frustration. 'I've just got to go to this place near Ide. I may not get another chance if they all get locked up after the canons get at them. But I couldn't get to Wonford and back in time to go there!'

His officer took it calmly. 'I can go with Thomas, just to view the body. You can see it again tomorrow, before you go off to Stoke.'

Their clerk looked worried, but de Wolfe assured him that he would be going about coroner's business to see a suspected murder, which was nothing to do with condoning heresy.

'Did the bailiff give you any details?' he asked Thomas.

'Only that it was obviously violence with a knife.'

Gwyn grunted and passed a thick finger across his throat. 'Not another Adam's apple missing?'

Thomas shivered. 'He didn't say so, but you can ask him yourself. He's waiting for us at Rougemont.'

'No, not his neck, but there's a knife still sticking out of his belly,' announced Robert of Wonford as he climbed into his saddle in the inner ward of the castle. 'Covered in blood all down his front. I think there are other stab wounds in his chest, but I'll leave that to you.'

Gwyn and Thomas were already mounted, and the three riders set off over the drawbridge across the dry moat and took their horses cautiously down the steep track through the outer ward to the gates in the stockade. As they trotted the mile or so to the village, Robert told them where they had eventually found the corpse.

'In an earth closet behind an abandoned toft, half a mile away,' he said with disgust. 'Thank God no one had lived in the place for a few years, but it was still stinking!'

They confirmed this when they reached the old cottage, a crumbling ruin built of wattle and daub on the road out of Wonford towards Clyst St Mary. It was an isolated place, an overgrown half-acre set between trees. The roof had collapsed, but the remains of a couple of small outbuildings still stood at the back.

'He's in here. We left him for you to see just as we found him.' He led the way to a small roofless hut made of planks, guarded by two villagers, though Gwyn thought that there was little chance of anyone interfering with the corpse in this isolated place. He looked inside the privy, where a rotting plank with a large hole formed the seat, but saw no sign of a dead man.

'He's around the back, in the pit,' explained Robert. The toft was on a slope and the back of the hut was lower than the front, with a wide hole for clearing out the ordure – apparently at long intervals, by the amount and smell of the contents.

The bailiff pointed at the hole and Gwyn bent down to look inside, a move not copied by the more squeamish Thomas. He first saw a pair of legs and, as he stooped even lower, glimpsed a whole body stuffed into the space.

'From above, you can see the knife and the blood through the shite-hole,' said Robert. 'Shall we get him out now?'

With the clerk standing well back, with the sleeve of his tunic over his nose, the two villagers came and hauled the corpse out on to the grass behind the privy. The back was smeared with the decaying contents of the pit, but thankfully a couple of years' disuse had moderated the smell. Hengist of Wonford was an elderly man, with a stubble of grey beard and lank hair to match. The legs were drawn up and the head flexed down on the chest.

'He's still got some death stiffness,' muttered Gwyn, testing the muscles. 'So he hasn't been dead for more than a few days.'

'We know he was alive last Thursday,' said the bailiff. 'What about that knife? Are you going to pull it out?'

Just to one side of the navel was the handle of a large knife, all of the blade being buried in the belly. It had a crude wooden hilt and looked more like a tool than a weapon. The brown serge tunic was soaked in dried blood from neck to thighs, though most of this appeared to be coming from a series of stabs in the front of the chest, as the fabric showed half a dozen rents, each about an inch long.

Gwyn touched the hilt with a finger, then shook his head. 'I'll leave this for Sir John,' he decided. 'He hates his corpses to be interfered with before he gets to see them!'

The face of the dead man was remarkably peaceful, considering the violence of his demise, but Gwyn knew from long experience, both in battle and as the coroner's officer, that the common belief that the expression on the features bore any relation to the act of dying was totally false.

'What's that stitched on to his tunic?' asked Thomas, venturing nearer to point at the shoulder of the dead man.

'He always wore that,' said Robert. 'He said it was a badge of his faith.'

'Looks like a bit of felt in the shape of a fish,' grunted Gwyn, not really interested.

'That's what it is, the *ichthys* sign,' explained Thomas, crossing himself. 'It's the word for "fish" in Greek.'

'I thought he was a leather-worker, not a fishmonger?' quipped Gwyn. 'We've already got one of those as a heretic.'

The clerk looked at his big friend with scorn. 'You ignorant Cornish peasant!' he said scathingly. 'It was the secret sign for the persecuted Christians in the first century, as the Greek letters stood for the first letters of "Jesus, Christ, God, Son and Saviour"!' He crossed himself yet again.

'Well, this one was certainly persecuted, as were Nicholas Budd and Vincente d'Estcote,' said Gwyn.

'Father Patrick didn't like him wearing that badge, but Hengist said that it was none of his business,' offered the bailiff.

'Heretics are Christians, so I suppose they are as entitled to wear it as anyone else,' conceded Thomas.

Gwyn became impatient. 'None of this helps to discover who killed the damned fellow,' he rumbled. 'Who would know of this cottage as a good hiding place?'

Robert waved a hand to encompass the whole countryside. 'Anyone who passed by, as well as our villagers, of course,' he answered. 'But none of us would slay Hengist. He's been accepted as being strange for years.'

Gwyn stood up and stared down at the corpse.

'Better leave him where he lies until the coroner comes in the morning. Cover him with something and keep him guarded against foxes. Sir John will no doubt hold an inquest, so gather together whoever found him and a dozen men from the village for a jury by the ninth hour.'

While his assistants were in Wonford, de Wolfe was setting off in the opposite direction, west of the city. He had obtained directions from the fishmonger and made his way down a lane off the highway to Crediton. The river lay between him and the small village of Ide a mile away, and at the edge of some common pasture which led to the start of dense woodland he saw a dilapidated barn that stored hay cut in the summer. The walls were made of crude boards, with irregular gaps between them, and the old thatch was lopsided and rotted. He rode past and entered the edge of the woods to tie up Odin in a small clearing, which still had some grass which had escaped the frost, then walked back to the barn.

There were no other horses about, and it was obvious that everyone else attending the meeting had come on foot. He silently approached the back of the barn but was suddenly confronted by Adam of Dunsford, who must have heard Odin's hooves on the track.

'You found us, then?' he asked abruptly, looking around suspiciously, as if uncertain whether the coroner had brought a troop of soldiers to arrest them.

'I doubt your attempts at secrecy are very effective, Adam,' scolded John. 'I suspect that half Devonshire knows where and when you meet.'

He was right, as unknown to him another pair of eyes was watching from the cover of a bramble thicket where the trees ended.

The fishmonger led him around the front and into the barn, which was about half-filled with this year's fodder. Seated or sprawled on this were eight men and two women, who seemed to have an air of resigned martyrdom about them. The men rose to their feet when the coroner entered and stood uneasily before him. Adam, who seemed to be the leader and spokesman, waved a hand around the small congregation.

'These are our brothers and sisters, but I won't give you all their names,' he said cautiously. 'But as four of us will be hauled before the bishop's tribunal on Thursday, our names will no doubt be bandied about the city within hours.'

He pointed at Oliver and Peter and Jordan Cosse of Ide, telling the coroner who they were. John remained standing, taller than any of them and looking like a predatory eagle in his black and grey clothing.

'I am not concerned with your religion, your beliefs, your faith,' he began in his sonorous voice. 'That is for other authorities to deal with. I am a king's law officer, and my only concern is investigating the death of two, probably three, persons who are of a similar religious persuasion.'

Jordan Cosse looked startled. 'You said *three*, Crowner? We know about Nicholas and Vincente, but who is the other one?'

All faces were turned towards him, waiting intently.

'A man called Hengist has been missing from Wonford for some days. I have just been told that he has been found stabbed to death.'

There was a shocked silence, then a buzz of whispering.

'We know of no one of our community by that name, sir,' said Adam.

'I understand that there are others who dispute the authority of the Roman Church, apart from your community?' De Wolfe made this into a question rather than a statement.

Adam nodded and explained. 'We have no name, like Cathars or Bogomils, but I suppose we follow the precepts of Pelagius, of whom I have read.'

'My learned clerk tells me that the cult of that man faded centuries ago,' objected John.

Adam, the philosophical fishmonger, smiled. 'Maybe his following under that name dwindled and was crushed, but the basic truths that he preached and wrote about remain in men's minds. We have revived them, and I know many others have similar beliefs.'

'I asked about other branches of heresy. I was told that this man Hengist was attracted to the Cathar beliefs.'

There was another murmur among the others and some nodding of heads.

'True, there are many pathways that a man can follow, without being chained by the Church to one narrow track,' said Adam. 'The Cathars are very numerous in France and pose the greatest threat to Rome. Not like us!' he added rather wistfully, looking around at his small group.

At the back of the barn, unseen by those inside, an eye appeared in a crack between the rough boards and a hand cupped to a ear listened intently.

'So this man in Wonford was not one of you?' repeated John.

Heads shook in reply and Peter of Ide expressed his sorrow. 'We revere all life, perhaps not like the Cathars, who consider the material world to be evil. I am saddened that any man or woman should be harmed, especially if it be for their faith.'

'I agree with you. I regret that I once killed many men in the name of my religion,' said de Wolfe – and the listening ear picked up his sentiments with satisfaction. He had heard enough and slipped away soundlessly back to the shelter of the trees, to find his horse tethered a safe distance away.

The coroner now got to the purpose of his visit. 'I came here today to meet you, to learn if any of you suspect who might be so incensed at your different view of Christianity that they would wish to slay you?'

There was some more murmuring and one of the women, a gaunt dame of late middle age with sparse hair straggled over a pink scalp, spoke up. 'Those canons – may they pay for their hatred when they meet their Maker – they are the ones who wish to persecute us!'

There was a general mutter of agreement, which again Adam put into words. 'One is a cathedral proctor, that Robert de Baggetor, so he can use his heavy-handed bailiffs to hound us.'

Oliver, the pale-faced younger man with the narrow face, spoke for the first time. 'That is so, but I find it hard to believe that priests, corrupt though so many might be, would stoop to foul murder, when they have the power of the Church to crush us, as they are plainly intent upon doing.'

'But has anyone attacked any of you, either by mouth or fist?'

Adam laughed sardonically. 'Plenty of abuse, when we speak publicly of our faith. I've had a punch or two aimed at me, but it was in the heat of the moment; it was nothing serious.'

'Even those proctors' beadles, Gale and Blundus, have never yet gone beyond a push and a shove,' added Jordan Cosse.

De Wolfe spoke to them for another few minutes, asking each individually whether they had any cause to suspect who might wish them dead. His suggestion that perhaps one of the other sects might be jealous or inflamed by their different beliefs was met with derision. 'We are all Christians and we respect each other's right to worship in our own way. We have no desire to convert the great mass of Romish folk; they are as entitled as we are to freedom of expression. I only wish they felt the same about us!'

There was no more to be learned and John wished them well, though, like them, he was apprehensive about what their interrogation on Thursday might lead to. He went back to find Odin, who was peacefully grazing in the wood, and rode slowly back to the city, pondering the multiple problems that were churning in his mind.

chapter eight

In which the coroner meets two ladies

De Wolfe took his big stallion back to Andrew's stables and, as he came out into the lane, saw his next-door neighbours leaving their front door. Immediately, Cecilia stepped forward and put a hand on his arm.

'Sir John, how is your brother? Please tell me he is much improved!'

The sincerity in her voice was unmistakable; it was not just a polite remark. John explained that he had ridden down there again and would be going again next day, hoping to hear better news.

'I am most appreciative of your accompanying me, doctor,' he said to Clement. 'My mother and sister also were gratified to have a physician examine William, especially as it took much of your valuable time.'

'You are welcome. It was the least I could do at such a difficult time,' replied the doctor. 'Now Cecilia and I are off to make our devotions at St Olave's,' he added. 'We are most grateful to your wife for introducing us to that excellent place of worship. In fact, we are having a meeting of the congregation there with the good priest Father Fulk, to discuss how we can best encourage the cathedral authorities to pursue this scandal of the heretics with the utmost vigour!'

He spoke with vibrant enthusiasm, his eyes glinting as he anticipated his vigilante role in 'cleansing the stables of the temple', as he had described it to his wife earlier that day.

Cecilia, wrapped against a rising east wind in a hooded mantle of blue velvet lined with white fur, was looking worried, but smiled at John and said she hoped that he would find a great improvement in William's condition next day. Her husband seized her arm and urged her towards the High Street, but as they went she looked over her shoulder and again gave him an enigmatic smile.

John felt confused about his new neighbours, as his initial dislike of Clement had subsided, particularly after he had so readily agreed to make the overnight visit to see brother William. Though full of his own importance – and too keen on religion for John's taste – he seemed a good enough man at heart. As for Cecilia, he could not make her out. She played the devoted wife, but his long experience of courting women told him that there was more to her than met the eye – though that was indeed pleasant enough!

He turned towards his own house and there, watching him with a scowl, was Matilda, also muffled up, with skinny Lucille trailing behind her.

'Ogling our neighbour again, I see!' she grated as she advanced upon him. 'Why can't you leave the sweet lady alone? You must see how it embarrasses her husband.'

John opened his mouth to argue, then closed it again, thinking it not worth the waste of words to spar with her in the street.

'I'm also off to St Olave's,' snapped his wife. 'Our diligent priest is preaching a sermon this evening about the dangers of heresy.'

'Why his sudden interest?' asked John. 'He never shifted himself before to take up any cause.'

'It seems the Archbishop of Canterbury has reminded all his clergy that blasphemy and apostasy are becoming rife in the land, another infection imported from France,' countered his wife. 'Father Fulk has taken this to heart and is to exhort us to be vigilant in seeking out those who would undermine Christ's Holy Church. A pity you do not have the same concerns!'

Julian Fulk was the odious fat priest who officiated at St Olave's, and who was Matilda's idol. For a time John had suspected that she was in love with him, until he realised that she was incapable of such a secular emotion.

'Our neighbour more than makes up for my defects,' grunted John. 'He seems intent on interfering in the bishop's duties by organising some protest meeting there.'

Matilda glowered at him. 'If all townsfolk were as devout and conscientious as Doctor Clement, Exeter would be a far better place,' she snapped.

'Why does a physician take such an interest in ecclesiastical affairs?' John retaliated. 'Better if he used his energies in offering medical help to those who most need it.'

'You are so godless yourself, husband, that you cannot conceive of men like Clement who have the interests of our beloved Church at heart!'

Having delivered her rebuke, his wife plodded past him without another glance, so he went indoors to find Mary and get something to eat from her kitchen-shed in the yard. He gave her a kiss in exchange for a platter of eggs fried in butter, followed by some bread, cheese and ale. As he ate and drank, his cook-maid brought him up to date with gossip in the market.

153

'The plague seems to have abated in the city,' she reported. 'It's now giving way to heretics as the favourite for the chatter around the stalls and street corners.'

'What are they saying about it?' he asked over the rim of an ale-pot.

'The usual exaggerations! That we are about to be besieged by hordes of pagans reeking of brimstone – and that a few brave canons are waging a war against the forces of evil!'

'Bloody nonsense!' grunted her master. 'The heretics I've met seem better Christians than most of us – genuine and sincere, anyway. And they are getting murdered for their faith.'

'They say that there's some kind of trial set for this week. Will they hang them or burn them at the stake?' asked Mary, with a frisson of morbid excitement.

John swallowed a lump of cheese and shook his head irritably. 'Stupid rumours! The Church itself can do them no harm other than excommunicate them – and I doubt that heretics will care a damn about that.'

Mary frowned at him. 'Well, you be careful, Sir Crowner! At the onion stall I even heard one man say that you had been seen consorting with a known blasphemer in a friendly fashion.'

John shook his head in wonderment. 'What a bloody town this is, Mary! You can't so much as belch without everyone discussing it on the street!' He assumed that long noses and flapping ears had seen him talking to Adam at the fishmonger's booth.

After he had eaten, he took Brutus on his usual perambulation to cock his leg everywhere along the familiar route to the Bush Inn. He had arranged to meet his two assistants there when they returned from Wonford, to tell him what they had found.

In spite of Mary's food, he succumbed to Martha's insistence that he had something more to eat, and by the time he had devoured a spit-roasted capon, Gwyn and Thomas arrived.

They sat with him at the table by the firepit and Martha brought more food for the two new arrivals, sitting with them as they ate and talked. A large, matronly woman of forty, she had a nimble mind and a tough, courageous spirit, which was just as well, with her husband absent with John de Wolfe for most of the previous twenty years.

Gwyn, between mouthfuls of mutton stew, told the coroner what they had found in Wonford. 'At least he hadn't had his tongue cut out,' added Thomas with a shudder.

'No, but there was far more violence than was needed to kill him,' countered Gwyn. 'I suspect that some of the wounds were made after he was dead, just for spite.'

John mused on what he had just heard. 'Is this a random killing, nothing to do with our heretics – or is it part of a campaign against them?'

'He was a poor man, with nothing worth stealing,' observed Thomas. 'His toft was little more than a workshop and a room to sleep in. Who would want to kill him for anything other than the same reason as the other two died?'

'He wasn't of the same religious persuasion as the pair in the city,' answered John. 'He was some sort of Cathar, according to the parish priest. But I agree with you, it would be a great coincidence if it wasn't connected, especially as he was on the canon's list of suspects.'

While the other two finished their food, he told them of his attendance at the covert meeting in the barn near Ide. 'None of them had any notion of who might wish them dead, apart from our friends the canons,' he said. 'And even they felt that those ardent priests would hardly stoop to murder, especially as they had just started on their campaign to bring all heretics before the bishop's court.'

Gwyn scowled. 'I wouldn't put anything past those bastards!'

The reason for his unwavering antipathy to everything ecclesiastical remained a mystery to John, but he now pursued another matter. 'Thomas, tell me more about the way that the Church deals with these people who disagree with their monopoly of religion. Why did Hubert Walter send out that reminder to bishops to be more vigilant?'

Hubert Walter was the king's Chief Justiciar, the head of the legal system, as well as being Archbishop of Canterbury and the Papal Legate, the Holy Father's representative in England. In fact, he virtually ruled as regent during the king's apparently permanent absence at the French wars. John knew him well, as he had been the king's right-hand man at the Crusade and when Richard was imprisoned in Germany. As the justiciar who introduced the coroner system two years before, their paths had crossed several times since.

The little clerk was in his element at being asked to spill out his knowledge. Gwyn gave an anticipatory groan, but this didn't deter Thomas.

'Some years ago, the rise of heresy all across Europe led Pope Lucius to issue a decretal called *Ab Abolendum* at the Synod of Verona, designed to root out heresy. That was in 1184, but nothing much was done about it until the Cathars, the Waldenses, the Poor Men of Lyons and many other groups became even more widespread and outspoken. So recently the present Pope, through his Legates in each country, has demanded more action from his bishops.'

'So what can they do about it?' asked de Wolfe.

Thomas rubbed his hands together in gleeful anticipation of giving another lecture.

'The decretal obliged the bishops and their officers – the archdeacons and others – to be vigilant in seeking out heretics. They were supposed to preach sermons against heresy several times a year and visit each parish regularly to enquire about it – though this was rarely done. They also were obliged to seek the aid of the secular authorities in enforcing their campaign – people like the sheriffs, burgesses and even the coroners!'

De Wolfe scowled at this, as the last thing he wanted was to get mixed up in some witch-hunt.

'So what could they do to heretics when they found them?' asked Martha, who leaned on the table with her chin in her hand, absorbed by Thomas's story.

'They were excommunicated, so could not be married or buried in a church, forbidden to hold any public office, could not make a will and could not inherit or pass on their property.'

'They might as well be outlawed!' said Gwyn.

'Exactly! Moreover, anyone else who gave them aid or concealed them was treated in the same way. When found guilty by a church court, they could be turned over to the civil authority for any further punishment that might be thought necessary. I suppose they could be hanged or imprisoned, if the local sheriff felt malicious towards them.'

John stared at the flames flickering from the logs in the fire and wondered if, in time, heretics would feel similar flames licking at their bodies. The zeal of the Roman Church to repress any who challenged their absolute despotism was sufficient for that to eventually happen, he feared. He sighed and turned his attention to other worries.

'Gwyn, I will go out with you to Wonford in the morning, to see this corpse and hold an inquest. Then we will go straight to Stoke, using the ferry at Topsham. If all goes well, we will be back before nightfall.'

There was little to be done at Wonford except to pull out the knife from Hengist's belly and look at the other wounds. The smell on his body from his sojourn in the privy-pit had abated a little overnight, and Gwyn and the bailiff dragged up his thin tunic to expose the injuries. They saw that the knife was a curved blade set in a rounded cylinder of wood for a handle.

'This is surely from his own workshop,' said Robert. 'There are others there with exactly the same sort of crude hilt. He probably made them himself to cut and shape the leather.'

On the chest and belly were six stab wounds, all of a size consistent with the same knife. In addition, John's probing finger found an area above his left ear which was swollen and boggy. When he pressed it, he could feel the crackling of the edges of broken bone grating together.

Rocking back on his heels, he rubbed the blood and filth from his fingers on the nearby grass and weeds. 'He wasn't stabbed in his cottage, for there's no sign of blood there. He must have been struck this severe blow on the head to stun him, then dragged outside, his heels making those marks on the floor.'

'Then brought here and stabbed – or stabbed on the way,' completed Gwyn.

'There's very little blood coming from the belly, so he may well have been dead by then, as it didn't bleed much,' noted the coroner, getting to his feet. 'But that doesn't help in telling us who did it.'

'Could only one man have hit him, dragged him out and brought him here?' asked the bailiff. 'It's half a mile from his toft.'

'One man couldn't have dragged him that distance,' said John confidently. 'But he might have had a horse, so that he could throw him across the saddle and walk him here.'

'It must have been during the night or they would have been seen,' said Gwyn.

They stood in silence for a moment, looking down at the corpse.

'That still doesn't help in finding the killer,' growled de Wolfe. 'So let's get on with the inquest and see if anyone knows anything – though I doubt it.'

As he anticipated, the inquest was a frustrating formality. The dozen men that the bailiff had rounded up from the manor stood around the cadaver while John officiated, but no one had heard anything during the nights of the past week. The harness-maker's croft and workshop was at the edge of the village, so when he was dragged out and taken away to the abandoned cottage, he would not have had to pass any of the other dwellings. The jury, directed sternly by the coroner, unhesitatingly brought in a verdict of murder, and John handed over the sad corpse for burial. The two sons claimed it rather reluctantly, for the parish priest was unwilling to allow it to be buried in the churchyard.

'He is a heretic and a sinner, a blasphemer cursed by God and man!' brayed Father Patrick angrily.

John walked up to him and bent down to glare directly into his face, his hawk-like nose almost touching the red bulbous one of the Irishman.

'Listen, priest! No court, not of Church nor king, has pronounced Hengist to have been a heretic. If you don't find him a nice quiet corner of your churchyard to rest in, I'll take you back to Exeter and drag you before your archdeacon, John of Alençon, understand? He'll tell you what you can and can't do in this diocese.'

He was bluffing, as for all he knew the archdeacon

would agree with Patrick, but the bluster worked and with a shrug the priest walked away.

'But don't expect me to hold a burial service over him,' he shouted over his shoulder. 'For all I care, he can rot in purgatory for the next thousand years!'

The rest of the day was uneventful, though worrying and depressing for de Wolfe, who was so concerned for his brother. From Wonford he rode with Gwyn to Topsham, the little port on the estuary of the Exe, where they were poled across the river with their horses on the flat-bottomed ferry. From there it was an easy canter across the flat lands to Dawlish, where de Wolfe steeled himself once again to ride past Hilda's house. On his last visit to Stoke-in-Teignhead, he had arranged for a message to be sent to Holcombe, to tell the reeve to let his daughter know that he was avoiding her, because of the risk of carrying the yellow plague. It was almost two weeks since he had last seen her, and he yearned for her company.

At Stoke they found little change in William's condition, though his fever had abated and his skin and eyes were slightly less yellow.

'I am concerned that he is passing almost no water,' said their mother, looking drawn and tired with worry. 'That nice apothecary you brought said that we were to try to make him drink more, but it is very difficult.'

'William still does not have his wits,' added Evelyn. 'He seems to sleep most of the time, and sometimes seems to know us, but it is hard to force food and drink between his lips.'

When John went in to sit with his brother for a time, there was nothing he could do but crouch on a stool alongside his pallet and watch his shallow breathing and closed eyes. There was a strange smell about him, which seemed to come from his breath rather than his sweat.

Sadly, he compared this wreck of a man with the robust, active man he had always known. Several years older than John, he had a marked resemblance to him, both in height, coloration and features, but he lacked John's habitual stern and grim expression, being a placid and even-tempered man. Unlike some brothers, these two had always got along amicably, and John was very fond of William, making the present situation all the more difficult to bear. He sat for an hour or two, while his mother and sister had a well-earned respite from their vigil. Eventually, they came back to keep him company at the bedside, until a meal was prepared in the hall outside.

'He has been hiccuping now and then,' reported John, mainly for something neutral to say. His mother nodded.

'The poor boy has been doing that for the past day or so,' she said. 'His breath smells peculiar, too. I wish I knew what more could be done for him.'

John had no useful suggestions, and Evelyn, a most religious woman, provided the only remedy by endlessly passing rosary beads through her fingers as her lips soundlessly prayed for her brother's life. The evening passed slowly, John helping his mother and one of the servants to clean William's body and to struggle a new bed-shirt over his limp limbs. William muttered a few incomprehensible words when he was disturbed, but he was in a stupor, if not actually a coma, and did not respond to any questions or attempts to rouse him.

At dawn the situation was unchanged and reluctantly John and Gwyn saddled up after a good breakfast and prepared to head for home. As his mother came to say farewell in the bailey outside the house, her tears touched John's heart, for he was aware that both of them were afraid that William would not survive.

'At least there have been no more deaths in the manor – nor new cases for a week,' she said, wiping her eyes and nose with a kerchief. 'And there have been none at all in Holcombe, thanks be to Christ and His Virgin Mother.'

He kissed her and his sister, who was also weeping silently, and with a promise to return in a couple of days he left with a subdued Gwyn riding alongside him. As the tide was in, they crossed the river by another ferry further upstream near Combe-in-Teignhead, and then made their way eastwards along the coast road.

'Strange how this bloody illness hits one village and not another,' ruminated Gwyn. 'Holcombe has had no trouble at all.'

He waved an arm to the left, where that manor lay just off the track, and John wondered if his officer was trying to hint at something. By the time they were in sight of Dawlish, a short distance further on, he had made up his mind.

'I'll speak to Hilda, but not come within coughing distance!' he announced.

In the little port, fishing boats were drawn up on the beach and larger vessels on the banks of the small river that came down from the hills behind Dawlish. At this stream, they turned off and found a short backstreet, parallel with the high road. Among the few houses there, one stood out by being both stone-built and larger than the rest. It had two stone columns at the front supporting an arch over a large door. Hilda's late husband, shipmaster Thorgils the Boatman, had modelled it on one he saw at Dol, in Brittany.

They reined in before the house, and Gwyn slid off his big mare to knock loudly on the door. Then he went back and climbed back into his saddle before Hilda's young maid Alice answered.

'Call your mistress to an upper window,' commanded John.

A moment later one of the upstairs shutters flew back and Hilda leaned out, a shawl thrown around her shoulders in the keen morning air. She was a lovely woman, her honey-coloured hair falling down her back, unfettered in her own house by any cover-chief.

'John, you must come in! I do not fear you bringing any contamination to me!'

He shook his head stubbornly. 'This is as near as I must come, though God knows I would wish to have my arms around you!'

'I had your message through my father,' she called. 'It is tragic what has happened in Stoke.'

John gave her the latest unhappy news from his brother's manor and they talked for some time across a gap of twenty paces.

'There have been no more attacks of the yellow plague in Stoke for a week, so we hope it has passed. But it seems that it has damaged William badly.'

Hilda offered to go to his mother to help nurse William, but John forbade it. 'You are a good woman, my love, but there is nothing you can do there that cannot be carried out by Evelyn and my mother. I would worry myself to my own early grave if I knew you were putting yourself at risk.'

Hilda pulled the shawl more closely around her against the cool morning air, and leaned further over the window sill, as if trying to get nearer to her lover.

'Now that the distemper seems to have passed, then it must soon be safe for you to visit me, John. I have missed you so much!'

They talked for a few more moments but, aware that their public conversation was starting to attract the attention of neighbours and passers-by, John reluctantly felt that he had to say goodbye, with a promise to call again within a few days. The two horsemen wheeled their steeds around and Hilda waved until they were out of sight, then the shutter closed.

CHAPTER NINE

*In which Crowner John
hears more bad news*

Having left at dawn, the coroner and his officer were
back in Exeter soon after the cathedral bells tolled for
High Mass in mid-morning. Gwyn went straight to his
family and another large breakfast at the Bush, while
John went up to Rougemont. He had not seen the
sheriff for a few days and felt he should tell him of yet
another murder, that of Hengist of Wonford.

'What in God's name is going on, John?' exclaimed
Henry de Furnellis as they sat on each side of his
cluttered table. 'Three heretics slain in a week? By
whom?'

De Wolfe turned up his hands in a gesture of
bafflement. 'Someone is taking the law into their own
hands, not trusting the Church or the king to deal
with these people,' he growled. 'These three canons
are the obvious suspects, but I can't see them getting
blood on their own hands in such a barbaric fashion.'

'Are they getting someone else to do their dirty
work?' queried the sheriff. 'What about these two
proctors' men?'

'William Blundus is ruffian enough, I suppose,'
answered the coroner. 'He is used to throwing drunks
out of the Close and beating a few hooligans with

his staff when the occasion arises. The senior bailiff is Herbert Gale, a more serious fellow altogether. But why should two men who are little more than constables or beadles take to murdering heretics?'

Henry, whose main concern was getting in Devonshire's taxes, was content to leave the problem to de Wolfe, but the latter reminded him what Thomas had told him about the Papal decretal.

'Our good friend and master Hubert Walter has sent a reminder to all the bishops about the need to stamp out heresy. My clerk Thomas tells me that we secular officers – and that especially means you, Henry – are obliged to give all necessary aid to the ecclesiastical authorities in detecting, securing and punishing these blasphemers. So we may not get out of this situation so lightly.'

De Furnellis sighed and pulled a face. 'You certainly know how to cheer me up, John! I need no distractions to scraping together the county farm, after this year's awful harvest.'

'We may have little choice after tomorrow, when they hold the first of these inquisitions,' replied de Wolfe. 'They are dragging in a handful of so-called heretics for interrogation and, if they are sent to the bishop's court, they may well call upon you to deal with them.'

John left the sheriff muttering under his breath at these extra labours likely to be piled upon him and went back to his chamber high in the gatehouse. He expected to find Thomas there, labouring away with his pen, ink and parchment, but there was no sign of the little priest, and John assumed he was either at one of the interminable services in the cathedral or working in the scriptorium on the upper floor of the chapter house.

With no new deaths reported and no hangings to attend that day, he felt rather at a loose end, so he settled down to a boring hour before dinner, trying to follow the reading lessons that Thomas had set him. He had been coached on and off for a year or so, by a vicar-choral from the cathedral, but had made little progress. Then Thomas had taken over, but their move to Westminster earlier that year had dislocated his tuition and he was no further forward, mainly from a lack of enthusiasm on his part.

He sat staring at a few curled sheets of parchment on which Thomas had carefully inscribed the Latin alphabet and some simple sentences, but his mind kept straying to Stoke-in-Teignhead and the vision of his brother lying so desperately ill on his bed. He found himself praying again, ill-formed words muttered under his breath, but nevertheless sincere in their plea to whoever was up above in heaven, asking him to deliver William from danger.

His lessons ignored, he sat gazing into space until the noon bell from the cathedral told him it was past dinner-time. Back in Martin's Lane, he endured another silent meal with Matilda, after he had told her of his brother's desperate condition and she had grudgingly admitted that she had prayed for his recovery or, if that was too much to ask of God, for the salvation of William's soul.

'I also hear that there is another outbreak of the plague down on Exe Island,' she added in a rare burst of loquacity. 'Not surprising, with such people living in those squalid shacks that dot the marshes there.'

He felt like telling her that not everyone had such a soft life as her, with a relatively rich husband, her own income bequeathed by her father from the de Revelle estates and a substantial house to live in. But he held his tongue, preferring silence to provoking another tirade.

News of a fresh attack of the yellow disease was worrying. He had begun to hope that the present sporadic epidemic had burned itself out. So far, about twenty people had died in the city, and the fear and tension that this engendered could be felt as he walked the streets. People seemed more bent and furtive as they hurried along, as if keeping inconspicuous lessened the danger of contagion.

After the meal, Matilda clumped up the outer stairs to the solar to take her usual postprandial rest until it was time for her to go again to St Olave's. John took a quart of ale and sat near his beloved stone hearth, nudging Brutus away with his foot so that he could be nearer the warmth from the glowing logs.

He had plenty to think about, as he stared into the flames. Apart from his brother's desperate condition, he was frustrated by the lack of progress on the heretic killings. There seemed nothing to grasp hold of in his search – the heretics themselves had no idea who was preying upon them and the only possible suspects, the canons, seemed too improbable a target to be seriously considered. The only people he had not questioned now were the two proctors' men, and for want of any other inspiration he decided to seek them out this very afternoon.

When he had finished his ale, he whistled to his old hound and went out into the lane, shrugging on his grey wolfskin cloak, though he found that the cold had moderated considerably as a dense mist had descended upon the city. When he went into the Close, the bulk of the cathedral was shrouded in fog, the tops of the great towers lost in a grey blanket.

The proctors' bailiffs had a small building alongside St Mary's Church, which was little more than a room for them to sit over a brazier and three cells with barred doors for incarcerating miscreants, most often drunks or aggressive beggars making a nuisance of themselves in the cathedral precincts – though occasionally it was someone in holy orders who was locked up.

De Wolfe rapped on the outer door and pushed it open, telling Brutus to stay outside. In the bare chamber he found Herbert Gale sitting at a rough table, eating from some food spread on a grubby piece of cloth. Half a loaf, a slab of hard yellow cheese and some strips of smoked pork appeared to be his late dinner. In one of the cells, a scarecrow of a man, dressed in rags and with filthy hair and a straggling beard, slumped on a slate shelf that did service as a bed. He was snoring like a hog and obviously sleeping off the effects of too much drink.

The cathedral constable got to his feet as he saw the coroner enter. Everyone in Exeter knew Sir John de Wolfe, though this particular citizen did not look too pleased to see him. About the same age as John, Gale was a thin, leathery man with a permanent expression of distaste, as if he disliked the world and all that was in it. He wore a long tunic of black serge, with a thick leather belt carrying a dagger. His cropped iron-grey hair was uncovered indoors, but a helmet of thick black felt lay on the table, alongside a heavy wooden cudgel.

'I came to talk to you and Blundus about these so-called heretics,' announced John without any preamble.

'They *are* heretics, coroner, not "so-called",' retorted Gale. 'And William Blundus is out about his duties.'

De Wolfe's black eyebrows rose. 'So they have been judged ahead of tomorrow's enquiry, have they?'

'If Canon Robert, who is a proctor and my master, thinks they are heretics, that's good enough for me, sir!' growled the bailiff.

John was not inclined to bandy words with a constable.

'I have no interest in their religious leanings, Gale. I am investigating two, probably three, murders. All of men you must have known.'

'What do you want from me, Crowner?' asked Gale suspiciously. 'This is a cathedral matter; we are independent of you in the castle and the borough.'

De Wolfe crashed his fist on to the table, making the remnants of Gale's dinner scatter on the cloth.

'Don't try to tell me my business, man!' he shouted. 'Firstly, these deaths took place well away from the cathedral precinct. And in any event, Bishop Marshal long ago agreed that serious crimes against the person are within the purview of the king's law, whether they are committed in or out of his territory.'

The bailiff remained silent, as when angry de Wolfe was not a man to be argued with.

'Now then, what dealings have you had with these dead men?' snapped the coroner.

'We received reports about them, starting some weeks ago. I passed these on to one of the proctors, as is my duty.'

'What sort of reports?'

'Accusations that they were either preaching sedition against the Church or that they were acting in some blasphemous manner. We have had many more such suspicions, not just about those who are either dead or will face the canons tomorrow.' He said this last with an expression of smug satisfaction, but just then the door opened and a large man burst in, already in full flow.

'Herbert, I've found another of the bastards ...'

His voice trailed off as he saw that Gale was not alone. Blundus was a powerful, pugnacious fellow, almost the size of Gwyn, but younger and darker. A short, thick neck supported a head like a large turnip, with small eyes and a flat nose that reminded John of a pig.

'The coroner wants to know about those dead blasphemers,' said Gale, a warning note in his voice.

'Best thing that ever happened to 'em!' snarled Blundus. 'Saves everyone the trouble of a hanging.'

De Wolfe controlled his temper with an effort. 'When did you last see them? Let's start with Nicholas Budd.'

Herbert Gale replied quickly, afraid of his partner's intemperate mouth. 'We warned him of this enquiry tomorrow and told him that if he didn't attend we would come for him. But he died before that.'

'And Vincente d'Estcote, the porter from Bretayne?'

'The same thing. We knew of his attendance at that barn near Ide, and the canons said to add him to the list. But he vanished, and I'm told he caught the plague.'

'God's retribution for forsaking Him,' muttered Blundus, but closed his mouth after a poisonous glance from Herbert.

The coroner could see that he would get very little help from these men, but he had to persist.

'And what about Hengist of Wonford? I suppose you know he's been killed as well?'

Gale nodded. 'Blundus here went out several days ago to give him a final warning for tomorrow, but he'd vanished as well. Now we hear he's been stabbed.'

'And you say you know nothing at all about their deaths?' rasped John.

'Why should we?' growled Blundus sullenly. 'We are but messengers in this, doing our masters' bidding, as is our job.'

The coroner scowled at the two men, for it was like pulling teeth to try to get information from them.

'How did you go about discovering those you suspect of non-conformity with the tenets of the Church?' he asked.

From the blank look on Blundus's face, he failed to understand, but the more educated Herbert Gale responded testily.

'Surely that is a cathedral matter, not part of a coroner's remit!'

John fixed him with an icy glare. 'Nothing is exempt in the search for a murderer. You seem keen on gathering folk for interrogation – so how would you both like to share a cell in Rougemont's gaol until your tongues are loosened?'

The expression on de Wolfe's face convinced the two men that this was no idle threat.

'We kept our eyes and ears open,' growled Herbert Gale. 'And the proctors gave us some funds to encourage others to do the same.'

'You mean you paid spies and informers?'

'Why not? Any means justify the end in doing God's work, which here was through the decretals issued by Rome.'

John realised that Gale was not only sanctimonious but had some education, certainly more than the coroner himself. He questioned them for a few more minutes but came to the conclusion that they knew – or would not admit to – anything other than the names of heretical suspects, corresponding with the list that Herbert had given the canons, plus a few more recently collected.

He left them standing in sullen silence and had no doubt that they would soon be reporting his unwelcome interest to the three canons, but that was of no concern to him. Collecting Brutus from outside, he made his way back up to the castle in case any more deaths, rapes, fires or assaults had been notified, as usually such messages were left with the sentries in the guard-room in the gatehouse. There were none, and he hauled himself up the steep stairs to find Gwyn alone in the bare room overlooking the city.

'Still no sign of Thomas?' he asked, slightly annoyed that his clerk was absent, even though there was little work to be done.

'Haven't seen hide nor hair of him today,' replied the Cornishman. 'I suppose he's scribbling away in that place above the chapter house.'

With a shrug, John sat down at his trestle table and Gwyn poured them each a mug of cider from a large jug standing on the floor. The jug was two-thirds empty and the remaining contents looked more like the bottom of a duckpond, with wreaths of turbid sediment swirling in the fluid. Neither man seemed bothered with this as they sat talking about the fog, which had thickened and had obscured most of the view from the slit windows. John thought about the road to Dawlish, which would be similarly blanketed by the sea-fret, which had rolled up the estuary of the Exe. That led his thoughts on to Stoke and his brother lying there so desperately ill. He must ride down there again tomorrow, the fog being no hindrance to a horse, but it might encourage the footpads who infested the roads to take advantage of its cover to surprise passing riders. Still, if Gwyn came with him again, they would be a match for all but the largest gangs.

He was distracted from his reverie by the sound of feet coming up the stairs, and a moment later the hessian draught-curtain was pulled aside and a hesitant face appeared.

'The man-at-arms downstairs said I was to come up, sirs,' said the visitor, whose projecting head bore the tonsure of someone in holy orders. His face looked vaguely familiar to John, but Gwyn recognised him.

'You are the vicar who shares our Thomas's lodgings in Priest Street,' he boomed. 'Come on in, we were wondering where the little fellow had got to.'

The cassock-clad young man came in and stood anxiously before them. 'Not a vicar, sir, only a secondary. Arnold is my name. But yes, that's why I came, for Thomas is sick and I did not know who else to tell.'

Both de Wolfe and Gwyn rose quickly to their feet, disturbed by the news. 'What's wrong with him, d'you know?' demanded John.

'He lies on his pallet, feverish and almost without words,' gabbled Arnold. 'I have been away for several days visiting my mother, so had not seen Thomas since Sunday, when he was quite well.'

De Wolfe grabbed his cloak and Gwyn was already making for the stairs, shrugging on the creased leather jerkin that he habitually wore. Within minutes, they had hurried down through the town to the street that housed many of the junior priests and clerks from the cathedral. Arnold led them into a narrow timber-framed house which was divided into a number of small rooms, in one of which they found Thomas de Peyne huddled on a hay-stuffed mattress on the floor. He was crouched under the coverlets, his back to the door.

'He was shivering, so I put my blanket over him as well, before coming up to find you,' said the secondary.

Gwyn, who was very fond of their little clerk, in spite of his endless teasing, squatted alongside the bed and put a hand on Thomas's shoulder.

'How are you, my friend?' he said, with a gentleness at odds with his huge size. 'Have you any pain?'

There was no response, so Gwyn gently rolled him over on to his back. 'Oh, God, no!' he whispered in an agonised voice as soon as he saw the priest's face.

'He must have caught it when he insisted on attending those burials,' muttered John an hour later.

They were in St John's Hospital, up near the East Gate, where they had examined the corpse of the slain woodcarver. As soon as they had seen the yellow staining of Thomas's eyes, Gwyn had wrapped him in the blankets and carried him as effortlessly as a child up to the hospital, where Brother Saulf had taken him in without demur, even though his single ward was already overflowing, half the patients suffering from the yellow plague.

'He's a selfless little bastard, always putting others before himself,' growled Gwyn, ignoring the fact that he had just carried a plague victim in his own arms halfway across the city. They were standing with the gaunt Benedictine monk alongside Thomas's mattress, in a corner of the large room that now held three closely packed rows of sufferers. Thomas was half-conscious, moving restlessly under his blankets and muttering incoherently to himself. His face was flushed and sweating, but a lemon-yellow tinge was obvious when his fluttering lids revealed his eyes. His lips were swollen and crusted with fever, and his fingers picked agitatedly at the bedcoverings.

'He had those under the clothes when he came in,' said Saulf, pointing to Thomas's precious copy of the Vulgate and a rosary that lay at the foot of the palliasse. 'I suspect that when he first fell ill, he began preparing himself for the worst.'

De Wolfe, worried and anxious beyond measure, looked around the ward at the legion of sufferers, some inert, others restless or moaning.

'Of those with this damned plague, how many will survive?' he asked, almost afraid of the answer.

'It is a strange disease, the like of which I have not seen before, though I know it has visited in the past,' replied the monk. 'Some die within a day of the first symptoms appearing, yet others who survive for a few days can make a rapid recovery.'

John looked down at the pathetic figure of his clerk, huddled and shivering under the blankets. 'What chance has he got, brother?'

Saulf held out a hand and rotated it several times in a gesture of uncertainty. 'At this stage, probably an equal prospect of living or dying, Sir John. I can say no more than that. This is the first such epidemic I have experienced.'

'Is there anything you can do for him? I could ask Richard Lustcote to visit, as he did with my brother, but he was honest enough to say that there are no medicaments that are effective.'

The Benedictine nodded his agreement. 'All we can do is keep him comfortable, and let God's will be done. We must all pray for him.'

Another monk came and claimed Saulf's attention and left Gwyn and de Wolfe at Thomas's side. They stood around awkwardly for a few moments until they decided there was little point in waiting.

'There's nothing we can do and we're just in the way,' muttered de Wolfe. As they went out, promising to return later that evening, Gwyn raised the matter of their clerk's family.

'They should be told, whatever is going to happen,' he said gruffly. 'His father is a minor manor-lord somewhere near Winchester.'

'I'll speak to Henry de Furnellis when we get back to Rougemont,' promised John. 'He has riders going regularly to Winchester. They can take a message to the cathedral, where Thomas was well known.'

He was as good as his word and the sheriff promised to add a letter to the pouch of a messenger who was leaving the next day with tax accounts relating to tin production from the Dartmoor stannaries. Leaving the keep, he walked across the inner ward with Gwyn, both subdued by their concerns over Thomas, which had come like a bolt from the blue, in spite of their knowledge of the risks the clerk had taken in helping to give plague victims a proper burial.

'Yet that may be nothing to do with him catching the distemper,' said Gwyn glumly. 'Look at these new cases down on Exe Island. The bloody poison could be blown on the wind, affecting anyone at will.'

John did not answer, as his attention was caught by a horseman who had just clattered over the drawbridge to stop at the guard-room. The man was dressed in black, and an icy hand reached into John's chest to rip at his heart, as he feared the rider might be Alfred, the reeve from Stoke-in-Teignhead, come to give him news of his brother's death. As the man finished speaking to the sentry, he slid from his saddle and began leading his horse towards the stables, when thankfully John could see that it was a total stranger.

Shaken, he began to wonder if these repeated blows of bad news were beginning to affect his mind – they were certainly diverting his full attention from his duties and the need to pursue whoever was killing these heretics. He said nothing about it to Gwyn, but mentally he hardened his resolve to keep on top of his various problems. Straightening his back from his habitual slight stoop, he set his mouth in a scowl of grim determination that frightened an old woman passing with two live ducks under her arms, then marched off home to warm himself by his hearth until the evening meal, after which he would go back to St John's Hospital.

His maid Mary was desolated to hear the news of Thomas's affliction, as she was very fond of the little fellow. In the days before he had been restored to the priesthood, he had lived a very frugal existence, sleeping in the passageway of the servants' quarters

177

of a canon's house, and Mary had often fed him in her cook-shed when Matilda was not around. John's wife treated him with utter contempt, as even after the accusations of indecent assault on one of his pupils in the school in Winchester had been proven wrong, Matilda always considered him a pervert and a disgrace to her beloved Church.

When John made his usual attempt to strike up some conversation over the silent supper table by telling her of his clerk's suffering, she offered only a grunt and the comment that many other people had also succumbed to the yellow murrain. Incensed by her indifference, he pointed out that Thomas had almost certainly caught it by his efforts to give other sufferers a Christian burial.

'Well, that's his sacred duty as a priest,' she retorted loftily.

Her husband glared at her for compounding her lack of charity. 'I wonder if that selfish fat parson at St Olave's, who you adore so much, would have risked standing at the edge of a plague pit!'

This started off yet another acrimonious argument, which as usual escalated into a shouting match. Matilda revisited all the old insults, such as his desire to stay away from home as much as possible, leaving his neglected wife alone.

'You use the coroner's job as an excuse to frequent alehouses and brothels,' she snarled and went on to list the various women with whom he had had adulterous affairs, ending with 'the Saxon whore in Dawlish'.

After five minutes of this, John could stand it no more. He already felt drained by the fear that his brother might be dying, and now Thomas was in the same situation. His wife's ranting inflamed him so much that he kicked back his chair, its legs screeching on the flagstones. Advancing on Matilda with clawed hands outstretched, the veins in his neck and forehead bulging with passion, for the first time in his life he felt murderous towards her.

'Shut up, woman, or I'll shut you up for ever!' he yelled.

Even as the words left his mouth, he realised that he did not mean them literally, but he needed to stop her battering his already overburdened mind with her spiteful tongue.

Unknown to him, those same words that left his mouth also percolated through the shutters into the narrow lane outside, where Clement and Cecilia were passing on their way to the cathedral. The physician's eyebrows rose and he stopped and leaned closer to the window, but his wife jerked at his arm and dragged him away.

Later that evening the coroner sat morosely in the Bush, his hands resting on the edge of the table, one each side of an untouched quart pot of ale. Gwyn was still in his brew-shed in the yard and Martha was getting him some food from the kitchen-hut, as he had walked out on his half-eaten meal at Martin's Lane. Edwin was stumping about serving other patrons and chivvying the two slatterns, girls hardly more than children, who helped carry the platters and collect the used mugs.

John's anger had subsided, to be replaced by despondency. Foremost of his concerns were his brother and his clerk, but also the fight with Matilda had been more virulent than usual and had depressed him markedly. He had never used violence against her, however much she had provoked him, and although tonight's episode was an empty threat on his part it showed how far relations between them had deteriorated. The only bright spot was that as he had stalked to the door to leave, she threw a final taunt after him.

'You can do me one last service, husband, by arranging a passage on one of the ships that used to belong to that Dawlish strumpet. I will go to stay with my relations in Normandy, where I will at least be safe from your murderous intentions!'

Her words echoed through his head as he sat by the fire in the Bush. 'If your poor bloody cousins will have you!' he muttered to himself. 'You battened on them last year, so maybe they'll not be so keen on repeating the experience.'

The other problem was that unless she went very soon, the sailing season in the western Channel would be over until the spring, by which time he might really have throttled the damned woman. As he sat staring into the fire, the old potman came up and pointed at the untouched ale.

'Something wrong with Gwyn's latest brew, Crowner?' he croaked. 'He was quite proud of it – though pride is often the sinner's downfall!' he added hastily, crossing himself as he remembered his newly acquired sanctity.

In spite of his gloom, John grinned at the silly old fool's antics and wondered how long it would be before he would drift back to cursing and blaspheming.

'I hear that some of those evil opponents of Christ's Holy Church are to be hauled before the canons tomorrow, Sir John,' Edwin cackled with relish. 'I hope you'll see their necks well and truly stretched when the bishop hands them over for their just punishment – unless this killer beats you to it!'

'Nothing to do with me, old man,' growled John. 'That's Church business. I'm only concerned with murder. Stabbing a heretic is just as much a crime as stabbing anyone else.'

Edwin snorted in disbelief but moved away as Gwyn advanced on John's table, still wearing his stained brewer's apron, which smelled strongly of malt.

'How did you find the little fellow, Crowner?' he asked, with deep concern on his rugged face. John had told Martha that he had called at St John's on the way to the Bush.

'Much the same. He's muttering under his breath, so he's not totally out of his wits. But the yellow tint of his eyes is worse and you can see it in his skin now.'

Gwyn nodded sombrely. 'I'll go up there first thing in the morning. No point in disturbing them again tonight.' He sighed deeply. 'I hear the plague is spreading even more. A carter came in earlier and said that there were many cases in Totnes now.'

This was a town in the centre of Devon, also a port even though it was several miles upriver from Dartmouth.

'It must be coming in with ship-men, as we suspected,' growled John. 'Perhaps that damned brother-in-law of mine was right for once – we should close the ports for a time.'

Gwyn shook his head. 'Don't see how it could be done! The whole trade of this area depends on sending out wool and tin and bringing in goods for ourselves. Folk would be dying of starvation instead of the distemper!'

Martha bustled up with a knuckle of pork on a large trencher of bread, with a side dish of boiled leeks and carrots.

'Get this down you, Sir John, it'll lift your spirits a little. I'd send Gwyn up to the priory with some choice bits for poor Thomas, but I gather he's not in a fit state to eat yet – but he'll survive, never fear.'

The motherly woman hurried away to quell some noisy argument between a farrier and a baker as Gwyn lowered himself on to the bench opposite to watch his master eat.

'Are you going to listen to this performance in the cathedral tomorrow, Crowner?'

De Wolfe spooned some boiled carrots on to his trencher before picking up the pork bone to nibble away at the succulent meat.

'No, none of my business! I'm riding down to Stoke after I've called to see Thomas, so that I can get back by evening.'

'I'd better go with you, then. You shouldn't ride alone,' said his henchman, worried about outlaws lurking along the roads.

John's teeth tore a strip of meat from the joint before he answered. 'No, I'll take Odin. He's slower, but no one will attack a knight on a warhorse. I want you to stay here and keep an eye on Thomas's condition, as well as looking into any new cases that are reported to Rougemont.'

After eating his fill, he and Gwyn spent an hour talking around the fire with some of the regular patrons, discussing the insidious spread of the yellow plague and also the other main talking point, the investigation of the heretics the following day. Being steeped in the all-pervasive power of the Church since infancy, most of the men were strongly opposed to any challenge to the dominance of the priesthood, but a few said that people should be able to choose their own way of worship. John had the impression that several might have been covertly in agreement with the religious mutineers but were too cautious to openly admit it.

When the distant curfew bell rang from the Guildhall at the ninth hour, John made his way back to his house. After curfew, all open fires were supposed to be banked down for the night as a precaution against conflagrations. Anyone walking the streets after dark was supposed to carry a horn lantern and have good cause to be abroad, but these regulations were held more in the breach than the observance, as with only two constables in the city it was almost impossible to enforce the rules.

When de Wolfe got back to Martin's Lane, he found the hall in darkness and when he walked around the passage to the backyard, Mary came from her hut to tell him that his wife was no longer there.

'The mistress is in a great huff, Sir Coroner,' she said, using the slightly sarcastic title she employed when he had done something to exasperate her. 'She's gone to stay with her brother, saying that she would be afraid for her life if she stayed here any longer!'

'Stupid bitch!' he growled. 'She knows damned well that I'd never hurt her. It was all words, though God knows she provokes me so.'

His maid stood with her fists on her hips, glaring at him accusingly. 'I know that well enough! But your tongue runs away with you sometimes. No doubt she's pouring her woes into the ear of Richard around in North Gate Street. It'll give him something more to use against you.'

He grunted, then gave her a chaste kiss on her cheek.

'After all the grief I've caused him over the past couple of years, he can now add my refusal to do anything about protecting his damned pig farms. Though I must admit that he may be right in thinking that the yellow curse is being brought in from overseas.'

He refused her offer of yet more food and found his way up the outer stairs to the empty solar and, stripping off his clothes, huddled under the blanket and bearskin. He was tired and despondent, yet sleep was a long time coming as he churned over all his problems. The wide mattress seemed strange without Matilda and, much as he disliked her, he missed her ample body snoring on the other side.

CHAPTER TEN

In which a convocation is held in the cathedral

Both canons and the other clergy were fond of their dinner, so on that November Wednesday a well-fed convocation assembled in the chapter house soon after noon, the cathedral community eating earlier than many folk outside the Close. This was not, of course, a regular chapter meeting, which always took place between Prime and Terce, two of the services held earlier in the morning. However, many of the canons, vicars-choral, secondaries and choristers attended again, mainly out of curiosity about this novel event. Robert de Baggetor had encouraged this, as he wanted the maximum publicity for his campaign against the heretics – even a few townsmen had sidled in without challenge, including Clement the physician.

As the senior clergy trooped in, John de Alençon followed them unenthusiastically. He took his place in the chair that had been set on a small dais alongside the lectern used daily by a secondary to read a chapter from the Rule of St Benedict, a ritual that gave the chapter its name. The benches were ranked in a half-circle before him, with another on each side of his seat to accommodate the interrogators. These were the three prime movers, the canons who had pressed for this enquiry, and the other senior proctor, Canon William de Swindon. In addition, the bishop was represented by his chaplain and the deacon who was his legal adviser, a wizen-faced man who looked as if he drank vinegar instead of wine. The two proctors' men, Gale and Blundus, stood one each side of the entrance door, looking as if they hoped for a riot, so that they could lay about them with their cudgels.

After the shuffling and fidgeting had subsided, the archdeacon nodded to the bishop's chaplain, who went to the lectern and read out a passage from the Vulgate, chosen by de Baggetor. Unsurprisingly, it was one of the more lurid and threatening parts of the Book of Revelation, obviously intended to emphasise the tortures of hell that St John alleged were waiting for heretics. John de Alençon then rose to his feet to intone a prayer. It was a fairly neutral supplication, asking for God's guidance in their deliberations, but free from any blood-and-thunder imprecations, which would have better pleased the canons. Then the two bailiffs went outside and marched in the five subjects of the inquisition, who were stood in a line before the dais, with Gale and Blundus at either end.

'Give us your names and where you live,' requested the archdeacon, in a mild tone that held no hint of threat.

Adam the fishmonger, Oliver and Peter and Jordan Cosse from Ide gave the details without demur, but the fifth man took a step forward, which made Blundus grab his arm and try to pull him back until de Alençon signalled to him to desist.

'I will give you my name, as it is no secret,' boomed the man in a deep voice. 'It is Algar, a fuller from the lower town. But I deny the right of this court to bring us here and to question us. We are all freemen who have done no wrong. By whose authority do you claim to hold sway over us?'

Before the archdeacon could respond, Robert de Baggetor had jumped from his seat, red-faced and furious.

'What authority?' he shouted. 'The authority of God in Heaven, transmitted through His vicar on earth, the Holy Father in Rome!'

Algar, a stocky man with wide shoulders and bulging muscles, was unrepentant. 'We acknowledge God and His precious Son as fervently as you, sir. We are no heathens or pagans, but we do not need a vast army of priests and their acolytes to intercede on our behalf.'

This blunt statement set the tone for the arguments, bluster and threats that followed for the next hour. John de Alençon did his best to act as an impartial referee, but the three canons became more and more intemperate as the men arrayed before them kept stoically to their principles.

De Baggetor was the most aggressive, but Richard fitz Rogo and Ralph de Hospitali attacked the five men with more penetrating vigour. However, whatever accusations and religious dogma were employed, the men stuck to their theme that they were entitled to worship their God in whatever way they chose.

'We are more steadfast in our beliefs than many priests, especially those in high positions,' claimed Adam. 'At least we do not sell absolution from sin as if it was a pound of herrings on my stall!'

This inflamed de Baggetor, especially as he knew it was true. He rose and pointed a quivering finger at the fishmonger.

'You add insults to Christ's Holy Church as well as your admitted sin of heresy! You condemn yourselves out of your own mouths!'

Again and again, de Alençon had to rise and attempt to quell what was becoming a tirade on one side and a stubborn stonewalling on the other. It was Algar the fuller and Adam of Dunsford who did most of the responding to the blistering if repetitive attacks of the canons. After they had angrily covered the same ground several times, the archdeacon held up his hands, demanding quiet both from the disputants and the audience, who were now calling out and arguing among themselves, though as they were virtually all in holy orders, there was nothing but support for the canons.

'This is supposed to be an examination of these men, not just an opportunity for invective and condemnation,' he called out sternly. 'Neither is this a trial, for which we require the express consent of the bishop and preferably his presence.'

De Baggetor swung around on his bench to face John.

'You are the bishop's vicar-general – you represent him and could make judgements here and now, archdeacon.'

'Indeed, you could send these men to the secular authorities – as well as excommunicating them on the spot!' added Richard fitz Rogo. A buzz of agreement rippled around the circle of benches.

'Not only excommunication, but anathema itself!' grated de Baggetor.

'They have not only failed to deny their heresy, but appear to revel in it!' snapped Ralph de Hospitali. 'What more do we need to hear? They are condemned out of their own mouths!'

'This is not the bishop's court, in spite of what you claim,' said de Alençon stubbornly. 'The matter must be put before Our Grace Lord Henry when he returns. It is too important a matter to be dealt with behind his back. Both the message from the Papal Legate and the terms of the original decretal of Verona specifically put the onus to prosecute heresy on *bishops*.'

A heated argument broke out between the three canons and the vicar-general, but de Alençon was adamant. Nothing would be done until the bishop was consulted. He swept his arm around to encompass the five men still standing resolutely before them.

'We know who they are. They have lived in the city or nearby for years. What else can we do with them except release them?'

Protests and argument welled up again, involving the people in the congregation as well as the angry canons, but the archdeacon stepped up to the empty lectern and rapped hard on it with the handle of his small eating-knife which he pulled from his pouch.

'This convocation is now closed,' he shouted, motioning at the five men below. 'For now, you are free to go. You proctors' men, make sure that they are allowed to leave the precinct safely, do you understand?'

Glowering, Gale and Blundus shepherded the accused out through the door, reluctantly pushing aside a number of secondaries and choristers who shouted, jostled and even spat at them. Inside the chamber, unexpectedly one of the listeners from the back benches strode forward and addressed the canons. It was Clement of Salisbury, arrayed in the traditional costume of a physician, a long black tunic with a narrow white apron running down from neck to hem and a black skullcap upon his head.

'I am but a layman, but a good Christian and a fervent disciple of the Holy Church!' he called in his strong voice, vibrant with emotion. 'I speak for many members of Exeter's devout worshippers in that we believe that these heretics are being dealt with far too lightly. They should be exposed to the full might of the Church's authority and then turned over to the king's officers for punishment – though I must confess that I have little faith in some of those officers, who seem to be too sympathetic to these heretical opinions!'

There was a chorus of cheers and stamping at that, ill suited to the usual solemn atmosphere of the chapter house. But the canons on the front benches seemed delighted with Clement's intervention, and fitz Rogo overrode the archdeacon's attempt at moderation by leaping to his feet.

'You see, we have the overwhelming support of our flock in this matter! Though the Holy Roman Church is quite capable of protecting itself, it is comforting to know that our congregations are of the same mind!'

Robert de Baggetor turned angrily to the archdeacon, eager to remonstrate with him for losing the opportunity to settle the matter quickly.

'Why are you so sympathetic to these blasphemers?' he snapped. 'You above all people are supposed to give a lead, not defend these vile men!'

De Alençon shook his grey head. 'I defended no one, and neither did I condemn them, for it is not within my remit so to do. You will have your chance to conclude this matter when you have placed it before Henry Marshal.'

He pulled the folds of his black cloak around him and walked out into the misty Close.

CHAPTER ELEVEN

In which Crowner John's faith is challenged

In spite of Gwyn's anxiety about John riding alone to Stoke, the journey was uneventful. A weak sun had burned off the mist before mid-morning, and he reached his brother's manor by noon, even though his heavy destrier Odin was appreciably slower than a rounsey or a palfrey.

Before leaving Exeter, he had called at St John's Priory to see Thomas and found him in much the same state as the previous day, still feverish and restless. Though he would not respond sensibly to any questions or seem to recognise his master, at least he was no worse. Brother Saulf was non-committal about his prospects, saying that some victims of the yellow distemper had recovered rapidly, while others had deteriorated after a good start. They prayed together over his pallet, John shedding his indifference about his religious belief in a genuine and heartfelt effort to persuade God to save this good little priest.

When he arrived at Stoke, he did much the same thing, as William was also in the same state as before, though the fever seemed to have subsided. He was even more yellow than on the previous visit, but Enyd, anxious to grasp at any shred of hope, reported that he had been passing slightly more water and that they had managed to force a fair quantity of water past his cracked lips. As with Thomas, he was semi-conscious and perhaps even more unreactive to any attempts to rouse him. At the table where Enyd had prepared her usual copious meal, she commiserated with John over Thomas's affliction by the same hateful illness, for like most people she was very fond of his clerk, who had visited them several times. Then she passed stoically to the almost unthinkable possibility that her son might die.

'The two manors are being run well enough for the present by the bailiffs and reeves, but what will become of us if we lose William?' she asked tremulously. 'He is such a good husbandman, for the crops, the livestock and the forest. Our servants, faithful though they are, cannot plan and organise in that way, and I am sure that neither Evelyn nor I have nearly enough knowledge to run an estate.'

John laid a comforting hand on his mother's sleeve.

'Do not seek problems before they arise, for I feel it in my bones that William will survive. But should the worst happen, I will come here to live, at least for much of the time, though I cannot pretend to have as much skill as my brother. I would have to find a competent steward to assist us, as happens in so many manors where there are absentee lords.'

His sister Evelyn, looking drained and weary from her ceaseless nursing of the sick in the village, as well as of her brother, dabbed her eyes with a kerchief.

'We only wish you could have been wedded to Hilda, though we realise that it would not have been possible in the old days, with her the daughter of one of our own reeves. But now she is a rich and independent woman, you could have brought her here to live.'

De Wolfe smiled bleakly. 'If only we had the gift of reading the future! So much would have been done differently.'

He told them of his latest spat with Matilda, which was more serious than ever before. 'She is like a millstone around my neck, my penance for all I have done wrong in my life,' he said sadly. 'Now she claims I intend to harm her, which is far from the truth, much as I dislike her.'

'You have not seen Hilda lately?' asked Enyd, who also would have liked her for a daughter-in-law in place of Matilda de Revelle, who always treated the Stoke family with disdain.

'I have been afraid to risk taking the distemper to her, though Dawlish already must be a vulnerable place, if it is true that it is being brought in on the ships.'

Enyd de Wolfe leaned to kiss her son on his forehead. 'You are a good man, John, but I think you should go to see Hilda. This foul affliction is so erratic in its attacks that I think it is pointless trying to avoid it. We have had no more victims in the village, and Holcombe had none at all, like Dawlish.'

So when he left Stoke in the early afternoon, John took his mother's advice and knocked on Hilda's sturdy front door. When little Alice opened it, he was going to tell her to ask her mistress if she wished to risk seeing him, but suddenly Hilda appeared and threw her arms about his neck, dragging him inside. Sending the giggling maid for wine and pastries, John's mistress pulled him by the hand up to her solar and, until Alice's feet were heard on the stairs, they kissed hungrily, grasping each other as tightly as if they wished to fuse their bodies together.

Soon, they were sitting decorously opposite each other on folding chairs, sipping the good wine that her late husband had brought back from France. Alice perched inconspicuously on a stool in the corner, watching with fascination as her beautiful blonde mistress was so obviously captivated by this forbidding, black-haired man who reminded her of some huge bird of prey.

Hilda listened to his sad news about both his brother and Thomas, but told him to have hope for them both.

'I have been praying constantly for Lord William,' she said. 'And now I shall do the same for poor Thomas, bless him. I am sure that God will not want to take such a good soul to heaven so soon.'

Unlike John, the blonde Saxon was very devout and was a pillar of faith and charity in Dawlish, where she looked after the well-being of a number of widows and families who had lost their ship-men husbands and fathers at sea, including those who had been murdered along with her husband Thorgils on his ship the previous year.

Hilda listened gravely to John's sour description of Matilda's increasing intransigence. 'She is such an unhappy soul, poor woman,' she said. 'But I wish she would not spread her bitterness all about her like a black cloud.'

Though de Wolfe would dearly have liked to have stayed with Hilda, preferably all night, the various troubles that assailed him seemed to tell both of them that this was not the right time. Soon he reluctantly made his farewell, promising Hilda that he would call each time he made the journey to Stoke. He walked to the inn, where Odin was being fed and watered, and hauled himself into the saddle.

As he trotted gently towards Exeter, he managed to drag his thoughts away from William and Thomas to wonder how the inquisition in the cathedral had gone that day. If he had not been so preoccupied with other problems, he supposed that he should have attended, in case any of the alleged heretics had confessed to any knowledge that might have helped in his investigation of the murders, though he thought that unlikely. He decided to go down later to see his friend the archdeacon, to hear what had transpired, but his priority was to visit Thomas, and when he reached the city he forced his big stallion through the crowded, narrow streets straight up to St John's Hospital.

He found Gwyn already there, crouched by the mattress, with Saulf standing at the foot. John's first thought was that something terrible had happened, but then he saw his officer's lips moving beneath his great moustache and, looking at his clerk's face, he was overjoyed to see that his eyes were open.

He dropped to his knees and bent over the little priest.

'Thomas, can you hear me? How are you?' It seemed an inane question, but it produced a result.

'I have felt better, Crowner,' whispered the clerk. 'But I will be back at my duties as soon as I am able.'

John, rugged soldier that he was, felt two beads of moisture appear in his eyes as he gave Thomas's shoulder a gentle squeeze, then climbed to his feet.

'Is this a miracle, brother?' he asked Saulf.

The Benedictine gave a gentle smile. 'I would like to think so, but every recovery is a miracle wrought by the Almighty. I told you that there are different degrees of severity of this yellow distemper, from rapid death to rapid cure.'

John looked down at Thomas and at Gwyn, who was looking as delighted as if he had found a barrel of gold pieces.

'Will he recover completely now?' he asked the monk.

'Only God knows, but I see no reason why he should not,' answered Saulf. 'He needs to expel all the yellow humour from his blood, which will take some days, but we will care for him here until that happens. He needs to rest and rebuild his strength.'

Taking the hint, John murmured his goodbyes to Thomas with a promise to visit him often, then motioned to Gwyn to leave their clerk in peace. On the way out, de Wolfe emptied his purse into Saulf's hand, with fervent thanks and instructions to purchase whatever was needed for Thomas's care. Outside, after celebrating Thomas's withdrawal from the brink of death, John asked Gwyn if anything had happened during the day.

'There's been an affray out near Honiton – two killed in a robbery, but both miscreants captured after the hue and cry caught up with them,' reported his officer.

'We'll have to go out there in the morning. Without Thomas to take a record, I'll have to borrow one of the sheriff's clerks. Anything else? What about this business at the cathedral?'

Gwyn ran a hand through his tangled ginger hair. 'I don't know what went on inside the chapter house, but there was a hell of a fuss afterwards!' he chuckled. 'They released those five men, but a crowd outside took against them and chased them out of the city. I can't see our fishmonger selling any more herrings in Exeter for a long time.'

As Gwyn enlarged on his story, John gathered that a mob had assembled in the Close and had started yelling abuse at the men as they left the chapter house. On leaving the Close, more protesters gathered and started jostling and punching the alleged heretics.

'Didn't the bailiffs or constables intervene?' demanded John.

'It seems that the proctors' men just stood back and did nothing while the mob was inside the cathedral precinct – outside, Osric and Theobald tried to keep order, but they had no chance against a hundred angry townsmen and women – in fact, the women were worse than their menfolk. Someone said that even that doctor who lives near you was there, shouting and shaking his fists!'

'That man is half-crazed! So then what happened?'

'The crowd got bigger as they went down Fore Street – it fed on itself. I suspect half the mob didn't know what they were rioting about, anyway; they were just itching for a fight. But the poor men from Ide had a rough time until they reached the West Gate, where the crowd seemed to lose interest in them. They were bruised and bleeding by then. It's a wonder we haven't got a corpse to deal with!'

'What happened to Adam the fisherman? I thought he lived in the city.'

Gwyn shrugged. 'I heard nothing more of him. Maybe he's lying dead in a gutter in Bretayne.'

De Wolfe put a foot in a stirrup and hoisted himself up into Odin's deep saddle. 'I'll see what John de Alençon has to say later this evening,' he promised. With another fervent thanks to God for Thomas's deliverance, he rode away, hoping against hope that a similar miracle would be granted down at Stoke-in-Teignhead.

The house in Martin's Lane was empty and, though Mary had a fire burning in the hall, it was too cavernous and bleak for him to sit eating alone. He went around to her kitchen-shed, as he had done many times before, and ate at her small table. He told her his news and, as he expected, she was delighted to hear that Thomas seemed mercifully delivered from the fear of death.

'Any word from your mistress?' he asked.

'She has gone to her brother's house, as you know. Lucille came around earlier to fetch some more of her clothes from her chests in the solar, but there was no message.'

John gnawed the last of the meat from a chicken leg. 'I wonder who'll get tired of each other's presence first,' he asked, 'Matilda or Richard?'

'Probably Eleanor de Revelle. She and the mistress are hardly best friends,' grinned Mary. Richard's icy and aloof wife considered that her own father had chosen too far down the social scale when he married her off into the de Revelle family. John washed his food down with some cider.

'So where can she go then? Polsloe won't take her in for the third time, I'm sure. She said she was going to batten herself on those poor bloody cousins in Normandy, but unless she is quick there'll be no ships sailing until the spring.'

Mary, in spite of suffering years of indignities and harsh words from Matilda, usually tried to heal the frequent breaches between John and his wife.

'You had better crawl around to North Gate Street tomorrow and try to make your peace with her,' she advised. 'That's what she'll be waiting for, and the sooner you grasp the nettle the better.'

Reluctantly, he agreed, as his sense of duty to a wife, however objectionable she might be, sat awkwardly on his conscience as he enjoyed the freedom her absence gave him.

After his supper he set out in the dusk to see his friend the archdeacon and again met his next-door neighbours as soon as he set foot outside his door.

They seemed to be almost as bad as Matilda for beating a frequent path to and from either the cathedral or St Olave's Church.

With the weather slightly warmer, Cecilia had discarded her fur-lined cloak and was attractively arrayed in a green woollen pelisse over her gown and a flowing cover-chief of white silk. The physician also wore a green mantle, his head encased in a close-fitting coif of crimson linen. He greeted John politely but made to walk on, whereas his wife stopped impulsively to enquire after his brother.

'He is much the same, perhaps slightly improved,' replied John, thanking her for her solicitude. 'My clerk also fell victim to the yellow plague several days ago, but thank God is rapidly recovering. No doubt the power of prayer was responsible!' he added, trying not to sound too sarcastic as he stared at Clement. This seemed to animate Exeter's only doctor.

'Never underestimate its power, Sir John!' he declaimed. 'I have been praying for the downfall of those evil blasphemers who were arraigned today at the cathedral. Did you hear that they were run out of the city by decent Christians?'

'I heard that they were set upon by an unruly mob! I must discuss with the sheriff and the portreeves how best these illegal riots can be prevented in the future.'

Clement became quite incensed. 'I cannot imagine why you have any sympathy for these evil men, Crowner!' he snapped. 'It was emphasised in the chapter house today that the secular authorities are bound to assist the Church in every way in bringing these blasphemers to justice!'

De Wolfe was unmoved, especially by this physician who seemed woefully short of sympathy for his fellow men.

'I will do everything that the law requires, if and when they are deemed guilty by a competent court,' he observed.

If the twilight was not so dark, Clement's face would have shown his angry flush.

'Surely your duty to God to preserve His Kingdom on earth comes before any duty to petty mortal laws!' he hissed. 'These agents of Satan wish to pull down the very foundations of the Holy Church, whose doctrines have been so painstakingly constructed over a thousand years! They should be exterminated, like pouring a boiling kettle over an ants' nest!'

John was in no mood to debate theology with someone who was so obviously obsessed with eliminating anyone who challenged the status quo.

'I'm afraid I have no say in these matters, sir. I am only a royal servant who does what King Richard and his justices expect of me.'

He bobbed his head to the doctor and smiled at Cecilia, who had stood uneasily during this exchange with her husband, then he turned on his heel and stalked away towards Canon's Row. A few minutes later he was sitting in de Alençon's bare chamber, with the inevitable goblet of good wine. The archdeacon was aware that his nephew Thomas was recovering, as several times he had called at the priory to see him.

'He's a tough little fellow, in spite of the hard times he has suffered in recent years,' he observed. 'He has often told me how much he owes you for saving his sanity and his life.'

De Wolfe told him of his brother's serious condition and found that de Alençon was yet another who had been praying for William, so hopefully the barrage of supplications to heaven might prove effective.

'Now what about today, John?' asked the coroner of his namesake. 'I suppose nothing came out in the proceedings which might give me some clue as to who is responsible for these deaths?'

The archdeacon shook his head. 'It was not that sort of enquiry, my friend. It was merely an attack by my colleagues on these fellows and an equally persistent denial of any wrongdoing by them.'

'They denied they were heretics?'

'No, but they claimed their right to practise as Christians in the way they thought best.'

De Wolfe sensed that de Alençon was torn between his ingrained lifelong acquiescence to Rome and his personal sense of tolerance. 'So what was the final outcome?' he demanded.

'Little better than chaos, John! My brother canons persisted in their inflexible condemnation, and like a lot of sheep virtually every vicar, secondary and even choirboy was infected by their enthusiasm.'

He paused to fortify himself with a sip of Loire red. 'Robert de Baggetor and the others even tried to force my hand, to convert this enquiry into a trial and to send those men to your secular powers for punishment. I refused, as I don't want their blood on my hands. Let the bishop deal with it.'

'So they've gone home?'

The archdeacon raised his hands in exasperation. 'They were chased out, as far as I could see. A mob was waiting for them and pursued them. I feared for their lives, quite honestly.'

De Wolfe was puzzled. 'These men were already known to many; that's how the proctors' spies picked them out. They've not been attacked before – apart from the three who were killed – so why should a mob suddenly set upon them?'

The archdeacon smiled wryly. 'It would not surprise me if the proctors' men did not pass the word – and a few coins – around to some who enjoy mayhem and persecution. Others will soon follow suit once some leading voice shouts loud enough.'

'Who are these agitators?' asked de Wolfe. 'I suppose they are those spies that your fellow canons have used to infiltrate the city?'

'I have heard of two men who have twisted their religious fervour into strange convictions. One is a lay brother from one of the parish churches, whose name escapes me, the other a former monk from St Nicholas Priory, a man called Alan de Bere, who was ejected some years ago for violent behaviour against foreigners, whom he considered heathens.'

John made a mental note to follow up these men as possible candidates for his murderers. While they finished their wine, they talked about the parlous state in which William remained and went on to speak of the progress of the yellow plague.

'It has been known for centuries, according to the old chronicles,' said de Alençon. 'There were two great outbreaks in Ireland in the sixth and seventh centuries – and the Welsh saint, Teilo, had to flee with his followers to Brittany to escape it around that time. Strangely, there was an eclipse of the sun on each occasion.'

He drank the last from his goblet. 'There are more outbreaks in Cornwall, and we have lost three parish priests in the diocese. It is difficult to understand God's purpose in sending this pestilence upon innocent people.'

John could not resist twisting his friend's tail. 'Then perhaps these heretics are right and there is no predestination. Man may be free to bring down his own problems upon himself.'

The archdeacon, who usually had a good sense of humour, did not smile at this. 'Be careful what you say and do, John. I have heard whispers that some may not take too kindly to you associating with these heretics.'

CHAPTER TWELVE

In which the Coroner rides to Honiton

Though weary and aching from his round trip to Stoke, that night John slept like a log until the first glimmers of light came through the shutters of the solar. After splashing water on his face from a bucket in the yard, he ate oatmeal gruel sweetened with honey and a small loaf of fresh bread in Mary's kitchen. As Odin had had enough exercise the previous day, he took a rounsey from Andrew's stable and rode up to meet Gwyn at St John's Hospital to check on Thomas's progress. Their clerk was still very weak, but he was fully alert and almost apologetic for being ill.

'He's been taking bread in warm milk,' reported Brother Saulf, who seemed very pleased with their clerk's progress.

John was never comfortable as a visitor to the sick, unlike Gwyn, who would have stopped and chatted all day. Once the coroner was satisfied that Thomas seemed out of danger, he wanted to be out of that depressing sickroom as soon as possible.

'Rest well and be sure to eat and drink,' he advised in a severe voice. 'No hurry to get back on your feet – you take your time.'

When he had prised Gwyn away from his little friend, they set off for Honiton, a large village about fifteen miles to the east, on the road to Ilminster and faraway London. It was one of the main highways out of Exeter on the line of the ancient Fosse Way, and they were rarely out of sight of either an ox-cart, a flock of sheep being driven or people on foot. The last tended to come together in groups for mutual safety, a mixture of pilgrims going to or coming from Canterbury, chapmen hawking their wares or priests and craftsmen going about their business.

It was a mild, still day, with a slight mist, and the dry weather had firmed up the usual churned mud of the track, so if the deep wheel-ruts could be avoided, the going was quite good.

They reached Honiton by mid-morning and had no need to seek out the bailiff, as there was a crowd of villagers waiting to conduct them to a barn where the offenders were shut in and well guarded.

'Caught the bastards within half an hour!' exclaimed the bailiff, a big, black-bearded man.

John insisted on having their horses watered and fed first, so they were taken to the village tavern where both steeds and riders were revived. Over a pot of ale and a bowl of thin potage, the bailiff described what had happened.

'Two strangers, probably outlaws from the forest, broke into a barton on the outskirts of the village in the early hours of yesterday,' he reported. 'They had beaten the farmer and his wife unconscious, ransacked the house, took some money stored in a jar, then stolen a horse from the stable. Thankfully, a young servant who slept in the barn raced down here to the village and raised the hue and cry!'

The reeve and the bailiff had turned out on horseback and had caught up with the robbers before they reached the shelter of the forest, as they were leading the stolen horse on a halter and trying to drive two fat pigs before them. A fight ensued but the mounted reeve felled one man with his staff and the bailiff ran the other down with his horse. A number of villagers had run after them and discovered that the farmer and his wife were already both dead. Enraged, they beat the two outlaws half to death before dragging them back to be thrown, bound hand and foot, into the grain store behind the mill.

The story told, de Wolfe got to his feet, anxious to get his business done and return to Exeter. 'Where are the two dead people?' he asked. 'They are my only concern.'

The bailiff's brow furrowed. 'What about the villains who did this, sir? What are we to do with them?'

The coroner considered for a moment. 'Either wait for the sheriff to send men-at-arms to take them back to Exeter, or get your lord's steward to try them at the manorial court. I'm sure you can find a good oak tree to hang them from!'

Strictly speaking, he should have insisted on having them brought before the king's justices or commissioners at the next Eyre of Assize, as one of the coroner's functions was to sweep as much business as possible into the royal courts. But he reasoned that in this case two outlaws would have no property to be confiscated for the treasury, and hauling them back to Exeter, keeping them in prison for months or even a year before trial, would be a drain on the royal purse, not a benefit.

This suited the bailiff well, and he took them to St Michael's Church to examine the victims, who had died of severe head injuries. A quick inquest with a vindictive jury brought in the inevitable verdict of murder upon the two bruised and battered renegades, and by early afternoon the coroner and his officer were back on the road to the city once again.

That same afternoon, Robert de Baggetor held a private meeting in his house in the Close. In addition to some of his fellow canons, which this time also included the other proctor, William de Swindon, he had invited the bishop's chaplain and the deacon who was the diocesan lawyer. A notable absence was that of John de Alençon.

'I fail to understand why our brother John is so lukewarm over this issue,' complained Richard fitz Rogo. 'Several months ago, a parish priest just outside the city sent me a crude pamphlet full of these heretical claims, which had been sent to him anonymously. I took it to the archdeacon and he promised to look into it, but nothing ever happened.'

'I have heard that some priests are secretly in sympathy with the arguments of the Gnostics,' contributed Ralph de Hospitali in a doleful voice.

'Our brother John has many claims on his energy and his time,' observed William de Swindon mildly. 'Perhaps he found it was just some chance tract that had found its way here from France.'

De Baggetor thumped the table impatiently. 'That is no excuse for de Alençon. He is the archdeacon and the bishop's vicar-general, and he should be in the forefront of our campaign to eradicate these dissenters.'

De Swindon hastened to agree. Though he had not been one of the first three to take up the crusade against the heretics, he now seemed equally enthusiastic. 'There is no question of our Brother in Christ John having any lessening of faith. He has been a pillar of strength and devotion here these many years. But it occurs to me that his well-known friendship with the coroner may be worth considering.'

Eyes swivelled towards de Swindon, as this was an unfamiliar suggestion. 'That's true, William,' said Ralph de Hospitali. 'His nephew is even the coroner's clerk.'

'What are you trying to imply?' fitz Rogo asked de Swindon.

'I have heard whispers – in fact, more than whispers – that John de Wolfe may be sympathetic to these blasphemers.'

There was a mutter of consternation around the table, but de Baggetor did not join in, as he already had heard the same whispers.

'As you know, our proctors' bailiffs have been charged with keeping a sharp eye out for any signs of heresy,' he said ponderously. 'In fact, virtually all our knowledge of their identity and their activities comes from their efforts. They have reported that de Wolfe attended a clandestine meeting of these creatures, only a few days ago, for they had a spy who was able to eavesdrop on that coven.' The others digested this for a moment.

'But the coroner is investigating the deaths of three of them,' objected fitz Rogo. 'Surely such a meeting would be a legitimate part of his enquiries?'

'At a secret meeting, skulking in a remote barn in the countryside?' said de Baggetor scathingly. 'In addition, he has expressed the opinion that it is none of his business to give any aid to our campaign, even though this was expressly demanded by *Ab Abolendum.*'

'Shall we add him to our list of persons to be interrogated?' suggested the young chaplain in a tone that suggested that he was being facetious. This was met with scowls from most of those facing him.

'Do not dismiss it too lightly,' grated Robert de Baggetor. 'It has not gone unnoticed that de Wolfe is a very reluctant and infrequent attender at Mass. He is rarely seen in a place of worship unless his devout wife drags him there.'

The lean and restless Ralph de Hospitali brought them back to more immediate issues. 'We need to decide how we proceed, after yesterday's convocation achieved so little.'

'It caused those devils a fright afterwards, with half the town chasing after them,' said de Swindon. 'It shows that we have popular support for our efforts.'

'We do not need popular support!' snapped de Baggetor arrogantly. 'It matters not what the rabble of Exeter think. We have the whole power of Rome behind us.'

'So how do we harness it?' persisted de Hospitali.

'Thanks to de Alençon's stubbornness, this has to go to the bishop,' grunted fitz Rogo. He turned to the chaplain. 'When is His Grace expected to return?'

'In the next few days, God willing. He has parish visitations to make next week and wishes to deal with accumulated business before then.'

'Well, we have some more business for him as a matter of urgency,' rasped de Baggetor. 'I would be obliged if you would arrange an audience with him as soon as possible, as we need him to agree to set up a formal court hearing without delay.' He turned to the others. 'Those swine we saw yesterday may have disappeared into thin air by now, but our bailiffs have collected more names for us, and next time they will go straight to the bishop's court – and from thence hopefully straight to the gallows.'

When he returned from Honiton, John went to see the sheriff, to tell him of the murders and the capture of the culprits by the villagers. Henry de Furnellis applauded John's decision to let the matter go to the manorial court there, as anything that saved him work was welcome, especially as there was no profit for the king in hanging penniless outlaws.

'You say the Honiton folk gave them a good beating – a pity they didn't kill them, it would have saved a lot of trouble,' he added. His attitude to justice was not as rigid as that of the coroner.

After leaving the keep, de Wolfe reluctantly decided to take Mary's advice and try to make peace with Matilda. He recalled some old country adage about 'taking the bull by the horns', which seemed an apt description of facing his wife. As he went across the inner ward towards the gatehouse, he had to walk around a troop of young soldiers being drilled by Sergeant Gabriel, an old friend and veteran who had shared several campaigns with de Wolfe. By the look on Gabriel's craggy face, the recruits were exasperating him with their lack of skill, but they had little chance to experience real fighting, as the last military violence in this area had been fifty years ago, during the civil war of King Stephen's reign.

As John neared the arch leading to the drawbridge, another friend hailed him. This was Brother Rufus, the garrison chaplain, who had just emerged from his tiny chapel of St Mary, set to the left of the gate. Rufus was a large, muscular Benedictine, with the jovial nature that big people often possess. He, too, had seen his share of battlefields, as he had been a military chaplain in the campaigns in France and Palestine, which gave him much in common with de Wolfe. He was a straightforward man, free from the pomposity and cant that many of the Exeter clergy exhibited. Admirably suited to his calling of a soldier's padre, he enjoyed his ale and wine and a game of dice in the guard-room, without forfeiting any of his compassion and devotion.

In no hurry to face Matilda, John accepted Rufus's invitation to sit with him on a bench outside the little church and enjoy the weak sun that had managed to penetrate the autumn haze.

'I hear that young Thomas is recovering, thank God and all His saints,' he said. 'We have prayed for him daily.'

John went on to tell him about his own brother's affliction, but of course the city grapevine had long ago spread the news. 'He seems no worse and we are hoping that he, too, will recover,' said John, almost afraid to be too optimistic in case it was dashed to the ground.

'You have been busy with our heretical competitors in the religious world,' grinned Rufus, who had an impish sense of humour. 'It seems that over this matter, the noble canons down in the Close are like a swarm of wasps that have had their nest stirred with a stick!'

Those in the monastic orders did not always see eye to eye with the diocesan priesthood, as Exeter cathedral was one of the dozen in England that was 'secular', in that it was not a monastery or an abbey.

'I saw many brands of religious belief on my travels in Outremer,' continued Rufus. 'Many were either different types of Christian, from Greece or Byzantium – and some were not Christian at all.'

He stopped to scratch an itch on his newly shaven tonsure. 'But many of them were intensely devout and scrupulously honest men, so I do not rush to condemn even the smallest deviation from our own Church. That does not divert me from my lifelong dedication to Rome, but I fear I cannot accept this current hysteria against a few sincere souls who wish to follow a different path.'

They talked for a while about the different types of heresy and then went on to wonder at the unpredictable ebb and flow of the yellow plague, which seemed to be maintaining its sporadic attacks. The incessant activity of the busy castle went on around them as they chatted, ox-carts lumbering in with fodder for the garrison horses, a blacksmith hammering a new shoe on a grey gelding and soldiers' wives passing by with small children clinging to their skirts. Then Rufus's eye was caught by someone running across the drawbridge on the outer side of the arched gateway. Even at a distance, he could see that the man was almost collapsing from the effort of hurrying up the steep track of Castle Hill, and waving his arms to attract attention.

'Here's our brave constable, Osric!' exclaimed the monk.

'What can be so urgent that he's running fit to burst?'

An unruly mob stormed down Rock Lane, gathering more people as they approached the Water Gate, which led out on to the quayside along the river. Mostly men, but with a few matrons on the fringes, they surged through the gate, brushing aside the pair of porters who were there to collect tolls on goods from the wharf.

The crowd, which numbered almost a hundred, was led by two men who capered and waved their arms to further inflame the mob. One was a skinny monk, dressed in a frayed black habit of the Benedictine order, and the other a stocky man in a brown serge cassock, both having shaven circles on their heads.

'Find the denouncers of the Holy Father!' yelled the monk, Alan de Bere. He waved a heavy stick, which ended in a crude hook like a bishop's crozier, and pointed with the other hand at the two vessels that were leaning against the quay, beached on the mud at low tide. The proctors' spies had discovered that four of the five men arraigned at the inquisition the previous day were trying to escape by sea, having decided that Exeter was too dangerous for them.

Not to be outdone, Reginald Rugge, the lay brother, screamed inaccurately at the top of his voice, 'Seize the disciples of the Antichrist!' as he brandished a rusty sword. A few stevedores, who had been carrying bales of wool towards a gangplank, dumped their loads and nervously retreated to the back of the quayside against the town wall, which here climbed steeply up towards the South Gate.

The mob, which contained quite a few drunks attracted out of the rougher taverns, was shouting incoherently, their excitement fanned by the two agitators. They spread out along the edge of the wharf opposite the two merchant cogs, from where bemused ship-men and dockers stared down at the angry crowd.

'Where are the bloody heretics? ... Give us the blasphemers!' came the cries. An unfortunate stevedore, a youth barely into his teens, was engulfed by the crowd as he ran for the gangplank of the nearer ship. Alan de Bere grabbed him with unmonastic violence and brandished his crozier at him threateningly.

'Tell me which vessel shelters these bastards!' he roared.

Without hesitation, the lad pointed at the next ship along, the larger of the two. 'They are aboard that one, sir!' he squealed and, ducking away as soon as he was released, scampered off along the quay to join his fellows huddled against the city wall.

Like a flowing liquid, the mob moved to the other ship, the *Saint Augustine*, and Reginald Rugge was first up the plank that led up to a gap in the bulwarks. A burly sailor blocked his way and, when the lay brother raised his sword in a threatening gesture, he lifted his foot and planted it on Rugge's chest. With a quick thrust, he sent the man staggering backwards into the man behind, almost pitching them both off on to the unyielding quayside.

A roar of anger went up from the crowd and a stone was thrown at the seaman, narrowly missing his head. A moment later, half the crowd was scrabbling on the ground for missiles, and a hail of pebbles and debris was soon being hurled at the luckless crew on the deck of the *Saint Augustine*. As it was not their battle, the half-dozen sailors retreated to the hold and sheltered behind the piles of wool that had already been loaded. Yelling with excitement, Rugge and de Bere led a cavalcade of rioters up the gangplank to the deck, where they spotted a few figures cowering in the low hut on the stern, which served as a shelter for crew and passengers.

With whoops of righteous triumph, they converged on this primitive cabin and dragged out four struggling figures and frogmarched them back down to the quayside, leaving three weeping and distraught women on the deck.

The mob had first formed outside the Saracen alehouse in Smythen Street, notorious for its ruffianly clientele, the frequency of bar fights and the poor quality of its cheap ale. Much of the violent crime in the city was connected with the Saracen in one way or another, and the landlord, a massive man named Willem the Fleming, enforced order only with the help of a bludgeon he kept always by his side. The inflammatory exhortations of Rugge and de Bere had attracted a score of men to gather around them in the road outside, collecting even more as they moved off towards the quayside. Their departure did not go unnoticed however, as Osric, the skinny constable, frequently kept a wary eye on the tavern, the seat of so many of his problems. Rapidly deciding that the odds of more than twenty to one were too great for his health and safety, he hurried away towards Rougemont, the ultimate seat of authority and law enforcement in the city.

Panting as he half-ran, half-trotted up the last incline, he passed through the gatehouse arch and thankfully saw the coroner sitting outside the chapel with the garrison chaplain.

'Sir John, Sir John!' he gasped, stumbling to halt before them as he leaned forward with his hands clutching his thighs, to get his breath back. 'You must come at once – and turn out a posse. There's likely murder being done down on the quayside!'

John and Rufus jumped up and lowered Osric down on to the bench to hear his urgent tale of the mob down on the river wharf. Wasting no time, the coroner turned and yelled across at Sergeant Gabriel, beckoning him urgently. Immediately, the sergeant hurried off to find Ralph Morin, the castle constable, to get him to organise an anti-riot squad, which would be comprised mostly of the recruits already in the inner ward.

'I can't wait for them to arrive. I'm going down there!' snapped de Wolfe and headed for a mare that was ready-saddled and tethered to a rail below the stairs to the keep. Heedless of who it belonged to, he swung into the saddle and cantered off through the gatehouse, scattering chickens and pigs on his way.

Knowing of the difficulty of running a horse through the crowded lanes of the city, he turned left at the bottom of Castle Hill and went out through East Gate, then followed the walls past the gardens of Southernhay and the South Gate to reach the gradient down to the river. As he slowed to let the mare feel her way down the steep path, he could both see and hear the commotion down on the quayside below. A mass of figures, looking from that distance like a disturbed anthill, was moving away from the moored vessels, along the wharf downstream to where the banks of the Exe began, covered with a tangle of bushes and small trees.

With some slithering, his horse got to the bottom and there he abandoned her to a group of cowering dockers and began racing across the quay towards the mob. As he ran, he hauled his sword from its scabbard and began adding to the tumult with his own voice.

'Stop, in the name of the king!' he yelled, but no one took any heed, apart from two women who were trailing along behind the crowd, wailing and sobbing.

'Save them, sir, they're going to hang our men,' screamed one of the women, a middle-aged matron with tears running down her face.

'Not if I can help it!' he growled back and, catching up with the edge of the crowd, began yelling again that he was an officer of the king and calling on them to desist from whatever they were doing. This time a few faces turned towards him and several men faltered and dropped back, but the bulk of the mob kept going, a straggling circle moving crabwise towards the end of the wharf.

Still shouting himself hoarse, de Wolfe began laying about him with the flat of his broadsword as he forced himself towards the front of the swarm. He caught a couple of men heavy blows on the shoulders, and one man collapsed after he hit him on the back of the head. At last, he was making the rioters notice his presence, and several of them, full of ale and cider, began to turn nasty. As he shouldered them aside, they began to push back at him, and a stream of foul language and blasphemy sat strangely with their supposed crusade against enemies of the Church.

One black-bearded ruffian spat at him and, lacing his words with some of the choicest oaths that John had ever heard, demanded to know who he thought he was. Obviously from out of town, he was ignorant of the coroner's identity.

'Clear off, you bastard!' he snarled and produced a dagger that he waved threateningly. De Wolfe had no time for niceties and promptly hacked at the man's arm and pushed him aside. Blackbeard howled, dropped his weapon and clutched at his arm, which was pumping blood from a deep slash. This certainly brought some attention, and those around stumbled and flailed about as they tried to get out of reach of this tall dark figure who was not afraid to cut a path through them. They fell back and, though many others were still yelling, John forced through to the centre, where a dozen activists were dragging four men across the stony surface of the wharf. Three of them were struggling in the grip of brawny captors, but the fourth was inert, the head that was slumped on his chest red with blood from a scalp wound.

In front of them, in the vanguard of rioters, were the two ringleaders, Rugge and de Bere. John yelled at them over the heads of the captives and their escorts.

'Stop this at once, do you hear!' he hollered, wishing Gwyn was with him, both for his brawn and for his stentorian voice. 'This is an affray against the King's Peace! As a law officer, I command you to break up this riot and release these men!'

The skinny monk de Bere turned as if realising for the first time that some interloper had arrived. When he saw the well-known black head of the county coroner, he faltered, but then decided to brazen it out, having God on his side.

'This is none of your business, Crowner,' he shouted. 'We are doing the Lord's work, not the king's.'

De Wolfe thrust his way nearer, pushing between two of the heretics and their captors.

'Everything that happens in England is the king's business!' he rasped. 'This is a riotous assembly and is therefore illegal and a felony. You can hang for this!'

He was jostled aside and took the opportunity to whack a few more shoulders with his sword, but the mood of the crowd was becoming ugly.

'Clear off, Crowner. Everyone knows you are a friend of heretics!' yelled one man, and the cry was taken up by others.

'Leave us be, we are cleansing the stables of Israel,' shouted one, illogically. 'We carry out the commands of the Holy Father. What business is it of yours!' screamed another wild-eyed drunkard, suddenly having discovered religion after a lifetime in the tavern. The mob pressed in on him so tightly that he was unable to lift his sword, but when someone tried to prise it from his hand John kneed him in the groin and then hit him in the face with the hilt, sending him staggering with a bloody nose.

But numbers were beginning to tell and as the hysterical mob became more excited he began to fear seriously for his own safety. Hemmed in by a ranting mob, he saw Rugge and de Bere moving away from him, their acolytes dragging two of the captives with them. For the first time, John saw that they already had rope nooses around their necks and that they were heading for some trees just beyond the end of the wharf. Though stunted, they were high enough to dangle a man by the neck, with his feet clear of the ground.

Desperately, John lashed out at those who were scrabbling at his clothing and landing fairly ineffectual punches on his back and arms. Struggling to get clear, he struck another fellow in the face with the pommel of his sword and punched another in the throat with his free hand. But things were getting out of hand and de Wolfe began wondering if he would survive as knives began appearing. In an almost detached manner, he considered how ironic it would be if he, who had survived so many battles and campaigns in France, Ireland and the Holy Land, were to be slain by a horde of drunken rioters just a few furlongs from his own doorstep.

'In the name of the king, I order you to let those men go free!' he yelled desperately, as his sword arm was grabbed by several horny hands.

Suddenly, he heard a bass voice roaring behind him and, craning his neck, looked expecting to see Gwyn coming to his rescue. In fact, the big Cornishman was there, but in front of him, thrashing his way through the mob, was Brother Rufus, commanding everyone in the name of God to get out of his way, a request he reinforced by swipes of the thick staff he was wielding. He struck one of the ruffians hanging on to John's arm, and with a yelp of pain he let go. Gwyn was close behind, cursing and also laying about him with a cudgel in each hand, virtually carving a path to the coroner.

In a trice, the three big men were standing together and the tide of battle turned almost immediately as they began moving apart, thrashing everyone within reach.

'Stop those bastards up at the front!' shouted John. 'They're trying to hang the fishmonger!'

They ploughed through the remaining protesters to reach the smaller group that were still dragging their prisoners towards the end of the quayside. John, now that his sword was free again, circled in front of Rugge and stuck the tip against his throat.

'Let that man loose or I'll cut your bloody head off!' he snarled.

219

By way of reply, the lay brother lifted his old sword in a futile gesture of defiance, but John swung his own heavy blade sideways against Rugge's wrist. The blow, though blunt, temporarily paralysed his hand, and the rusty weapon clattered to the ground. Adam of Dunsford, the Pelagian fish-vendor, jerked the rope from Rugge's other hand and hauled the noose up over his head, wincing as it rubbed against his bloody face and black, swollen eye.

'Thanks be to God, Sir John. Another five minutes and I'd have been swinging from that tree.'

The crowd was now more sullen than aggressive, but a new factor soon changed their mood more dramatically. Several yelled out a warning and pointed up at the steep slope that led to the South Gate. A score of men-at-arms, led by another giant and a sergeant, were pounding down towards them, bearing a variety of weapons, including some lances, ball-maces and heavy staffs.

Just as a flock of birds will change direction simultaneously without a command, so the mob dispersed as if it had exploded. The captives were abandoned and men ran in all directions, some along the riverbank, others back through the Water Gate and the remainder northwards towards Exe Island and the West Gate. By the time Ralph Morin and his men arrived, they could grab only a few stragglers, which included the two leaders, Alan de Bere and Reginald Rugge. John and his two rescuers were more concerned with the victims than with rounding up the rioters.

'This one's coming round,' said Gwyn, bending over Peter of Ide, the unconscious one who had been dropped to the ground when his captors had run off. Brother Rufus had knelt alongside him, ready if necessary to give him the last rites, but Peter groaned and tried to lift his bruised face towards them.

They laid him on the ground again and the castle constable detailed two soldiers to guard him.

'Will he be safe here?' asked Adam, who came limping over to them, followed by the other two, Jordan Cosse of Ide and Oliver, both of whom were bedraggled and bruised.

'I've told those two men of mine to stay with him until we know what the hell's happening,' grunted Morin. 'Though what the hell *is* happening?' he asked the coroner.

'Some of our noble citizens seem to have been disappointed with the failure of the cathedral to deal with these dissidents, so they took it upon themselves to mete out their own type of justice,' answered John bitterly.

'We've lost most of the bastards,' growled Morin. 'We arrived a couple of minutes too late.'

'Never mind. You've got the two ringleaders,' said John. 'Lock those swine up in the cells at the castle – the rest are of no importance. You might as well let those fellows go free.'

'What about these other men we rescued?' asked Sergeant Gabriel. De Wolfe looked at the trio of heretics and the one on the ground, who was starting to drag himself to his knees.

'They've committed no crime that I know of,' he growled. 'They were lawfully aboard a vessel, seeking passage. What grounds have we for interfering?'

The women who were aboard the *Saint Augustine* had hurried down the gangplank and were now hugging their husbands, including the wife of Peter, who was now recovered enough to be helped to his feet. John strode across to the vessel and called up to the shipmaster, who with his crew had been watching the turmoil ashore with consternation.

'Are you leaving on the next tide?' he shouted.

'Yes, if we can get those porters to finish loading.'

'And did you promise to take these men and their wives as passengers?'

The burly captain nodded. 'They paid their fares as far as Rye. We go on from there to Calais,' he explained.

John looked around at the bedraggled victims of the mob and walked back to Adam of Dunsford. 'Are you still willing to leave on this ship?'

The fishmonger nodded. 'There is nothing left for us here – either the mob will kill us or the canons will find a way to destroy us. But will you let us go?'

De Wolfe shrugged. 'You were the victims, not the aggressors! You have committed no breach of the peace, to my knowledge.' He waved a hand towards the gangplank of the *Saint Augustine*.

'Go now, and I hope you will find a quiet life wherever you end up. I would suggest that you keep your religious beliefs to yourselves in future.'

The small group of men and their wives seemed half-afraid that the soldiers would prevent them from leaving, but with profuse thanks to John they shuffled to the ship, supporting the injured Peter between them.

'I'll leave a few men to guard the ship until she sails,' suggested Ralph Morin, 'in case some of those unruly bastards creep back to cause more trouble.'

As life settled back to normal on the quayside, Gwyn collected John's 'borrowed' horse and, together with Brother Rufus, walked it back to Rougemont, the garrison commander and Sergeant Gabriel marching the remainder of the troops in front of them, their two prisoners in the centre, protesting loudly.

'You'll be in bad odour with the cathedral for this, John,' warned the chaplain as they went through the

West Gate. 'They already have you marked down as sympathising with these heretics. There are a few people vindictive enough to make a lot of trouble for you.'

John felt that with all his existing problems, another one would be barely noticed.

In the keep of Rougemont, Henry de Furnellis listened gravely to the news that de Wolfe and Ralph Morin gave him. Riots and civil disturbance were uncommon in Devon. At the fairs and local tournaments, there was always some trouble from brawling drunks, armed robbers and purse-snatchers, but they could usually be dealt with either by the constable's heavy staffs or by a few soldiers sent down from the castle. But today's riot involving a hundred people was most unusual.

'The last time was a year ago, when those poor women were hounded by a mob who raved that they were chasing witches,' recollected Morin.

'And they hanged one, as well,' said de Wolfe. 'At least today we were in time to stop that happening.'

'Get a couple of ringleaders agitating and the rest follow like a lot of sheep!' growled the sheriff. 'As with that witch-hunt, some kind of hysteria arises that feeds on itself.'

'So what are we going to do with these two troublemakers?' asked John, referring to Rugge and de Bere, who were incarcerated below their feet in the foul cells of the castle's undercroft gaol.

'Haul 'em before the county court next week,' suggested the castellan. 'Charge them with fomenting a breach of the peace. That'll keep them locked up until the justices come.'

The king's courts were the Eyres of Assize, whose royal judges trundled around the counties very slowly to dispense justice. As it was sometimes years between

223

their visits, additional courts had been added, where Commissioners, usually barons or senior court clerks, came more often to carry out 'gaol delivery'. It was part of the coroner's duty to prepare all the cases to put before these justices, though as the delays were so great, many of the accused had either escaped from – or died in – prison before justice could be dispensed.

'So you let these heretics escape, John?' observed Henry, leaning back in his chair. 'That won't increase your popularity down in the cathedral Close!'

'What else could be done?' grunted John defensively. 'They had committed no crime against the King's Peace, so we couldn't lock them up. And did you want extra mouths to feed for God knows how long, down in the cells?'

'We could have told them to go to their homes, I suppose?' said Morin. 'But then we would have to mount a guard, in case some of those madmen from the cathedral had another go at them. They've killed three already, according to John here.'

'The Church has been trying to rid the county of heretics, so now we've done it for them, as far as four are concerned,' said de Wolfe. 'They can go and cause problems in Rye or wherever that ship lands them. At least they are no longer our concern.'

Gwyn, who had been standing quietly by the door, joined the discussion. 'We sent four on their way, with some wives. But what happened to the fifth man who was hauled before the canons yesterday?'

De Wolfe had been told about him by the archdeacon.

'It was a fuller called Algar, who lives in Milk Lane. I know nothing more about him, but it seems he was the most defiant of those arraigned yesterday and virtually told the canons that they had no right even to question him.'

The sheriff groaned. 'The canons will be after him again; they won't let him get away with that. I hear they have a list of other suspects, drawn up by the proctors' men and their spies.'

'I agree. He'd better stay at home after dark,' said the coroner. 'Otherwise he'll find himself without a tongue or voice-box one of these nights.'

By the time he left the castle, it was early evening, when he would normally be going home to have supper with his wife, cheerless though that usually was. But with no Matilda, he reluctantly decided to go to her brother's house in North Gate Street to see if he could pour some oil on the very troubled waters – at least it would satisfy Mary.

His brother-in-law kept a town house in the city, though he also had two large manors, one at Revelstoke near Plymouth and the other in the opposite direction up at Tiverton. His glacial wife Eleanor spent most of her time at the latter place, but these days Richard favoured the Exeter house, where he could supervise his various business ventures and consort with loose women, which was one of his main pastimes.

When John reached the tall house in North Gate Street, the door was opened by the timid Lucille, who had gone into exile with her mistress. She showed him into a small room off the hall, for the house was larger than John's and had two extra chambers, as well as a solar. Matilda was sitting on a cushioned settle, with a brazier of glowing charcoal nearby. She scowled at her husband by way of greeting.

'What makes you think I wish to set eyes on you?' she snapped.

Determined not to lose his temper, he dug his nails into his palms and found some conciliatory words, even apologising for any hasty language he may have used.

'You threatened me, John! What kind of behaviour is that?' she responded ungraciously.

He tried to dismiss the claim by making light of it. 'We have shouted at each other for the past sixteen years, wife,' he said earnestly. 'All married couples do; it's part of wedded life. It was merely words; you know damned well I didn't mean any of it.'

She sniffed and looked away, pretending to be indifferent, but John knew from experience that she was weakening. Even a day or two with her brother and sister-in-law was enough to make her pine for home. She and Eleanor de Revelle were mutually incompatible, as Richard's wife made no effort to conceal her disdain for her husband's family.

John was stumbling through more platitudes and apologies, which he knew were an essential part of the forgiveness ritual, when the door opened and Matilda's brother entered. He stiffened as soon as he saw John, their long-standing dislike of each other crystallising into contempt on de Wolfe's side and sheer hatred on Richard's.

'What are you doing here?' he demanded. 'I don't trust you to be alone with Matilda!'

'Don't be so bloody silly, she's my wife,' glowered John. 'I don't come spying on you and Eleanor when you are having a spat in your own house!'

'You offered violence to my sister,' brayed Richard, his pointed beard wagging in indignation. 'I heard you threaten to kill her!'

Vehemently, John protested that it was merely talk generated by high temper, and for several minutes they argued back and forth, that same temper beginning to show itself more on both sides as they went on. It was brought to an abrupt end by Matilda herself, as she lumbered to her feet and screamed at them both.

'Enough of this! My husband is an impulsive fool

with a foul humour, but my place is at home with him, for better or worse! I shall return there tomorrow, Richard, when my maid has packed my belongings.'

De Wolfe noticed that though her brother huffed and puffed and warned her again about the danger she would be in, he made no real effort to persuade her to stay, as a little of Matilda was more than enough for him or his wife and she could outstay her welcome in a matter of hours.

John decided there was no point in further discussion and, with a muted farewell to his wife until the morrow, he left the room. Richard followed him to the front door, strutting as if to make sure he did not steal anything or assault his staff.

As de Wolfe stepped into the street, his brother-in-law made one last parting shot. 'Behave yourself, John! My sister is very dear to me,' he bleated with false sincerity. 'If any harm befalls her, I will know where the blame lies!'

Resisting the temptation to punch him on the nose, the coroner stalked off, not deigning to offer a reply.

CHAPTER THIRTEEN

In which various meetings are held in Exeter

After the chapter meeting next morning, ten of the twenty-four canons stayed behind in the chapter house after the vicars and secondaries had left. The three keenest heretic-crushers had been joined by the other proctor, William de Swindon, as well as the precentor, the treasurer and three other prebendaries. The tenth was John de Alençon, who as archdeacon and the bishop's vicar-general, could hardly absent himself. Henry Marshal's chaplain and the legal deacon were also in attendance as Robert de Baggetor took it upon himself to lead the meeting without seeking any approval from the others.

'We are in an intolerable situation!' he boomed. 'The cathedral, and indeed the Holy Church itself, has been slighted and insulted by the arrogant and high-handed actions of those barbarians in Rougemont!'

Though the archdeacon had intended to keep as low a profile as possible, this was too much for him. 'Come, my brother, that is putting it too strongly!' he retorted. 'There was a major riot in the city, one man was injured and another almost hanged – what did you expect the law officers to do? Ignore it?'

'The citizens were displaying their anger and abhorrence of the presence of those cursed unbelievers in the town,' snapped Richard fitz Rogo. 'They are not fit to live and if we, as guardians of the faith, failed to take proper action, then I do not condemn the townsfolk for taking the law into their own hands.'

'A failure, I regret having to point out to you, de Alençon, was in no small measure due to your unhelpful leadership at the inquisition on Wednesday, archdeacon,' added Ralph de Hospitali waspishly.

John de Alençon remained silent, not wanting to fuel the tirade by responding, but de Baggetor was unwilling to let the matter drop.

'Not only have they arrested two men in holy orders, but they set the blasphemers free – and in fact assisted them in leaving by ship!' he blustered. 'How do you view that piece of defiance to the Church, archdeacon?'

Questioned directly in that way, de Alençon had no option but to reply.

'There seems no doubt, according to eyewitnesses among the stevedores and ship-men on the other vessel, that Rugge and de Bere were the instigators of the riot and were central to the seizure and threatened execution of the alleged heretics, so is it at all surprising that the sheriff's men arrested them?'

'Not alleged heretics – they were self-confessed heretics!' interrupted de Hospitali hotly. 'They boasted as much before us on Wednesday.'

The archdeacon ignored this and carried on. 'Those men had committed no civil or criminal offence and were quite entitled to go about their business until such time as the bishop's court passed a judgement upon them. And part of that business was the right to take ship, if they so chose.'

This was too much for Robert de Baggetor, who almost exploded into loud speech. 'Brother John,

229

you seem suspiciously sympathetic to these wretches who defy the might of the Church of Rome! Are you losing your faith, man, to be so partial to the cause of those who would mock and seek to bring down the very structure that for over a thousand years has steered the unlettered common herd in the true path of Christianity?'

Pale with anger, the archdeacon turned upon his fellow canon. 'I beg you, do not dare to question my faith and my devotion to the Church I have served all my life! But like our Saviour Himself, I seek to tread the path of justice and compassion. As yet, those men have been convicted of nothing and do not deserve to be hounded by a mob, half of them drunk, who wished to string them up from the nearest tree.'

He pointed a quivering finger at de Baggetor. 'And whether you like it or not, those same men are avowed Christians, who merely wish to think their own thoughts about their faith and not be dictated to by the likes of us as to how their minds must function!'

De Baggetor laughed sardonically. 'The next thing you will be advocating will be a translation of the Vulgate into English and then teaching the peasants how to read it!' he sneered. 'Would such a catastrophe please you, archdeacon? It would make us priests redundant as their means of intercession with the Almighty!'

William de Swindon, who seemed to be a late convert to the anti-heretic camp, broke in to stop this personal squabble between de Alençon and de Baggetor. 'Let us direct our minds to the immediate problems, brothers. We seem to have lost those four men who came before us, though I understand that the fifth, the fuller Algar, chose to remain in the city, no doubt to defy us further.'

'He will be attended to very soon,' interjected Robert de Baggetor. 'I have already given instructions to our proctors' men to seize him and place him in the cells in the Close.'

The archdeacon, his sense of justice overriding his caution, objected at once. 'At the end of that inquisition, I gave orders to the bailiffs that the five men be guarded from public assault. Now you are going back on our direction not to let them be interfered with.'

'It was not *our* direction, brother – it was entirely *yours*!' snapped de Hospitali. 'Personally, I would have welcomed the crowd stoning them to death, as the Old Testament prescribed for those who denied the Lord God.'

The archdeacon could see that it was futile to again point out that the accused men had denied no one except the autocracy of Rome and were equally as good Christians as the entire chapter of canons. He was conscious that he had already put himself in a difficult position and there was no point in making matters worse.

The other proctor, William de Swindon, returned to his practicalities. 'The other aspect is most urgent. We have two men now incarcerated in the castle gaol, who, however hasty their actions yesterday, are still in holy orders. I hear that they will be brought before the sheriff court and thence probably to the next Eyre of Assize, though God knows when that will be. Are we to let them rot there without protest?'

A gabble of indignation rippled around the circle of priests, but again Robert de Baggetor raised a hand and took over the proceedings. 'By no means! I am sending our law deacon up to Rougemont this very morning, with a demand to the sheriff that they be released forthwith into our custody. They can be lodged in the proctors' cells for a time, though I see no reason why they should not be dealt with very

231

leniently, as they were only doing what they saw as God's will.'

'Who exactly are they?' asked one of the canons who had not previously spoken. He was Jordan de Brent, the cathedral librarian and archivist, an elderly, amiable man, more immersed in books and manuscripts than with everyday events.

'One is Reginald Rugge, a lay brother who helps out at St Olave's Church,' replied fitz Rogo. 'The priest there, Julian Fulk, came to see me last night, entreating me to help in getting Rugge released.'

'But St Olave's is not part of our cathedral enclave,' objected the archivist gently. 'It is not even within the jurisdiction of our bishop, for it belongs to St Nicholas Priory, which itself is a cell of Battle Abbey in Sussex.'

There were some muted mutterings among the others about the old canon being more concerned with church history than current emergencies, but de Baggetor ignored them. 'All the more reason for us to assist them, as it might take weeks to get any action from Sussex. This Alan de Bere is in holy orders and deserves our protection, whatever his affiliation. That goes for the other one, too.'

'But everyone knows that he is half-mad!' objected the precentor, Thomas de Boterellis. 'A monk he may have been, but he is surely crazed, running around the city in a ragged habit, talking to himself!'

'He still wears the tonsure and is one of our brothers,' declared fitz Rogo, conveniently forgetting that Alan de Bere had been an embarrassment to the clergy for half a decade. He was obviously slightly deranged, but had been given a menial job in the cathedral to occupy some of the time in which he would otherwise be on the streets chanting some incomprehensible message of salvation and damnation that fermented in his disordered mind.

John de Alençon, who had no disagreement with this desire to retrieve the two men from the secular powers, felt on safer ground when he asked if they were going to plead 'benefit of clergy' to get them released.

'Of course, there is no question of them not being eligible,' snapped de Baggetor. 'Rugge has some education, for all that he is now but a lay brother. He can read and write a little, and even the mad monk can easily deliver the "neck verse".'

To prove they were entitled to plead 'benefit of clergy', the supplicant had be able to read, a prerogative almost confined to the clergy – but in fact if they could recite a short section of the scriptures, that was sufficient. As it might save them a hanging in the king's courts, it became known as the 'neck verse', usually a few words from the fiftieth Psalm of the Vulgate, though many illiterates merely memorised the words.

The discussion in the chapter house continued about the details of getting the two men released and also about further action against suspected heretics.

'We have had four of them snatched from under our noses, but there are many more lurking in the shadows,' proclaimed Richard fitz Rogo. 'The list compiled by our bailiffs contains another six names, and more will be unearthed as the days go by.'

De Baggetor turned to the bishop's chaplain. 'It is still urgent that we have a meeting with His Grace as soon as he returns to Exeter,' he said aggressively, as if it was the chaplain's fault that the bishop was so often absent. 'We shall not let these other heretics slip through our fingers so easily!'

John de Wolfe needed to go to Stoke again to see how his brother was faring, but he knew that it would

be a grave mistake not to be at home when Matilda
returned. He rose at dawn and had his breakfast of
honeyed oatmeal gruel, bread and cheese in Mary's
kitchen-shed, reassuring her that her mistress had
agreed to come home that day. Like his maid, John's
feelings about his wife's return were mixed – though
she was cantankerous, sullen and bad-tempered,
both of them were used to her being there, and the
gloomy house seemed strange without her brooding
presence.

'Make something she particularly likes for dinner,'
John suggested to her. 'That should please her after
the dishes she probably suffered at her brother's
house, as he has a lousy cook!'

He wanted to go up to St John's to see how Thomas
was getting on, but again was afraid that Matilda might
turn up when he was out.

'Why don't you go up to North Gate Street with old
Simon and offer to carry her bundles home?' suggested
Mary. 'That might put her in a better mood.'

As usual, she talked good sense, and John
commandeered the old man who chopped their
firewood and cleaned the pigs and privy. Marching
ahead of Simon, he went through the streets, full of
people doing their morning shopping at the stalls. As
his servant was stone-deaf, he had no need to attempt
any conversation and they arrived at the de Revelle
house just in time to find Matilda leaving. Lucille
was staggering under an armful of cloaks and gowns,
but his wife had left behind a large bundle of her
belongings to be collected later.

There was no sign of Richard de Revelle, for which
John was grateful, and in silence they set off for
Martin's Lane, Matilda grasping his arm possessively
to show the city that she was still married to the second
most important law officer in the county.

The two servants trudged along behind as they pushed through the crowds in the narrow streets, Matilda using her free hand to lift her skirts up out of the ordure that covered the ground, especially where the central gutter was filled with a sluggish ooze of debris that included dead rats and an occasional decomposing cat.

When they reached the tall house in Martin's Lane, John gallantly held the door open for her and at last got a muttered word of thanks. The weather was dull, though not particularly cold, but Mary had a good fire blazing in the hearth, and Matilda sank into her favourite monks' chair with a sigh of relief.

'John, send Mary with a hot posset for me,' she commanded, knowing that for a time, at least, he would be polite and subservient. 'Then I shall go up to my solar to make sure that that stupid Lucille puts my clothes properly in the chests.'

He did as he was ordered. When his wife had had her cup of hot milk curdled with wine and spiced with cinnamon, he announced that he must go to his chamber in the castle to attend to his duties, omitting to mention that he was first calling to see Thomas, which might have jolted her out of her present relatively benign mood.

At the little hospital, he found his clerk remarkably recovered and could only hope that his brother William might be making a similar improvement.

'God must have listened to all the prayers for me offered up by so many good people,' said Thomas brightly, crossing himself as he spoke. He was sitting on the edge of his mattress, but had been walking about the ward, visiting other sick people to deliver comfort and consolation in his usual selfless fashion.

'Your colour has greatly improved, Thomas!' said his master, giving him the present he had bought on the way, a fresh meat pasty from one of the cook-stalls. Certainly, the yellow colour of his skin had faded, though there was still a noticeable tinge in the clerk's eyes.

'I am almost well again, Crowner,' agreed Thomas eagerly. 'Brother Saulf, who has been kindness itself, told me that I may go home in the next day or two. I am now no danger to anyone else, he says, so I can return to my duties later next week.'

John shook his head at his clerk's enthusiasm. 'You came very near to death, Thomas. I am amazed that you have recovered so quickly. But do not strain your good fortune. You must rest until you feel quite well again. Gwyn and I can manage, though I admit we miss your prowess with a pen and parchment.'

Thomas wriggled with happy embarrassment at this rare praise, then went on to enquire after William de Wolfe's health.

'I am riding down there to see him after dinner and will be back tomorrow morning,' replied John. 'I fear that when I last saw him he had not made your miraculous recovery, but your progress gives me more hope.'

'Brother Saulf was also surprised by the way the fever subsided and my colour faded,' said the clerk. 'Unfortunately, two of those poor people in here who also had the yellow curse died, but five more are recovering, two almost as rapidly as myself. The ways of the Almighty are certainly mysterious.'

John grunted. 'It's bloody mysterious why He sends the plague in the first place!' he muttered, but not wanting to offend his clerk's deep religious feelings he changed the subject and told Thomas all that had happened down on the quayside.

'No doubt the cathedral will be clamouring for the release of these two scurrilous bastards who fomented the riot,' he concluded.

'I know of that monk Alan de Bere,' said Thomas. 'There is no doubt that his mind is unhinged, poor fellow. He was ejected from St Nicholas Priory several years ago for beating up another brother over some obscure point of religious belief. It was not the first offence, it seems, for he was originally in the mother house at Battle, but was posted out of there for some such similar offence.'

'What about this Reginald Rugge?' asked the coroner. 'Do you know anything of him?' Thomas was usually a mine of information about all things ecclesiastical, but this time he had little to impart.

'I know the name and have seen him about the town – but your wife might know more, for he has some connection with St Olave's. He helps the priest keep the place in order and assists in a lowly way at the Mass. I think he actually lives in a hut at the back of the church.'

They talked for a little while longer, though de Wolfe was a poor sick visitor, never knowing what to say. Thomas told him that the monks at St John's had kept abreast of the outbreaks of plague in the locality, and it seemed that no new cases had been reported for a few days, raising hopes that the present epidemic might be over.

He left the priory after seeking out Brother Saulf to thank him for his care of Thomas and leaving some more money as a thank-offering, then went up to Rougemont. Here he found Gwyn playing dice in the guard-room with Sergeant Gabriel and a couple of soldiers. They chatted for a few minutes about the drama down on the quayside the previous day, and Gabriel confirmed that the *Saint Augustine* had sailed on the tide with the fugitives without any further interference.

'What about those two troublemakers you have in the undercroft?' asked the coroner.

'Ha! The cathedral have already demanded their release,' growled the sergeant disgustedly. 'Some lawyer fellow from the cathedral is with the sheriff at this very minute.'

Hearing this, de Wolfe hurried across the inner ward to the keep and clattered up the wooden steps to the high entrance door. In the sheriff's chamber he found the weaselly deacon from the bishop's palace seated across the table from Henry de Furnellis. The sheriff looked relieved to see the coroner walk in.

'John, I'm glad to see you! It seems that the cathedral want me to release those two instigators of yesterday's riotous assembly.'

De Wolfe had half-expected this turn of events, as he knew that the Church was jealous of their jurisdiction and objected on principle to the secular authorities dealing with anyone with the hair shaved from the top of their heads. But from sheer perversity, he did not want to make it easy for them and immediately objected.

'How can that be, sheriff? These two ruffians are charged with serious offences. Encouraging citizens to become an unruly mob, to assaulting and unlawful imprisonment, to grievous bodily harm – and if they had not been stopped in time, to murder by hanging!'

He winked at Henry, out of sight of the deacon, and the sheriff carried on with giving the man a hard time.

'Yes, that is indeed the case, Sir John! They must be brought before the king's justices or his Commissioners, who will probably get to Exeter within the next few months or at most a year!'

'That is not acceptable!' squeaked the lawyer, a drab little fellow by the name of Roger de Boltebire. 'The bishop will not countenance such a delay. These men are in holy orders and must be tried by a consistory court held by the bishop's chancellor.'

John decided to persecute de Boltebire a little further by contradicting him.

'Several years ago, Bishop Marshal agreed that he would renounce his ecclesiastical jurisdiction for the most serious offences – which these most certainly are.'

De Boltebire waved his hands vigorously in denial of John's provocation. 'That is not strictly true, sir. He said he would allow it for crimes committed within the cathedral precinct, which as you well know is outside the control of the city and county authorities.'

The sheriff shrugged. 'Then serious offences committed down on the quayside, far away from the cathedral, are even more correctly dealt with by our secular courts!'

'No, no, no!' howled the deacon. 'I am instructed to say that if you are unwilling to allow "benefit of clergy" in this matter, we will take it to the Archbishop in Canterbury!'

'Who is Hubert Walter, also the king's Chief Justiciar, the head of the legal system in England,' said John mischievously. He knew this was a contest they could not win, once the bishop returned, but was determined to make the clergy work for their success.

But the decision was the sheriff's, not his, and after a further period of wrangling Henry de Furnellis gave in, as John knew he had little choice.

'But how do we know they are really in holy orders?' demanded the coroner, awkward to the last. 'Anyone can shave their head or put on a monk's habit.'

There was a further argument about proving their literacy and being able to read the Vulgate, but by then Henry had tired of the game.

'Take the damned fellows, will you! They've had a taste of prison down below, under Stigand's tender care for a night, so that alone might curb their desire for rabble-rousing.' Stigand was the evil, obese gaoler in the cells under the keep, a sadistic moron who revelled in inflicting the tortures of the Ordeal. Roger de Boltebire jumped to his feet, eager to leave these two big men who enjoyed baiting him.

'I'll send up the two proctors' bailiffs to take them back under guard. They will be lodged in the cells in the Close.'

'Sheer luxury compared with our accommodation here,' grinned the sheriff.

While John was helping Matilda to settle back in Martin's Lane, a man on remand for robbery with violence decided to turn 'approver', choosing to try to avoid execution by turning 'king's evidence' against his accomplices, who had escaped when he himself was arrested by the hue and cry.

So the coroner spent the rest of the morning in the warder's tiny room at the base of one of the towers of the South Gate, which acted as the city gaol. The few cells in the keep of the castle were for short-term prisoners and those to be subjected to the tortures of the Ordeal, but suspects awaiting trial at the burgess courts, the sheriff's county court or the very intermittent Eyres and Commissioners' courts were housed in the South Gate.

John's function was to take his confession for eventual submission to the royal justices and, in the absence of Thomas, he had one of the sheriff's clerks to make a record.

As the terrified man's confession was punctuated by sobbing, screaming and grovelling on his knees before the coroner, the process took up most of the time until dinner, when John went back to Martin's Lane. Treading delicately, he managed to survive the meal without any major outburst or denunciation from his wife, before announcing that he must go again to Stoke to visit his brother.

'It is too late for me to go there and then return tonight,' he said cautiously. 'I will have to stay with my family and come back early in the morning.'

He expected Matilda to launch into her usual whining about being left alone once again – not that she ever relished his company when he was there, he thought bitterly. But she made no protest as she informed him that it mattered little, as she had an important meeting at St Olave's early that evening.

'Father Julian has called his congregation together to organise a protest to the canons about the shockingly lenient way in which those heretics were allowed to escape!' she said in the strident tones of a determined campaigner. 'We are going to send a deputation to demand proper action against this hateful seed of ungodliness that is being allowed to take root in our city! Some of the canons are of a like mind, but we need to influence the bishop into taking a firmer stand, as the Holy Father has commanded!'

Glad that his wife's new-found crusade was at least turning her attention off himself, he encouraged her to tell him more.

'Is this Julian Fulk's own idea?' he asked. 'Or are all the parish priests being encouraged to do the same?'

She gnawed some more meat from the capon's leg she was holding before replying. 'The idea was suggested to him by our neighbour, Doctor Clement,' she admitted. 'He is a forthright man with increasing influence in the town, and no one else I know has greater devotion to the well-being of the Holy Church.'

De Wolfe held his tongue but thought that it was a pity that the physician did not use some of this enthusiasm to help the poorer people when they needed medical aid.

241

As soon as his wife had lumbered up to her solar to sleep off the effects of a large meal, John collected Odin from Andrew's stables and began his journey down to Stoke-in-Teignhead. On previous trips he had seen no sign of footpads on the road, so he decided against taking Gwyn as an escort, as with Thomas out of action there was no one else to attend to any coroner's business if some new case cropped up. With the weather cool, but dry and frost-free, the going was good, and he covered the thirteen miles to Dawlish at a steady trot in three hours, stopping once at an alehouse to water Odin and himself.

Riding resolutely through the little port without diverting to Hilda's house, he reached the River Teign to find the tide had not dropped far enough on the ebb to ford across, so he led his horse on to the flat-bottomed ferry and paid a penny to cross to Shaldon with dry legs.

Soon afterwards, he was riding into Stoke, nestling in its sheltering valley, and turned into the manor yard with some trepidation, unsure of what he might find. He left Odin with one of the stable boys and hurried into the square-built manor house. His mother and her steward were coming to meet him, and from their expressions he knew that, unlike with Thomas, no miraculous cure could be expected.

'How is he?' he asked as soon as he had hugged and kissed his mother and sister, who had hurried out of William's sickroom on hearing John arrive.

'Very little changed, I'm afraid,' said Enyd sadly. 'The yellowness has faded somewhat and he is half-conscious some of the time.'

He followed them into the sickroom, where the steward's wife was bathing William's brow with scented water. His brother looked haggard and drawn, cheekbones standing out under stretched skin, giving his face almost the appearance of a skull. His eyes were half-open, but they were dull and failed to focus on John, even when he stood over him and spoke softly to him.

'We had an apothecary over from Totnes yesterday,' said Evelyn. 'A sensible man, but he admitted there was little he could do. He said the actual plague seems to have receded, but that it must have damaged the balance of William's humours.'

John sat on a stool alongside the bed for a time, holding one of his brother's bony hands and talking quietly to him. He spoke of their boyhood together, their adventures in the surrounding woods and the ponies they had ridden, but William made no sign of understanding what he said. Eventually, John went back into the hall for a meal and to discuss domestic matters and the running of the manor.

'So far, our steward, bailiffs and reeves have coped well, both here and at Holcombe,' said his mother. 'But soon there will have to be decisions made about the ploughing and what stock can be kept over the winter. Without William, we are not sure that we can make the right decisions.'

'I will do what I can to help, Mother,' said John. 'But I am no farmer, God knows!'

He stayed another hour, but there was nothing useful he could do, apart from listen to the steward and bailiff as they tried to explain the rudiments of estate management to him. It was dusk when he set off again, this time aiming only to ride the few miles back to Dawlish. The tide had dropped in the meanwhile and he was able to ride Odin in the twilight across the river, between the sandbanks. Then slowly and carefully he traced his way back along the coastal track to Dawlish, thankful for a half-moon shining in a clear sky.

Hilda was surprised to see him turn up on her doorstep in the dark, but nonetheless delighted. When he had settled Odin in a nearby livery stable, he came back for another meal in Hilda's kitchen, before spending a blissful night in her bed up in the solar.

Just as the coroner was sloshing his way across the shallows of the River Teign, back in Exeter two score parishioners were converging on the small church of St Olave. They assembled expectantly on the earthen floor of the nave, beaten rock-hard by generations of worshipping feet. Some were there because of their obedience to Father Julian's summons, others from a burning antipathy to heretics – and the remainder out of sheer curiosity. Matilda was escorted in by Clement and Cecilia, whom she had met as they all came out of their front doors. She had a ready-made excuse for her husband's absence, by explaining that he had to go to his manor to visit his very sick brother, which set Cecilia off on an anxious enquiry as to how William was progressing. Matilda had no real idea, but muttered some platitudes until she could change the subject.

'I think it very virtuous of your husband to encourage our reverend father to call this meeting,' she said earnestly to Cecilia. 'I wish more eminent people in the city would show such public spirit.'

The doctor's wife made no reply, but looked at Clement as if to pass on the burden of response to him, which he gladly took on.

'I *suggested* it, rather than merely encouraging the good priest,' he said smugly. 'It is time that some firm action was taken, after the fiasco of that enquiry and then the blasphemers being allowed to walk free and vanish from the country.'

He assumed an expression of sad piety as he continued. 'I regret to say that the law officers, including your husband Sir John, did not come out well from that episode.'

Matilda tried hard to conceal her anger, mainly directed at John. He had shamed her before this devout physician, who was gently, but pointedly, condemning her own husband. But some of her ire was kept for Clement himself, for being so insensitive as to publicly criticise her spouse. She tried to recover some merit for de Wolfe and regain her own lost face.

'It is difficult for him, sir! He is a senior law officer, sworn to uphold the King's Peace. Whatever his own feelings might be, he has to abide by the statutes set down by his masters in London and Rouen.'

'I am sure Clement was aware of that,' hastily broke in Cecilia, anxious to cover any embarrassment caused by the doctor's gaffe. 'The Church and the state are always uneasy partners, as old King Henry discovered at Canterbury.'

Any further awkwardness was thankfully erased by the appearance of the parish priest, who appeared from the tiny sacristy to stand on the single step that separated chancel from nave. Julian Fulk was a short, rotund man, unctuous in manner and full of his own self-importance, though secretly frustrated by his lack of advancement in the Church, feeling that he had the potential to be a canon or even a bishop and resenting being kept back in one of the smallest churches in the city. He seized every opportunity to make his presence known and saw this current heretic scare as another chance to make his name before the more senior figures at the cathedral.

Fulk raised his arms to command silence, the embroidered chasuble over his white alb rising like a pair of wings. Then a sonorous stream of Latin emerged from his mouth, which, apart from the physician, not a single person present could understand, but assumed it was a prayer.

Reverting to English, he asked for God's blessing on those present and their families and added a profound wish that the yellow plague would now leave them in peace. Round-faced and completely bald-headed, apart from a narrow rim of sandy hair, the priest then launched into a tirade against those in the city and the surrounding countryside who were denying the right of the Holy Church to mediate with God on their behalf. There was nothing new in what he had to say, but he was a good orator and a number of the congregation began mouthing 'Amens' and other more earthy condemnations of the blasphemers.

'The ease with which these disciples of the devil escaped any justice cannot be tolerated,' declaimed Fulk as he wound up his exhortations. 'Though the bishops, the archdeacons and the canons are the captains of our faith, we are the army they lead and we must impress upon them that we desire that this corruption in our midst is stamped out!'

After more in this vein, the portly priest made a beckoning gesture at the front row and invited Clement of Salisbury to stand alongside him on the chancel step.

'We are fortunate in having not only a renowned physician in our congregation, a true disciple of St Luke in the healing arts, but one who is also a true soldier of Christ, unafraid to speak his mind and to demand the action we wish to see employed against these evil-minded heretics!'

He stepped to one side to allow Clement centre place, and the doctor threw out his arms as if to bless the audience and summon down the angels at the same time. Tonight he was soberly dressed in a long black tunic, without the central white apron that was affected by many physicians. His head was encased in a tight-fitting helmet of white linen, tied under the chin.

If Julian Fulk's exhortation was forceful, it was nothing compared with the dramatic version which Clement delivered. Starting in measured tones, he rapidly escalated his passion until he was almost manic in his condemnation of anyone who diverged more than a hair's-breadth from the tenets and ceremonies of the Holy Roman Church. Displaying a wide knowledge of the various types of heresy, he castigated Cathars, Waldensians, Gnostics and Pelagians, working himself up into a frenzy of denunciation that drew cries of agreement from the listeners. Matilda was afraid that her neighbour, red in the face, wide-eyed and with a trace of spittle at the corners of his mouth, might drive himself into an apoplexy. Glancing sideways at Cecilia, who stood alongside her, she saw that the wife was tight-lipped and rigid. Assuming that the younger woman was afraid for her husband's health, she laid a reassuring hand on her arm, but then realised that the expression on Cecilia's face was not one of concern, but disapproval or even hatred.

Surprised and concerned, Matilda took her hand away and turned back to watch Clement, who was coming to the crescendo of his diatribe, demanding that anyone suspected of heresy should be immediately arraigned before the bishop and subjected to the most rigorous penalties.

'Excommunication, even anathema, is utterly insufficient!' he thundered. 'Those who undermine God's holy institutions must be removed so that they can cause no more mischief! We all know and accept that if a lad steals a pot worth more than twelve pence, he is hanged! So is the price of a pot more important than preserving our beloved Church?'

He raised clenched fists over his head and bellowed his final words. 'They must be expunged from the earth! In the days of the prophets, those who worshipped false gods were stoned to death – surely we must rid ourselves of this contagion, which is more dangerous than the yellow plague itself, by the gallows or the stake! Not let them sail away on the first convenient ship!'

To cheers and shouted support, he stepped down from the chancel, allowing the priest to return and hold up his hands for order.

'Tomorrow, we will progress together down to the cathedral and stand outside the chapter house when chapter ends, so that we may respectfully approach the canons with our requests. We all know that there are many more blasphemers lurking in and around the city, and they must not be allowed to get away with their evil activities again!'

He gave a rapid blessing in Latin, and immediately many of the crowd clustered around Clement, showering him with congratulations and promises of support. Matilda noticed that a sizeable minority did not do so and quietly made their way out of the little church, looking uneasy at some of what had been said. She turned to Cecilia, who had made no effort to push her way to the front to join her husband among his circle of admirers.

'The doctor is certainly an accomplished and forceful speaker,' she said to Cecilia. 'Though he is a renowned physician, he told us that he had once wished to take holy orders. I feel his sermons would have been outstanding.'

Clement's wife turned a sombre face to Matilda. 'And I feel that his passions and obsessions will one day be the death of him.'

*   *   *

In the early morning the little maid Alice stared at John coyly as she made them oat porridge and poached eggs, by now accepting that this menacing-looking man was entitled to sleep with her beloved mistress. Hilda walked him to the stable to watch his destrier being saddled, now becoming indifferent to any gossip that their affair might arouse among the neighbours.

'I will go down to Stoke often, now that it seems likely that the plague has run its course,' she promised. 'I will try to help your mother and sister as much as I can, though I am no nurse.'

The handsome blonde rested her hand on his as he prepared to leave. 'Don't worry about matters down here, John,' she said reassuringly. 'I'll make sure that my father keeps closely in touch with the bailiff at Stoke to make sure that they get any help they need from Holcombe.'

With a heavy heart at leaving behind all the people he loved, John hoisted himself on to Odin's broad back and turned his head towards Exeter. He reached the city a few hours later, with some of the morning left, so he called at Martin's Lane before going up to Rougemont. His main purpose was to prove to Matilda that he was back home, trusting that she would believe that he had made a swift journey from Stoke, rather than the shorter one from Dawlish. However, there was no sign of her, and Mary informed him that his wife had gone to the cathedral.

'The mistress was full of this meeting at St Olave's when she got home last evening,' reported the cook-maid. 'She even deigned to speak to me about it. It seems that Clement the physician was the leading figure. They have all gone off to petition the canons after the chapter meeting.'

De Wolfe glowered at her as if it was her doing. 'Why is this damned doctor sticking his nose into Church business?' he growled. 'Let him keep to his pills and potions. The bloody canons have got enough power and money to look after their own affairs, without him meddling!'

'From what your wife said, he wants to hang all heretics,' replied Mary. 'I gather from gossip in the markets that you and the sheriff are not looked on with much favour for letting those men on the quayside get away.'

John made a rude noise to indicate his indifference to public opinion. 'Those rioters were just about to string them up from a tree when we rescued them! I only hope the one man that stayed behind is lying low, or his life won't be worth a clipped ha'penny!'

He marched out of the house bound for the castle, intending to call in to see Thomas on the way. As he passed the door of his neighbour's house, it opened and Cecilia emerged so opportunely that he suspected that she had been looking out for him since he had come from the stables opposite.

'Sir John, can I detain you for just a moment?' she asked in a low voice, but with an urgent ring to it. He bowed his head politely to her and moved across to stand with her on the doorstep. She did not invite him inside, and from her quick, nervous glance back into the house, she seemed not to want to speak within the hearing of her handmaiden.

'Can I be of some service to you, mistress?' he enquired courteously, always glad to be close to an attractive woman, especially if he could gain her favour. She wore no cover-chief, and her dark hair was plaited into two long ropes, each hanging down her bosom, the ends encased in silver tubes.

Standing in the cool autumn air, she wore a fur-edged blue velvet pelisse over a long gown of fine cream wool. John thought she looked delightful, and if he had not long left his lovely Hilda he might have been dangerously smitten.

'It is a delicate matter, but I know you for a discreet and considerate man, with a well-deserved reputation in this county.'

Her large eyes regarded him appealingly, but he saw that there was nothing of the coquette about her manner, for she looked genuinely worried.

He waited expectantly for her to continue, but for a long moment she remained silent, as if summoning up courage.

'I am concerned about my husband, sir,' she said hesitantly.

'Is he unwell – or in some kind of trouble?' asked de Wolfe with a frown of concern.

'His body is in good health, thank God. But my concern is for his mind and what trouble that may lead him into.'

John was puzzled – though he disliked Clement for a being a supercilious snob, he did not see him as either a madman or an evildoer. He waited for her to explain further.

'As you may know from your goodwife, Clement is very much concerned with this problem of heresy in the city,' she began in a low voice. 'He has always been of an unusually devout nature, passionately concerned for our religion. But I fear that it has become an obsession and I am deeply worried about where it may lead him.'

He stood close to her and, though she was tall for a woman, he looked down into her upturned face, which was tight with suppressed emotion.

'You are no doubt referring to this meeting last night in the church,' he said. 'I understand it was held mainly at your husband's instigation, but I have no knowledge of what transpired there, apart from a few words Matilda offered to our maid.'

Cecilia sighed. 'He virtually took over the meeting! After Father Fulk gave a strong, though reasoned condemnation of the heretics, Clement became an impassioned orator, designed to whip up the anger of the congregation against these misguided people. He even demanded that they should be killed, drawing on biblical images of stoning to death!'

She shook her head and de Wolfe saw tears appearing in the corners of her eyes. 'I sometimes fear for his sanity, Sir John! Though he can be cold and calculating, especially in his dealing with his patients – and with me, for that matter – once his religious zeal is aroused, he becomes a different man!'

John resisted an impulse to put a reassuring arm around her shoulders, in case Matilda had chosen to appear at that moment. 'Is there anything I can do to help?' he asked lamely.

Cecilia dabbed her nose with a lacy kerchief which she pulled from her sleeve.

'He is leading this delegation of parishioners to demand that the cathedral takes sterner action against the heretics. He is there at the moment and I think your wife is also attending.' She sniffed back her tears. 'He wanted me to go with him, both to the church last night and now to the chapter house, but I refused. I do not want to be associated with a persecution that might lead to the deaths of people who only wish to follow their own roads to God. Clement was very angry with me, for not sharing his outrageous views.'

'He has not offered you any violence, I trust?' snapped John, his chivalrous senses at once alerted, but Cecilia shook her head.

'No, nothing like that. But I know you are of a like mind to myself over this issue, though I must warn you that many voices are being raised against you for it.'

'Is there nothing I can do?' he asked harshly. 'This distresses me greatly, to know that you are in such an unhappy situation.'

'You are a friend of the archdeacon, I know. He is also known to be moderate in his views, even though as a senior churchman his position is difficult. I thought perhaps you could warn him of my husband's extreme views and his somewhat unstable mind.'

John promised that he would use all the influence he had, though privately he was unsure whether John de Alençon was either willing or able to stand up against his fellow canons' thirst for blood, which would be greatly reinforced by Clement's obvious obsession and the groundswell he had whipped up among the public.

They spoke for another few moments, but then several groups of people came from both directions in Martin's Lane and it became difficult to continue this clandestine conversation. With a whispered 'thank you' and a quick press of his hand, Cecilia hurried back into her house and the door closed.

John regarded it thoughtfully for a moment, then loped off towards the High Street.

When he walked into the ward at St John's Hospital, he saw a complete stranger on the pallet that Thomas had occupied and for a sickening moment thought that his clerk might have had a sudden relapse and died. Then Brother Saulf hurried towards him from a nearby patient, his smile telling John that all must be well.

'He has gone home, Crowner! He insisted early this morning that he was restored to health, apart from his still-yellowed eyes.'

'Was he really fit to go?' asked de Wolfe, concerned for Thomas's well-being.

'To be honest, there was nothing more we could do here except try to make him rest – and we desperately need the space for other sufferers.'

'I suppose he's gone back to his lodgings?'

'Yes, I impressed on him the need to rest and take regular meals to restore his strength. He claims the cleric who shares his room will keep him fed.'

On his way up to the castle, John was determined to make sure than Thomas was looked after, so when he met Gwyn in the gatehouse chamber, he arranged with him for Martha or one of the serving maids at the Bush to go around to Priest Street twice a day with nutritious food. The Cornishman reassured him with a big grin of pleasure.

'Don't worry, Crowner, we'll see the little fellow is well fed. God knows his scrawny body could do with some fattening up!'

It was a great relief to both of them to know that their clerk seemed out of danger and likely to be back at work very shortly, in spite of the monk's exhortations to rest for a while.

They brought their minds back to the business of the day. In the absence of any new dead bodies, rapes or fires, Gwyn wanted to know what was to happen to the two instigators of the quayside riot.

'The sheriff has had to bow to the demands of the cathedral and give them back to the bishop's jurisdiction,' said John bitterly. 'Though, as usual, the bloody bishop is conspicuous by his absence and I doubt if he would be very interested in such mundane matters, when he has the politics of England to amuse him.'

The coroner rose from his bench at the mention of the two renegades.

'They were to be collected from the castle gaol yesterday. If they're still there, I'd like a word with the bastards before they leave. I still wonder if they were the ones who killed our three heretics.'

With Gwyn clumping behind him, he hurried down the stairs and out into the inner bailey, where a cold rain had begun to fall from a leaden sky. They strode across to the keep but, instead of climbing the wooden stairs to the hall above, went down a few stone steps to the undercroft, a crypt partly below ground which occupied the whole of the base of the keep. A gloomy, damp cavern with stone arches supporting the building above, it was part prison, part storehouse and part torture chamber. Ruled over by the sadistic Stigand, the gaol consisted of a few filthy cells locked behind a rusty iron grille that divided the undercroft into two halves.

As they reached the bottom of the steps, Gwyn bellowed out in the near-darkness, lit only by a couple of guttering pitch-flares stuck into rings on the walls.

'Stigand! Where are you, you fat evil swine?' The gaoler was not one of Gwyn's favourite people.

There was some grunting and shuffling and the man appeared from an alcove formed by one of the supporting arches. This was where he lived, between stone walls slimy with green mould, the floor covered with dirty straw. He had a hay mattress and a brazier for cooking and heating branding irons and the torture devices used in Ordeals.

The gaoler shuffled across to them, his flabby face appearing to join his gross body without the need for a neck. Two piggy eyes surveyed them and his loose lips quavered as he saw the coroner and his officer, as he had suffered from their tongue-lashings several times in the past.

'Are those two men still here, the ones who are going down to the cathedral proctors?' demanded de Wolfe.

Stigand noddcd, but said nothing, and ploddcd across towards the iron grille. This reached up to the low ceiling and had a gate in the centre, secured with a chain and padlock. They followed him, regarding with distaste the short and filthy tunic he wore over bare legs. His unshod feet were black with dirt, and his leather apron was spattered with dried stains, the nature of which John had no desire to contemplate.

A ring of keys hung from his belt; he took one to unlock the gate. 'They are in the first two cells,' he said thickly, speaking as if his tongue was too big for his mouth.

The two visitors went into the prison, where a short passage led between half a dozen crude cells, each with a door of rusty iron bars. Only the first on each side were in use and as soon as the coroner and his officer appeared, the occupants began shouting at them.

'I thought you were the proctors' men – where are they?' demanded Alan de Bere arrogantly. 'We don't want you bastards. We want to be taken out of here!'

Gwyn poked a brawny arm through the bars and hit the renegade monk in the chest, making him stagger backwards into the filthy alcove, where the only furnishings were a stone slab for a bed and a wooden bucket for slops.

'Watch your tongue, brother, else Stigand here might feel inclined to cut it out,' he said amiably.

De Wolfe turned to the other side, where Reginald Rugge was glowering at them through the bars.

'Talking of cutting out tongues,' said John, 'do you know anything about the death of Nicholas Budd? For if you do, your good bishop may be handing you back to us for hanging!'

Blustering, but uneasy at the prospect the coroner had forecast, Rugge loudly denied any knowledge of the bizarre killing of the woodworker.

De Wolfe swung around to Alan de Bere. 'And you, monk, did you take a knife to his throat? Or was it

Vincente d'Estcote you killed and left to be dropped into a plague pit?'

Rapidly, he went back to the lay brother. 'And was it you who took a trip to Wonford and stuffed a murdered man into a privy?'

John knew full well that he was unlikely to get a sudden confession from these men, but he always felt that if you shake a tree hard enough something might fall out.

When their loud protests of innocence had subsided, he changed the direction of his provocative questions.

'Right, if you are as white as the driven snow over those killings, then tell me instead who put you up to inciting this riot on the quayside, eh?'

Rugge grasped the bars of his cage and glowered at de Wolfe. He looked like some madman, with his tousled dark hair stiff with dirt from the cell, bits of straw sticking out at all angles.

'Why should anyone put us up to it?' he ranted. 'It is a Christian duty to cleanse the world of such vermin, who are increasing like the rats they are, procreating new blasphemers!'

Alan de Bere joined in from the other side, beating on the rusty iron barricade in his frenzy. 'We need no one to encourage us in our God-given task!' he brayed. 'The good canons and proctors do their best, but they are frustrated by such as you unbelievers.'

Rugge returned to the tirade. 'Even the bishop and his archdeacon are little help. They are too concerned with the trivial rituals of the cathedral and the finances of their treasury to bother with the cancer that is rotting the Holy Church in the shape of these heretics!'

The coroner was not impressed by their fervent denials. 'You were only too willing to murder those men on the wharf!' he shouted back at them. 'If I and other forces of law and order had not arrived in time, you would have hanged them out of hand! Is that the act of the Christians who you are so keen to defend? I thought that kindness and compassion was the code that they professed.'

Reginald Rugge had a ready answer for him. 'Like the compassion you Crusaders showed at Acre, when you and your king beheaded almost three thousand Saracen prisoners?'

'That was an entirely different matter; that was war!' retorted John, but he felt uneasy, as it was an episode that had shaken his respect for his hero, Richard Coeur de Lion. 'And anyway, as Mohammedans, were they not the ultimate heretics in your eyes?'

What promised to become a theological altercation conducted at the tops of their voices was interrupted by the sound of boots on the steps outside and calls for the gaoler. Stigand shuffled out through the gate and a moment later the two proctors' bailiffs appeared, clutching their long staves. Herbert Gale also had a coil of thin rope in his other hand. Like his colleague William Blundus, he was not pleased to see the coroner and his officer.

'These are our prisoners now, Sir John,' grated the senior bailiff with reluctant deference to the coroner's rank.

'And you are welcome to them, for now,' snapped de Wolfe. 'I suspect we may have the pleasure of their company here again, when the bishop decides to turn them over to the secular powers for sentencing.'

He said this more for his own satisfaction than in any hope of it being true, for he knew that the Church liked defying the king as a matter of principle, especially as Bishop Marshal was a supporter of Prince John in the latter's striving to depose his elder brother from the throne of England.

He stood aside with Gwyn as Stigand unlocked the chains around the two cell gates and let the prisoners out into the passage. They watched as Blundus took the rope from Herbert Gale and tied one end around the wrists of the wretched monk and the other in a similar fashion to those of Rugge.

'Come on, then, down to the Close with you!' commanded Herbert Gale, grabbing the centre of the rope and tugging the two men out into the undercroft. With a smirk of triumph at the coroner, Alan de Bere followed, stumbling alongside his fellow prisoner. With William Blundus bringing up the rear, they climbed the steps to the inner ward and vanished.

Gwyn spat contemptuously on the ground. 'Did you see the wink that bastard Blundus gave them as he tied them with those knots that a newborn babe could undo? I'll wager they'll be on the loose again before the sun rises tomorrow!'

At the dinner table John thought it politic not to mention to Matilda his meeting with Cecilia that morning, as it would only be asking for more sneers about his trying to inflict his lustful desires upon the fair lady. However, given what the physician's wife had had to tell him, he wanted to know what Clement had been saying in the chapter house that morning.

For once, Matilda was only too ready to talk. 'It was a great success, thanks be to the doctor!' she effused. 'Some of the canons were most receptive, and Robert de Baggetor actually apologised for the leniency with which those blasphemers were treated.'

Then she glared at him over her bowl of hare stew. 'Your friend the archdeacon tried to play down the whole affair and came in for some criticism – and your name was bandied about, much to my shame!'

He ignored this and asked, 'Did your delegation actually go into the chapter meeting?'

She shook her head sourly. 'The archdeacon forbade it. He said that it was a private conclave of the cathedral. We had to stand outside in the cold and petition the canons as they came out.'

De Wolfe speared a leg of hare with his eating-knife and added it to the broth in his pewter bowl. 'And what part did our neighbour play in this enterprise?' he asked in a neutral tone, not wanting to arouse any more of his wife's antagonism.

'He was our leader, rather than Father Julian,' she said proudly. 'He was most eloquent, polite and deferential to the higher churchmen, but still firm and persuasive. He emphasised that the population of the city were the soil from which the cathedral and other churches were nourished and it was only right that their voices were heard.'

'A courageous man,' observed John dryly. 'If he dared to voice opinions like that to most of the barons or the king's court, they would have had him hanged for sedition and fomenting revolution!'

Matilda failed to recognise his irony and preened herself in the reflected glory of the outspoken doctor. 'He is a remarkable man. I feel he is wasted as a physician, noble though that profession may be. He could have been a major cleric or an officer of state.'

'And what was the outcome of his efforts?' asked de Wolfe.

'Four or five of the canons, including the two who are proctors, promised to press the bishop most strongly as soon as he returns. They will insist on his arresting all known heretics and those suspected of such evil leanings, to bring them before a properly constituted ecclesiastical court – and to demand the most stringent penalties allowed by the Papal edicts. They will also insist on the proper harnessing of the secular powers, as prescribed by the Holy Father and his Legates.'

She scowled at her husband even more fiercely. 'So you and that lazy idiot of a sheriff will not be able to slide out of your responsibilities in future!'

Matilda suddenly seemed to realise that she was failing in her long-lasting campaign of ignoring her husband, after all the indignities and disappointments that he had heaped upon her. She fell silent and attacked an inoffensive boiled capon as if it was John himself, savagely tearing off a leg and gnawing at it to indicate that the conversation was at an end, but her husband doggedly pursued the subject, as he needed to know what was in store, especially if it led to more unrest, riots and even murders.

'So what will happen until the bishop eventually arrives home?' he asked with false innocence. 'Have they found more heretical victims to persecute?'

She stared at him suspiciously but put down her chicken leg to take a drink from her wine-cup. 'Canon William de Swindon, one of the proctors, told us that they will be sending out their bailiffs again, together with other agents, to seek informants who will trawl for unbelievers, both in the city and the county. They already know of one, the man who did not escape on that ship, no thanks to you!' she snapped. 'But they admit that until Bishop Marshal returns, there is little point in arresting him, as there is no competent tribunal able to try him.'

'I suppose they mean that fuller, whose name I forget,' he mused. Silently, he hoped the man would see the dangers and quietly leave the city, together with his family, if he had one. His wife made no reply, concentrating on her stew, her fowl and then the dessert that Mary brought in, a rosy almond cream with cinnamon and ginger.

After the meal, when Matilda had stumped off to the solar for her afternoon rest, John sat by his fire with a jug of ale, as the day had turned colder, though the rain had stopped. He mused that autumn had not yet seemed to make its mind up to turn into winter, the flurries of snow that fell a couple of weeks earlier having turned to cold rain and occasional fog. He threw on a couple more oak logs from the stack alongside the hearth, stamping out some glowing embers that flew from the fire on to the stone floor. That was one fad of Matilda's that was useful, as she had insisted on having the hall flagged, instead of the usual reeds or straw scattered over beaten earth. At least, he thought, it saves having the bloody stuff catching fire every time a spark spits out of the fire.

When his ale was finished, he prodded Brutus, who was snoring near his feet, and together they went out into the vestibule. Taking his cloak from a peg, John went out into the lane and looked hopefully at the house next door, but there was no sign of Cecilia. Though he had no real designs on her, the sight and company of a beautiful woman was always pleasant. Turning the other way, he followed his hound as he zigzagged his erratic path from bush to grave-mound across the cathedral Close.

As they passed St Mary Major, one of several small chapels in the precinct, he looked towards the small building that housed the proctors' men, but there was no sign of either the bailiffs or their prisoners. Like Gwyn, he suspected that their incarceration would be far from rigorous – and probably brief. He doubted whether they would ever appear before the Consistory Court to answer for their behaviour in leading a raucous crowd through the streets of the city – and in getting very close to lynching the heretics. With a mental shrug, he decided he had no interest in their fate, but he still suspected them of involvement in the deaths of the three murdered men, though neither had he eliminated the two proctors' bailiffs as candidates for those crimes.

As they neared Idle Lane, Brutus was confounded, as from long experience the dog turned into the lane from Priest Street, assuming that his master was going to the Bush. Instead, de Wolfe carried on down the slope, where some of the small houses were given over to lodgings for the more junior clerics from the cathedral. Every canon had a vicar and usually a young secondary living in his house as part of his establishment, but a number had no such patronage and found accommodation in Priest Street.

Thomas, since his restoration to favour after his years in the wilderness, shared a room there, and now John went to call upon him to make sure that he was well enough to fend for himself. Leaving his dog outside, he found the little clerk in his small chamber, eating heartily of the food that Martha had sent around from the tavern. Gwyn and his wife had already been to see that Thomas was comfortable back at his lodging, and John was sure that the little fellow would lack for nothing until he was fully recovered.

'Fresh mutton pasties, Crowner!' he said proudly. 'And a trout baked with chestnuts.' He displayed a wooden platter now devoid of all but a few crumbs and bones. 'Gwyn also sent a gallon jar of good cider.' He hoisted it on to the small table and insisted that John joined him in a cup of the powerful liquid.

'You have made a remarkable recovery, Thomas,' he said, lifting the mug in a toast to his clerk's continuing health. 'But you must not tempt Fate by assuming you are utterly recovered.'

'But I feel so much better, master!' protested Thomas. 'God must have decided that there are still tasks that I can usefully perform on this earth – and one of them is serving you to the best of my ability.'

John grinned at his clerk's earnest devotion. He certainly had recovered so rapidly that even the sceptical coroner wondered if the Almighty really had taken a hand in the cure. Apart from the lingering yellowness in his eyes, Thomas looked as well as he had ever seen him, probably helped by the mild euphoria that deliverance from death had generated. John only wished that a similar miracle could be worked upon his brother.

After they had talked for a little while, Thomas asked if any progress had been made on the murders while he had been lying in St John's.

'None at all, to my shame and regret,' admitted de Wolfe. 'I have four prime suspects, those bailiffs belonging to the proctors – and the two crazed fellows who have used holy orders to escape their involvement in the riot. But there could be others in the city demented enough to kill out of religious zeal.'

He was thinking of the ease with which Julian Fulk and the physician had roused the congregation at St Olave's into marching upon the cathedral chapter. If such a normally placid group of people could be so easily inflamed, then there might well be some others out there who would feel it their sacred duty to carry out God's will in exterminating any opposition to the Church.

In a little while the coroner left his clerk with further admonitions to build up his strength by eating well and resting, though he suspected that the conscientious little priest would soon tire of inaction and wriggle his way back to his former duties. Brutus was glad to see his master emerge from the house and even happier to find him turning into Idle Lane. The Bush was one the hound's favourite places, where

Gwyn or Martha would always find him a bone or scrap of meat as he lay under a table while the others talked above him.

Over a quart pot, de Wolfe and Gwyn discussed a few cases that were pending at the next county court and began to think about some others that would need work on them if the threatened Eyre of Assize came to Exeter in the near future.

'We really need Thomas back in action as soon as possible,' mused John. 'It's not the same trying to use the sheriff's clerks in his place; they don't understand the system like him.'

Gwyn was more realistic about the likelihood of the royal justices getting to the city. 'It takes them years sometimes. We'll have to make do with the Commissioners for a bit, I suspect. They're easier to deal with than these bloody barons, who want everything written down and presented to them in duplicate.'

As neither he nor the coroner could read, they were totally dependent on Thomas to keep their records and depositions in order.

De Wolfe told his officer what he had learned from Matilda about the deputation to the canons concerning the leniency they had shown the heretics. 'We are in the cathedral's bad books for letting them sail away – though I am not happy about the fate of that fuller who decided to brazen it out here. I hope we don't find *him* in a back lane with his voice-box lying alongside him!'

Gwyn nodded soberly. 'I hear from the gossip in the tavern here that the search for new heretics goes on. It seems that those damned proctors' men have openly offered money to anyone who will lead them to any folk suspected of deviating from the straight and narrow path laid down by Rome. I even heard that they

265

are going to question all those who do not regularly go to Mass on a Sunday!'

De Wolfe scowled at this. 'That will include you and me, Gwyn! Maybe I'd better accompany Matilda to the cathedral in the morning. It might save my neck in the long run!'

CHAPTER FOURTEEN

In which the coroner attends a fire

Partly because of his half-serious remark about going to Mass, but mainly because of his revived hope in the power of prayer to affect the course of his brother's sickness, John volunteered to escort his wife to the cathedral next morning. She grudgingly accepted, mildly surprised that for once she did not have to nag him into this duty.

The nine devotional offices each day were for the benefit of the clergy in their endless glorification of God and, except on high festival days, they were not concerned about the participation of the public, considering this to be the responsibility of the many parish priests. However, Masses were said for the locals before the small side altars, and so on Sunday morning de Wolfe found himself standing alongside Matilda in the base of the massive North Tower. This formed one arm of the cruciform plan of the cathedral begun by Bishop Warelwast some seventy years earlier.

There were two altars against one wall, one dedicated to the Holy Cross and the other to St Paul. A small crowd had gathered before the latter, and they joined the back of the score of townspeople as the

Mass began. The celebrant was a vicar-choral, aided by a secondary and another lay brother. John stared at him for a moment, hardly believing what his eyes told him, for the man was Reginald Rugge, whom he had last seen only the day before in the cells under Rougemont's keep.

Unable to say anything to his wife, he suppressed his annoyance with difficulty. The sight of this near-murderer, who should have been hanged or left to rot in chains in a dungeon, being allowed to serve at the altar as if he was the epitome of devotion and innocence, made him grind his teeth in frustration. Presumably, the other bastard, the mad monk Alan de Bere, was also at liberty somewhere, even after the promise that they would be incarcerated in the proctors' cells.

But he tried to dismiss the aggravation and concentrate on the actions and incomprehensible Latin of the priest, for it was for William's sake that he had come today, to offer up his stumbling prayers for his brother's recovery.

After the taking of the Eucharist, he marched Matilda back to the house, not a word passing between them, though she held his arm when in public view, in the usual possessive way she had, showing that she had a knight of the realm and a king's officer for a husband. As soon as they were in the vestibule, she dropped her hand from his elbow as if it had become red-hot and yelled for Lucille to come and help her out of her cloak and pelisse, ready for dinner.

John would like to have gone down to Canon's Row to talk to his friend John de Alençon, to learn what was happening about the heretic issue and the likely stance the bishop would take when he eventually returned – but he hesitated to do that when Matilda was around, as the archdeacon was certainly not in favour with her anti-heretic faction at the moment.

Mary soon arrived with the first remove, a small cauldron of steaming vegetable potage which she ladled into pewter bowls. Fresh bread sopped up the fluid, then she arrived with a 'charlet', a hash of chopped pork and egg, with milk and saffron, served on a bread charger. When this was demolished by the silent but hungry couple, the cook-maid brought her 'Great Pie', a small version of one usually served at Christ Mass. Under the crust, a mixture of chopped beef, chicken and pigeon was cooked with suet, spices and dried fruit. This was washed down with ale, but when a slab of cheese was produced, a jug of red wine from the Loire helped it to end the meal.

For once, Matilda could find no fault with the food and wordlessly pushed past Mary at the door, stumping up to her bed for the rest of the afternoon, until it was time to go to St Olave's. John followed her example, snoring before the hearth after he had finished what was left in the wine jug. Exhausted from his frequent journeys up and down to Stoke, he slept for hours.

When he awoke, to his surprise it was getting dark and he could hear his wife's voice berating Lucille about some offence against her hair or her dress. There was a narrow slit in the wall between the solar and the hall, high up to the side of the stone chimney-piece, which allowed a restricted view downwards and some sound, when the voices were shrill enough. He gathered that she was being got ready for yet another foray to praise the Lord at her favourite church in Fore Street. Shaking himself fully awake, he called softly to the dog and slipped out of the house, grabbing his cloak as he went, for there was a chill wind outside.

He made his usual journey down to the Bush and spent a pleasant couple of hours talking to Gwyn, Martha and a few drinking friends who were regulars at the alehouse. Some had been old soldiers, and John liked nothing better than to relive past campaigns in Ireland and France with them. Even Edwin forgot his religious mania for a time, to join in with reminiscences about the battle of Wexford, where he had lost his eye and damaged his foot.

Outside, a chill east wind had come up, but the taproom of the Bush was warm and snug, the atmosphere being a heady mix of woodsmoke, spilled ale and unwashed bodies. Martha brought him a trencher bearing a pork knuckle, with a side dish of fried onions, and after he had chewed off the succulent meat, he dropped the bony joint on to the rushes under the table, where Brutus slavered over it for the next hour.

This convivial evening was suddenly disturbed by a man bursting in through the front door, a familiar figure to John and Gwyn. It was the beanpole shape of Osric, one of the constables, obviously in a state of agitation as he stared around in the flickering light from the fire and the few rushlights on their sconces.

'Crowner, there you are!' he cried. 'There's a fire started in Milk Lane. You'd better come quickly!'

De Wolfe jumped up at once, as did Gwyn and a number of the other men. Fires in the city were a very serious matter, as many a town had been razed to the ground from a single house going ablaze. Part of the coroner's remit, irrespective of whether there were deaths, was to hold inquests into fires with a view to trying to prevent similar ones in the future.

The men hurried out, jostling through the door after the coroner, and began jogging to the end of Idle Lane, then up Smythen Street towards The Shambles. Darkness had fallen several hours earlier, and the pulsating glow from the fire was plainly visible over the roofs to the left. Before they reached The Shambles, Milk Lane branched off to the left, meeting Fore Street just above St Olave's Church on the other side.

As they ran, Osric was alongside John and panted out what he knew of the conflagration. 'It's in one of the dairy houses, halfway along. Thank God they are well spaced out because of the beasts, so there's less likelihood of the fire spreading!'

Milk Lane was named after the half-dozen cottages that kept cows and goats in their large yards, the tenants – or usually their wives – milking the animals and selling dairy products around the city streets. The beasts were fed with hay and cut grass and often taken on halters down to Bull Mead or Exe Island to crop the grass on the common land.

As they reached the corner, they saw a low dwelling well ablaze, with a crowd of people outside doing what they could to quell the flames. There was little water available, other than what could be carried in wooden and leather buckets from a couple of wells, but half a dozen men were dragging down the blazing thatch with long rakes.

As they hurried up to the cottage, Gwyn looked up at the sparks and shreds of burning straw that were flying into the lane.

'This damned wind is making it worse!' he shouted. 'Better if those men threw some water on to the thatch of the houses opposite. It's too late to save this one.'

Osric raced off on his long legs to divert some of the men with buckets, while John and his officer ran into the garden, keeping upwind of the flying embers. Cattle were lowing and goats bleated in fright, but those belonging to the burning house had been taken out into adjacent yards to keep them safe.

'Is there anyone inside?' he shouted to one of the neighbours labouring to pull off the burning straw.

The man, his hair singed and face blackened, came up close. 'It seems so, but we can't get near enough to get in until this thatch is taken down!'

He was right, as over the front door, the only entrance, a cascade of flame dripped down from the low roof.

'I'll try a window,' boomed Gwyn and lumbered off around the back, dodging sparks and handfuls of burning straw. He saw that a low shed, used as a dairy, projected from the back wall, but it had no door and was well alight. In each side wall of the cottage was a small window opening, firmly blocked by heavy shutters barred on the inside. John came after him with another man, and they cast around for some way to get into the building.

'Use this as a ram!' hollered de Wolfe, pointing to the ground. A stout feeding trough, made of long planks nailed together, lay on the earth. In a moment he and Gwyn had lifted it up and smashed one end against the shutters on the nearest window. These were strong and the bar inside must have been even stronger, but half a dozen blows shattered both the trough and the window frame. Gwyn tore at the splintered wood with his big hands and pulled the whole structure down on to the ground. He stuck his head into the ragged aperture, but withdrew it instantly, coughing and gasping, his eyes running with tears as a blast of hot, suffocating air rushed out to meet him.

John pulled him out of the way and shoved him back to recover his breath, while he grabbed an empty oat-bag that was lying on the ground nearby.

'Bring that bucket here!' he yelled to a man who was bringing water to throw on the fallen thatch. Dipping the coarse cloth in the bucket, he wrapped it around his head, with only a slit for his eyes, and advanced on the window. The burning straw above gave plenty of light, and in the moment before his eyes filled with tears he glimpsed several bodies lying inert on the floor inside.

Forced to draw back, he grabbed Gwyn's arm as he pulled off the soaking bag.

'There are people in there – at least one is a child!' he gasped. 'We must get in straight away!'

Two other men heard him and instantly set about knocking down the house wall. The window was set between two oak uprights that stretched from ground to eaves, the wall below being made of cob, a mixture of lime, mud and straw plastered on to a framework of woven wattle. The men ran to the front gate and rocked out one of the posts, a length of tree trunk the thickness of a man's thigh. Using this as a heavier battering ram than the trough, they rapidly smashed the brittle wall from between its supports, making a doorway out of the window.

Gwyn, the ends of his red hair and moustache singed from his earlier attempt, was first through, and he dashed in and grabbed the smallest body from the floor. A rain of burning and smouldering thatch floated down on him, but the main structure of rough rafters and hazel-withies was still intact, though beginning to burn through. As he came out with the inert little body, John and three more neighbours ran in and took out a larger child, then struggled out with two adults.

All were laid on the earth well away from the burning cottage, immediately surrounded by a ring of concerned men and women.

A quick examination in the flickering light soon confirmed the worst – all were undoubtedly dead. The wives began sobbing and wailing, especially over the pathetic bodies of the two children, a boy of about three and a girl of four years.

'They haven't been burned to death, thank God,' muttered Gwyn, trying to wrest some comfort from the tragedy. 'Look, they have no burns worth talking about, apart from what's fallen on them from bits of roof straw.'

John, saddened as much as any of them, nodded. Experience had taught them the signs of fatal burning, thankfully absent in these bodies.

'Look at the faces of the mother and father,' he murmured to one of the rescuers. 'Pink, that's what they get when they breathe in these noxious fumes.'

He stepped back and turned to the shocked neighbours, all the wives – and some of the men – openly crying at the tragedy. 'These are the folk who lived here?' he asked, just to officially confirm who they were.

A grizzled man wearing a smith's apron nodded. 'I live next door to them. My wife also keeps a couple of cows. These did the same, though Algar was a fuller, just as I am an ironworker in Smythen Street.'

John stared at him. 'Algar the fuller? This is the man?' He pointed down and then bent to get a better look at the face in the poor light, as the flames were now dying as all the thatch was pulled down.

'Yes, that's Algar, God rest his soul, even if he did have some strange ideas.'

'The same Algar who was hauled up before the cathedral canons last week?' persisted John.

The smith looked at him suspiciously. 'Do you think there's some connection, then?'

De Wolfe rubbed some smuts from his eyes. 'I don't know, but I'm damned well going to find out!' he said grimly.

The inquest held next day was different from almost all the others that John de Wolfe had held in Exeter. This was mainly because of the size and mood of the crowd who attended. Usually, it consisted of a dozen or a score of reluctant jurymen, plus the immediate family, unlike in the countryside, where the whole village turned out to watch and listen.

On this Monday afternoon, well over a hundred people gathered in the churchyard of St Bartholomew's. This was the nearest available burial ground to Milk Lane, as the canons had denied burial of a self-confessed heretic in the cathedral cemetery in the Close. This in itself had angered many townsfolk, given the tragic circumstances of the four deaths, especially of two children and their mother.

The little church, in whose yard the mound of soil was still fresh over the plague pit, also had a crude mortuary, an open lean-to shed built against one wall, where the corpses had lain overnight. The coroner and his officer arrived and were surprised by the large crowd who had assembled – and by the sight of none other than Thomas de Peyne, complete with his writing pouch, ready to record the inquest.

'You should be in bed!' protested de Wolfe. 'What are you doing here?'

The clerk was unrepentant. 'I am almost completely recovered, Crowner,' he said firmly. 'This awful event needs a proper record made, and you said yourself that the sheriff's man was not satisfactory.'

Grudgingly, but with some concealed admiration, John muttered that as he was now there he might as well make himself useful. Gwyn fussed around getting him a stool from the church and a box to set his parchments on, then they got on with the proceedings.

The sheriff appeared, another unusual event, together with Ralph Morin and Brother Rufus from the castle.

It was noticeable that no one from the cathedral was present and that the only cleric, apart from Rufus and Thomas, was the incumbent of St Bartholomew's.

The horror of the fire also brought out the two portreeves, Hugh de Relaga and Henry Rifford, as well as a number of the burgesses. The reason for this unusual interest was made obvious when, as soon as Gwyn had bellowed out the official call to order, the coroner began the proceedings.

'This is an inquest into both the cause of the fire itself and the causes of death of the four victims,' he boomed, standing up on an old grave-mound with his back to the wall of the church. 'Such verdicts are usually of accident, but in this instance I have no doubt that you, the jurymen here assembled, will find that it was murder!'

A rumble of anger, shock and dismay passed like a wave over the deep half-circle of faces ranged before him, even though many either knew or suspected the fact already.

'We must enquire into the deaths of Algar, a fuller of Milk Lane, together with Margaret his wife and his children, Peter and Mabel.'

The jury, eighteen men who had been at the scene the previous night, were ranged in the front of the crowd. They stared at this tall, dark man with an intensity driven by the anger in their hearts, and hung on his every word.

'As you well know, myself, my officer and the city constables were at this conflagration last evening and we were there again this morning. We found certain evidence that makes it certain that this was no accident!'

His voice was harsh as he made it carry over the crowd, and they responded by a low growl of anger at what he was telling them.

'Firstly, in spite of the damage by fire, we found a baulk of wood the length of my leg, jamming the only door, so that it could not be opened from the inside.'

He waved at Gwyn, who came to his side bearing a scorched length of timber, as thick as an arm. The coroner grabbed it and waved it in the air. 'The bottom of this was set in a crack in the stones of the path so it could not slip, and the upper end was jammed under the middle cross-member of the door. It could not possibly have got there by any other means than deliberate malice.'

He handed the wood to the nearest juryman, who looked at it and passed it along to his companions.

'When I entered the burning house to help retrieve the victims, there was a definite smell of naphtha, and this can be confirmed by Gwyn of Polruan, Osric the constable and several of you jurymen.'

He paused and Gwyn again handed him something.

'This morning, when we searched the yard, we found this earthen jar against the fence.'

De Wolfe brandished a rough pottery flask of about a quart capacity above his head. 'It smells strongly of naphtha, and there were a few drops of an oily liquid smelling strongly of that fiery substance still inside.'

Naphtha was a distillate imported from the Levant, an ingredient of 'Greek Fire', a highly inflammable substance used in grenades and naval warfare. John passed the jar to the jury, who sniffed it and muttered over it as it went along the line. But he had not yet finished with his indictment.

'Inside the cottage, when we were able to enter it

this morning, were the broken remains of yet another flask, lying in a corner.' Gwyn provided a small wooden bucket, inside which were some shattered shards of a finely made pottery flask with a narrow neck still intact.

'This can only be a container for brandy-wine, an expensive concoction from France, which has much pure liquor in it and is very easy to ignite.'

He beckoned to the next-door neighbour, whom he had designated to be the foreman of the jury, and handed him the bucket. 'Tell me, from your close knowledge of Algar, was he likely to have brandy-wine in his house?'

The tone of his voice suggested the answer he wished to receive, but the man had no need of prompting.

'By God's truth, sir, not at all!' he said firmly. 'Algar was an abstemious man and also without any riches to spend on liquors. What they drank in that house was weak ale and good milk!'

The dramatic part of the inquest was over, but for form's sake John called several of the neighbours to describe the suddenness of the fire late at night and the rapid conflagration of the straw roof, which made any approach to the front door impossible.

'I think that incendiary stuff was thrown up over the front of the thatch. That broken flask must have fallen through when the roof came down later,' claimed the foreman harshly.

'Would most folk in Milk Lane be in their beds at the time the fire started?' asked John.

'Indeed so, sir! We are all milking people, with work to do before dawn, so we get abed very early. That is why the fire was so well ablaze before anyone noticed last night, as we were all asleep ourselves.'

There was no more relevant evidence, and the growling crowd had little need of anything further.

John had one last order to make, a poignant and pathetic one.

'It is part of the king's law that the inquest must include a viewing of the cadavers by the jury. However painful this must be to you men who knew this family as neighbours and friends, you must see the bodies and confirm who they are and observe any wounds or other significant appearances. You will see that though there are numerous surface burns, there are no other injuries and that the skin of the victims is pink, showing that they drew down noxious gases into their lights before dying. This may be some consolation, as this can obliterate their wits and render them virtually dead before the fire reaches them.'

With a mixture of reluctance and suppressed wrath, the jury filed past a handcart which Gwyn pushed out of the mortuary shed. On it were four still figures, shrouded in clean linen, the wrappings turned back to expose the faces.

The man lay next to this wife, and nestled in the crook of each of her arms were her children. All the faces were tinted pink like ripe cherries, together with scattered burns from fallen thatch. There were sobs from some of the men and outright wailing from women in the crowd, who had a more distant view of the pathetic remains on the handcart.

De Wolfe watched impassively as the men returned to their places before him, though there was cold fury in his own heart at this atrocity. He scanned the crowd as he waited, identifying those from the castle and Guildhall – and was surprised to see Matilda at the back, attended by Lucille and Cecilia. At dinner he had told her briefly of the calamity and the findings of incendiary devices and the blocked door. She had listened in silence, but he sensed that it was not the silence of her usual indifference, but from horror and dismay. He had not known that she intended to come to the inquest, but there she was at the rear of the crowd, along with so many others who had come because of the killing of two innocent children and their mother.

When the last juryman had shuffled into place, John's deep voice again boomed out over the crowded churchyard.

'The duty of a coroner is to determine who, where, when and by what means persons came to their deaths – and where necessary to send any persons suspected of causing those deaths to the king's justices for trial.'

He paused and glared around as if to deny any contradiction.

'The first four of those tasks is not difficult in this instance. We well know who the victims are, we know where and when they died and we know they died from the effects of fire. As to who caused their deaths, at this stage that remains unknown, except to God himself.'

He pulled himself up on his mound to his full height, his grey-black cloak stretched over his bony arms like some great bat or avenging angel.

'But I and your other law officers will not rest until we have discovered what evil person did this cowardly deed – barricading the door and throwing combustibles to ensure that a man, a woman and two innocent children would be done to death!'

Another throaty growl of angry agreement rolled across the churchyard as he continued.

'It is not the business of a coroner to probe into *why* certain acts were committed, but in these hideous and appalling circumstances I feel obliged to say something of what I and probably many of you must feel about the matter.'

There was a mutter of agreement as he went on speaking, an expression of cold ferocity on his long face.

'No one traps a man and his family in his house and then deliberately sets it alight, just because he is a fuller! You know as well as I do that events in this city in the last few days have shown the animosity that many folk have to those whose religious views do not sit well with their own.'

There was silence at this, and John could almost feel the guilt that crept over the crowd. He continued remorselessly.

'As King Richard's coroner, I am not interested in the whys and wherefores of that dispute. I am here to uphold the law, as is your sheriff and his officers. On the quayside last week, only good fortune allowed us to intervene in time before several men were hanged. I do not want to know if any of you were involved; that episode is past!'

Again there was silence, with only the shuffling of feet and sideways glances to indicate the unease that pervaded the crowd.

De Wolfe's voice suddenly became louder and took on a harsher tone. 'But all of you – and I include myself – should be ashamed to live in a city where an evildoer took the lives of a goodwife and her two infants, over the issue of how Jesus Christ should be worshipped. Let us not be mealy-mouthed about this. There can be no other motive for this foul act, other than to destroy a man for his beliefs, uncaring whether innocent children and their mother perished with him!'

He glared around the subdued crowd, as if challenging any other explanation.

'God knows, I am no saint, not even a devout enough Christian, yet I remember something of the Gospels.

Did not the Good Lord say "Suffer the little children to come unto me"?'

He raised his fists in the air in a final explosion of frustrated anger.

'Is this how whatever fiend did this terrible act brought little children to Him? Killing innocent mites in the name of some argument about how best to worship God? He must be found and made to pay for his sins!'

De Wolfe reached the crescendo of his wrath and suddenly his arms dropped to his sides as he slumped into despondency.

'Jury, consider your verdict. I challenge you to find any other decision than wilful murder, though unfortunately against a person or persons unknown!'

At supper that evening Matilda was unusually subdued. Though it was now normal for her to ignore her husband, especially at mealtimes, John sensed that this was something different. She was not snubbing him with her usual air of dislike and discontent, but seemed more pensive and abstracted. He realised that the inquest had affected her, as it had many people, due to the cruelty of the deaths, but as a childless wife who had never shown any maternal interest, he had never expected her to be so distraught. His attempts to talk to her were met with a shrug or a shake of the head, and he soon abandoned any attempt to lighten her mood.

John had escorted her back from St Bartholomew's, together with Cecilia from next door, and whereas Matilda remained in frozen silence, the physician's wife, tears still wet on her cheeks, quietly praised his handling of the inquest.

'It was a terrible thing, Sir John, but you said what needed to be said. I think it has jolted the consciences of many who heard it, and hopefully dampened this hysteria that has been pervading the city these past few weeks.'

De Wolfe was afraid that this might have inflamed Matilda's defence of the anti-heretic faction, but she remained silent, almost as if she had not even heard the words.

When supper was over, to which unusually his wife failed to do justice, she called for Lucille and soon made her way out again, cloaked and hooded. Breaking her silence, she informed him that she would be at St Olave's, praying for the souls of the victims from Milk Lane.

Equally unusual, John did not feel like going down to the Bush that evening and slouched in front of his fire, drinking ale and then wine. He felt depressed by all that was going on: his brother's illness, the lack of any progress over the increasing number of murders associated with the heresy issue – and now his wife's strange moods. He wondered sometimes if she was losing her mind, as a result of her brother's repeated falls from grace, the disappointment over his own abandonment of the Westminster coronership and, not least, his own infidelities.

As he drank more and more, he slid towards sleep, his thoughts churning in his mind. Would William live or die, could the miracle of Thomas be repeated? How would he cope with Stoke and Holcombe if he did die? Who killed the four heretics? Was it the same assassin in each case?

Mary came in later to add logs to the fire and shook her head sadly at the sight of him slumped on the settle, a mug of ale spilled on the floor where it had slipped from his hand as he snored the evening away. 'This houschold is falling apart,' she murmured to Brutus as she mopped the flagstones with a rag. 'Things can't go on like this. I can see me out of work and living with my cousin before long.'

The hound opened one watery eye to look at her, but made no reply.

CHAPTER FIFTEEN

In which Crowner John is confounded

Early the following morning Crowner John sallied
forth in grim determination. The inquest on the
previous day seemed to have cast a shadow over the
city and, though the usual number of people were
on the streets, there seemed to be a pall of unease
hanging over them.

His object today was to descend upon those whom
he thought most likely to be the perpetrators of the
awful crime in Milk Lane. All had some connection
with the cathedral, and it was towards the Close that
he directed his steps on leaving the house. The two
bailiffs working for the proctors were certain to be
found there, and he assumed that the lay brother,
Reginald Rugge, would also be in the vicinity. As to
the weird monk, Alan de Bere, he would seek him
later.

John went alone, as he hoped that Thomas was
taking his advice and resting in his lodging, while
Gwyn was up at Rougemont in case there were new
deaths requiring attention.

At the small building which housed the proctors'
cells, he found both the bailiffs in residence, busy
eating their breakfast bread and cheese and drinking

small ale. Throwing open the door with no ceremony, he marched in and confronted them.

'I see that unlike so many of our citizens, you made no effort to attend the inquest yesterday!' he grated. 'Perhaps you had guilty consciences?'

The two men stared at him with their food halfway to their mouths, indignation being swamped by anxiety that this menacing figure might do them an injury. Herbert Gale struggled to his feet and stared anxiously at the coroner. 'I don't know what you are talking about, Sir John!' he muttered uneasily.

'You know damned well what I mean,' snarled de Wolfe. 'A house is burned down and the whole family deliberately killed! Do you not think it strange that the householder was the one man left from your crusade against heretics?'

William Blundus glared up at the coroner from his stool. 'We had nothing to do with that! You can't come here unjustly accusing us with no evidence.'

Angrily, John kicked a spare stool across the room to relieve his feelings.

'Don't tell me what I can and can't do! I am investigating four deaths, and I intend getting the truth from the most likely perpetrators, for which you are good candidates.'

Gale, the senior bailiff, had recovered much of his confidence and began blustering at the coroner's intrusion.

'We are just servants of the cathedral. Why should we take it upon ourselves to commit such a crime?'

John leaned forward and banged their table with his fist.

'Perhaps because you were so dissatisfied with the release of the other heretics, you wished to mete out your own type of justice?'

The exchange carried on in this vein for some time and became more heated with every minute, but

John could get no trace of a confession or unearth any incriminating signs. They obdurately denied both involvement in the deaths and his right to accuse them.

'The canons shall hear of this!' threatened Herbert Gale. 'And the bishop when he returns.'

'Then tell them to ask their Archbishop at Canterbury why he introduced coroners two years ago,' snapped de Wolfe. 'They will find that it was exactly to investigate events such as this.'

As he saw that at present he would get nowhere with these men, he marched out with a promise that he would be back as often as it took – an empty threat, but it relieved his feelings.

He made enquiries in the cathedral precinct and eventually traced Reginald Rugge to the cloisters on the south side of the great building. The lay brother was sweeping dead leaves from the garth, the central area of grass between the arcades on each side. When he saw the coroner loping towards him, he went rigid and gripped the handle of his besom as tightly as a drowning man grasping a floating plank.

'You are supposed to be locked in the proctors' cells!' barked de Wolfe. 'But for your convenient rendering of the "neck verse", you would be awaiting trial for attempted murder before the king's justices!'

Rugge had a hangdog look, laced with defiance, as he knew he was protected by the invulnerable ecclesiastical machine.

'I was released on condition I stayed within the Close,' he muttered.

'And did you?' demanded John. 'Or did you just happen to sneak out on Sunday night with some naphtha and a flask of brandy-wine, eh?'

Rugge glared at him sullenly. 'Where would I get such things? I don't even know what that naphtha stuff is!'

'Last week, I saw you trying to hang men with the same beliefs as the man that died in Milk Lane. Why should I believe that you didn't make another attempt?'

Rugge's temper flared up briefly. 'Well, I didn't, see! Though that blasphemer deserved to die, by rope or fire or any other means. A pity about his family, though no doubt they would have had the same evil beliefs.'

It took an effort for de Wolfe not to strike the man for his callous words.

'You are the one with the evil beliefs, you cold-hearted bastard!' he shouted, making several clerics walking in the cloister turn their heads. 'If your guilt is proven, I will come to see you swing from the gallows and cheer at every spasm of your jerking limbs as your poisonous life is choked out of you!'

The lay brother went pale at the vehemence of the coroner's words and gazed about, looking for someone to rescue him from this vengeful knight. A young vicar came hesitantly out on to the grass towards them, but John waved him away imperiously.

'Rugge, I will fetch a priest from the castle, a priest with a copy of the Vulgate. And you will swear upon that holy book that you did not leave this precinct on Sunday. Is that understood? If you lie, then as a devout man of the cloth you know you will suffer eternal damnation!'

As several other figures under the cloister arches were now pointing at him and debating about intervening, John saw no point in provoking them further and left the garth. Outside, on the paths through the Close, he found that he was quivering with suppressed emotion, an unusual state for the normally phlegmatic coroner.

He felt that Reginald Rugge could well have committed this heinous crime, but there seemed no chance of getting him to confess. John wondered if the man confessed his guilt to a priest, whether any cleric might be so appalled that he would break the sanctity of the confessional. He knew this was a futile hope, but as he was in the Close he decided to seek the opinion of his friend John de Alençon, so made his way to a side door into the great church. It was the time of the morning when Prime, one of the early offices, was in progress, and he stood alone in the huge, empty nave of the cathedral to wait for a break between the prayers and chanting that endlessly praised God behind the ornately carved wooden screen that separated the nave from the quire.

As he waited, with only chirping sparrows for company, he looked up at the screen and recalled that it was exactly a year since he had had to climb up it, to retrieve the severed head of a murdered manor-lord, impaled on one of the spikes at the top. It seemed as if violence and religion were never far apart, even in Devon.

The distant chanting eventually ceased and a final benediction allowed the black-robed celebrants to file out of the chancel and disperse themselves in the crossing, where the two great towers flanked the axis of the cruciform building. John walked around the side of the enclosed quire and saw the archdeacon in conversation with several other canons and vicars, some young secondaries hanging around the outside of the group. He waited, and in a moment John de Alençon noticed him and broke away to come to speak to his friend.

'I suspect I know what brings you here, John,' he said.

His voice was subdued, and he looked over his shoulder to see if anyone was in earshot, as Canon Robert de Baggetor and William de Swindon were among those to whom he had been talking.

'Yes, this abominable tragedy in Milk Lane,' growled de Wolfe. 'There can be little doubt that it was a deliberate assassination – and equally certain that it was because Algar was the only one of those heretics who stayed behind in the city.'

The grizzled-haired priest nodded sadly. 'I only wish I could contradict you, John, but any other explanation seems unlikely. My heart is saddened by the thought that differences in faith could lead to such suffering.'

'Not even differences of faith, for surely everyone concerned professes to be a Christian,' replied the coroner bitterly. 'It is over differences in how to pursue that faith which makes it all the more tragic.'

'I cannot believe that anyone connected with the cathedral could stoop so low as to commit this outrage,' murmured the archdeacon. 'But no doubt it is your duty to investigate the possibility.'

'Where else would I look for candidates, other than those who have already plainly exhibited their hatred of these people?' asked John with suppressed ferocity. 'It is but a few days since a mob, egged on by the dictates of some of your colleagues, tried to kill a few harmless folk down on the quayside. Only the intercession of your ecclesiastical rules saved two of them from facing trial for murder. Can you wonder that I now come looking at these same people?'

De Alençon's shoulders slumped and he gave a great sigh.

'I appreciate your position, John. But what can I do to help? I am in an even more difficult position here, as you know. I am supposed to give a lead in defending the Church in this matter, though you know my heart is not in this particular persecution.' He looked behind again and saw that the other priests and clerics were moving away. 'I must go to chapter, John. There is no time now, but come to see me later.'

De Wolfe nodded, but then held up a restraining hand. 'One question, John. If the perpetrator of this foul crime confessed to a priest, are there any circumstances where that confidence could be broken, given the outrageous nature of the crime?'

De Alençon laid a hand his friend's shoulder. 'The eternal question, John! The answer is "no", as that confession is made to God. The priest is but a passive channel to the Almighty, then conveying back God's absolution to the one confessing.'

'Even if by allowing that man to stay free, it might permit him to repeat his crimes?'

The archdeacon groaned. 'It would be a personal decision by the priest. I have heard of only one such instance and then the priest left his vocation, becoming a hermit, as he felt that he could no longer continue in office after breaking his vow of silence.' He backed away and lifted a hand in farewell. 'I must go to chapter, John. I will see you soon.'

The coroner made his way slowly out of the cathedral, unsure of what to do next. The illness of his brother hung over him all the time, like some dark cloud under which he had to go through the motions of daily life. Even thoughts of Hilda rarely entered his mind these past few days, it being filled with the horror of this multiple crime, as well as concern over his deteriorating relations with Matilda and her odd behaviour since the deaths of those children. He thanked God that at least the added worry about Thomas seemed to have receded and that faithful Gwyn, his rock in this turbulent life, seemed as stable and reliable as ever.

On the way out of the nave and again as he crossed the Close, he enquired of several clerks and lay brothers if they knew where Alan de Bere might be found. He went again to the proctors' office, partly to annoy them with his persistence, but neither bailiff was there. He thought of trying St Nicholas Priory, in the backstreets near Bretayne, but decided it was a futile quest to seek Alan there, as he had been ejected by them a long time before. The only other people who might know of him were in the constables' hut at the back of the Guildhall; though Osric and Theobald were there when he called, neither had anything useful to tell him.

'Not a sign of that crazy bloody monk,' growled Theobald, the fat constable. 'No one seems to have laid eyes on him since he was taken from the castle gaol.'

De Wolfe turned to Osric, the Saxon with an emaciated body and a thin face to match. 'Were there any sightings of a stranger in Milk Lane that night?' he demanded.

'I've asked everyone in the lane and up and down nearby Fore Street,' he said nervously, his prominent Adam's apple bobbing up and down his scrawny neck. 'Everyone is keen to help, but the trouble is they invent things in their urge to be useful. I've had reports of all manner of folk being seen there, from the portreeves to the bishop himself!'

John sighed. He had come across this warped imagination of witnesses before. 'But nothing definite? The same person being seen by two different people, for instance?'

Osric shook his head. 'As that neighbour told us, they go to their beds early there, with the morning milking to do. It's a side street; not many people use it unless they come to buy butter, cheese or milk, and that's in the daytime.'

Theobald put in a sensible question. 'Where would anyone get this naphtha stuff, Crowner? I'd only heard of it as something used in warfare. Would it have to be a soldier of some sort?'

The coroner shrugged. 'I know little about it myself. I heard of it being used at the siege of Constantinople, as an ingredient in this Greek Fire they shot from catapults. But who in Devon would possess it, God alone knows.'

'We'll keep asking around for this Alan de Bere, sir,' promised Osric. 'He must be hiding somewhere, unless he's already left the city.'

'I'll question all the gatekeepers,' offered Theobald. 'But most are so blind or so stupid that they'd not notice if an elephant passed through!'

On this pessimistic note, John left and went back to his chamber at Rougemont, where Gwyn had news of a serious assault in Polsloe, a mile north-east of the city.

'The Serjeant of the Hundred rode in to say that a woman there had been robbed, ravished and beaten. She's been taken into the priory in danger of her life.'

'Have they caught the assailant?' demanded de Wolfe, already sickened by the increase in violence lately.

'The hue and cry was raised and they seized two men. They're locked in a cowshed waiting for you, with half the men of the village eager to hang them from the nearest tree.'

'People are too damned ready to hang anyone they dislike,' grumbled the coroner. 'What do they think the king's courts are for?'

Gwyn had his own opinion on that, but he kept his thoughts to himself.

An hour later they rode into Polsloe, a village which had a small house of Benedictine nuns nearby. John knew it well, not least because it was where Matilda had taken refuge twice, though she never stayed long enough to take her vows. They were met at the edge of the hamlet by the Serjeant of Cliston Hundred and the manor-reeve, who took them to the small barn where a couple of angry villagers were guarding two men locked inside.

'Who are they?' asked John, peering through a crack in the rough planking at the pair of ruffians sitting disconsolately on the floor, already feeling the gallows rope around their necks.

'Strangers, passing through,' answered the serjeant, a tall, muscular man named Thomas Sanguin, who was responsible for upholding the law in his Hundred, a subdivision of the county. 'One claims his name is Martin of Nailsea, the other just David the Welshman. Both say they are ship-men, stranded at Exmouth and walking back to Bristol.'

'Have they confessed?' asked Gwyn.

'No, have they hell! They deny everything, though they were seen running away from the woman's house.'

'Any stolen goods on them?'

Sanguin shook his head. 'She had nothing to steal. A young widow, living on the parish, so they beat her and ravished her for spite, the swine!'

'Will she die?' asked John.

'Best ask the nuns at the priory; they are caring for her. But the poor woman is beaten badly.'

John scratched his head as an aid to thought. Where victims were badly injured, they could be given into the care of the assailant, who would usually do all he could to keep them alive, for if they died within a year and a day of the assault, he would be tried for murder. However, a couple of rascally sailors were unlikely to be of much use to the poor woman, compared with the care she was getting at the nunnery, which was well known for its expertise in dealing with childbirth and women's ailments.

'Get them sent into the city. They can be housed at the South Gate gaol. The sheriff can decide what to do about them, depending on whether the woman lives or dies. I'd better go down to the priory to make enquiries.'

He and Gwyn went to the woman's cottage on the way, a desperately poor place, where he was told that the woman eked out an existence after her husband died of poisoning of the blood caught from an injury in the fields with a hayfork that stabbed his foot. The single room was so barely furnished that it was hard to tell if an assault had taken place there, apart from the bloodstains on the pile of rags that was her bed.

'Better keep those to show at the court, if it ever gets that far,' said John to the serjeant. 'Now I'll go to see the woman – or at least talk to the nuns about her.'

The nunnery was in a compound behind a stone wall, with a gatehouse guarded by a porter. John knew the place well, not only from visits concerning his wife, but from several cases concerning women, where Dame Madge, a formidable nun who acted as the sub-prioress, had been of great help to him in matters of rape and abortion.

Leaving Gwyn at the gatehouse with the horses, he sought out Dame Madge and she came to the steps of the main range of buildings to meet him.

'The woman is too ill to talk to you, Sir John,' she announced firmly. A tall, stooped woman with a gaunt face, she was almost a female version of John himself, a humourless, no-nonsense person who spoke her mind and whose honesty was beyond question. He did not even attempt to persuade her to let him see the victim, but accepted her word.

'Has she been ravished?' he asked.

'Undoubtedly and repeatedly,' replied the grim-featured nun. 'She has been damaged in her woman's parts, as well as beaten sorely about the head and face. Her wits are disordered at the moment, but no doubt they will return.'

'She will recover, then?'

Dame Madge nodded. 'She is young and strong and her body will heal up. I am not so sure about her mind, after such an ordeal from those swine.'

'They will pay for it, never fear, lady. I will see to it myself.' He sighed and shook his head at the amount of evil in the world.

Though sequestered in a priory, the nuns were always avid for news of the outside world, and he told the old sister of the evil calamity in the city two nights earlier. She crossed herself and murmured a prayer for the dead children and their mother.

'There are sinful people about, Sir John. Though I cannot condone heresy, which eats at the fabric of our Mother Church, no one can approve of such random and vicious cruelty.'

'It seems to have affected my wife very much,' said John. 'Though she was very active in a campaign to rid the city of these heretics, since these deaths she seems to have turned in on herself and has become silent and morose.'

Dame Madge gave him a sudden sweet smile. 'Your wife is a strange woman, Crowner! We have had ample opportunity here to get to know her, from her two fruitless attempts to take the veil. I think she despairs of life, since her brother fell from grace – and you have not helped at all, sir, with your absences and your amorous adventures!'

De Wolfe nodded sadly. 'We should never have married, sister. It was not of our doing – we were pushed together by our parents.'

The dame nodded but was unforgiving. 'What the Lord has joined together, let no man break asunder, even until death itself.'

With this uncompromising finale, de Wolfe left the priory, with an assurance that the nuns would let him know when the woman was fit enough to be questioned. He rode back to the East Gate in silence, Gwyn knowing him well enough not to intrude on his bleak mood. At Rougemont, they returned the horses they had borrowed from the castle stables, and John went to bring the sheriff up to date on events. When he had told him of the latest crime in Polsloe and of the failure to make any headway with the Milk Lane fire, he went back to Martin's Lane and waited for his dinner. Matilda was up in her solar at the back of the house, so John went to sit in Mary's kitchen-hut in the yard, drinking ale and watching her gut some fish that she was going to spit-roast over the fire that burned red in its pit in the middle of the floor. She was a brisk, competent woman, and John was always impressed by the variety of good food that she managed to produce with such primitive facilities.

As she worked, he told her of the morning's visit to Polsloe, and as usual she was angrily sympathetic to the victim's plight.

'You men are such evil creatures!' she complained. 'Look at the harm that has been done to women and children in the space of a few days. You treat animals better than that!'

Few would let a maid speak to them so frankly, but John and Mary understood each other far beyond the usual relationship of master to servant. He cocked his head upwards towards the solar stairs.

'What mood is your mistress in today?' he asked. 'She seems oddly subdued since yesterday, hardly bothering to abuse me!'

Mary nodded as she slid long skewers through the herrings to place across the forked supports over the fire. 'There's something bothering her, that's for sure. But her tongue is recovering, for I heard her shouting at Lucille not long ago.'

The wraith-like French maid lived in abject subjection to Matilda's bad temper. Recently, when her mistress had gone into retreat in the priory, Lucille had been farmed out to Eleanor de Revelle, but when John's wife had returned to the house she was reclaimed, as if she was some piece of furniture.

John sat drinking for a while, watching the cook adding herbs to an iron pot of hare stew at the edge of the fire and peeling onions to go with the fish. Suddenly, she looked up.

'I hear the solar door opening. You had better make yourself scarce,' she warned.

John took the hint, as Matilda frowned upon his fraternising with the lower classes – especially as she had a shrewd suspicion that in the past John had known Mary a little too well, in the biblical sense. Taking his jug of ale, he slid out of the hut, which faced away from the solar, and hurried around the house, through the covered passage that led to the vestibule.

When she lumbered into the hall, her husband was sitting by the fire, fondling his hound's ears. She looked at him suspiciously but said nothing as she made her way to her usual seat, the hooded monks' chair on the other side of the hearth.

From long practice, John was sensitive to her moods and detected that her recent preoccupied depression was now giving way to suppressed anger. She glared across at him as he sat with his ale-pot in his hand.

'Are you not going to get me something to drink?' she snapped, her small eyes dark and penetrating.

Relieved that at least she was speaking to him now, John went to the table, where he kept his wines, and filled a pewter cup from a skin of Anjou red. As he handed it to her, he took advantage of the slight thaw in her mood to tell her about the attack in Polsloe. 'I went to the priory to see the poor woman, but Dame Madge told me she was too ill. She asked after your health, by the way.'

Matilda grabbed the cup and swallowed half the contents in one draught. 'I suppose that old crone slandered me, telling you what a difficult woman I was when I was there!' she said bitterly.

'She did no such thing,' retorted John indignantly, annoyed by his wife's lack of charity in ignoring the plight of the ravished woman.

'The world is full of evil people,' she muttered obscurely, slipping back into silence until Mary came in some time later to set the table for their dinner. Most households ate directly off the scrubbed boards of their tables, but Matilda had long insisted on wooden or pewter platters to hold the bread trenchers and bowls for potage and stews. When the carrot and herb soup and the grilled herrings were finished, the cook-maid brought a dish of diced fat pork with winter-sweetened parsnips.

The pair champed their way through the courses in surly silence, until Matilda suddenly grunted and fished inside her mouth.

'That useless woman – she could have broken my teeth!' she snapped, throwing a small piece of bone down on the table.

John tried to be conciliatory, though he knew that his wife seized on every chance to denigrate Mary. 'We should build a better cook-shed for her,' he suggested mildly. 'It's very difficult for her to prepare food properly in that tiny place, where she has to live and work.'

Matilda took instant exception to his innocent remark. 'You contradict me at every turn, John!' she flared. 'You always defend the woman – and don't think I don't know why! No doubt you employ your

299

lechery on her at every opportunity. Lucille is not blind, you know; she sees plenty from that room of hers!'

The injustice of this accusation melted John's restraint like the sun on morning frost, especially as he had not laid a lecherous finger on their cook-maid for several years.

'You see adultery and fornication in every breath I take, woman!' he shouted across the table. 'For the sake of St Peter and all his angels, why did you not stay in that damned nunnery and not inflict yourself upon me?'

For answer, she grabbed her platter, which still had some pork gravy on it, and threw it across the table at him. It hit him on the shoulder, and a greasy mess slid down the front of his grey tunic. His quick temper was instantly ignited and he leaped up to yell imprecations at her, while she for her part launched into a screaming diatribe about the years of shame and humiliation she had had to bear from him. It was a familiar pattern for their differences, though the intensity was extreme. Even in the midst of this torrid exchange, John managed to feel a morsel of relief that her former abstracted mood had reverted to something more familiar.

At the height of their abusive exchange, a pale, frightened face appeared around the hall door as Lucille peered in, having heard her mistress's voice from her den in the yard. Fearing that she might miss a summons and all the castigation that would follow, she peered in to enquire if she was required – but before she could open her mouth, John spotted her and roared at her.

'Get out of here, you damned spy and carrier of tales!' he yelled and threw an empty wooden salt-pot at her. It bounced off the draught-screens inside the door but had the desired effect as Lucille's head vanished abruptly and the door slammed shut.

'You not only persecute me, but my poor maid as well,' screeched his wife, ignoring the fact that she made the 'poor' maid's life a misery with her endless demands and scoldings. However, the interruption had dampened their ardour for fighting, and Matilda marched out imperiously, heading for her solar, where she no doubt would continue to harass Lucille. John slumped back into his chair, emotionally drained once more. He wondered how his life could go on like this, but as the anger receded so the problems that beset him began to flood back into his mind. His brother – how was he? He must get down there again very soon, as he had a permanent fear of the manor-reeve riding into Exeter to tell him that William was no more.

Almost guiltily, he again realised that no progress had been made at all on any of the murders of the past week or two. Most killings, certainly in the countryside that contained the majority of England's population, were either solved almost instantly or never solved at all!

If a house were robbed and someone attacked, then in a village everyone knew within minutes who had done it, except in the rarer cases of some stranger passing through, as at Polsloe. But even there the sharp eyes of nosy old men and curious goodwives usually spotted something unusual happening.

Even in towns and cities, each parish or district had a village attitude and often knew exactly what was going on from moment to moment. It was the casual killings, the robberies with violence by outlaws on lonely roads or the gangs that sometimes came marauding through hamlets that left the rudimentary law-enforcement system paralysed. John felt that lately he had had more of his share of unsolvable crimes.

If he felt guilt about failing to solve a single murder, he had more of the same emotion concerning Hilda, who he felt he was neglecting with all the problems circling around him. He recalled that he had lost his former lover, Nesta, partly because his preoccupation with his duties had led her to feel shut out from a large part of his life.

But soon his common sense pulled him back to earth, and with a muttered curse at the world in general he hauled himself to his feet and went around to the yard to find Mary. After all, he consoled himself, it was just another row with his wife, one of hundreds over the years, though he could not recall her ever throwing a platter at him before. He went into the kitchen-shed to get Mary to swab off the mess on his tunic with hot water and a rag. She did so, clucking her disapproval at the spoiling of a good linen garment.

'Lucille told me there was a fine row going on,' she said severely, 'but I could hear it from here – this household goes from bad to worse!'

'I think she's going mad,' said John gloomily as Mary rubbed at his shoulder. 'She wallows in self-pity and doesn't have a good word for anybody or anything – except that bloody church of hers.'

He went back to the vestibule and threw on his cloak to hide the wet patch on his tunic, then went out into the lane. At a loss for a moment as to what to do next, he turned towards the High Street, deciding to go back to Rougemont. At the corner he saw the massive figure of Gwyn coming towards him, ploughing through the crowd like a ship breasting a choppy sea.

'Crowner, I think I've found the bastard!' he bellowed from several yards away.

'Found who?' demanded John as his officer came close.

'Alan de Bere! Gabriel says one of his men-at-arms swears he saw him this morning coming out of one of those ramshackle huts on Exe Island. Shall we see if we can find him?'

They hurried down to Carfoix and then down the steep slope of Fore Street to the West Gate. Outside, the river ran sluggishly past, separated from the city walls by a wide area of grassy swamp and mud, criss-crossed by leats and ditches. This was Exe Island, sometimes flooded when there was a cloudburst up on distant Exmoor, though a number of poor wooden houses and shacks dotted its unstable surface. Near the walls, a row of slightly better dwellings formed Frog Lane, and at the northern end, where the river bent around, there were fulling mills and other small factories belonging to the thriving cloth trade.

'Any idea where this soldier saw him?' asked John, looking at the rickety footbridge across the river and the ford just below it.

'He said not far from the new bridge,' answered Gwyn, pointing to where a number of spans of a long stone bridge ended abruptly at the edge of the river. It was an ambitious project of Nicholas Gervase, but the money had given out before it was finished.

There were a few huts dotted about in that area, where some sheep and goats were cropping the sparse grass. The coroner and his officer made their way towards them, jumping across ditches filled with brown mud and turbid water. Some of the shacks were empty, but a few had forlorn families living in them, though none of the occupants admitted to knowing Alan de Bere. A few of the shanties had collapsed and others teetered on the edge of deep leats, ready to fall in at the next flood.

'That one's nearest the bridge,' said Gwyn, pointing at a wooden hut with a roof of grassy turfs, which was almost under one of the stone arches of the unfinished bridge. They walked towards it and were within a dozen paces when the sacking that covered the door-hole was suddenly thrown aside and a thin figure shot out, obviously intent on making his escape.

'That's the swine!' yelled Gwyn and set off in pursuit, with John close on his heels.

The more nimble fugitive, his monk's habit tucked up between his legs and secured by a belt giving his long legs the freedom to go fast, might well have escaped had he not gone in the wrong direction. The doorway of the hut faced the river and de Bere had run straight ahead, being cut off by the deep main channel of the Exe. John and Gwyn fanned out on each side of him as he stood at bay on the bank and, converging, grabbed him almost simultaneously. He wriggled violently, but Gwyn threw him to the grass and planted a large foot on his chest.

'You were released from the king's gaol to be confined in the bishop's cells,' growled de Wolfe. 'So how is it that you are lurking on Exe Island?'

The skinny man in his tattered habit glared up at the coroner, his pale blue eyes having a glint of madness. 'You have no authority over me. I am a servant of God!' he screeched.

'Aren't we all?' answered John grimly. 'You are a miserable little toad, and I want to know where you were on Sunday night.'

'I was in this hut here, minding my own business.'

Gwyn slid the toe of his boot up until it was pressed against Alan's throat.

'You're a liar. You were in Milk Lane setting a fire. Was Reginald Rugge with you, eh?'

'I was not, I swear it!' gurgled the man. 'I had nothing to do with that.'

Gwyn pressed down harder and the renegade monk began to go blue in the face as he could not breathe.

'You tried to hang those men last week – and the one who didn't sail away was Algar the fuller,' snarled de Wolfe, half-convinced that this was the man they wanted.

'So you decided to get rid of him in another way, blast you!' boomed Gwyn, screwing his heel into Alan's chest.

'I didn't, I swear by God and the Virgin!' gasped the monk. 'It may have been Rugge for all I know. I've not seen him since we were let out by the proctors' men. Father Julian wouldn't let me go back to my hut at St Olave's, so I came here.'

John sighed, as without proof his sense of justice prevailed over his revulsion for the man. He motioned to Gwyn to let the man get to his feet.

'If I get any evidence that you were responsible for this mortal sin, I'll see you on your way to hell personally!' he threatened.

De Bere staggered to his feet, his face contorted in hate. 'You have no right to hound me like this. The bishop will hear of this.'

'That's what your accomplice in crime said – and much good it will do you both,' snapped John.

'Can we take him back to Rougemont and let Stigand get some practice on him with his branding irons?' suggested Gwyn, holding Alan's arm in a grip of steel.

'I wish we could, but some of us still keep to the letter of the law, thank God,' answered de Wolfe. 'You'd better let him go for now. We know we can always find him in some pigsty or under a flat stone!'

They were standing on the edge of a deep leat that ran under the bridge. As Gwyn released the man, John sent him on his way with a shove, which overbalanced him into the ditch. He fell face down into the glutinous mud and struggled up covered in filth.

'That's for trying to hang those men on the quayside last week!' declared de Wolfe. 'Now clear off, you evil bastard!'

De Bere scrambled up the opposite side of the leat, wiping mud from his face and spitting dirty water from his mouth. When he had moved a safe distance away, he turned and screamed back at the coroner. 'You'll pay for this, de Wolfe – I'll get even with you yet!'

Back in Rougemont, John and his officer went into the hall to warm themselves at the firepit and to get something to eat and drink. They found a heated discussion going on between the sheriff and Sergeant Gabriel and came nearer to discover what the trouble might be.

'I'll have those two idiots in chains for a week,' fumed Gabriel. 'This is what comes of having milksops as soldiers, boys who have never seen a sword raised in anger!'

'What's the problem, sergeant?' asked the coroner, but it was Henry de Furnellis who answered.

'Those two bastards you saw at Polsloe, the rapists,' he said bitterly. 'They've bloody well escaped!'

'And committed another crime already,' added Gabriel, fuming with anger at the incompetence of his men-at-arms. 'We sent two men to drag them back here to await trial in the gaol and what happens? Those two fools I thought were proper soldiers were overpowered and lost them!'

When the story was told in full, it appeared that Martin of Nailsea and David the Welshman while in the cowshed had managed to free themselves from the ropes that bound their wrists and ankles. They had armed themselves with baulks of timber prised from the stalls and, as soon as the two soldiers opened the door to take them away, had beaten them to the ground and ran away into the nearby woods.

'Where they'll no doubt remain as outlaws!' glowered de Wolfe.

Gabriel shook his head. 'No such luck! The swine came back into the city within the hour, for they attacked a merchant in an alley off North Gate Street, choking him near to death before stealing his purse and making off into the lanes of Bretayne!'

The coroner sighed at the futility of arresting people only to let them escape. 'Are you looking for them now?' he barked.

The sheriff nodded irritably. 'It's like a bloody rabbit warren, that Bretayne! Half the folk there are thieves themselves and they'll readily give shelter to any evil brethren. But we'll get them in the end, though it may take a day two, knowing that place.'

Though he shook his head in disgust, John was preoccupied with his other problems. The sergeant marched away, ready to give another roasting to his incompetent soldiery, while the sheriff joined Gwyn and the coroner in another pot of ale as they bemoaned the way the world seemed to be going to the dogs.

CHAPTER SIXTEEN

In which the coroner is in dire trouble

Heavy cloud banks and a cold drizzle combined with the advancing days of November to bring an early dusk, and when John came down from the castle into the town it was already twilight. After the particularly virulent quarrel with Matilda at dinner-time, he decided to miss his supper at home and instead went down to the Bush, where Martha would be happy to feed him. On the way to Idle Lane he called on Thomas and found his clerk in good spirits. The yellow tinge had virtually vanished from his eyes, and he declared himself eager to resume his duties.

'I have already spent a few hours today in the scriptorium,' he said proudly, referring to his work cataloguing the manuscripts in the cathedral archives on the upper floor of the chapter house. 'So I see no reason why I cannot return to scribing for you, Crowner.'

He seemed so keen that John agreed to let him come each morning that week, provided he sat quietly at his table. When Thomas asked after the coroner's brother, John had to tell him how concerned he was that William seemed to make no progress – at least, he had not improved the last time John had seen him.

'I must visit him again very soon,' he said. 'I hope to go down to Stoke tomorrow, depending on what duties await us in the morning.'

As always, the little priest was very solicitous about his master's problems and promised to continue praying earnestly for William's recovery. He also passed on some encouraging information.

'When I was in St John's, Brother Saulf explained to me that sometimes even when the poison of the plague has left the body, it can have already damaged some of the entrails, so that they cannot function properly. Maybe that is what has happened to your brother – and hopefully those functions will slowly return.'

John hoped he was right and told Gwyn and Martha about it when he got to the tavern.

'Both that Saulf and our dear Thomas are clever, learned people,' said Martha. 'Perhaps when you get to Stoke tomorrow, you will find William much improved.'

John sat at his usual table, glad of the warmth of the firepit as a cold, wet wind had arisen outside. While he waited for Martha to chivvy her cook-maid into making him a meal, he sat over a quart of Gwyn's latest brew, talking to the Cornishman and several other acquaintances. Old Edwin hovered nearby, clutching empty pots and eavesdropping on the conversation. His religious fervour seemed to have diminished markedly since the quayside riot and especially since the outrage in Milk Lane. When John mentioned finding Alan de Bere down on Exe Island, the ancient potboy's indignation overflowed.

'An evil lunatic, that man!' he croaked. 'I'd not put it past him to have set that fire. I hear that he's found another three so-called heretics in the city since last week and reported them to the proctors.'

Another man, a florid baker and pie-maker from the High Street, chipped in with similar news. 'One of my customers told me today that Herbert Gale, that miserable proctors' bailiff, had heard from his spies of two more from Alphington, just outside the town.'

There was a rumble of discontent from those sitting nearby.

'I reckon that folk in the city have lost their appetite for hounding heretics, since that awful business on Sunday night,' said a brawny smith from Smythen Street. 'Time we let the bishop sort out his problems in his own way, not by taking affairs into our own hands.'

John was glad to hear that common sense was re-establishing itself in Exeter, but then he was diverted by the arrival of Martha with a wooden bowl of steaming potage, smelling deliciously of thyme and mint. She was closely followed by a young maid with a platter bearing a shank of mutton with beans and boiled leeks.

'Get that down you, Crowner!' she said cheerily. 'It will raise your spirits in these dark days.'

He found that he was ravenously hungry, having left part of his dinner behind in his fight with Matilda and now gone well beyond his usual supper-time. He attacked the food heartily and soon finished it all. When he ended with a bare mutton bone, he realised that he had no Brutus beneath the table, as he had left him with Mary, where the dog spent most of his time when John was away from the house. He recalled that she was going to visit her cousin in Curre Street that evening and would probably have taken the dog with her, as Matilda had no time for the old hound and was probably at St Olave's anyway.

The evening passed pleasantly in drinking and gossiping, but after a couple of hours John decided that he had better go home to bed, as tomorrow would be another hard day, if he was to ride to Stoke-in-Teignhead and back. He bade goodnight to his friends and trudged back along the familiar route to Martin's Lane, a path he had taken a thousand times before, so the darkness was no hindrance.

In the cathedral Close he passed the guttering pitch-flare at Bear Gate and aimed for the next one stuck in a ring on the wall of St Martin's Church, fifty paces from his house. As he reached the front door, he frowned because it was ajar. Though they rarely locked it, it was normally closed against the draughts that blew through the lane. He pushed it open and went into the small vestibule that connected the inner door to the hall with the passage to the backyard. A tallow dip in a wall niche gave him light enough to hang up his cloak, before he went into the hall.

The fire was burning low, but two more tallow lamps on each side wall dimly illuminated the high, gloomy chamber. No one was sitting near the hearth, so he assumed that his wife was still at her devotions. Going to the fire to throw on a couple of the logs stacked at the side, he suddenly saw a pair of feet sticking out beyond the further monks' settle. Aghast, he thrust the seat out of the way and saw that his wife was lying motionless on the flagstones.

'Matilda! Matilda, what's wrong?' He dropped to his knees alongside her, fearful that she had had a stroke or a seizure. She was lying on her side, and he tugged at her substantial body to turn her on to her back. Then, even in that poor light, he could see the bruises on her throat. She was dead – stone dead.

De Wolfe had seen too many corpses in his time to even attempt to revive her, and he rocked back on his heels, stunned by the realisation that his wife was dead. To his credit, the thought that he was now free of her never entered his head. Though he had made many empty threats in the past, these were just an angry retaliation to her jibes and he had never contemplated her demise as the answer to his marital problems. Now he felt confused, as if this was all happening to someone else.

'Matilda, what the hell happened to you?' he croaked, then berated himself for being such a fool. A practical man of action, he pulled himself together and stood up, a cold fury slowly overtaking him at whoever had robbed him of his wife, however undesirable to him she might have been.

He stared almost maniacally around the chamber, as if he might see some murderer skulking in a corner. Was this anything to do with the heretic hunt or was it some random robbery with violence? What about those two evil bastards from Polsloe? They had already attacked someone inside the city – and that was also an attempted throttling.

Or could it be someone getting back at him for his actions against those who wished to exterminate heretics? Perhaps that madman Alan de Bere? Or the lay brother Reginald Rugge – he knew Matilda well, as he was always lurking around St Olave's. The possibilities swirled around in his head, confusing him, making him yell out in anguished frustration.

But he was the coroner, he told himself sternly … For God's sake, pull yourself together, man!

He suddenly realised that he was now the First Finder. It was different being on the other side of the fence that usually divided a law officer from the people in the street or the village. What was he to do? Should he raise the hue and cry?

He stood indecisively, looking down at the inert body of the woman he had been married to for over seventeen years. For once unsure of what to do next, he stood transfixed, trying to get his thoughts in order.

There was a click behind him as the hall door opened and he swung around in a crouch, automatically whipping out his dagger to confront the return of the killer.

'For Christ's sake, what are you doing, John?' came a familiar voice. 'Put that damned knife away.'

It was Richard de Revelle, his detested brother-in-law, who came cautiously towards him, as John's knife hand slowly subsided.

'I came to visit my sister. Is this the welcome I get?' he brayed in his high-pitched voice. Suspecting from John's manner that something was amiss, he hurried forward, keeping his brother-in-law at arm's length until he reached the chairs near the hearth. Finding them empty, he dropped his gaze and saw his sister lying motionless on the floor. With a cry of horror, he dropped to one knee and, like John, instantly recognised that she was beyond any mortal help.

'What have you done, you bastard?' he shrieked, looking up fearfully at de Wolfe, as if he expected him to jump murderously upon him. 'You've killed her, you swine!' He struggled to his feet and backed away from the coroner.

'I knew this would happen! I've heard the many threats you've made against the poor woman!' He stumbled backwards a few more steps. 'It was bound to happen sooner or later, but you'll not get away with it, damn you! I'll see you hang for this!'

His hysteria seemed to jerk John back into rational thought. 'Don't be so bloody silly, Richard!' he said dully, dropping his knife carelessly on to the flagstones. 'I found her like this when I came in, not three minutes ago. It must have been those two swine who attacked that woman in Polsloe. I must send for the sheriff. He'll know what to do.'

'Damned right he will!' shrilled de Revelle. 'He'll arrest you for murder if he knows what's good for him!' He moved warily towards the door, half-afraid that de Wolfe was going to jump on him.

'Where are you going?' snapped John. 'You must help me get her decently laid out, not left crumpled on the cold floor.'

'Don't you dare touch her!' shouted de Revelle. 'You've done enough damage already. And nothing must be moved until the sheriff and his men get here – you should know that, as so-called coroner!'

He sidled to the door. As he vanished, he shouted, 'I'm off to raise the hue and cry – though they'll not have far to search for the killer!'

John slumped into his chair and stared across the room at where his wife's feet pointed at him accusingly. The fire had livened up and he could see her more clearly, lying there murdered before her own hearth. The feeling of unreality began to creep over him again and he leaped up to dispel it, but again hovered indecisively over her still form.

Then the door opened again and Mary entered, straight from the street with a woollen shawl draped over her head and shoulders.

'What's going on, Sir John?' she asked briskly. 'Your brother-in-law is hammering on the door of the next house.'

He looked at her dully and wordlessly waved a hand towards the hearth. His cook-maid came forward to stare at what was behind the chair. Typically of her, she neither screamed nor shouted but dropped to her knees and felt Matilda's face with the back of her hand.

'She's still warm,' she said harshly.

'But dead, Mary! She's been strangled by some bastard.'

His voice was flat and desolate. The maid stood up, pulling the shawl from her dark hair and spreading it gently over the body of her mistress.

'She must be covered up. It's not seemly for her to be left like this,' she said briskly. Not for a moment did she think that John was responsible. Her mind was on what needed to be done.

'You sit down and I'll get you some brandy-wine, then you can go for help, before her brother causes you more mischief.' She hurried to the side table and brought him a cup of strong spirit, the same stuff that had been used to start the fire in Milk Lane. He swallowed it in a couple of gulps and then stood up again.

'I must go to the castle to see if Henry de Furnellis is still there,' he announced thickly. 'Can you send old Simon down to the Bush to tell Gwyn what's happened?'

She nodded and went to the door, pushing Brutus out of the way, as he was peering in, wondering what was happening. 'I'll take him with me out of the way.'

She disappeared, and with leaden feet he made for the street door. As he reached it, he collided with Richard de Revelle, who pushed him back inside before John could resist.

'No, you don't, you stay here!' screeched Richard. 'Help, he's trying to make a run for it!' he yelled at a higher pitch. Behind him came Clement the doctor and then two men John vaguely recognised as belonging to the house around the corner in the Close, some minor lay functionaries from the cathedral. They all crowded into the vestibule, almost filling it, before de Wolfe could retaliate.

'What the hell are you doing?' he shouted. 'Get out of my house this minute!'

315

Richard grabbed him by the arm. 'We are the hue and cry, and you are under arrest!' he yelled, an almost maniacal look of triumph on his face as he saw a chance of repaying all the indignities that de Wolfe had heaped on him over the past years.

For answer, the coroner pulled his arm free and landed his brother-in-law a punch on the chest, then another on the jaw that sent him reeling backwards to hit the wall behind.

'Don't you dare handle me, you madman!' he hissed and advanced on Richard, prepared to strike him again.

Clement seized his arm and tried to calm him down. 'Sir John, I beg you to behave like the gentleman you are. Just let us see what the situation is in your hall.'

Breathing hard, de Wolfe pulled himself together and allowed the physician and the other men through the inner door. By now, two other men from the corner house on the High Street had been summoned, together with Andrew from his stables opposite. Cecilia and Lucille hovered behind them, the maid attracted from the yard, wide-eyed with apprehension. They all trooped into the high chamber, where the new logs were now burning brightly enough to give a good light. As John led the way across to the chairs standing before the hearth, Richard pushed his way forward, rubbing his chin with one hand and gesticulating with the other.

'You are all witnesses to his assault upon me!' he babbled. 'He is a dangerous man. Be careful. He has already killed, he is violent and not to be trusted!'

His protests were ignored, as the sight of Matilda's body had transfixed them. Mary's shawl covered her head, but Lucille gave a piercing scream and collapsed sobbing on to the floor, in spite of the fact that her mistress had made her life a misery. It was Cecilia who ran forward and crouched at Matilda's side, gently pulling back the woollen cloth and feeling for a heartbeat in the woman's neck.

'Clement, come here quickly!' she commanded. 'See if anything can be done for her.'

Her husband joined her on his knees and, pushing her out of the way, felt Matilda's throat and then lifted up her eyelids one at a time. 'She is dead – she cannot be revived.' He crossed himself, as did several of the men standing around.

'I told you, de Wolfe killed her,' rasped de Revelle. 'You can see the grip marks of his fingers on her throat!'

Clement got up, while Cecilia reverently replaced the shawl over the dead woman's face. Then she went across to where Lucille was crumpled on the floor making whimpering sounds.

'Come on, my girl, I'll take you next door away from all this trouble.' She put an arm around the maid and led her sobbing to the door, leaving the men looking at each other in consternation, though the physician advanced on the coroner.

'What do you say to all this, sir?' asked Clement sternly.

John glared at him. 'I say that this is none of your damned business!' he snapped. 'But if you must know, I came home a short while ago from the Bush alehouse to find the street door open and my wife dead upon the floor!'

'Ha! A likely story!' brayed Richard. 'I found him standing over my poor sister's body, still warm after his murderous assault. He tried to silence me with his dagger. Look, there it is, still upon the floor!'

He pointed dramatically at the knife which lay on the flagstones. Seven pairs of eyes stared at de Wolfe, as if waiting to hear his explanation, but they were disappointed.

'I don't have to answer your ravings, de Revelle,' he snarled. 'You are expert at causing trouble where none exists. I shall wait for the sheriff, who holds the office in which you were found so wanting in honesty.'

One of the men from the Close, a lawyer in the bishop's service, frowned at his response.

'This is a difficult situation, Sir John. What is required is a coroner, as you well know. But you yourself are the coroner here, so what is to be done?'

'Let the sheriff decide,' snapped John. 'He is the king's representative in this county.'

'And your bosom friend, of course!' sneered Richard, still rubbing at his aching jaw to emphasise how badly he had been assaulted. 'What chance is there of him going against your interests?'

As if in answer to the question, there was a commotion outside and the doors were flung open as Henry de Furnellis and his chief clerk came in. He had had only a short distance to travel when summoned, as though he had a manor outside Exeter he also had a town house near the Guildhall.

A gabble of explanations was hurled at him, but Henry ignored them and walked straight up to de Wolfe. His lined old face, resembling a tired bloodhound, looked calmly at the coroner.

'What's going on, John?' he asked mildly.

'I found my wife lying there on the floor, strangled,' he replied. 'And this idiot thinks I did it!' He jerked his head at his brother-in-law.

De Furnellis looked down at Matilda's body for the first time. 'Good God, John! I'm so sorry. Who could have done this awful thing?'

This provoked another cacophony of chatter, above which Richard's reedy voice rose in protest. 'What did I say? We will get no justice here!'

He thrust his way through the men thronging the chamber and vanished into the night. The sheriff scowled at those remaining.

'Clear the room! This is now king's business. My clerk will take your names in case you are needed as jurors or witnesses.' He hustled them all outside, and when the last had gone he slammed the door. 'Now, John, tell me what happened.'

His down-to-earth manner cleared the turmoil in de Wolfe's mind, and in a few succinct words he explained what had happened.

'Of all things that I needed at that moment was that bloody fool de Revelle appearing on the scene,' he said bitterly. 'It was manna from heaven for him, of course, to catch me in what he imagined was a compromising situation!'

The sheriff looked down at the still shape on the floor. 'What are we to do with her, John? It's not decent for her to be left lying there.'

De Wolfe grabbed his hair in a gesture of consternation. 'In one thing, Richard is right. We need a coroner, for I am not above the law and that is what is demanded. They have raised their hue and cry and I am First Finder. There must be an inquest, and the coroner, whoever he is, should be able to view the corpse where it lies.'

As he uttered the word 'corpse' he shivered, the realisation seeping over him that his wife was now just a dead body. Though he could generate no affection for her, she had been a part of his life for so long that he found it hard to believe that she was no more.

Henry de Furnellis pulled at the jowls under his chin as he thought what to do next. 'Can we get Nicholas de Arundell back just to deal with this?'

This was the manor-lord from near Totnes who had temporarily taken on the coronership when John had been called to Westminster.

319

John shrugged and gave a great sigh. 'I suppose so. He's the obvious answer. He must be sent for straight away, so that he may be here in the morning.'

The sheriff looked down again at Matilda. 'But can we leave the poor woman here until then?'

'A sheriff and a coroner can hardly go against the rules laid down by the king's justices,' said John. 'The body must be left undisturbed until the coroner has the opportunity to view it.'

Eventually, they decided to leave her where she was, as in any case the alternatives were difficult. Taking her to lie in the usual mortuary in the castle cart-shed was not to be contemplated and putting her before an altar in either the cathedral or St Olave's was too much of a departure from the legal process.

'I will send down a soldier from Rougemont to stand guard over the door,' declared the sheriff. 'And another can ride at dawn to Hempston Arundell to fetch Sir Nicholas. With forced riding, he could be back here soon after noon.'

With a last look at the shrouded body near the hearth, Henry firmly shepherded his friend from the hall and closed the door.

'I didn't do it, you know,' said John suddenly as they stood in the vestibule.

The sheriff gripped his arm in a gesture of friendship. 'It never entered my mind that you did, John! But that bastard de Revelle is going to squeeze every ounce of trouble for you out of this.'

He opened the door to the lane. 'What are you going to do tonight? You can't stay here.'

'I'll sleep down at the Bush – not that I'm likely to get much sleep,' he answered. 'Now I must see to Mary.'

When de Furnellis had left, he went around to the yard, where Brutus was whimpering at Mary's feet.

Though he had been treated with disdain by Matilda, the hound knew that something was very wrong in the household.

'What will you do tonight, Mary?'

The cook-maid raised her hands. 'What can I do but stay here, as usual? I'm not afraid of ghosts.'

'I didn't harm her, Mary,' he said, repeating the assurance he had made to the sheriff. She reached up and kissed his bristly cheek.

'Of course you didn't, Sir John!' she said vehemently. 'But I fear for your safety now, all the same.'

De Wolfe went back to the Bush and told his dreadful tale to the horrified Gwyn and Martha. Already patrons were coming into the tavern who had heard the news higher up in the town, spread by the men who had been turned out for the hue and cry. Some looked askance at the coroner, but others came across to offer their sympathy and support.

'It must be those bloody ship-men that ravished that poor woman,' said a carpenter he knew. 'Flood Bretayne with soldiers, I say, to flush them out!'

Gwyn sat John at his table and pressed a jug of ale upon him, as the only way he knew to express his feelings, while Martha tried to get him to eat again, which he declined.

'De Revelle is out to make trouble for me over this, Gwyn,' he said soberly. 'He sees this as his big chance to even up old scores.'

'It's nonsense; no one will take him seriously,' scoffed his officer.

'I hope not, but I have a bad feeling about this. He found me standing over her still-warm corpse – and I pulled a knife on him, as I thought it was the killer returning.'

Gwyn still dismissed his fears, and soon Martha

persuaded him to go up to the loft and lie down on one of the better feather mattresses. In spite of his fears, John slept dreamlessly for a few hours before dawn, but as soon as he awoke all his troubles came tumbling down on him again.

By the time he finished his morning oatmeal gruel, Thomas appeared in a highly agitated state, as by now everyone in Exeter knew of Matilda's death. He was almost beside himself with concern and fear for his master's welfare, as already rumours were circulating that the coroner himself was a suspect.

'And I'll wager I can guess who is promoting that notion,' growled Gwyn. 'I'll wring the swine's neck myself if he causes you serious trouble, Crowner!'

Together, the three set off for Rougemont, after John had arranged with Andrew for one of his ostlers to ride to Stoke-in-Teignhead with a hasty note which Thomas had penned for him. His sister Evelyn could read fairly well, as she had spent time in a nunnery when young. In the note, John explained what had happened and expressed his sincere hope that William was improving. He also asked that a message be sent to Hilda, explaining his inability to visit any of them for the time being.

Up at the castle, John went straight to see Henry de Furnellis, who confirmed that a soldier had already left on their swiftest horse to bring Nicholas de Arundell back to Exeter.

'Is there any news of Richard de Revelle yet?' demanded John. 'No doubt he'll be abroad soon to make as much trouble as he can.'

The sheriff shook his head. 'Not a sign of him here, but Sergeant Gabriel says the porter on the South Gate saw him riding out with a servant as soon as it was opened at dawn.'

'He's up to something,' growled Gwyn. 'He'll not

just ride away and lose an opportunity like this.'

The sheriff agreed. 'He can't be going to his manor at Tiverton. He'd have used the East Gate for that.'

It was afternoon before they discovered where the former sheriff had been.

CHAPTER SEVENTEEN

In which Crowner John is in dire peril

The sheriff was being too optimistic when he expected Sir Nicholas de Arundell to arrive by noon. Though the messenger he sent at dawn to the manor near Totnes went as fast as his good rounsey could take him, de Arundell was not at home. He was out supervising his men assarting the edge of the woodlands, and it took an hour to find him and to persuade him to come to Exeter to resume his former duties as a coroner. His reluctance was all the more stubborn when he discovered that he was expected to hold an inquest on the wife of the existing coroner, a man for whom he had the greatest respect, as well as gratitude for past help. Being told that John de Wolfe was also the prime suspect was even worse, but eventually, when his literate steward read out the letter penned by Henry de Furnellis's clerk, he felt obliged to comply with what was essentially the king's command, conveyed through the sheriff.

By the time he reached Exeter, it was well past the middle of the afternoon. He met de Furnellis, and they went to the house in Martin's Lane for his obligatory viewing of the scene and of Matilda's body, a task for which he had the greatest distaste.

His examination was cursory, just a glance to identify the deceased and a quick confirmation of the bruises on her throat, which by now had become more prominent, as commonly happened after death.

'What about the viewing by the jury?' he wanted to know. 'Surely we cannot make the poor lady suffer the indignity of being pushed up to the castle on a handcart!'

De Furnellis had already pondered on this, as Rougemont was the obvious place for the inquest. The Guildhall was the only other venue large enough, but he had no jurisdiction over the burgesses and portreeves, who jealously guarded their independence.

'We must use Rougemont, and Matilda can be laid out decently there in the garrison chapel,' announced Henry. 'I'll arrange for a closed wagon to take the body up there straight away.'

To allow time for this and to provide Nicholas de Arundell with some food and drink after his hard ride from Totnes, the sheriff took him to the New Inn in the High Street for the better part of an hour.

When they eventually reached the castle, a considerable crowd had gathered around the gatehouse and quite a number had already pushed their way inside. As an inquest was a public affair, they had every right to be there, but the sheriff drew the line at letting a mob into the hall. He had decided to use the inner ward and had soldiers bring out a chair for the coroner and some benches for the senior officials and clerks.

Gwyn and Thomas de Peyne had come up from the Bush with John de Wolfe, but due to the late arrival of de Arundell they had been cooling their heels in John's chamber, high in the gatehouse. De Wolfe was in an icy mood, tense and internally seething with anger at the mischief that Richard de Revelle was causing – but he acknowledged the need for an inquest and a proper disposal of his wife's body. The fact that she was irrevocably dead and gone had still not fully sunk into his mind, and he seemed to be gliding along on some superficial plane of consciousness. However, he was still able to worry about the condition of his brother and whether his family and Hilda had had the message explaining his absence.

When they went down to the inner ward for the impending inquest, Thomas flatly refused to act as clerk in a case where his master was being suggested as the culprit, but he hovered behind one of the sheriff's clerks to make sure that he wrote down an accurate record.

As the main players assembled, Nicholas de Arundell hastened to de Wolfe's side, where he stood brooding at the edge of the twenty people marshalled as a jury.

'Sir John, this is a terrible tragedy,' he said solicitously. 'When you aided me in my predicament last year, not only you showed me kindness, but your wife was also very supportive to mine.'

Nicholas was a tall, fair man, an ex-Crusader like John, but some years younger. Now obviously embarrassed by the role he was being forced into playing, he tried to excuse himself to John, but de Wolfe set his mind at rest.

'I know how difficult this must be for you, but there is no one else to turn to. You at least had a few months' experience of a coroner's duties, and I am sure you will act with honour and fairness.'

Reluctantly, the country knight moved to his place before the crowd, fervently wishing himself back at his manor and his agricultural pursuits. He sat in the only chair, which had been placed in the centre facing the jury, and on each side the benches were occupied by Ralph Morin, the castle constable, the two portreeves,

Archdeacon John de Alençon and the sheriff himself. As Gwyn had also gruffly declared himself unavailable, his role as coroner's officer was taken by Gabriel, the sergeant of the castle garrison, who called the inquest to order and declared it in session.

The crowd, which now numbered at least a hundred, fell silent. The whole assembly made a strange tableau in the inner ward, surrounded by high castellated walls of red sandstone, which gave Rougemont its name. Uneasily, Nicholas de Arundell got to his feet and began the preamble, confirming that they were there to enquire into the death of Lady Matilda de Wolfe. He was just starting to charge the jury with their duty to discover 'where, when and by what means' the lady came to her death, when there was a disturbance at the gatehouse end of the courtyard. A crowd of more timid onlookers was scattered as four horsemen clattered through the entrance arch, the leader shouting as he came.

'Stop these proceedings!' he yelled. 'They are outwith the law!'

He reined in at the edge of the crowd and slid from his saddle, one of his companions doing the same. He stalked forward, pushing through the onlookers, and advanced to face the row of benches. The sheriff leaped to his feet, his old face red with anger.

'De Revelle! What in Christ's name do you think you're doing? Get out of the way, blast you!'

Nicholas, who had been another adversary of Richard in the past, also advanced on him.

'Have you not already caused enough trouble in this county?' he demanded angrily. 'What mischief have you dreamed up this time?'

De Revelle, his dandified clothes dusty from hard riding, stood his ground. 'This so-called inquest is invalid! You are not a coroner, you cannot officiate here!'

'He is here at my invitation and, indeed, my direction, as I am the king's representative,' yelled the sheriff.

'He is no longer a coroner and does not now hold the king's writ,' retorted Richard. 'Nor has his appointment been ratified by the county court, as is necessary.'

His voice had the smug satisfaction of one who knows he has the weight of the law behind his argument.

'So what do you suggest we do?' snapped de Furnellis angrily. 'Just bury the poor lady without any enquiry?'

For answer, Richard stood aside and with a sweep of his hand indicated the man who had accompanied him. 'This is a genuine coroner, Aubrey de Courtenay, appointed by the king and confirmed by a county court. He holds the jurisdiction of West Dorset and will officiate at this inquest!'

De Courtenay stepped forward and saluted the sheriff with a hand across his breast. He was a short, pigeon-chested man with a florid face and a big nose. Under his heavy riding cloak, a dull brown surcoat could be seen and on his head was a woollen cap with a large tassel hanging at one side.

'Sir Richard has summoned me from my home at Lyme for this purpose. He is correct in saying that in these circumstances only another coroner can officiate.'

A few yards away, John de Wolfe viewed this interruption with consternation. It now came back to him that this de Courtenay was a distant relative of Richard's wife Eleanor, who was connected to the powerful Courtenay family. The former sheriff had obviously seized the opportunity to obtain someone who might be persuaded to be partisan in this affair.

Henry de Furnellis began to argue with de Revelle and the new arrival, denying both the need and the legitimacy of changing coroners in midstream, but they would have none of it.

'Everyone here is biased in favour of John de Wolfe,' shouted Richard, sweeping an arm around to encompass the seated worthies. 'If you insist on continuing with this farce, I will take this matter to the royal judges, the Justiciar and the king himself!'

Aubrey de Courtenay also weighed in with his own insistence on taking over the proceedings, on pain of bringing everyone before the king's justices at the earliest opportunity. Their demands might have been rejected, but Nicholas de Arundell suddenly capitulated.

'I cannot continue in these circumstances,' he announced in a tone that allowed no argument. 'It is quite true that I am no longer a coroner. Neither am I sufficiently versed in the law and the practice of that office to stand in the way of an accredited man.' Suiting his words with his actions, he walked to the end of the line and stood alongside John de Wolfe, muttering his apologies to him.

Henry de Furnellis made one last stand against this conspiracy. 'Why have you thought fit to interfere in this matter, de Revelle?' he snapped. 'What business is it of yours how justice is administered in this county? You took little interest in it during the short time you were sheriff – from which post we all know you were dismissed for malpractice!'

Richard's skin was as thick as one of Hannibal's elephants and he ignored the jibe. 'Because it is my only sister who lies so brutally murdered!' he retorted. 'And I will not stand idly by while the killer is standing there, absolved by all of you, who are John de Wolfe's friends!'

The sheriff still struggled manfully against the inevitable. 'You have no right to prejudge the issue before a single word of testimony is heard!' he shouted. 'De Wolfe has every right to challenge you for defaming him!'

'Then he may have to do it from inside a prison cell while he awaits the gallows!' screeched Richard, by now so carried away that he was careless of what slander he uttered.

The stocky coroner from Dorset became impatient. 'Am I or am I not going to hold this inquest?' he asked plaintively. He stepped forward and sat himself in the chair that Nicholas had vacated so abruptly. 'Let us hear what the jury has to say on the matter.'

Though juries in the countryside were supposed to be composed of all the adult men from the four nearest villages, this was often patently impossible, and in towns even less practicable, so anything from a dozen to a score were usually empanelled.

The idea was to include all those who might know something useful about the event, so in addition to being the jurymen who delivered a verdict, they were also the actual witnesses.

Somewhat to his surprise, John realised that he was also one of the jury, being the person who had first found the body.

The new coroner called for evidence of identity, but before John de Wolfe could step forward, Richard had virtually hopped in front of him.

'She is my sister, Matilda, a lady of good Norman stock, in her forty-sixth year,' he exclaimed.

By the time he had uttered the words, John had marched across from where he stood on the end of the line and pushed his brother-in-law out of the way with a thrust of his shoulder. There was a gasp from the crowd, as many half-expected him to strike de Revelle a hammer blow with his fist.

'I am Sir John de Wolfe, and Matilda was my wife,' he glowered. 'A husband undoubtedly takes precedence over a mere relative when it comes to identification. Yes, she was of Norman blood, so there is no question of presenting Englishry.'

De Courtenay nodded his agreement. 'Let the clerk so record that fact. I will leave the matter of a murdrum fine to the royal judges when the case is presented to them in due course.'

'I am also the First Finder,' continued de Wolfe. 'I will give evidence as to the situation when I arrived at the scene.'

The locum coroner looked irritated at having his role being anticipated for him by one of the witnesses, but nodded for John to continue.

'There is little to tell. I returned home some time in the evening, went into my hall and found my wife lying dead on the floor. She had bruises on her throat indicating that she had been throttled by some unknown assailant.'

'So you no doubt raised the hue and cry?' asked de Courtenay.

'I had no opportunity. As I stood there, I heard the hall door opening and feared it was the killer returning. But it was just this man, my brother-in-law, arriving at a suspiciously opportune moment!'

He managed to inject a note of sheer contempt into his voice as he waved a hand dismissively at Richard, who was still standing nearby.

'That is only half the truth!' shrilled de Revelle. 'I came to visit my sister and found this evil man standing over her, while she was still warm! He pulled a knife on me and made to attack me. I was afraid for my life!'

'Attack you be damned!' snarled John. 'I wouldn't need a knife for that! Just shouting "Boo!" at you would be sufficient, you craven coward!'

'So you failed to raise the hue and cry?' persisted de Courtenay.

'This interfering rascal did it for me!' snapped de Wolfe. 'Before I could gather my wits, the house was swarming with people he had dragged in from all around – the stable-keeper, the physician, neighbours, God knows who!'

Laboriously, the new coroner called all those who had responded to Richard's raising of the hue and cry. They all told much the same story, some embellished, but basically confirming that Matilda was dead on the floor, John de Wolfe was present and that there was a dagger dropped nearby.

The evidence of Clement of Salisbury amounted to considerably more in John's disfavour. After repeating the bare facts of being called by de Revelle as part of the hue and cry, de Courtenay asked him if he knew of any reason why Matilda might have been the victim of such violence.

With a sorrowful expression, Clement admitted that he knew there was friction between John de Wolfe and his wife, for he had several times heard violent arguments going on in their hall. This aroused a murmur of interest among the crowd, and many heads turned to stare at John.

'You actually heard such disputes?' demanded de Courtenay. 'How could that be?'

'Their house stands immediately on to the lane, sir. The window shutters allow the sound of voices to escape.' He looked crestfallen, but assumed an air of righteous honesty. 'On one occasion my own wife was present with me and can confirm what I say.'

'Perhaps we should hear from her later,' said the acting coroner. 'But for now, did you hear what was said?'

'I cannot recall the words, but it was of an angry, threatening nature,' replied Clement.

Richard de Revelle was moving restlessly from foot to foot, desperate to have his say, and now he saw his opportunity.

'I can confirm what the good doctor has testified,' he declared, moving to the centre, directly in front of de Courtenay. 'I repeat what I said just now – I called to see my sister last evening and found him standing over the body. As I entered the hall, he turned upon me and drew a dagger!'

'Did he attack you with it?'

'He was very threatening, but I remonstrated with him and he threw it on the floor.'

'You bloody liar, Richard!' called de Wolfe from the side, but the coroner held up a restraining hand as de Revelle continued his tale.

'As Clement of Salisbury has said, my brother-in-law has repeatedly threatened his wife and quite recently, in my presence, I heard him promise to kill her! I am sure that their servants will confirm this.'

This provoked a loud ripple of muttering across the audience, which was strengthened when Lucille, Mary and Cecilia were called to be questioned.

Cecilia did her best to be non-committal, but when directly asked by Aubrey de Courtenay if she backed up her husband's allegation, she reluctantly agreed that on one occasion, when passing their next-door neighbour's window, she had heard a noisy altercation between Sir John and his wife.

'But I am sure it was no more than the frequent raising of voices that occurs between man and wife,' she added, trying to mitigate the damage that was being caused.

Mary the cook-maid was similarly reticent and gave evidence so grudgingly that the coroner had to warn her that she might be in trouble if she told less than the truth. Under this duress, Mary was forced to admit that her master and mistress sometimes had differences of opinion that developed into raised voices, but that she never heard Sir John ever seriously threaten his wife. It was Lucille who did the most damage, in that her evidence related to the time of the killing.

Looking like a frightened rabbit, she stood frail and shivering before the crowd as she related her knowledge of the previous evening.

'The mistress and I had come home from church and I was folding her outdoor clothing in the solar upstairs,' she whispered with chattering teeth. When de Courtenay barked at her to speak up, she almost fainted from fright but managed to get out the rest of her story.

'The mistress was in the hall, taking some wine and cold meats that Mary had left for her, as the cook had gone to visit her cousin. Between the solar and the hall is a small window-slit, high up on the wall. I could hear voices and soon one was raised in anger, but I often heard them arguing or in violent contention, so I took little notice.'

'Could you hear what was being said?' demanded the coroner.

Lucille shook her head. 'No, sire, I was busy packing garments into a chest at the other end of the solar. It was just a distant noise of voices.'

'Did you recognise who was speaking, then?' asked de Courtenay irritably.

Lucille managed to shrug her drooping shoulders. 'I thought it was the master, as they often shouted at one another. Who else would it be, in the hall alone at night with Lady Matilda?'

This time a buzz of excitement gripped the audience, and men and women were turning to stare openly at John de Wolfe. For his part, John listened to the litany of accusers with a sinking heart. Unless he was careful

– or fortunate – he was going to be condemned by default of any contrary evidence on his behalf.

'You wish to deny anything that we have heard, Sir John?' demanded de Courtenay, in a tone that suggested that he was not really concerned with any disclaimers but was required to go through the tiresome motions.

De Wolfe strode to the front again, flinging his black cloak over one shoulder in a dramatic gesture.

'Deny? Of course I deny!' he roared. 'I have heard some travesties of the truth in my time as coroner, but never such a concoction of nonsense as this!'

'You are saying that you never had violent disagreements with your wife, the latest last night, as heard by her handmaiden?' asked de Courtenay in a tone that conveyed his incredulity.

'That was not me who the stupid girl heard!' snarled de Wolfe. 'She may well have heard voices through that slit, but they certainly did not include mine. My wife was dead when I arrived.'

'She said she heard you!' brayed dc Revelle, breaking in from a few feet away.

'She did not say that! She assumed it was me, because she expected any voice at that time and place to have been mine.'

Aubrey de Courtenay returned to chip away at John's denials. 'But your neighbour – and his wife – say they have heard you shouting at your wife in anger, as did your own cook-maid. And Sir Richard here claims you threatened to kill your wife in his presence. Do you say that they are all liars?'

De Wolfe fumed in impotence at being unable to forcefully deny what had been said.

'They were idle words, uttered in temper, without true meaning! Every husband and wife falls out with each other from time to time; it would be unnatural to do otherwise!'

'So you admit to often having angry scenes with your wife?'

'They were not often, as you imply. I will admit that she was a difficult woman and our views on many things were sometimes at variance.'

'Like your frequent infidelities that drove my poor sister twice into a convent,' cried Richard.

John rounded angrily on his brother-in-law. 'If you wish to trade personal insults and evidence of infidelity, I can supply details of seeing you with whores in the sheriff's chamber – and recall that I once rescued you from a burning brothel!'

Aubrey de Courtenay held up his hands to restrain the two men from coming to blows, and Sergeant Gabriel moved nearer, motioning two of his men-at-arms to close in.

'Enough of this! It is unseemly to rake up past happenings, except where they are relevant to this inquest,' exclaimed the Dorset coroner, getting up from his chair and wrapping his dusty cloak around him. 'It is an appropriate point for us to view the deceased, as the law directs. Both myself and the jury will satisfy ourselves that the cadaver is indeed that of Matilda de Wolfe and that she has injuries upon her consistent with the facts that have been heard.'

He led a procession of the score of jurors across the inner bailey towards the tiny church of St Mary, which stood to the left of the gatehouse. It was little more than a stone box with a small bell-arch at one end of the roof and a simple porch on one of the side walls. Gabriel's soldiers kept back the rest of the onlookers, but the front row followed the jury, including the sheriff, constable, archdeacon and portreeves. As the acting coroner neared the chapel door, the portly monk Brother Rufus hurried ahead of him to open it, as he was the garrison chaplain and incumbent of St Mary's.

336

They all filed in, half-filling the small nave, which was separated from the tiny chancel by only a step up from the earthen floor. In front of the linen-covered table that served as the altar, a bier on four stout legs bore a shape shrouded in a crimson velvet cloth.

Sergeant Gabriel, who was carrying out all the duties that Gwyn normally performed, stepped behind it and folded down the red drape to expose Matilda's head and neck. The jury solemnly shuffled past, peering at her face, which seemed to repose quite peacefully in death. They gaped at the six blue-black bruises, each half the size of a penny, that lay on the upper part of her throat and under her jawline – and at some crescentic marks alongside them.

'See the evidence of a strong hand, from a powerful man!' brayed de Revelle triumphantly. 'And the scratches nearby, from my poor sister desperately trying to prise her husband's murderous fingers away!'

Aubrey de Courtenay made no effort to silence the prejudicial ranting, but the sheriff turned on de Revelle.

'Keep your slanderous remarks to yourself, blast you!' he hissed. 'If this were not a church, I would fell you to the ground!'

John de Wolfe stared woodenly at his wife's face, not approaching closely, as he wanted to say his farewells in private, not with half the town gawping at him. As he stood rigidly at the end of the row, Brother Rufus came up to him and laid a comforting arm about his shoulders and murmured something into his ear. John thought for a moment, then nodded at the burly monk, as Aubrey began leading the way towards the door. The jurors filed out into the pale wintry sunshine, and the more elite audience followed them until only Rufus, de Courtenay and John were left.

Aubrey pointed to the door. 'It is time to ask for the jury's verdict, de Wolfe. Go back to your place, please.'

There was a pause, then John shook his head. 'I'm not going!' he said.

Aubrey scowled. 'What d'you mean, you're not going?'

Calmly, de Wolfe took a step backward into the empty nave. 'This is a church, a consecrated place. So I claim sanctuary for forty days, as ordained by the state and the Church!'

CHAPTER EIGHTEEN

In which Crowner John spends some time in church

To say that consternation gripped the company would be a gross understatement. The locum coroner's eyes bulged and he made fluttering gestures with his hands.

'Sanctuary? You can't claim sanctuary. You are a juror in the middle of an inquest!'

'Is this, or is this not, a properly consecrated House of God?' asked John coolly. He looked towards Brother Rufus for confirmation.

'It is indeed,' said the priest. 'The chapel of a royal castle, under the direct control of Canterbury.'

Unlike most castles, Exeter had been built by William the Bastard as a penalty for the Saxon town's revolt of 1068 and had remained in the possession of the Crown ever since, rather than of some local baron.

'But you are a knight, the county coroner and the dead person is your own wife!' spluttered Aubrey de Courtenay.

'And where, may I ask, does the law lay down that any of those prohibit the gaining of sanctuary?' said de Wolfe.

The other man's mouth opened and closed like a fish, but he could find no answer. By now, a few people were coming back into the chapel, wondering at the delay. The first was de Revelle, and Aubrey found his tongue again.

'De Wolfe refuses to come out, Richard!' he exclaimed. 'He says he is claiming sanctuary.'

A thunderous expression came over de Revelle's face. 'Impossible! Drag the man out! He is trying to ridicule the law!'

The stout monk advanced on him angrily. 'You'll not violate sanctuary in my church, sir! Recall what happened after Thomas Becket!'

Henry de Furnellis now hurried in from the porch. 'John? Is this true?' he asked anxiously. 'You have thought of the consequences?'

De Wolfe nodded. Now that the die had been cast, he felt calm and resolute, knowing that there was only one way forward.

'I need time to discover who is the true culprit, Henry. These vultures are only intent upon condemning me, without seeking any other explanation.'

The Dorset man was still trying to deny John's right to sanctuary. 'You are still part of a coroner's jury. I command you to come out and take your place in the inquest,' he protested.

'I decline your kind invitation,' answered John sarcastically. 'I am well aware that the verdict was decided beforehand by you and your cousin's husband here.'

'Then I shall have no option but to continue without you,' huffed Aubrey. 'That will deny you the opportunity to say anything more in your defence.'

'Why, is this a trial, then?' snapped de Wolfe. 'And does anyone think for a moment that anything I say will have the slightest impression on what you have already decided?'

Richard de Revelle, who had just railed against John's right to sanctuary, suddenly reversed his attitude. 'Let him stay here, Aubrey,' he said gaily. 'It proves his guilt, for why else would he abandon the chance to maintain his innocence? Only the guilty run for sanctuary, so he has condemned himself by his own actions!'

He pulled at de Courtenay's arm, but as they went to the door Aubrey called over his shoulder. 'On your own head be it, de Wolfe! I am going to complete the inquest forthwith.'

Henry de Furnellis, John de Alençon and Ralph Morin remained in the chapel with John and the chaplain.

'Archdeacon, is sanctuary valid in these circumstances?' asked the sheriff, his drooping features heavy with concern.

De Alençon nodded. 'I see no reason why it should not be. As de Wolfe has said, there is nothing that prevents it. Sanctuary is denied only to those committing sacrilege against the Church.'

'But how can you go about proving your innocence when you are cooped up in here, John?' boomed Ralph Morin.

'I have forty days to think of something,' replied de Wolfe. 'If I stay out there, those bastards will see that I get thrown into some gaol or other to await trial God knows how far in the future!'

'We had better get back and discover what mischief those two have managed to perpetrate,' growled de Furnellis, leading the way back out into the inner ward. Aubrey de Courtenay was just finishing haranguing the jury, before ordering them to consider their verdict.

'The poor woman clearly was strangled in her own home,' he cried with a flourish of his hand. 'She was still warm when the hue and cry saw her, and her husband, John de Wolfe, was present in the room, waving a dagger about and claiming he found her dead.'

He stopped and glared from one end of the jury to the other.

'You have heard that he regularly quarrelled with his wife and that his brother-in-law has heard him threaten to kill her. His next-door neighbour, a physician and his wife, both of impeccable character, told you that they had heard altercations through the shutters. The dead lady's maid heard voices raised in anger at about the very time that she must have been killed.'

He reached the climax of his damning speech, gesturing with outflung arms. 'John de Wolfe has not denied those facts – and who else would or could have strangled her? It flies in the face of reason to think otherwise! And now he has sought sanctuary – is that the act of an innocent man?'

He dropped his hands to his sides as his histrionics ceased. 'Now you must debate among yourselves as to how Matilda de Wolfe came to her death. This is not a trial and you are not judging anyone's guilt – that is the task of the king's justices when they next come to this city.'

The outcome was both inevitable and rapid. After a few moments' muttering, the man appointed foreman, a pastry-man from the High Street, stepped forward, still wearing his flour-dusted apron.

'We find that the poor lady was murdered and that her husband can be the only man responsible.'

Aubrey de Courtenay nodded his approval. 'Then I so pronounce my verdict,' he said pompously. 'That Matilda, wife of John de Wolfe, was killed with malice aforethought on the twelfth day of November in the seventh year of the reign of our sovereign lord, King Richard. And the jury name the said John de Wolfe as the perpetrator.'

He drew a deep breath, as he had never done this before to a knight of the realm and a king's coroner.

'I therefore use my power as a coroner to commit him for trial before the royal justices and command that he be kept in close custody until that time.'

There was an urgent murmuring among the crowd, broken by a stentorian voice from Henry de Furnellis, Sheriff of Devon. 'How can you commit him, when he is in sanctuary?' he demanded.

De Courtenay shrugged. 'That is now your problem, sheriff! My jurisdiction ceases at the end of an inquest. He either emerges from that chapel and is arrested, or he stays there for forty days and is then starved to death – unless he confesses his crime and abjures the realm, in which case you will need me to come back to take his confession.'

He walked away from his chair as if distancing himself from any further involvement, but Richard de Revelle hurried towards him and began to speak urgently into his ear. The Dorset coroner stopped and beckoned to the sheriff, who from the look on his face would like to strangle Aubrey himself.

'What is it now?' he growled.

'I have been reminded of your close friendship with the accused. I demand that you will not let your personal feelings allow him to escape from sanctuary – nor from your prison, if and when he emerges to be arrested.'

'If he shows his head outside that chapel door, you are entitled – indeed, obliged – to hack it from his shoulders!' added Richard de Revelle with obvious delight.

Henry glowered at the two men. 'I need no reminding of my duties, thank you!' he snarled.

De Courtenay wagged an insolent finger at him. 'I'm sure you don't, but I shall be kept well informed of any mishaps and I will see to it, through my noble family if needs be, that the Curia Regis be immediately made aware of any failure to keep this man in custody!'

With this last threat, he walked away with Richard de Revelle to fetch their horses. Then they rode away to Richard's house to stay the night before his return to Lyme next morning.

'Bastards!' was Henry's succinct comment as he watched them vanish through the gatehouse arch.

'Can you not look the other way when John takes a walk one night?' suggested Ralph Morin, who admired de Wolfe as much as he detested de Revelle.

The sheriff sighed. 'I dare not. Richard will be watching like a bloody hawk! I'll wager he'll station one of his servants here in the bailey during the daytime, to check that John is still here.' He spat on the ground, livid that de Revelle seemed to have got the better of them at last. 'As the king's officer in this county, I have sworn on oath to uphold his peace. Even for such a good man as de Wolfe, I could not break that obligation – and I know that John would not wish me to.'

'I suppose something will turn up,' said Ralph with an optimism that he did not really feel.

That evening was a very strange one for John de Wolfe. As the early dusk approached, the castle bailey lost its daytime bustle and an eerie quiet fell over Rougemont. The gawking crowd from the inquest had dispersed, as John was no longer on show, and soon he was left alone in the empty chapel.

Brother Rufus had brought him a fresh loaf, some cheese and a jug of ale, then went about his business. Gwyn and Thomas had stayed with him for a while, then the Cornishman went off to the Bush, promising to bring up a decent supper when Martha had finished cooking. Both men seemed somewhat ill at ease, unsure how to react to this new situation where their master was virtually a prisoner and accused of murder.

The possibility of him being guilty never crossed either of their minds, but they needed time to adjust and to work out how they might best help him prove his innocence.

It was indeed a bizarre situation, locked in a stone box with only his murdered wife's corpse for company. He wandered over to the bier, a wooden stretcher with four legs, normally kept hanging by ropes from the rafters at the back of St Martin's Church, from where it had been borrowed.

'Matilda, what's to become of me?' he murmured, getting the same lack of response that he usually received when she was alive. 'I never wished this upon you, even when you were at your most obnoxious. We have our fathers to blame for this, God rest their interfering souls!'

As their parents had pushed them into a marriage which neither desired, it was little wonder that two such different personalities as John and Matilda had never found contentment, let alone loving happiness.

He sighed and ambled back to sit on the stone ledge that ran around the walls. Normally, worshippers stood on the packed earth floor, but for the old and infirm there was this comfortless resting place. It gave rise to the expression 'going to the wall', to indicate where failures ended up, John thought wryly.

He chewed listlessly at some of the bread and drank an earthenware cup of Rufus's ale. Sanctuary seekers were entitled to be fed by the parishioners, an obligation that was often resented, especially in times of hardship or famine – which accounted for the number of 'escapes' from sanctuary, as the villagers were often eager to look the other way when they were supposed to be guarding the unwelcome inmate of their church. The law was hazy about the right of access to the sanctuary seeker by family and others

– in this case, there was little likelihood of anyone challenging it, as apart from Richard de Revelle no one really wanted their Crusader coroner locked up.

As well as Gwyn and Thomas, Henry de Furnellis and Ralph Morin had been in to visit him, followed by John de Alençon. His friend the archdeacon said some prayers over Matilda's body and told John that she would be moved to the cathedral next morning, to lie before one of the side altars.

'Whatever her faults, John, she was a genuinely devout woman and will have no problem in finding her place in heaven,' he said solemnly. 'Tomorrow I will begin making arrangements for her funeral and have no doubt that you will be able to leave this place for that, even if I have to get a special dispensation from the bishop, who returned today.'

Typically, he did not ask John whether he was guilty or innocent, but offered to take his confession at any time he cared to give it.

'My only confession would be to having murderous intentions upon whoever did this awful act!' de Wolfe had replied angrily.

Now, sitting upon the cold stone ledge, his mind roved over all the events of the previous day, since he had discovered his wife's body in their hall. Who could have done this? This was the question that drummed endlessly in his mind.

Why Matilda, who, though she had been the bane of his life, was never a threat to anyone else? In fact, her public face in church and in the social life of middle-class Exeter was one of devout respectability and even gracious affability.

Over and over, he went through the catalogue of potential suspects. Top of his list was either Reginald Rugge, the fanatical lay brother, or Alan de Bere, the equally malicious monk. Both were crazed religious extremists and had grounds for hating de Wolfe for breaking up their riot and their attempt to hang the heretics, as well as for getting the pair of them arrested afterwards. But why kill Matilda, unless they felt that it was an easier option than trying to harm the formidable coroner himself? He suspected one or both of them had set the fire that killed Algar and his family, but what relevance could that have had to Matilda's death?

His thoughts moved on to the two proctors' bailiffs, Herbert Gale and William Blundus. Again they were possible suspects, though God alone knows what possible motive there could have been. Of the two, John disliked Herbert Gale the most, as he sensed that he had a cold, unemotional nature that had little regard for human life.

This led him to once again review the other men who were so violently opposed to the survival of anyone with heretical leanings. The canons themselves, especially Richard fitz Rogo, Robert de Baggetor and Ralph de Hospitali – and possibly the other proctor, William de Swindon – were the motivators of this campaign against the Cathars and the latter-day Pelagians, but try as he may, John could not bring himself to see any of those as murderous arsonists and stranglers.

There was one person left in his catechism of suspects. What about Richard de Revelle? It took a wide leap of the imagination to accept that a man could kill his sister, even in the course of a violent quarrel. But in recent months their relationship had become very strained, as Matilda had become progressively disillusioned about her brother. Formerly, he was the apple of her eye as her successful big brother, who had become rich and been made sheriff of the second-largest county in England. But disclosure of his various scandals had shown her that her idol had feet of clay. His involvement in the treachery of Prince John against the king, his dishonesty in dealing with the county finances and various other sins, including personal cowardice, had turned her against him. This situation had been made worse by the fact that her own husband had been largely instrumental in exposing Richard's failings.

But to kill his own sister? It was unthinkable – yet he had turned up at the very moment that John had discovered her body. A coincidence or clever planning? Could de Revelle have been so devious, cunning and evil as to arrange this as a means of at last getting even with his hated brother-in-law, who had so shamed him before all their peers?

He shook his head in bewilderment, unable to focus any longer on the problem. Walking to the door, he looked out into the twilight, where the first stars were appearing in the clear, cold and windy sky. A lone sentry stood a few yards away, a token posted there by Ralph Morin, though as there were two more in the guard-room of the gatehouse, the only exit to the inner ward, it seemed unnecessary. If John had ideas of escape, he would have to think of a better plan than just walking out under the portcullis.

A figure was striding over the drawbridge across the dry moat, and from its rolling gait, a legacy of his fisherman youth, John recognised Gwyn, clutching a basket no doubt containing Martha's supper. He suddenly realised that he was hungry, in spite of the vicissitudes of the day, and soon he was sitting with his officer at the back of the chapel, devouring a meat pie and a couple of capon's thighs, washed down with a wineskin of Anjou red.

'No doubt you'll hear from Stoke and Dawlish tomorrow,' said Gwyn consolingly. 'I saw Andrew at the stables and he said he sent his most reliable man down on a good horse.'

After he had gone, Rufus the chaplain held a late service for half a dozen men-at-arms and several of their wives, but John stayed discreetly at the back of the nave, virtually invisible in the dim light from half a dozen rushlights placed around the chancel. Rufus wished him goodnight after a simple prayer, then John lay down on the floor, wrapped in his cloak and two blankets that Gwyn had brought. Used to far worse sleeping places on many a campaign, he was quite comfortable, and even the knowledge that Matilda's cold body was only twenty paces away did not deter him from sleeping dreamlessly until dawn.

True to his word, Archdeacon John de Alençon came soon after dawn with his nephew Thomas and a covered wagon drawn by a black mare. They all said prayers over Matilda's body, Thomas being very concerned that she had not received the last rites before her dying breath. Then several lay brothers from the cathedral carried the bier out to the wagon and John was left alone again.

During the morning, all his usual friends came in to talk to him and keep him company for a while, but he was fretting to get news of his family in Stoke-in-Teignhead and of Hilda in Dawlish. He expected either the bailiff or reeve from Stoke to come and possibly the reeve from Holcombe, Hilda's father, whom he had known for almost all his life.

Around noon, he was waiting for the dinner that Gwyn had promised to bring him, spending the time in anguished thought about how he could possibly track down his wife's killer. If no other means offered itself, he decided he would somehow break out of the castle and go into hiding in the city, though with his distinctive appearance that would be very difficult. Even his height alone, apart from his black hair and great hooked nose, made him stand out in a city where virtually everyone knew him by sight. He was morosely contemplating these problems when a voice hailed him from the doorway.

'John, I've brought you your dinner!'

His head jerked up and delight filled his face when he saw Hilda coming across the nave, with his mother close behind. Lurking near the door were Gwyn and Thomas, holding back from this family meeting.

Hilda, grasping a basket in her hands, stood aside while Enyd de Wolfe rushed forward and hugged her son to her breast. Though a tough, resolute woman, there were tears in her eyes, as there were in Hilda's, when she in turn fell into John's arms.

When the emotion of the moment had passed, they sat on the stone ledge, with John between the two women.

'Gwyn and Thomas have told us all the details of this ridiculous arrest,' began Enyd, but her son cut her short.

'First, I must know about William. I am almost afraid to ask!'

His mother's face broke into a smile, though tears appeared again in her eyes. 'Dear Thomas's fervent prayers, added to ours, have been answered, John!' she said. 'You brother is recovering, though slowly. His wits returned yesterday and his bladder functions again for the first time in weeks.'

Overjoyed, John grasped Enyd around the waist and kissed her fervently, then turned to give several more kisses to Hilda.

'That news puts all my troubles in the shade,' he boomed. 'Hear that, Gwyn and Thomas? William is on the road to recovery!'

'It will take some time,' warned his mother. 'On Saturday a White Canon came from the new Torre Abbey, learned in physic. He confirmed what Thomas had said, that with the yellow plague, many die, some recover quickly and others take weeks or months to get back to health.'

Immensely relieved by the news, John allowed them to pass on to Matilda's death and all the drama that had followed, which again reduced the two women to tears of concern over his present precarious position.

'What can you do to destroy this vile accusation?' sobbed his mother. 'That evil man de Revelle – I would like to tear his heart out!'

'Maybe I will, if you can't get out of here to do it yourself, John,' said Hilda, rubbing her eyes with her sleeve. De Wolfe recalled that this was the stalwart woman who the previous year had gone looking for her husband's assassins and had actually killed one of them with her own hand.[*]

His mother soon insisted that he begin eating the game pie and grilled trout that the good Martha had sent for him.

'She is a wonderful woman. You are lucky to have her for a wife, Gwyn!' she said. 'We are staying at the Bush until this nonsense is settled.'

John soon learned that the two women had ridden all the way on horseback, shunning any form of cart or litter. With a bailiff and a reeve as escort, his mother had travelled from Stoke across the Teign on the Shaldon ferry and stayed with Hilda the previous night, coming on to Exeter that morning.

When the food had been eaten and every detail of the story recounted, John made them tell him again of

[*] See *The Elixir of Death*.

the way in which William had showed signs of recovery and the degree to which he was improving.

'He is now quite rational in his speech, thank God, though very weak,' said his mother, crossing herself in unison with Thomas, who stood behind, smiling benignly. 'He recalls almost nothing of the many days that he was delirious and without speech, but already he is planning the crops he wants planted in the spring! Evelyn has stayed behind to care for him; otherwise she would have been with us.'

After an hour Enyd pleaded fatigue, though she looked as energetic as ever, but she made Gwyn and Thomas escort her back to the Bush for food and rest – an obvious ploy to leave Hilda alone with her son.

The two sat side by side on the cold stone, holding hands, the most they felt able to do in this consecrated place.

'What will become of us, John?' she asked quietly. 'I know you can hang for this unless the real killer can be unmasked.'

'That will never happen, Hilda my love,' he said with a confidence that he did not fully believe. 'I have forty days' grace, but I shall not stay in here for long. Henry de Furnellis is in a difficult position and I would not wish to get him into deep trouble by allowing him to connive at my escape. But I will manage it, never fear. I have given no promise not to try.'

Neither of them wished to mention the obvious consequence of Matilda's death, that he was now a free man. With her body as yet unburied and John committed to trial for murder, it was a forbidden subject, yet both of them knew that the possible outcome hovered unbidden over them.

Eventually, he reluctantly sent her away to join his mother at the Bush, with her promise that she and Enyd would come again that evening. All his friends came one by one during the rest of the day, including Mary, who brought Brutus up to see him at the door of the chapel. His first news for every visitor was the recovery of his brother, not a discussion of his own predicament. He even joined Brother Rufus on his knees at the altar in solemn and genuine thanksgiving for William's escape from death.

Henry de Furnellis came to see him late in the afternoon and again pleaded for John's understanding of the difficult position in which he had been placed by Aubrey de Courtenay.

'He is strongly under the influence of Richard de Revelle, who detests me for replacing him as sheriff,' he said bitterly. 'Though God knows I did not seek the bloody job! All I want is a quiet life down at my manor, but if I put a foot wrong over this affair he will see that I am dishonoured and ruined.'

Once again, John tried to assure his friend that he knew the problem and he forbade Henry to take any risks with his honour and reputation. 'But that doesn't mean that I will miss any opportunity to find a way out of this damned place!' he added vehemently.

They went over the same old ground again, trying to think of possible suspects and ways to flush them out, but made no progress.

'I suppose I could re-arrest those two swine we had here in the undercroft, if they poke their noses outside the cathedral Close,' suggested the sheriff. 'Then I could set Stigand on to them and see what he can wring out of them with his persuasive instruments!'

'That will get you into trouble with the bishop, Henry,' warned John. 'Best let things lie for the moment. I'll think of something. I still have Gwyn and clever little Thomas to work for me on the outside.'

When Henry had gone, John sat slumped on his flinty ledge as yet another dusk began to creep over the city. He rubbed his chin, where a black stubble was forming, as he had missed his weekly wash and shave on Saturday. His black hair, worn long at the back, was greasy and tangled, and he felt generally grubby and unkempt. 'Forty days of this and I'll be looking like some wild hermit from a cave on Dartmoor!' he muttered to himself.

In desperation he began plotting how to escape from Rougemont, the fortress on the hill. John had noticed an old Benedictine habit belonging to Rufus hanging in an alcove at the back of the chapel. He thought he might pass himself off as the chaplain, if he padded his belly with a blanket to imitate the fat monk's figure and pulled the hood well over his face. Getting past the sentry at the gate was the problem, but maybe Gwyn could cause some sort of diversion to distract him, such as a fire at the other end of the inner ward. He decided to broach the subject when the Cornishman brought up his supper that evening. But once again Fate had other plans.

Mary was seated in her kitchen-hut at the back of John's house, thinking what she might take up to him tomorrow for his dinner. When she had visited him earlier, she demanded to be allowed to feed him, as well as the supply from the Bush.

'I am your cook, Sir Coroner!' she claimed, using the title she employed when she was annoyed or sarcastic. 'You house me and pay for the food we eat, so I am going to feed you.' Her mild impertinence was a cover for her deep concern for him, as well as for her own future if he ended up swinging at the end of a rope. She sat fondling the old hound's ears and trying to decide between another meat pie, which was easier to eat at the back of a church, or a grilled fowl in a basket.

As she sat in the fading evening light, she gradually became aware of a moaning sound nearby. Brutus pricked up his ears and padded out of the shed, his head cocked on one side as he listened.

'What is it, lad?' she asked him, as he stared at the high wooden fence that separated their yard from the one next door. The dog gave a deep woof and went to the bottom of the fence and scratched at the rough boards. Mary put her eye to one of the narrow cracks but could see nothing in the poor light. Then the sound came again, a gasping croak, followed by more soft moaning.

Unable to see over the fence, the cook-maid turned and ran up the wooden steps that led to the solar, the room that projected high up from the back of the house. Halfway up, she peered over into the next-door yard and saw someone lying on the ground, moving feebly. Mary shouted down, but there was no response. As she hurried back down the steps, Lucille emerged from her cubicle underneath, disturbed by the footsteps and the shouting.

'What's happening, Mary?' she said fearfully, her nervous nature already stretched to its limit by all the recent troubles. The two women were not good friends, as Mary knew she had often carried tales to Matilda, but the present upheaval in the household had submerged their differences.

'It looks as if Mistress Cecilia has been taken ill. I hope by every saint in the calendar that it's not the plague!'

The dark-haired cook jogged around the side passage to the vestibule and went out into Martin's Lane, Lucille following timidly in her wake. Mention of the plague had abruptly dampened her willingness to help, but she felt obliged to see what was happening.

Mary ran to the front door of the doctor's house and saw that it was wide open. At the threshold, she called out, as a servant had no right to barge in to someone else's dwelling, but there was no response. With Lucille close behind, she stepped straight into the darkened hall, as there was no vestibule as in the de Wolfe house.

The door to the yard was at the back of the large chamber, and a faint rectangle of light showed that it, too, was open. Mary made towards it but was pulled up by a piercing shriek from the French woman behind her, who had veered off slightly to her left and tripped over the legs of a body on the floor.

Their eyes now better used to the gloom, Mary saw that Cecilia's young maid was crumpled on the rushes. When she knelt near her, she was relieved to hear her still breathing, though in a jerky, snoring fashion. She smelled blood and, feeling with her hands in the girl's fair hair, found a sticky patch, already swelling under her fingers.

Lucille was blubbering with fright, but Mary was made of much sterner stuff. She rose to her feet and shook the maid by her thin shoulders.

'Stop that stupid noise, girl!' she commanded. 'Now run over to Andrew in the stables and tell him that someone has been attacked and to raise the hue and cry. Hurry, damn you!'

She pushed Lucille towards the door and bent over the maid again. There was nothing she could do for her in the dark and moving her might cause more damage. The unexpected finding had momentarily driven from her mind the fact that there was someone else moaning outside. She sped to the back door and went out into the yard, where there was still some twilight.

'God preserve us from more bodies!' she muttered as she saw yet another figure lying on the cold earth, between the privy and the well. 'At least this one is still moving.'

Once more, she dropped to her knees. This time alongside Cecilia, for it was the mistress of the house who was sprawled face down on the dirt, making harsh, guttural noises, alternating with pitiful moans. Mary tried to lift her up but only managed to roll her on to her back, where her croaking breaths became more laboured. Squatting on the ground, Mary hoisted her shoulders up and cradled her on her lap, feeling powerless to do any more for the ailing woman.

'At least it's not the damned plague,' she murmured distractedly. 'But is someone trying to assassinate all the women in Martin's Lane?'

Thankfully, there was the noise of boots in the hall and Andrew, the red-headed farrier from across the lane, appeared with one of his stable boys.

'I've sent for help. The constables and some neighbours will soon be here!' he announced tersely. His groom held a lantern, a pair of candles behind a window of thin horn, which was enough to dimly illuminate the scene. By its flickering light they could see that Cecilia's face was congested and puffy, with a speckle of blood spots in the whites of her eyes. Mary pulled away her coverchief to release a cascade of black hair and, in case it was impeding her breathing, loosened the silken gorget which ran from ear to ear under her chin.

'Look at her neck!' exclaimed the farrier. 'Covered in bruises, poor lady!'

Mary recalled that it was the second time in a few days that she had seen marks like this, then her mind soared! Surely two such stranglings, not fifty paces apart, must have been made by the same attacker? And that could *not* be John de Wolfe, as he was incarcerated in St Mary's Chapel!

Her elation was promptly interrupted by Cecilia, who grasped the arm that was supporting her and began croaking unintelligibly.

'You are safe now, mistress,' soothed Mary. 'Help is coming soon, then we will get you to bed.' She almost added that they would also send for a physician, until she realised that the only doctor this side of Bristol was the woman's own husband.

In spite of Mary's reassurance, the injured woman persisted in trying to speak. Putting her ear closer and telling Cecilia to whisper instead of trying to croak, she managed after several attempts to make out a few words.

'Clement ... my husband ... tried to kill me ... just as he killed poor Matilda!'

John de Wolfe was sitting on his ledge in the garrison chapel, thinking rather selfishly that they were late with his supper tonight, as his stomach was rumbling. For the moment he was dwelling more on his hunger than on his serious predicament.

It was now virtually dark and he had lit one of his thin rushlights from the single candle that burned on the altar, sticking the grease-soaked reed between two cracks in the masonry.

Suddenly, he heard running feet echoing in the gatehouse archway and some indistinct shouting. Before he could get to the porch, the bulky figure of Brother Rufus burst in, shouting for him.

'John! Gwyn has just come up from town, seeking the sheriff. He told me to tell you that your next-door neighbour has been attacked!'

'What! Clement the physician?'

'No, it's his wife! Their maid is injured as well.'

'Did Gwyn say who did it? What the hell's going on?' demanded de Wolfe.

The chaplain shook his head, dimly seen in the gloom. 'I don't know, your man didn't stop. He was heading for the keep to get Henry de Furnellis.'

'Henry's not there. He told me he was going back to his house,' exclaimed John, agitated that something important was going on and he was not a part of it. He fumed for a moment, then pushed past Rufus to get to the door.

'I'm going out and to hell with the consequences!' he snarled. 'I must know what's happening out there.'

The monk grabbed him with a very strong arm. 'Wait, John! If you break sanctuary, you may pay for it with your life. I'll go and find out what all this is about, before you do anything rash.' He vanished and, moving quickly for such a big man, hurried over to the keep. At the foot of the wooden stairs that went up to the entrance, he met Ralph Morin clattering down, Gwyn close behind him.

'We must collect the sheriff from North Gate Street and get down to Martin's Lane as fast as we can!' shouted the castle constable.

As the three men set off across the inner ward, Ralph yelled at a passing soldier and told him to collect Sergeant Gabriel and half a dozen men, to follow them down to the town.

'De Wolfe was on the point of breaking out when he heard the news,' panted Rufus, his bulk beginning to slow him down. 'I managed to stop him, but not for long, I suspect!'

Morin stopped dead near the gatehouse. Tugging at his forked beard, he made a decision. 'He can come with us now! I'll vouch for him. I'll say he's my prisoner under parole.'

Gwyn shot towards the chapel and immediately emerged with the coroner, who had been standing in the porch in a fever of anxiety.

'We're all going down to find Henry,' snapped Morin, starting to jog again. 'Officially, you're my prisoner, John, so please don't make a run for it!'

359

'Why the hell should I do that now?' retorted de Wolfe. 'It sounds as if this might vindicate me, though I'm still not clear what's happened.'

'Nor am I, so let's find out!' growled Ralph.

They trotted down the hill and along the High Street and when they reached the corner of Martin's Lane they heard and saw a crowd of people milling around outside the two houses that stood side by side opposite the livery stables.

'Gwyn, go to the sheriff's house and drag him out,' commanded Morin. 'Tell him what you know and bring him back here as fast as you can.'

With John and Rufus at his side, Ralph pushed his way through the throng, where Osric and Theobald, the city constables, were trying to organise a hue and cry from the disorderly crowd. Inside Clement's hall, a couple of local matrons were bending over the young maid, who was still unconscious.

'She's had a bad blow on the head, poor lamb,' said one. 'We've sent for Richard Lustcote the apothecary, but I think she should be taken to the monks at St John's.'

A few candles had now been lit, and John, who suddenly became a coroner once more, suspected that by the look of the large bruise on her jaw, the girl had been punched in the face and had then fallen backwards, striking her head.

There was cry from outside the back door, and de Wolfe recognised Mary's voice. He hurried out ahead of Morin and the monk, to see his cook-maid sitting on the earth in the gloom, still cradling the head and shoulders of Cecilia of Salisbury.

'She has been throttled, John!' said Mary, forgetting the 'Sir' in her agitation. 'But she seems in no danger, though her voice has almost gone. But she managed to tell me that she cannot remember anything since he attacked her.'

'He? Who's he?' demanded John, almost demented with mixed rage and relief.

'Yes, what evil bastard did this?' bellowed Ralph Morin from behind him.

'She says it was her husband,' answered Mary in a voice choked with emotion. 'And she said that Clement also strangled my mistress, may God curse him!'

An hour later some order had been made out of the chaos in Martin's Lane. The apothecary had examined both Cecilia and her maid, who was slowly showing signs of regaining her wits. Richard Lustcote decided that neither would gain anything by being carried off to St John's Priory and that bed rest and some soothing potions would be the best treatment.

John had sent Gwyn down to the Bush to fetch Enyd and Hilda and soon they arrived, weeping tears of relief at his sudden deliverance from the accusation of murder. His mother clutched him to her breast as if she wanted to crush him back into the womb that had borne him, while Hilda braved his black stubble to give him tender kisses of thankfulness. Once they had vented their emotion, they willingly agreed to help tend to the two victims in Cecilia's own house.

Instead of a solar, there was a bedroom partitioned off the hall, and here the lady of the house was gently laid on her couch. Lustcote applied some soothing balm to her bruised throat and gave her a honeyed draught to ease her battered voice-box. The maid normally slept in the warm kitchen-shed, as they had no live-in cook, so after her head wound had been cleaned and bandaged she was laid there, under the watchful eyes of a benign neighbour.

John had looked at the damage to Cecilia's neck while Richard Lustcote was anointing it and saw typical finger bruises and nail scratches on the skin.

'Almost exactly the same as those on Matilda's throat,' he told Henry de Furnellis when the men were standing around the fire in his own hall next door, drinking some ale after all the commotion. A dozen neighbours and a few men-at-arms had gone off around the city streets as the hue and cry, this time looking for Clement the physician.

'Why the scratches, as well as the blue bruises?' asked Brother Rufus, who did not intend to miss any of this drama.

'From fingernails,' explained de Wolfe. 'Usually from the victim trying to tear away the strangler's hands.'

'Why should her husband want to kill her, for Christ's sake?' demanded Henry de Furnellis. 'And why kill Matilda, as she claimed?'

John shrugged, though he badly wanted to know the answer himself. 'When she can speak more easily, no doubt all will be made plain. In the meantime, where is that murderous bastard?'

The sheriff for once looked optimistic, a rare mood for him. 'We'll get him, never fear! I've sent soldiers down to each of the city gates, to make sure that tonight no one goes in or out. Hopefully, not a mouse can leave the city, so he must be in here somewhere.'

Leaving the women to look after the victims, they decided to join the hunt and, after placing a man-at-arms on the door, dispersed to join the various groups who had formed the hue and cry about the town. By now, the city grapevine had alerted almost the whole population; one of these was Thomas, who hurried up just as John and Gwyn were leaving.

His peaky face was creased in smiles when Gwyn explained that their master was now free from suspicion, and he crossed himself repeatedly as he murmured a prayer of thanks for John's deliverance.

'We're off to look for this damned doctor now,' rumbled Gwyn. 'You're the clever one among us – where do you reckon he might be hiding?'

'Have you tried the place where he holds his healing consultations?' suggested Thomas. 'I think it was in Goldsmith Street.'

They hurried to the lane near the Guildhall, but found it was one of the first places that the men of the hue and cry had thought of. Theobald, the fat constable, was still standing outside the shop when they arrived.

'Osric told me to keep watch in case Clement came back,' he explained.

'Came back? So was he here before?' snapped de Wolfe.

Theobald waved a hand at the premises behind him, which was a former cordwainer's shop with a wooden shutter on the front which was lowered to form a display counter.

'The door was open and there's some disorder inside, bottles and pills scattered on the floor, but no sign of the doctor.'

Thomas had a quick look inside the single room and came out nodding. 'Looks as if he was searching for something in great haste,' he reported.

The coroner looked from face to face. 'Now where do we look?' he asked angrily. He had collected his sword from his hall and was swishing it aggressively, as if practising to lop off the head of the man who had slain his wife.

As usual, it was Thomas who had the best suggestion. 'The physician is a very devout man, perhaps abnormally so, by all accounts,' he observed. 'So perhaps he has taken himself to a church to seek absolution for his many sins?'

'Perhaps he's also seeking sanctuary!' said Gwyn with unconscious irony, after de Wolfe's recent manoeuvre.

The coroner rasped a hand over his bristly cheeks as he thought of the various places Clement might have gone to.

'Not the cathedral, it's too obvious and too many people hanging about there. But what about St Olave's; he is very friendly with that poxy priest, Julian Fulk.'

For want of any better idea, they set off down the High Street and across Carfoix to the little church at the top of Fore Street, founded by Gytha, the Saxon mother of King Harold. Outside, de Wolfe hesitated and beckoned to his clerk.

'Thomas, I can't go storming in there with a naked sword and I'm not leaving it in the street. You're a priest. You go in and see if there's any sign of him.'

He waited with Gwyn at the edge of the road, listening to the cries of other searchers lower down towards the West Gate. The fitful light of a gibbous moon appeared through a gap in the clouds and illuminated another group of men coming out of Milk Lane almost opposite, their tramping feet echoing in the night air.

Then their attention was jerked back to the church as Thomas's face appeared in the doorway, looking even paler than usual, given the poor light.

'You'd better come in, master!' he said in a very subdued voice. 'Sword or no sword, this is more important.'

John and his officer followed the clerk into the bare nave lit only by a pair of candles on the altar.

As Thomas led them towards the chancel step, he began intoning, '*Domine, requiem aeternam dona eis, et lux perpetua luceat eis.*'

A moment later they saw the outline of a man spreadeagled across the step, his arms outstretched as if in supplication to the cross on the altar table. De

Wolfe bent and grasped the back of his hair and lifted the head to see the face.

It was Clement of Salisbury, his features contorted in a final grimace of agony, his mouth twisted into a rictus of pain. Smashed alongside him was a small pottery bottle, a trickle of dark liquid still seeping down a crack in the chancel step, just as the physician's life had seeped away a short while earlier.

Next morning the main participants assembled again in the hall of Clement's house. Mary had brought in pastries, ale, cider and wine from her kitchen, and they sat around the large table where some time ago John and Matilda had eaten supper with the physician and his wife.

'How is the young maid today?' asked the sheriff, who sat at the head of the table.

'Recovering, thank the Blessed Virgin,' said Enyd de Wolfe, who had appointed herself chief nurse. 'She has regained her senses but has a severe headache and her face is sore from that bruise. The apothecary, bless him, has given her a strong draught to let her sleep today.'

'The poor child must have had a heavy blow to the face,' added Hilda, who sat next to John and held his hand under cover of the table.

'My husband hit her when she tried to stop him assaulting me,' whispered Cecilia. She had insisted on leaving her bed when the others came, saying that it was her throat that was afflicted, not her legs or brain. She wore a heavy blue brocade surcoat over her nightgown, the collar turned up over a swathe of bandage that Richard Lustcote had wound around her neck to hold his poultice in place.

'Don't strain your throat, dear woman,' advised Enyd solicitously, but Cecilia said that whispering was not a problem.

'I want to expose all the facts of this terrible matter, so that no one carries any further blame,' she breathed earnestly. 'The fault lay entirely in this household, I fear, for my husband was quite mad, though I did not fully realise it until last night.'

The others listened in horrified fascination as she slowly and quietly revealed the extent of Clement's obsessions.

'He did not move to Exeter to set up a better physician's practice,' she said. 'We were forced to leave Salisbury because of his behaviour.'

'In what sense, lady?' asked Brother Rufus in a gentle voice.

'His obsession with religion, which he must have had all his life, grew more extreme there. His first choice was to become a priest, not a doctor, but his parents would not allow it. Perhaps even then they suspected his strange notions.'

'Which were?' prompted Thomas, fascinated by this story of religious distortion.

'That the perfection of the Church was established by the early founders in Rome and this was the only thing that mattered. Adherence to their precepts was the salvation of the world and any deviation from their rituals was the work of the devil.'

'But many priests, especially in the higher orders, would fully agree with that!' objected Rufus mildly.

Cecilia coughed and paused a moment to rest her voice, Enyd patting her shoulder and offering her a cup of watered wine.

'Not to the exclusion of every other topic,' she continued after a while. 'He preached at me continually, always on the same theme of the purity of the Church of Rome and the need to be always vigilant against its enemies and detractors. It became so monotonous that I tried to turn away from God, but he punished me for it.'

'Punished? You mean by force?' asked Hilda aghast.

For answer Cecilia pushed up the loose sleeves of her surcoat and exposed her arms. They bore many yellow and green bruises, some of considerable age.

'He often pulled and punched me, if I dared disagree with his ranting or was reluctant to go to devotions with him. But he took care to mark me only where it did not show in public.'

'The bastard!' muttered John. 'Who would have guessed it?'

'The people in Salisbury, for a start,' replied Cecilia. 'Though he was an effective physician, as long as he was paid well enough, he could never resist preaching at his patients and became unpopular as a result.'

'Was that cause enough to leave?' asked Rufus.

'The end began when he struck one woman who told him to leave religion to the priests and stick to prescribing pills!' replied Cecilia. 'The last straw was when he refused to treat a sick infant when he discovered it had not yet been baptised and it later died.'

'And you say he was violent towards you – did he ever try to strangle you, like last night?' asked Henry de Furnellis.

'No, it was always shaking and striking,' she said with tears in her eyes. 'And he would also punish me by his strange ways in the bedchamber,' she whispered, her pallid face flushing as she dropped her eyes in embarrassment.

The sheriff hurried to cover up her distress by changing the direction of his questions. 'We need to know why he tried to kill you and how that was connected to the death of Lady Matilda next door,' he said gravely.

Enyd held up her hand and then gave Cecilia a cup of warm honeyed milk. 'She is talking too much, important as it is. Give her a moment's rest, please.'

Mary, who was hovering in the background, occupied the break by handing round the platter of pastries filled with chopped meat and herbs and refilling empty cups from the jugs that stood on the table. Soon, Cecilia finished her soothing draught and handed the mug back to John's mother with a grateful smile.

'It all happened so quickly last night,' she continued. 'Clement had claimed he had a sore throat since the previous evening and had bound up his neck with a length of flannel, just as I am now!' She smiled wanly at the ironic similarity. 'Last evening he came in from his work and said he was going to apply more liniment to his throat, so went into the bedchamber. A few moments later I happened to walk in on him and found him with his tunic opened at the neck, as he pulled off the long strip of flannel.'

She stopped and stared down at her hands on the edge of the table, as if reliving that cataclysmic moment in her life.

'And then?' prompted John gently.

'I saw that the skin of his neck was covered in scratches, running downwards under his chin and jaw. I knew what they were; they were made by fingernails clawing at his neck. Instantly, he tried to cover them up again with the cloth, to hide them from me, so I knew they came from some wrongdoing. My first thought was that they were from some woman's passion in love-making, but then they should have been on his back and chest, not under his chin.'

There was a silence, partly from further embarrassment at the carnal nature of the explanation, but also because Cecilia's eyes had again filled with tears.

'I was afraid to challenge him on his infidelity in case he began beating me, but he started ranting about heretics, claiming that this was all their fault. If it had not been for them and the need to exterminate every one, he raved at me, he would not have been in this predicament!'

'What did he mean?' asked the sheriff mystified.

De Wolfe was quicker off the mark in his understanding. 'Was he confessing to having set the fire that killed the fuller in Milk Lane?'

Cecilia started to nod, but the movement hurt her neck and she grimaced before replying. 'Yes, Sir John. Without my even asking, he started to complain about the forces of the devil being against him, when he was trying to perform God's work in ridding the city of those who denied the omnipotence of the Holy Church. Those were his actual words!'

She shuddered as she recollected that awful moment. 'He said that as he was leaving Milk Lane after carrying out his duty as ordained by the Almighty, he saw Matilda de Wolfe standing in the doorway of St Olave's and was sure that she had recognised him.'

John groaned with dismay as he heard this, recollecting his wife's strange mood the following day, which must now be put down to her suspicions of the physician. For God's sake, why did she not confide in him? he agonised.

Enyd offered Cecilia another cup, but she shook her head.

'By now, my husband was advancing on me, his hands reaching for my throat, as he knew he had fatally compromised himself.' Her whispers were vibrant with emotion, and John's mother slipped a comforting arm around her shoulder.

'But my wife?' croaked John. 'What had happened?'

'Clement said that he could no longer bear the suspense of waiting for her to denounce him and went into her house to confront her. She admitted she had seen him slink out of Milk Lane immediately after the fire had started. Not sure of his guilt, she was going to tell her husband the next day, as it was her duty as wife of a law officer.'

De Wolfe groaned at the explanation. Matilda was prepared to follow her conscience, in spite of her antipathy to him – but she had left it too late.

'So he silenced her, just as he tried to silence you?'

Cecilia sobbed and Enyd held her tight. 'He came for me and I ran in here, but he seized me by the throat. My poor little maid heard the commotion, ran in and tried to pull him off, but he felled her to the floor. He ranted that I was a heretic at heart, avoiding church when I could and refusing to join their petition to the canons. I shook him off and ran into the yard, trying to escape, but he followed … and that was the last I remember until you kind people revived me. He must have thought that he had left me dead!'

'She has had enough now!' said Enyd de Wolfe firmly. 'We'll put you to rest for a while, my dear.'

As the other women went to settle Cecilia on her bed, the men continued to sit around the table in a subdued mood.

'What happens now?' asked Ralph Morin, who had been a silent listener to this drama. 'Where does John stand in this?'

Henry de Furnellis poured himself a pint of cider and drank half of it before replying. 'Legally, he's a sanctuary seeker and stands committed by a coroner's jury to trial before the king's judges,' he said. 'But as that idiot de Courtenay was so grossly influenced by Richard de bloody Revelle, I intend ignoring his verdict in the light of what has happened since.'

'The facts will have to be put before the Justices of Assize, as a matter of record,' said John doggedly, even though it might be to his disadvantage.

'I hope so – otherwise that persistent troublemaker de Revelle will wriggle out of it once again,' growled Morin.

Thomas de Peyne ventured a suggestion, which was always worth heeding. 'The Chief Justiciar knows the situation in Devon very well, sir. Should not a letter be sent to him, explaining what has happened? As he's Archbishop of Canterbury as well, the fact that this grew out of a heresy problem makes it all the more relevant.'

Archbishop Hubert Walter was an old Crusader and knew John de Wolfe better than most other men. It would be a good insurance against any repercussions over this affair, and the sheriff approved of the idea.

'The next time I go to Westminster with the county farm for the Exchequer, I'll take such a letter – and see Hubert myself to explain what's been going on here.'

They sat drinking for a moment longer, then Gwyn opened up a different aspect of the drama.

'What about these other killings?' he grunted. 'Are they all down to this doctor fellow?'

De Wolfe reflectively scratched a flea bite on his head. 'Maybe we'll never know! With Clement's confessed guilt about my wife and to burning that family to death, as well as attacking his wife and her maid, everyone will be happy to lay all other crimes at his feet.'

'I suppose there's no reason why he couldn't have done them,' boomed Ralph Morin. 'As a physician, he travelled about outside Exeter. It's no distance to Wonford, and the other murders were actually in the city.'

The sheriff shrugged. 'As John says, we'll never know the whole truth, though he seems the most obvious culprit. The way that poor man's voice-box was cut out smacks of medical knowledge to me.'

'Yet that mad monk Alan de Bere and his fanatical friend Rugge were crazy enough to have been the killers,' countered John.

'And I wouldn't put it past those proctors' men, either!' added Brother Rufus darkly. 'Whoever it was, God will know well enough when it comes to the Day of Judgement.'

Thomas nodded fervently and crossed himself, and with a sense of anticlimax the meeting broke up, John taking Mary back next door, leaving his mother and Hilda to care for the bruised and battered women.

Gwyn and Thomas thought it best to leave their master to his own thoughts, so John settled in his chair in the empty hall, with only Brutus and a cup of wine for company.

He sat brooding darkly on what he had just heard. This was the very chamber in which that bastard Clement had ended his wife's life, and though John was not sufficient of a hypocrite to shed crocodile tears, it was still his wife and the woman who had shared his life for so many years, albeit intermittently. What right had that swine to take her away in such a violent fashion? The sudden horror of that episode even overshadowed the obvious liberation that it had given him, the freedom now to be with Hilda. His blonde mistress and lifelong friend was sensitive enough to avoid the subject for now, until the emotional avalanche had levelled out.

She said she would stay at the Bush for another two nights, to attend Matilda's funeral, which John de Alençon had arranged for tomorrow in the cathedral. Then she would have to go back with Enyd, who was keen to return to help Evelyn look after William, who was still very weak. John was determined to escort them back himself, as he was desperate to see his brother returning to health.

He sat for a while longer before going up to Rougemont, where Gwyn said a local case needed his attention. He would also have to hold an inquest on Clement of Salisbury later that day – on reflection, it was fortunate that he had killed himself, as John had been fully prepared to run his sword through him if he had found him alive, getting himself into more trouble.

Richard Lustcote, whom John called to look at the body and the broken flask, had said that from the smell and tentative taste, the black fluid was a strong extract of monkshood and belladonna and possibly other poisons that the physician would have had in his pharmacopoeia.

With a sigh he hauled himself out of his chair and, with a final pensive glance at the empty one on the other side of the hearth, he went out of the hall to carry on with his life.

epilogue

Three months later, on a clear winter's day, Sir John de Wolfe was married to Hilda of Dawlish in the porch of St Andrew's Church in Stoke-in-Teignhead, the parchment with the banns still nailed to the door as they faced it for the ceremony, as was the tradition.

The slim blonde, in a long gown of blue satin under a fur-lined pelisse of dark blue velvet, was attended by a beaming Evelyn as maid of honour. John, in a new grey tunic and mantle, had his brother William as his wedding squire, still thin and pale but happy to be back in charge of his beloved manors.

After Father Martin, assisted by Thomas de Peyne, had completed the ceremony and taken them inside the church for the nuptial Mass and a blessing, they all adjourned to the nearby Church Hostel for the 'bride-ale', a lavish feast, which overflowed on to the street, where trestles were spread with food and drink for the whole village, the festivities lasting until well after dark.

Many guests had come down from Exeter by cart and on horseback the previous day, so that all John's friends were there to wish them good fortune. Gwyn, Martha, Mary, Henry de Furnellis, John de Alençon, Hugh de Relaga, Ralph Morin, Gabriel were there – even

Andrew the livery man, who provided the transport. A further large contingent came across the river from Holcombe, including all Hilda's extensive family.

As John stood with an arm around the slim waist of his lovely bride, a hand grasping a cup of mead, a thought penetrated the haze of his happy confusion. He wondered where Nesta was at this moment, the Welsh woman whom he had undoubtedly loved, as he now loved Hilda. Was she still happily married to her stonemason in Chepstow and was there perhaps a chubby infant at her breast? Would she ever learn of Matilda's death?

Another person who did not attend the wedding was Cecilia, who, as soon as she fully recovered, left the house and returned to live with her family in Worcester, taking Lucille with her as her maid, as her own did not wish to leave her folks in the city. Cecilia had confessed to John that she felt out of place in Exeter, being a reminder to the citizens of the harm that her husband had done there. Though de Wolfe did not appreciate it, the perceptive Mary suspected that Hilda was secretly pleased that the handsome widow was going far enough away not to be a temptation to a susceptible next-door neighbour!

Yet another notable absentee was Richard de Revelle, whom John had not laid eyes on since Matilda's funeral, when they both studiously ignored each other. That sad occasion had also been well attended, as Matilda's many friends from St Olave's and the cathedral had been augmented by a large number of sympathetic citizens. The Requiem Mass was conducted by the archdeacon, and she was laid to rest under the floor before the altar of St John in the nave, right up against the rood screen. Since then, John had had it covered by an inscribed granite slab, which recorded Matilda's name for posterity.

John had heard nothing more from Aubrey de Courtenay, the Dorset coroner. The sheriff had gone on his routine visit to Westminster with his pony-train of panniers filled with silver coins and had seen Hubert Walter, who had sent his condolences to John and told him to ignore any legal complications that the Justices in Eyre might raise when they eventually came to Exeter. He also forcibly expressed the wish that John continue as county coroner, for de Wolfe had had some qualms about his position, given that he had been arrested, committed for murder and had sought sanctuary as a common criminal, even though the allegations proved unfounded.

This hardened his resolve to stay in the city, rather than move to Hilda's fine house in Dawlish, as she had suggested. She did not want to move permanently to Exeter, so they compromised by living part-time in each place, with Hilda spending at least one week a month at the coast and John going from there to visit his family at Stoke far more often since the scare over his brother's health.

The yellow plague vanished from Devon as mysteriously as it had arrived, but reports from other parts of the country showed that it struck sporadically here and there. However, it claimed one last victim in the city and simultaneously cleared up one last mystery. The mad monk, Alan de Bere, had been living in his hovel on the marshes near the river, when he was struck by the dreaded disease. As someone in holy orders, however renegade he had become, he was taken to St John's Hospital, where it was soon all too apparent that he was dying. Brother Saulf urged him to make a last confession and, surprisingly, de Bere gasped that he wished to confess to murder and wanted a law officer to be present. John de Wolfe was away at his brother's manor, so Gwyn and Thomas were called instead. In their presence, the monk admitted that he and Reginald Rugge, the weird lay brother from St Olave's, had taken it into their own hands to cleanse the world of two heretics whom the Church seemed unable to deal with. These were the porter from Bretayne and the man from Wonford. The first they smothered and hid among the plague victims, the other man they stabbed and hid in the earth closet.

'And what about the woodcarver whose throat you tore out?' growled Gwyn, standing uncaringly over the yellowed man who lay dying at his feet.

Alan de Bere stared up at the massive Cornishman. 'I swear to God we had nothing to do with that,' he whispered. 'That must have been one of the doctor's.'

As they left the priory, Gwyn and Thomas walked in silence for a while. 'Is that confession going to be any use, given that two priests were present?' grunted Gwyn.

Thomas nodded. 'He asked for a law officer, so he intended it to be known far and wide. It had none of the inviolacy of the confessional, so it can be disclosed to the coroner. Sir John will welcome it to clear up two uncompleted inquests.'

'So what about the woodcarver, Nicholas Budd? That bloody monk back there says he didn't do it – and I can't see why he should tell anything but the truth on his deathbed.'

Thomas crossed himself jerkily. 'God rest him, however evil he's been. If it wasn't that awful pair, then it must have been the doctor. We thought at the time that someone with medical skill may have cut out that voice-box so neatly.' He shuddered at the memory, as they walked on. There was no way to squeeze the truth out of Reginald Rugge, as he had vanished immediately after Clement's death and by now was probably living rough somewhere in the forest.

The heretics had also vanished – or, at least, were

keeping such a low profile that no more was heard of the canons' crusade against them. De Wolfe suspected that the revulsion against the burning of the fuller's family had quenched everyone's appetite for pursuing them. Certainly, John de Alençon told him that the bishop had no desire to make an issue of the matter, in spite of the Papal Legate's letter. Henry Marshal was more concerned with keeping an eye on Prince John's chances of becoming king, which should lead to his own advancement in the hierarchy of government.

In Martin's Lane life went on almost as usual. Mary was content to keep house for John and his new wife, with whom she got on exceedingly well. Gwyn and Martha revelled in their tenancy of the Bush Inn, though the big Cornishman still acted as John's officer. Thomas continued as his clerk, but also managed to fit in his teaching at the choir school and his duties in the scriptorium.

Six months later the Eyre of Assize came at last to Exeter and John half-expected to be summoned before the justices, but he heard nothing of it and it appeared likely that the Chief Justiciar had warned them off. Richard de Revelle sold his town house in Exeter and no one of John's acquaintance had laid eyes on him for months, so he was probably lying low in his manor at Revelstoke in the far west of the county.

'And long may the bastard stay there!' was de Wolfe's heartfelt comment to Gwyn and Thomas.

hISTORICAL NOTE

'Heresy' in the religious sense is any significant dissension from an accepted (usually majority) view of faith and doctrine. Almost every religion has, or had, its heretics. Islam has many contentious factions, especially the Sunni and the Shia, who each consider the other as heretical, as well as Alawis, Ismailis, Sufis, Ahmadis, etc. Orthodox Judaism has various dissenters but Christianity has had the most diverse variations, about forty 'heresies' having been recorded during its long history.

The oldest is Gnosticism, which originated in the Near East and predates Christianity but later competed with its doctrines, believing that the material world was evil and that knowledge was given by God to those who placed it before blind faith. They claimed that the teachings of Jesus were more important than his death and resurrection.

Arianism, named after a priest of Antioch in the fourth century, claimed that Christ was mortal, being only an intermediary between God and Man. The cult was condemned by the Council of Nicaea in AD 325, which declared that Christ was one with God, but Arianism persisted until at least the seventh century.

Pelagianism was founded by Pelagius, a Welsh monk probably from the monastery of Bangor-on-Dee, who was in Rome about AD 400 and attacked the Church's corruption and the contention, championed by St Augustine of Hippo, that all men were born with original sin and only the intervention of the Church could save them by supplying the grace of God. He believed that men had innate goodness and the free will to save themselves without the intervention of priests, and he denied the concept of predestination. Pelagianism became powerful in Dark Age Britain, and the Pope sent St Germanus, Bishop of Auxerre, here twice in the mid-fifth century to try to combat the heresy. The essence of Pelagianism survived for many centuries and its concepts are accepted by many to this day.

The Cathars or Albigensians, as well as similar groups like the Bogomils, the Poor Men of Lyons, Publicani, etc., were widespread between the eleventh and thirteenth centuries in France, Italy, Bulgaria and Germany. They were dualists, believing in two gods, one good, one evil. Like the Gnostics, they claimed that the material world was evil, created by Satan, and that man's body was evil, but his soul was godly. They were extremely ascetic, denied the Cross and rejected marriage and procreation. The cult became widespread in France and Italy, having eleven Cathar bishoprics by the twelfth century. They posed such a threat to the Catholic Church that in 1209 the latter mounted a Crusade against them under Simon de Montfort, Earl of Leicester, who crushed them with terrible slaughter and cruelty, especially in south-western France.

POCKET
BOOKS

Bernard Knight
CROWNER ROYAL

London, 1196. At the command of King Richard, Sir John de Wolfe has left his beloved West Country for the palace of Westminster, where he has been appointed Coroner of the Verge. But with the Lionheart overseas, embroiled in a costly war against King Philip of France, Sir John is dismayed to discover that the English court is a hotbed of greed, corruption and petty in-fighting.

The murder of one of the palace clerks, stabbed in broad daylight and thrown into the Thames, leads John to suspect that there's a conspiracy underway to overthrow King Richard. Could there be a link to the daring theft of gold bullion he was escorting from the Tower? With the visit of the dowager Queen Eleanor fast approaching, the new Coroner must do whatever it takes to prove his suspicions are right, root out the traitors within and prevent a national catastrophe.

ISBN 978-1-84739-328-9
PRICE £6.99

POCKET
BOOKS

Bernard Knight
THE MANOR OF DEATH

April, 1196. When an unidentified body is discovered in the harbour town of Axmouth, twenty miles from Exeter, Sir John de Wolfe, the county coroner, is summoned to investigate. The manner of the young man's death is a matter of some dispute. But, as Sir John discovers, it was no accident. The victim did not drown, as the manor reeve alleges, but was strangled to death.

The ensuing murder enquiry is frustrated by what appears to be a conspiracy of silence among the seamen and townsfolk. Just what is the local population trying to hide?

In order to root out the truth, Sir John hatches a cunning plan. But is he playing with fire? There are those who would go to any lengths to ensure the shocking truth remains hidden, and Crowner John must draw on all his resources of courage and ingenuity if he is to escape from Axmouth with his life.

ISBN 978-1-41652-594-3
PRICE £6.99

POCKET
BOOKS

This book and other **Pocket Books** titles are available from your local bookshop or can be ordered direct from the publisher.

978-1-84739-328-9	Crowner Royal	£6.99
978-1-41652-594-3	The Manor of Death	£6.99
978-1-41652-593-6	The Noble Outlaw	£6.99
978-0-74349-215-7	The Elixir of Death	£6.99
978-0-74349-214-0	Figure of Hate	£6.99
978-0-74344-989-2	The Witch Hunter	£6.99

Free post and packing within the UK
Overseas customers please add £2 per paperback
Telephone Simon & Schuster Cash Sales at Bookpost
on 01624 677237 with your credit or debit card number
or send a cheque payable to Simon & Schuster Cash Sales to
PO Box 29, Douglas Isle of Man, IM99 1BQ
Fax: 01624 670923
E-mail: bookshop@enterprise.net
www.bookpost.co.uk

Please allow 14 days for delivery. Prices and availability are subject to change without notice.